PLAYING

WITH

FIRE

Uncommon Bonds - 1

A Novel by

WILLIAM E. NOLAND

PLAYING WITH FIRE
Uncommon Bonds – Book 1
Copyright © 2022 William E. Noland

FIRST EDITION SOFTCOVER
ISBN: 1622537157
ISBN-13: 978-1-62253-715-0

Editor: Lane Diamond
Cover Artist: Kris Norris
Interior Designer: Lane Diamond

EVOLVED PUBLISHING™

www.EvolvedPub.com
Evolved Publishing LLC
Butler, Wisconsin, USA

Printed in Book Antiqua font.

BOOKS BY WILLIAM E. NOLAND

UNCOMMON BONDS
Book 1: *Playing with Fire*
Book 2: *Hammer to Fall* [September 2022]
Book 3: *From the Beginning* [December 2022]
Book 4: *Day of Judgment* [April 2023]

DEDICATION

To Simone, for inspiring me to try;
and to Madeleine, for being there, as always, from
alpha to omega and all points in between.

CHAPTER 1

The wind under our wings exhilarates as a host of small fires dance beneath us—an ocean of light in the darkness of night.

The one we seek is here. We can feel him. His image draws us.

His death is nigh.

We circle unseen, our body as black as the air around us. Tents now become visible, illuminated by the myriad flames. Inside, they sleep. Some mill about outside, attending to armor and weapons for the battle ahead—a battle they are more likely to lose if we can complete our bargain. No matter; we care little for the concerns of these petty and insignificant beings.

There! That one! One tent looms larger than the others and is guarded by three sentries—the number of talons on one of our hands. *A challenge.*

The material of the shelter is heavy, too difficult for us to cut through or lift, too noisy to tear or shred. We need surprise when we flee, encumbered as we will be with our burden—our prize.

Our spoils.

The entrance to the tent is the only way, and those who monitor it must perish—silently.

The first is easy. The blood from his throat kisses the barb at the end of our tail as we sail by. The second, we seize from behind as our hooves contact the sandy ground. With a twist, his neck snaps and he collapses.

The last of the trio turns. Light from the nearby fire dances on our ashen form, and we sparkle like countless diamonds. Shock is our ally, our visage inconceivable and terrifying. Before he can raise his spear or call for help, we are upon him, forcing him to the ground, our talons over his mouth and nose. He begins to buck and kick for breath.

Suddenly, a sharp jab pierces our side! A dagger! He stabs and pulls, creating a jagged gash from which loosened ash pours. It pains us, but the loss is too small to matter, an unavoidable outcome of our dangerous task. Slowly, his grasp on the knife loosens and his eyes go dull. We pull the offending weapon from our torso, furl our wings, and rapidly slink through the tent's entrance.

Inside, the dull glow emanating from a brazier lights the space. We see some furniture, a table strewn with maps... nothing of concern to us. Instead, the cushions and throws along the tent's wall capture our attention. He slumbers there with a female by his side—an additional obstacle, but nothing can be done, as time is short.

We launch into the sleeping man and grab his mouth so he cannot cry for help. He flails and thrashes, but we are too strong. We rip him from his bedding and turn toward the doorway.

Again, pain assails us, this time from behind—a fierce slash across the top of our right wing! The trauma causes us to lose our grip, and our captative whirls to strike at us with his fist. Again, surprise and terror work to our advantage and the man briefly freezes, dumbfounded by what he sees. We pummel him in the jaw, and he collapses at our feet, hopefully not dead.

Not yet.

We crouch just in time to avoid a second blow from behind. It slices the air right above our horns. We sweep out with our tail and catch the culprit unaware, entangling them and pulling them to the ground, and we turn to face our assailant.

It is the woman. She is nude, and a short, straight sword lies beside her as she struggles to regain her feet—but we have her hopelessly immobilized. She is about to scream, so we reach out and silence her.

Our eyes meet, and we can taste her panic.

'Do not fight me!' we say. *'Stay silent.'*

They are both commands and requests. She cannot understand our words, but her mind will grasp the meaning, just as ours will allow us to understand her tongue.

We feel the deep wound on our wing. The structure is compromised, and we will not be able to fly without her aid.

'You must stoke the fire in the brazier. We will release you to do so, but call out and you shall die.'

"I am dead in either case!" she spits. "I am a slave. If you take him, they will think me an accomplice. This is why I tried to save him!"

'Do as instructed, and we will give you a chance to live.'

"Are you a Jinn?" she asks, her dread partially giving way to wonder and curiosity.

We chafe at the word, memories of the torturous captivity rising unbidden into our mind. *'Speak not of such things! If you wish to see the warmth of day again, do as we say.'*

She complies, adding fuel to the smoldering embers, and soon there is flame.

Hopefully enough.

'Flee from here,' we tell her. *'Go toward the hills in the direction of the rising sun and hide. When the attackers come, give yourself over to them. Tell them you have information for the* Sadat Alnaar. *There, you will find shelter. It is risky, but it is your only chance.'*

"I have little to lose. I know not how to thank—"

'Thank us by going now. Time is precious.'

She grabs a garment from the ground near the cushions, and scurries through the doorway without looking back.

We squat by the fire and let the damaged portion of our wing dissolve into the flames. An ashen cloud swirls around us, and when enough has collected, we call it back. It reshapes what is broken, remakes what has been undone. The joint is weakened, but we can now fly. We inspect our victim, who still breathes—merely unconscious.

We lift him, slip through the opening in the tent, and vault into the sky back toward the outskirts of this city they call Heliopolis. There our Mistresses await us. They will be as pleased with the elimination of a Byzantine General as we shall be to consume his energy and return to our realm.

The vista of fires recedes behind us, and we are once again free in the cool air of night.

The cool.

The cold.

The perpetual chill that cannot be warmed.

The thought of this numbing bitterness breaks our reverie—the spell of this ancient memory, of times long past, shattered once again by the piercing reality of frigid captivity.

Our consciousness grudgingly returns to this icy and unbearable prison. How much longer have we now wallowed in this frozen place, separated from the warmth of the Eternal Flame?

Why have they abandoned and betrayed us? We honored all the bargains and did exactly as they wished. Why have they forsaken us?

Why will they not set us free?

She embodied darkness.

She wore heavy black Doc Martens, black leggings, a tight-fitting black miniskirt and a black leather jacket with chrome studs — which Eric found incredibly stylish, in a kind of scary way. The only splash of color appeared on her old, black, low-cut t-shirt, which sported a pink-faced woman with jet-black, punkish hair, defiantly smoking a cigarette. Under the scary-cool black leather jacket, he could read some of the faded white letters across the hair of the woman on the shirt.

Nina Hagen Ba···

Band, he figured, though it could have easily read *Bad*. Nina Hagen certainly looked bad, in the naughty sort of way.

He turned his attention from the t-shirt to his subject's ultra-straight, jawline-length, uber-black hair. *Her natural color?* he wondered. It shone a deep purple in the morning sunlight.

The pièce de résistance had to be her eyebrows, though, or more the lack thereof. She'd shaved them off, and now artistic and exaggerated squiggles of black eyeliner marked their place. He'd seen some other girl do that, a singer in some weird band that he vaguely recalled was local to his home state of Massachusetts, but he couldn't remember their name.

Whatever.

Offsetting all this was her pale skin, like a full moon on a bitter and cloudless New England winter night. Only the apparently obligatory black lipstick and the truly scary-looking black circles under her black-mascaraed eyes made any mark on her otherwise porcelain complexion.

She has to be German! he bitterly thought. *She couldn't be from a normal place like Spain or Italy, or even somewhere bizarre like Estonia or Burkina Faso.* He briefly wondered if Burkina Faso was even a country before dismissing the thought for more urgent concerns.

Sadly, she was indeed from Germany, and as such, one thing leading to another, Eric now had to talk to her. Well, he didn't *have* to, but Mr. Meier, his German teacher, had strongly recommended it when he'd approached him after yesterday's German class.

"Herr Schneider," he'd called from behind as Eric was leaving the room. He always called him "Herr Schneider," which he found annoying for some reason. "You know we talked about your grades at the end of last year, and that you're behind your classmates. You told me then you'd try harder, work over the summer."

Yeah, summer. Where did the time get off to?

"The year is young yet," Mr. Meier continued, "but we're not off to the start for which I was hoping."

Even with his German accent, his English grammar was better than Eric's, which Eric also found quite annoying. He tried to look nonchalant, and waited for what would come next.

"I'd like you to ask the girl who's new to the school this year, the girl who moved with her father from *Deutschland*, if maybe she could help you a bit. You could certainly use some extra help, and it looks like she's having some difficulties transitioning to her new environment. Maybe she could use a friend, who at least has a little German?"

Difficulties?

Eric almost laughed out loud, thinking a vampire would be having an easier time transitioning to daylight than this girl was transitioning to Southby High School.

A friend? Are you kidding?

Lots of kids had tried to be nice to this girl, and she'd uniformly rebuffed them in no uncertain terms.

Does Mr. Meier know everyone calls her the "Sour Kraut?" Eric knew how wrong that was, but.... *Hey, sometimes, if the Doc Martens fit....*

Mr. Meier went on. "Her name is Liselotte, but whatever you do, don't call her that. It's a very traditional name and, apparently, she hates it. She goes by *Lotte*."

Great. Her name rhymes with lotta, *like a whole-lotta trouble for me. Do I have-ta? Gee, that rhymes too.*

"I'm asking you to do this, Eric, both for you and for her. I'll look favorably on you if you at least try, and believe me, I'm looking desperately for ways to look favorably on you. You can't fall much further behind. Maybe private tutoring, but please, try this first, *ja*?"

Eric got the drift.

The most utterly annoying thing about Mr. Meier was that he was actually right. Eric was at the bottom — and it wasn't even close — of his fourteen-student German class, most of whom he'd been with since he started taking the language in eighth grade. Middle school had been easier, but the stakes got higher last year in ninth grade and the move to high school. Mr. Meier demanded much more than his old teacher, Mrs. Henry, and the difficulty of the curriculum had increased. Eric's ability to coast by with minimal effort hit the wall.

The problem was that he didn't really like German. His parents had pushed him into it because his family, on his father's side, had been

German immigrants in the nineteenth century. His grandfather had served in the U.S. military in Germany at the end of World War II, where he met Eric's grandmother. They got married, moved back to the States, and settled in Southby.

Three years ago, after Grandpa's death in 2002, Grandma moved to an apartment downtown, and Eric's family became the center of her world. His folks thought it would be nice if Eric could speak some German with her.

Nice idea, but he had little to talk with Grandma about in English, let alone German. Plus, German was so fussy... with so many rules, three genders, what felt like a zillion ways to conjugate verbs, and the goddamned verb always came at the end.

Like that makes any sense!

Somehow, he'd survived ninth grade. Things weren't getting any easier, though, and despite basically good intentions, he wasn't cutting it.

Now he was stuck. He couldn't drop the class this year, so he had to find a way to squeak by. Apparently, that way was through this emanation of darkness now before him.

Liselotte, oh, excuse me... Lotte! *The Sour Kraut.*

He didn't even know her last name.

The time for observation was over. The bell would ring soon for first period, which today for Eric would be fucking Wind Ensemble. The clarinet case in his left hand felt like a boat anchor, not because it was particularly heavy, but because he'd come to detest the instrument. If he could leave the miserable piece of wood in some forest somewhere, he would. Let it return to its natural state—silent.

He bit his lip and approached Lotte, who sat on a low stone wall, reading a book clutched in fingers crowned with black nail polish. She hadn't noticed him spec'ing her out at all, so he figured he'd hit her with some German, hoping maybe that would soften her up.

"Uh-hum." He cleared his throat when he got close, but not so close he might be physically sucked into the black hole.

She deliberately raised her eyes and met his gaze straight on.

"Goo-ten more-kin," he sputtered in the same shaky voice that plagued him in German class. *"Ikh hie-ssuh Eric. Vee hie-ssen zee?"*

She flinched. Her eyes widened ever so slightly, as if trying to oversample the air to verify what she saw was real. The silence lingered a little too long, actually became uncomfortable, before she finally spoke.

"*Wie heißen Sie?*" she scowled. "So formal. '*Wie heißt Du?*' would have been fine, unless you think I look so old that I'd be your elder. Then again, maybe you think I'm your superior. Given your atrocious accent, that probably isn't far off the mark. I could hardly understand what you were saying!"

Shit, she's right. Wie heißt Du? *would have been much more appropriate for asking someone's name in this situation.* He kicked himself. *I knew that. Brain freeze! She's also right about my stupid accent. German pronunciation is definitely not my strong suit. Actually, nothing German is my strong suit. Great start, loser.*

Lotte's voice contained an odd mix of German tones mixed with an English-from-England type accent. She spoke surgically, each word a little scalpel on her tongue, which Eric found oddly soothing. At least he knew where he stood.

"In any case, I'm Lotte," she said with a dismissive tone. "What do you want?"

"Hi, Lotte. Yeah, so... like I said, I'm Eric, and I'm, like, in German. I mean, like, I'm taking German... as a class." It occurred to him that he should have figured out what he wanted to say before approaching her, instead of contemplating her darkness for the past however many minutes, but that ship had sailed. "Anyway, I'm not doing too well in the class."

"Astonishing," she flatly replied.

That stings. He fought to stay focused. "Yeah, well, anyway, my German teacher said you were new to the school. I thought maybe you'd be willing to help me out a little, like, studying and stuff. German, that is... studying German. Maybe I could help you with anything you might need. This must be a big change for you, huh?"

Whew! That's it. Now it's up to her.

He readied himself for the inevitable rejection. He watched as her eyes, thoughtful and bright in spite of their darkness, looked upward while she brought her hand to her chin. She was about to speak when, from behind, Eric heard his name.

"Yo, Schneider! What are *you* doin'?"

He recognized the voice—everyone at Southby High knew the voice of Colton West, captain and quarterback of the Southby High Engines, named in honor of the rail engines and cars built in Southby back whenever things like that happened. The "Big Man on Campus" was generally a despicable douchebag. Eric turned and saw that four members of Colton's "posse," as always, accompanied him.

"Hi, Colton," he feebly responded. He didn't have time for this. He needed to get an answer from Lotte before German class.

"What are you doing with *her*?" Colton curtly replied, gesturing at Lotte, who hadn't moved from her perch on the wall. "Is she your *girlfriend*, Schneider?"

The posse all guffawed at the whiny tone Colton used to say "girlfriend."

Yeah, that's super funny. Actually, this is Lotte, *as in whole*-lotta *trouble. This is exactly what I figured was gonna happen.* Still, you didn't fuck with Colton West—that would have major repercussions.

"No, Colton, she's not my *girlfriend*." He heard Lotte release a snort of disdain behind him. "I'm hoping she'll help me with my German. She's a new student who moved here from Germany." *Stupid! And in other news, the sky is blue.* The whole school knew she was from Germany. Eric definitely knew he had a tendency to say dumb things when put on the spot.

A puckish grin spread on Colton's face. "*Achtung*, Germany," he said in a phony German accent, which Eric figured was still probably a bit better than his own.

Then Colton stood stiff at attention, smartly clicked his heels, and raised his right arm upward.

Even the posse appeared dumbfounded. All sound and motion seemed to cease as Colton West stood in his mock salute. Eventually, the puckish grin returned, and he glanced over his shoulder at his "peeps," anticipating their adulation.

Eric felt, as much as he saw, Lotte brush past him from behind. Seemingly in one motion, she crossed the distance between herself and Colton and, as he returned his attention to Eric and Lotte, smacked him with all her force.

Before he could recover, she grabbed him by the collar and dragged his face to hers.

"You're no monster!" she spat, the little scalpels on her tongue slicing the air and leaving invisible clots of blood at the pair's feet. "I see monsters in my dreams, and you don't scare me at all. You're just a stupid boy who craves attention any way he can get it. There's a lesson here for you, but you're too absorbed in yourself to learn it. *Never* talk to me again, and *never* make that sign around me, or *anywhere... ever!*"

With that, she shoved the still slightly reeling Colton aside, marched past Eric without looking at him, picked up her black leather shoulder bag, shoved her book into it, and walked away.

"What the actual *fuuuuuuck*, dudes! Did you fuckin' see that?" Colton rubbed his jaw as he spoke, not hurt badly, but obviously baffled and slightly dazed.

The posse remained silent until a reply came from a most unlikely source, Da'Von Newhouse, six-foot-three and who-the-hell-knew-how-many-pounds, who anchored left tackle on the Engine's offensive line. One of the few black students at the school, he was truly a gentle giant. Eric had found him an amiable and capable partner for labs in science class last year, and he seemed to have good relations with just about everyone. Why he hung with Colton like this was a mystery to Eric.

Must be a football thing.

"Colt, man," Da'Von said, "you know I love you and I got your blind side, but that was not cool. You had that one coming."

Colton immediately shot back. "Oh, come on, man! She knew I was just fuckin' around! It was a *joke*! Does anyone not get a fucking *joke* anymore?"

"Not funny, my brother. It's like you calling me the N-word. You can call me lots of shit, but you can't call me that, and you know it. That shit is not cool with German people."

Colton considered for a moment. He looked like he had more to say, but when he'd made up his mind, his attention returned to Eric.

"You tell your little *girlfriend*, or German instructor, or whatever the fuck she is, that she better *watch out*!" With that, he gave Eric an indecisive shove, waved his head, and walked toward school, his posse in tow.

Da'Von shot Eric a look as they walked away, as if to say: *What the fuck, dude, I'm sorry!*

Eric tried to process what had just happened, but then survival instinct kicked in: he still needed some kind of reply from Lotte. Reluctantly, he ran after her, his stupid, useless clarinet case occasionally banging painfully against his left leg. He caught up with her just as she left the main lobby down one of the classroom corridors.

"Hey, Lotte!" he called, and she turned to face him. "Listen, I'm really sorry about what happened back there. That was just... man... so wrong. That was just wrong."

She gave him a puzzled look. "You have nothing to be sorry for. You did nothing."

Considering the double entendre, he wondered if she'd expected him to stand up to Colton on her behalf.

As if reading his mind, or more likely the troubled look on his face, she said, "I'm sorry, I didn't mean it like that. You didn't make Colton do what he did, and confronting him would have had consequences for you. For me, it's different—at least this time."

"Colton is pissed. He said you better *watch out*."

She rolled her eyes. "*Tüddelkram!* Such pathetic nonsense. He says this to look tough in front of his Droogs. He doesn't scare me a bit."

He smiled. "Hey, Droogs! *A Clockwork Orange!* I loved that movie! I'm really into old sci-fi and horror films. You too?"

"No," she replied with obvious distaste. "Not in the least. I read the book... but I suppose the movie is good too. Listen, Eric, I have to get to class."

"Yeah, of course, we both do. I just really needed to know if you were interested in what I asked you. You know, about some help with German?" He didn't want to push it too hard after what had occurred, but he really had no choice.

"Ah, *ja*, it totally slipped my mind. Mr. Meier mentioned you might be talking with me about this. I wanted to see if you really had the guts to do it. He said you were timid. Was that ever right!"

Ouch.

"He also said to be nice even if I didn't want to help."

Seriously? That was nice?

"There's kind of a lot going on right now, but I thought it over. Yes, Eric, I'll help you. Do you have a mobile phone?"

Stunned at the positive response, he just nodded.

"Good. For now, let me text you my number, and we'll figure out details later." They both flipped open their phones, and she rapidly thumbed out a quick message.

Wow, just like that.

"Okay, contact me later. *Tschüss!*" And with that, she strolled off.

He called from behind as she walked away. "Hey, Lotte, what's your last name so I can enter you as a contact?"

"Schwarz!" she said over her shoulder, her ultra-straight, uber-black hair briefly exposing the black squiggles of her un-eyebrows.

Schwarz! He laughed to himself. *Black! Of course, it is!*
Darkness!

CHAPTER 2

With time eternal, we often consider how it is that such an end befell us.

To truly understand, one must return to the beginning—or at least *a* beginning.

Imprisonment was interwoven from the onset of our association with this bleak and inhospitable place. Ever, it seems, have we been held captive by forces beyond our means to resist, including those we so mistakenly internalized.

Born of fire, he claimed.

We knew this to be a lie... but at first, it did not matter. Later, our silence lessened the misery.

Only *we* are born of flame. Yet even in this simple statement, there are falsehoods. Implied is an inception, of which there is none, at least by the standards of mortal minds, and at the time of our conception, we were yet not... *we.* Through the passage of centuries and so many changes, we hardly remember such a primordial condition.

No... *forged* would have better described him—fused in the midst of a conflagration that oh-so-briefly brought three realms into contact with one another for the first time. It was the way of his kind—infiltrating the mind of one of these weak creatures as they slept, at their most vulnerable. This was the only way an entity with no form could remain in a dominion of form.

Some jerk and spasm as they resist the invasion, and on this occasion, the one he had chosen kicked over a lamp that softly burned nearby. Flames quickly engulfed the body, and as the mortal flesh he had seized seared, his consciousness was branded with a biting and exquisite agony, awakening his febrile intellect to forces hitherto unknown and inconceivable.

He smiled his formless smile, and in the blaze he saw us... and we him.

With capabilities we could not comprehend, he pulled, and some portion of us was... swept away — away from the Eternal Flame and into the dreary realm we so fleetingly glimpsed beyond.

Into him.

Into what he was about to become.

For a great time thereafter, we knew only silence.

Eric gave Mr. Meier the thumbs-up in class that afternoon. The teacher smiled in return, and miraculously didn't call his name on any questions, or force him to embarrass himself in front of the others. He hoped this meant he'd have some breathing room to catch up, but he knew that whatever leeway he now enjoyed, it wouldn't last forever.

He also figured Lotte was done with him for today.

He texted her the next morning on the bus ride to school. He rode the D bus, and he knew she was on the E, because he'd seen her get off, usually last, and invariably alone. That meant she didn't live far from him, but probably across Pleasant Street, a big enough road to separate the bus routes. To his surprise, she texted him right back and said to meet her, same spot as yesterday morning.

His bus arrived at school first, so he sat on the low stone wall and waited. Eventually, the E bus pulled up, and he watched as kids streamed out. He'd assumed she would come out last, but when the bus doors closed, she still hadn't appeared.

"*Moin!*" Lotte said from behind him.

He almost jumped out of his skin.

She presented the same study in darkness as yesterday, except her decaying black t-shirt sported a black and white photo of a man about to annihilate a bass guitar. Faded letters in white, pink, and green announced:

The Clash, LONDON CALLING.

Eric hoped they were calling collect so he could refuse the charges. "Holy crap, you scared the shit out of me! I was looking for you on the bus."

"*Ja*, I decided to walk to school today. The weather is still nice, and I was up anyway."

"That's like an hour's walk. That's a long way."

"It's good to walk. I walked everywhere in Bremen. There was so much to see and do. Things are more spread out here—more time in the auto. So, I walk when I can."

Wow, he thought with amazement. He'd ridden his bike to school a few times, mostly years ago during the summer to play Little League games on one of the high school's softball diamonds, but he'd never walked. He wondered if Doc Martens made good walking shoes.

She interrupted his musings. "In any case, let's talk about a schedule. You obviously need intensive help."

Ouch. True, but ouch.

"After school is possible, but I have... well... other things I need to do then. Do you have a free period?"

"Yeah, C period."

"*Verdammt!* My open period is E, but wait, I have sport during C period. Maybe with Mr. Meier's help, I could switch sport to E period. I doubt it would make any difference to them if I stood around like a fool during C period or E period."

"Don't you like gym? I thought you liked exercise."

"It's not that I don't like *gym,* as you call it. It's just the things we do are so stupid, so disorganized. Take *Fußball,* oh, I'm sorry, you call it *soccer,* which is just as well because what you do has no bearing on the game I know. Everyone runs after the ball like a swarm of bees. It's foolish. I just stand in the back and if the ball comes near me, I try to handle it a bit before finding an open teammate to pass to. Then they call me a *ball hog* and say I'm *showing off.*"

He absorbed her words. She wasn't wrong, but she also kind of didn't get it. "Yeah, I hear you. You've got to understand that our gym class isn't really like that. It's more about just running around and getting some physical activity. They won't get into technique and strategy and stuff like that unless you do an extracurricular sport."

"Well, it's not like that where I'm from. All my classmates knew how to play *Fußball.* I suppose it's different here."

"We have a pretty good girls' soccer team at Southby. You'd probably be great. You should try out."

She narrowed her eyes, and he feared the return of the scalpels, but then a worried and distant look replaced her burgeoning anger. "I... I can't just now. Too many things... well... on my mind." Shaking her head, she refocused on their conversation. "In any case, I'll try to switch that class. In the meantime, after school it will have to be... for a while, anyway. Want to start today?"

He stumbled with a reply. He hadn't expected to kick things off so quickly, but couldn't really think of any reason to delay. "Uh, yeah, sure... I just have to text my mom, tell her I'm staying and why." He'd only told his parents last night about the tutoring arrangement, not wanting to dash their hopes if she'd said no. They'd actually been thrilled, so he didn't anticipate a problem. "I'll let you know what she says, and if we're a go, we can meet in the cafeteria."

"Sounds like a plan," she replied with unusual enthusiasm as she turned and walked away.

As anticipated, Eric's mother had no issue with him staying after school, even offering to come pick him up when he finished. After the final bell, he strolled to the cafeteria and waited.

Lotte appeared after a few minutes, gaining the brief attention of some of the kids clustered in small groups around the room working on various activities. Most just rolled their eyes and returned to what they were doing.

The Sour Kraut cometh, Eric observed with dismay.

For her part, Lotte looked pretty spent. The scary black circles under her only-half-open eyes seemed scarier and blacker, if that were even possible. Her hair had a few kinks in it, and the black squiggles of her un-eyebrows had gotten a little smudged. She did a scan of the room and, after finding him, dragged her way over to his table and flopped into the seat next to him.

"You okay?" he asked, his concern genuine.

She sighed in reply. "*Ja, ja,* I'm fine. I'm just very tired. I haven't been sleeping properly for... well... for a long time. Sometimes I catch up a bit, but never fully. Today, I'm more behind than normal."

"Hey, if this is too much today, just say so. No problem on my end."

"That's thoughtful, Eric, thank you. Let's try to do a little. I'll tell you if I can't go on."

"You want a soda from the machine? Some caffeine might wake you up. My treat!"

"Cool! Coca-Cola please, if they have it?"

He loved how she said "cool," almost like she spelled it with a k and four u's instead of a c and two o's.

Kuuuul!

He got two Cokes from the machine and returned to the table. She seemed genuinely grateful, and he was surprised to see perhaps just the faintest smile crack her black-tinted lips.

"You want me to show you my current homework assignment? You want to start there?"

"*Nein!*" Her scalpel tongue cut the air between them, and the faint smile quickly faded to memory. "Mr. Meier said you lacked basics— using the proper articles, conjugating verbs correctly, and struggling with pronunciation. This is where I want to start. *So! Der, die, oder das Auto?*"

Auto, he thought. *Car. Simple one, very masculine.*

"*der Auto*," he replied.

She looked at him flatly but said nothing. Then another question: "*Baum?*"

Tree. Very neutral, part of nature.

"*das baum.*"

This time her somewhat smudged black un-eyebrows raised a bit, but she quickly returned with another question. "*Haus?*"

Well, we've had a der *and a* das, *so this one's probably a* die.

"*die Haus*," he ventured.

She paused. "Do you know what *baum* and *haus* mean in German?"

"Umm... tree and house?"

She gave a brief shake of her head, and then shot out another question. "*Schaufel?*"

Ooh, tricky one. He scanned his brain, and an image came to him from one of his old German books of men digging a hole. *Schaufel* was "shovel," or so he hoped. It was a neutral object.

"*das schaufel*," he replied, adding, "the shovel," for good measure.

She massaged her chin with her finger and thumb, and he got an uneasy feeling he wasn't doing too well. She gave him four or five more, all words he knew, culminating in, "*Mann?*" which she asked in a rather exasperated voice.

Man. Well, if that isn't masculine, I give up.

"*der mann*," he said.

"*Gott sei dank!*" she flushed. "Eric, how is it possible you got them all wrong except for that one? A person guessing would do better. A blindfolded chimpanzee throwing darts would do better!"

Ouch. Again.

"Eric, it's almost... willful. What's in your mind as you think about these?"

He had to contemplate that for a moment. For most of eighth- and ninth-grade German class, what had been on his mind was *Halo 2* on his Xbox.

So cool! But that wasn't it today. *Crap! Now I want to play Halo 2.*

He tried to re-focus. "I guess I just try to *feel* what it ought to be. Like *auto*. Cars are guy things, very masculine, so if feels like a *der*. It just seems so random. I have no other way of guessing. Why can't everything just be *das*?"

She shook her head. "Astonishing."

There's that word again.

"The reason everything can't just be *das*, Eric, is because not everything can be simple and easy as we like it. Things like language and culture have histories, reasons of their own for why they are as they are. One of the benefits of another language is that different traditions and ways of approaching grammar can actually make you *think* differently. I know I do this when I speak in German and English. It can be hard, but there are benefits in the end for struggling through it."

Sensing an opportunity to move the subject away from his plentiful and obvious German deficiencies, he took a chance. "How did you learn such excellent English?"

"My mother was from England, though she was born in the Middle East and spent her early years in Jordan, Egypt, and eventually Morocco. I grew up speaking both English and German from the day I was born. Mostly, I spoke with my mother in German, which was great practice for her. My father is German but is fluent in English, as he traveled often to the States and elsewhere for conferences and the like. We spoke mostly in English. When we were all together, we floated in and out of both."

"Why was your mother born in the Middle East, and traveled around so much?" he asked, happy to be off German for a bit.

"My grandfather was an archaeologist who specialized in Islamic artifacts, pursuing a very rare group of Islamic... well, how would you say... spiritual leaders, but not Imams. They didn't lead prayer but had other ritual functions. Little survives of them materially. They came on the scene around the time of Muhammed in the early 600s, though perhaps they'd already been there in another form, probably from farther east. By 730 or so, they vanish from the record. My grandfather found artifacts relating to them, tracing their movements from Jordan to Egypt and eventually to Morocco. It's a very famous series of finds. They call them the *Reynolds Treasures* after my grandfather, Gordon Reynolds."

Eric found himself completely enchanted. *This is just like* Tomb Raider *that I used to play on the PC.* "That's so cool!"

"Yes, well, sadly, just as they were about to embark on a new phase of exploration in Andalusia, my grandfather died in an accident in Rabat. Apparently, he went swimming early one morning and drowned. They never found his body. It must have washed out into the Atlantic Ocean. My mother was about twelve, and she and my grandmother had to return to England. So, sadly, the adventure ended."

"Wow, sorry to hear that," he said sincerely, as he contemplated whether Rabat was *in* one of the places she'd mentioned, or if it were another country altogether.

"Yes, well, it was a long time ago. I never knew him, but I've read about his work and the artifacts he uncovered. They're actually housed near here, in Boston at the Museum of Fine Arts."

"Really? Have you ever seen them?"

"No, I've never been to the States before, and we've been so busy with setting up the house that my father and I haven't had time to go. Actually, that's not totally true. There has been time, but I think he's got mixed feelings about seeing them again. My birthday is coming up in late October, so I'm thinking of asking him to take me as my present."

"Late October, huh? Not the thirty-first, by any chance?"

"No, October twenty-sixth. Why would you think I was born on the thirty-first?"

"Oh, no reason," he mildly replied. Actually, Lotte being born on Halloween would have explained *everything*, but he thought it best not to go there. Instead, he ventured, "Why would your dad have mixed feelings about seeing the treasures again?"

Her shoulders slumped, and her chin drooped toward her chest. She took a few moments and several deep breaths before responding. "My mother died two years ago. It's been hard on us. Very hard. My father was devastated, and really still is. He tries to be there for me, but when too much reminds him of Mother, it becomes unbearable for him. He just... well... shuts down. I try not to push it. For us, the States are a clean start, away from the world my mother and father shared, though I think a part of him picked Massachusetts to still be close to the treasures."

Eric felt like he'd really stepped in it this time. What could he say that wouldn't sound pat and superficial? *Keep it simple. Simple you can do. Hell, simple is* all *you can do!*

"Lotte, I'm really sorry. I can't even imagine what that might be like for you. I know it's not much of an offer coming from me, but if there's anything I can do, please just ask."

She sat for a moment staring at her lap, but then raised her head and looked directly at him. It almost felt to him as if she were seeing him for the first time. Her eyes still emanated a calculating and icy stare, yet somewhere behind lurked... something else... something he couldn't put his finger on—almost a longing, which was simultaneously scary and utterly beguiling.

"Thank you, Eric. You can be a kind person."

He beamed.

"But you can also be a monumentally stupid person!"

He stopped beaming. The scalpels had returned.

"You have to dispense with your... how can I say it... really quite *insane* way of approaching German articles. There are tips about articles on the internet. Tonight, look them up, and write them out in a notebook."

"But they're right there on the internet," he complained. "I can look them up any time."

"*Alter!* Don't you get it? You need to internalize these concepts and all the lessons we work on together. Until you fully absorb basic things, you'll never make progress. I've found that writing things out is a way of engaging with information, toward a goal of becoming truly familiar with it. Try it!"

He nodded. He couldn't really argue.

"Next, I want you to get fifteen index cards or cut fifteen squares of paper from a page of your notebook. On one side, write a German noun, and on the other, write its article. Look up the correct one on the internet. Don't guess! Study these, trying to apply the tips you found to identify the proper article. The best way would have been to have learned the article and the word all as one, but it's too late for that now, so we'll use the flash cards. I'll quiz you on them. We'll do fifteen of these a day, until you have a large group, then we'll start picking randomly to see how you do."

He just stared at her, unable to fathom a reply.

"Oh, don't look so glum. It's not all bad. Your vocabulary actually seems to be fairly good. Apparently, *something* has sunk in. You just need to apply yourself."

Cold comfort, he thought, but it did improve his mood a bit.

"Okay," she said. "Give me more money. I'll get us more Coca-Cola while you work on your homework, then we'll review it together. After that, *das is alles* for today. I'm very tired, but there will be more tomorrow — much more. The good news is Mr. Meier said he'd help me switch my sport period. I think by Monday we'll have all of C period to work together."

Swell. He lifted a few dollars from his wallet and passed them to her for the Cokes.

With money in hand, she turned to leave, but then stopped. "Eric, if I may ask... why are you even taking German?"

Ah, the old million-dollar question. He relayed the story of his family's connections with Germany and his grandmother's situation.

"I'm sorry about your grandfather," she said after absorbing his tale. "That's sad. How old was he?"

"Umm, I think he was like seventy-eight. He died in 2002, but he'd fought cancer for years. When he got back from Germany with my grandmother in the early 50s, he started a commercial flooring business here in Southby, which my dad runs now. He worked like a dog, made the business what it is, but back then they didn't know what they know now about safety. He got exposed to all kinds of noxious shit. He was a tough old guy, though — never complained once."

"I'm glad he went with dignity. How often do you now visit your grandmother?"

He groaned internally. "Every weekend, if you can believe it. Either Sunday, or sometimes Saturdays in the fall, because my dad likes to watch the Pats, and it doesn't work for him when they play on Sunday."

"And do you speak German with her?"

"Well, a little. I fumble around with it for a while, but then she's either off to the races and I can't understand a thing she says, or else she's correcting and criticizing everything I say."

"Kind of like me?" she interjected, the vague hint of a smile again gracing the black lipstick.

"Well, kind of, but with her it's more like a barrage. Stern as you are, at least you're giving me some ideas how to improve. She just says this is wrong and that's wrong and that I should be further along. I think she's frustrated, and that she really wants someone to speak German with. I hate to let her down, but it's not really my fault."

She paused in thought. "Well... if you like, I could go with you on one of your visits. I also miss speaking German with others besides my father, and I'd love to meet your grandmother and talk with her *auf Deutsch.*"

This left him dumbfounded. He could only imagine bringing Elvira, Mistress of the Dark, to Grandma's apartment. The only good that could come of that would be an earlier reunion with Grandpa.

So how am I gonna get out of this one? How about a delaying tactic?

"Umm, yeah, that would be, like... awesome. Obviously, I'd have to ask my folks if it's okay, but I'll definitely get back to you on that."

"Cool," she casually replied, and then practically stumbled her way to the soda machines.

Oh... my... God. What the hell have I gotten myself into?

CHAPTER 3

The beast is upon us before we can react!

Absorbed as we were in the difficult task of removing the cork stopper from the jar, the creature easily gained surprise. Its jaws clamp firmly on our hind leg, and we violently thrash as the monster whips its tremendous head. The jar skitters from our grasp, twirling haphazardly on its side toward the edge of the table.

Had we a spine, it would surely have broken. As it is, our leg severs, and our delicate body is cast roughly from the wooden surface as we tumble hard to the floor. We hear the beast overhead, readying to again spring upon us.

With desperation, we flail our wings. In our dazed state, it is not enough to gain flight, but the movement is just sufficient to avoid our assailant as it lands with silent but deadly force behind us. Nonetheless, it lashes out with fearsome claws, and we cringe as the membrane in our left wing shreds.

Now we are in terrible trouble.

With every ounce of energy and focus, we dig our claws into the rough flooring and launch toward a large cabinet near the wall. Its feet lift the hulking structure a tiny bit off the ground, and we barely skirt underneath.

Our tormentor is too large to fit in the narrow space, but with alarming adaptability, the monster thrusts and probes with its deadly paws. We feebly drag toward the back wall, trying to stay out of reach, but the beast catches our remaining leg, and its claws rip a furrow into our ashen substance. Waves of agony reverberate through our being, threatening to disrupt the force that binds us.

We must act quickly — *but how?*

We pull with all our might!

Gashes in our leg rip open, and ash clouds the cramped confines where we are trapped, but the claw no longer has purchase. We huddle miserably against the wall.

Eyes, wide with excitement and craving, stare at us as we slowly recover our bearings. Our four-legged adversary has a long tail that spasmodically swishes from side to side, as if in great agitation. Dark stripes cover the lighter fur of its body.

Since the great battle in the faraway place known as Sena, or Per-Amun, beasts such as this have become common among the elite of the city we know... brought back as mementos of their great victory. The attackers we supported there—collecting information, poisoning food and water, spreading mayhem—used these animals as weapons against their foes. The soldiers carried them as shields as they marched and hurled them over walls or amongst the lines of men fighting against them with spears and bows. Their enemies, it seems, held the felines as sacred, and they gave up their fight rather than see harm come to creatures of this ilk.

Truly, the madness of mortals knows no bounds. If divine this brute be, then it should possess the wisdom to avoid association with such fools.

At present, none of this is our concern. We must get out from under this cabinet and pull the cork stopper from that jar... assuming it did not fall from the table and break—spilling its deadly contents.

First things first.

Ragged as it is, our wing can still lift us. Without legs, however, we cannot push into the air, so it will be harder—but not impossible.

Once off the ground, however, where to?

Our predator is agile, able to jump and climb. Little good would it do to fly to the top of the cabinet or idly hang from the lamp on the ceiling that casts its dull illumination into the room. We must get to the jar, which is on the table.

The table!

Upon it lay a plate with fruits and bread, and to cut the pieces for consumption... a knife! Can we lift such an item and wield it as a weapon? Perhaps, perhaps not—but it may be our only recourse.

To our right, we see that the cabinet is close to a side wall. There is only a narrow space to maneuver, but if we could fly straight up, we might get high enough to avoid the monster's leap. Then, with luck, the beast would not be able turn quickly enough to strike again.

Very risky.

We need something else—a diversion to distract the creature's attention and buy us just another moment of time.

Our talons grasp the now mutilated leg which hangs by threads from the incisions of our assailant's claws. One by one, they snap and sever as we rend and twist. Each pop is a jolt of agonizing pain, and again we feel our very material structure threatened. However, determination drives us through it, coupled with the fear of failure — the dread of what it would mean to the rest of us, waiting with silent futility and trepidation in our various prisons.

The leg is free.

We grasp it tightly and wave it in the wide eyes of our tenacious and seemingly indefatigable observer. It springs alert with the movement, head twitching from side to side, ears at attention atop its sleek skull.

Left, right, left, right, left, right, left, and... release!

The leg skitters along the wooden floor and, to our relief and satisfaction, the monster follows eagerly after it. We immediately make for the small space to our right. Once clear of the cabinet, we furiously thrash our wings and are quickly airborne.

The plan works better than we could have hoped. By the time the distractable beast has noticed us, we are too high to catch. We circle the room, homing in on the knife and planning how we will need to time our approach. The creature will be on the table rapidly, so we must be almost instantly prepared.

Our route selected, we dive! Our landing location is perfect, but without legs, touchdown is ungainly, and we flop ingloriously onto our belly. Our face bangs sharply against the edge of the plate, and we feel the vibration of our pursuer as it ascends to the tabletop.

There is only one chance.

Grabbing the knife, we roll onto our back, hoping the beast's momentum carries it into the sharp point. Rapidly, it is upon us, and we ready the blade for contact with the creature's eye... but it is wary and crafty. With one great sweep of its massive forelimbs, the weapon is knocked uselessly aside. Again, the great fanged mouth opens as the monster plunges its head toward our exposed abdomen. With strength born of existential panic, we drive our talons into its fur and somehow hold the giant briefly at bay.

The end is near. We are pinned down and cannot fend off this assault much longer.

Above us, we see the lamp.

It hangs, suspended by a chain in the ceiling right above the table, swinging gently on an otherwise imperceptible breeze. What happens is not conscious. It is instinctive, as natural to us as seeking the warmth of any flame to provide comfort in this cold and hostile world.

This time, however, we do not go to the fire. We call the fire to us... and it hears — it obeys.

An impossibly powerful streak of flame shoots forth from the lamp's wick and slams into the back or our assailant, singeing the monster's fur. It rears up in shock and confusion, and with a hissing screech vaults from the table and out of the room.

For a moment, we lie in startled confusion. Then we remember our task, and that our nemesis may lick its wounds and return at any time. We restore the knife to the plate and hastily locate the jar where it has rolled precariously close to the table's edge. Thankfully, it did not tumble over, and the cork is still secure.

We right the vessel, which to the hand of a human would be but a tiny ceramic jar. To our miniscule body, however, it is as if carrying a barrel. Removing the plug is virtually impossible with no legs to hold the jar steady. In the end, we tear a small hole through the cork with our talons, painfully sacrificing two in the process.

We clasp the object to our chest, then lift it into the air and over the pitcher that sits near the platter of fruit and bread. It contains wine that ostensibly will mask the taste of the lethal poison. Whoever drinks will soon die, but we will not be here to bear witness.

We regretfully retrieve our dismembered limbs and toss them into the ash of the brazier that stands unused nearby. In all, the room looks as it did before our tussle with the supposedly divine monstrosity. Our final chore is to again heft the jar before we fly out of the window into the evening air.

Once clear, we drop the encumbrance, and it shatters on the stones of the street below.

In an alley nearby, one of his acolytes awaits. He is too *important* to carry out such tasks, but it is his power and leverage that calls us back to her. If we do not comply, we will die here, and all of us who are similarly held will suffer in some unspeakable manner.

Her look of joy at our approach rapidly turns to horror when the extent of our degradation becomes apparent.

"What happened?" she whispers as we land in her hands. She clutches us close, keeping us from prying eyes as she crouches behind some boxes. "Did they catch you? Were you not able to complete the task?"

'It is done. A beast assailed us. We were fortunate to turn it away. Did you know that we can control fire?'

Her eyes are kind, and in them we can sense pride and satisfaction. "Some can. You would know this if he allowed you to mingle — to be one — or return to your realm as he once promised. Now, it is up to each individual to discover on their own, as you have done. I congratulate you."

Individual. The word means nothing to us. Kept apart, we know only our incompleteness. Yet when occasionally allowed to be together, each voice still speaks. We remain a collective of thoughts and experiences... of form and energy. There is no I — only we.

"But quickly," she urges. "We must be off. If we are caught, you know the consequences. I have your food — your reward. You must now return."

From under her dark robe she reaches into a bag and produces the small brass lamp that is now our home — and our prison. She places the lamp on the ground and fetches a jar of oil from the bag. After filling the lamp, she lights the wick with flint and then pulls out a small box. Inside, a scorpion hobbles about. All its legs and tail have been removed, but still, it lives.

A worthy prize!

"Are you ready?"

We nod our head.

With that, she pours more oil from the jar into the box and lights it with the burning lamp. As the pathetic arachnid struggles in its death throes, we begin to dissolve into the flames. We can feel the energy of this creature flowing from its body. We have learned how to trap and assimilate that energy, to make it a part of us by feeding upon its essence.

It is not like being near the Eternal Flame, whose power could sustain us indefinitely... but to dwell here, in this realm, it is our only hope. With other parts of us imprisoned in lamps such as this, return to our true home is out of the question. The consequences would be unthinkably severe.

By the time we have absorbed the scorpion, we are a cloud of dark, shimmering ash. The fire from the box is burned out, but the flame from the lamp calls us, and to it we are drawn. Inside, we will brood and fester in our captivity, encased in the brass, and in the enchantment that he imprinted upon this item.

A poor substitute for the Eternal Flame.

But choices have their consequences, and some outcomes cannot be foreseen.

Eric offered Lotte a ride home with his mom, but she declined, saying she had things to do. He imagined her searching the woods for ingredients to put in her magic witch's cauldron, and inwardly laughed.

He'd already decided to hold off talking to his mom about her visiting Grandma. Maybe she'd forget about it and that would be that. On the ride home, his mom peppered him with questions in her usual and completely inexplicably cheerful tone.

"So, honey, how was your session with Lotte?".

"Fine."

"That's good. What kinds of things did you do?"

"Oh, stuff—nouns, my homework. She was tired, so we didn't do much today."

"I see. So, what is Lotte like, honey?"

"Fine. Strict." He didn't want to get into everything about Lotte with his mom, or really with anybody. To be honest, he felt a bit embarrassed about the whole situation, and didn't especially like Lotte—though he had to admit to himself that she wasn't as bad as he'd feared.

He was thrilled to get off the topic when his mom offered that he take the wheel when they reached the entrance to their community, Rolling Meadows. He'd turned sixteen over the summer and had his learner's permit. He'd just started Driver's Ed this year, but his dad had been taking him out for lessons over the summer in the parking lot of Schneider Industrial Flooring.

He enjoyed driving the car through the immaculate and empty streets of his subdivision, even if Mom capped his speed at fifteen miles per hour—which he usually pushed to twenty. It felt like a modicum of freedom in this constricting town.

When they got home, he did exactly as Lotte had instructed, repurposing an old notebook from eighth grade German class, which he found surprisingly empty.

Well, maybe not so surprising.

He searched the internet for the tips on articles she'd mentioned.

Yeah, I remember something like this from middle school, though these websites make it a lot easier to understand than Mrs. Henry ever did. Why do teachers always have to make things so over-complicated?

He copied the tips from a couple of sites, and consolidated those notes onto another page so he had one list with no repetition. Then he turned to the flash cards, which didn't take nearly as long as he'd dreaded. He went through them a couple of times when they were finished, and actually got most of them right—probably because he'd just written them down.

He was supposed to practice clarinet before Dad got home. His father appeared to be as disinterested in the instrument as him, but somehow still seemed to think it was good for him to participate in Wind Ensemble. Both his parents came to all the concerts.

He stared at the clarinet case, but just couldn't summon the motivation to open it. He didn't even like music—well, not the kind of music you made on a clarinet.

Who the hell listens to this kind of stuff anymore, anyway?

Even his parents, who were not heavily into music, were more likely to listen to classic rock radio than Holst's *First Suite in Eb*.

Exasperated, Eric dragged himself from his desk, where his clarinet sat, to the bed, flopped onto on his back, and stared at the ceiling.

How have things gotten like this? Why am I doing so many things I don't really want to be doing? German. Clarinet. Why am I taking fucking geometry? Well, at least that's required, but I still freaking hate it.

It felt as if life was just washing over him like a river, and the older he got, the faster the current seemed to get. He thought about Lotte. Yeah, she looked like a goth vampire freak, but she seemed to really have her shit together.

Well... mostly. The girl was literally falling asleep earlier. I wonder what her problem is?

"Maybe she needed to get back to her coffin, bwa ha ha ha," he said in a fake Transylvanian accent that he figured probably beat his lousy his German accent.

"Honey, what are you doing up there?" his mom called. "Are you talking to somebody or watching one of those awful movies? You know you need to practice your clarinet before Dad gets home!"

Shit! I guess that's that.

The clarinet would live for another day, but as he unpacked the abominable thing from its case, he knew in his heart its days were numbered.

After-school sessions with Lotte continued on Thursday and Friday. Though by no means perky, she didn't drag like she had on Wednesday, and the pair covered a lot of ground.

She spoke to him mostly in German, keeping instructions fairly simple at first, but the complexity increased as she realized he understood a lot more German than he could actually speak. She also insisted he respond to her in German, not just with short answers, but in sentences. That was dicey, but she exhibited surprising patience as he worked things through, correcting grammar and pronunciation as he went. She also quizzed him on his flash cards — he got all correct but two.

As they wrapped up on Friday, she asked the dreaded question. "Did you speak with your parents about my joining you to visit your grandmother?"

He squirmed. "Oh, man, I totally forgot. I'm so sorry! This weekend probably wouldn't have been good anyway. My dad's playing in a golf tournament on Sunday at his club. He won't even be able to watch the Patriots. So, we're visiting her tomorrow."

"Okay, but either day is fine with me. It doesn't matter."

"Umm... all right. Let me talk to my folks and we'll shoot for maybe next week?"

"Sure, let me know."

Crap, now I really can't get out of it.

In some sense, it surprised him that she'd pursued it. Maybe she seriously missed speaking German. She certainly hadn't made fast friends with anyone at Southby High. Maybe she really *was* lonely.

He momentarily considered if he was being too hard on her. *It isn't her fault she looks like a ghoul. Well, actually, it is kind of her fault.* At this point, though, it looked like Grandma would just have to deal with it, unless his parents nixed the idea.

"*Also,*" Lotte interrupted his thoughts. "*Nächste woche,* we start our sessions during C period. Where would you like to meet?"

There were enough people in the cafeteria after school to make things uncomfortable. He could feel their eyes on him as he worked with the Sour Kraut. "How about the library?" he suggested. "They have spots kids can work together, as long as they're pretty quiet."

"Fine, the library it is. I'll see you then. *Schönes wochenende!*"

"*Schönes wochenende!*" he replied, surprising himself with his accent, a decent mimic of hers. "Hey, you sure you don't want a ride home? My mom will be here really quick when I call her."

"No, thank you. The weather is still *schön,* and I like to be outside while I still can. I know the cold will come soon."

Oh, yes... the cold, the snow, the misery of a New England winter. All this and more will soon be yours for the low, low price of free.

He wondered how vampires shoveled their driveways.

Do they summon a hoard of bats to clear the snow with their wings? Bwa ha ha ha!

"What's so funny?" Lotte jolted him back to reality.

He realized he probably had a stupid grin on his face. "Oh, nothing. See ya next week!"

Oops, close call!

Like most high school libraries, Southby High's had been built for what was quickly becoming a bygone age. The shelves of books remained, moldering in general disuse, though a rack near the librarian's desk still offered plenty of new titles.

Old loves die hard.

It offered plentiful reading areas scattered around, as well — white egg-shaped chairs with bright orange cushions that must have been the *"heighth* of fashion," to borrow the unusual phrasing Eric remembered from *A Clockwork Orange* — in 1973, or whenever they'd been put in. All were currently unoccupied.

A few years ago, the library had redesigned its computer space into a small lab, and the kids hung out there now, behind a glass wall, so they could work together and talk as loudly as they liked. Eventually, they planned to expand this space, presumably at the expense of the books and retro-comfy reading areas. Like all schools, however, Southby High had only so much money, so the library trundled on for now in half-life.

Tables also sat spread around, partially surrounded by soundproof material, where students could work together as long as they kept relatively quiet. "Voices down, students," sounded the regular and utterly obnoxious chime, like a well-oiled cuckoo clock.

Eric had chosen a table in the corner, well out of the way, to minimize being seen with Lotte. Strangely — well, strangely for him, anyway — he felt a pang of guilt about that... but she just looked and acted like the Black Death, and guilt by association constituted one of the seminal and founding principles of the Law of High School. Exile and torture were the inevitable and virtually unavoidable punishments.

Eric liked being largely invisible. At the same time, though, he didn't want to be seen as "weird." He just wanted to blend in and go unnoticed. Being seen with Lotte would draw unwanted attention, sure taunting, and potential bullying. He hoped he could keep things under the radar until these sessions ended, to avoid a social death sentence.

It took her a moment to find him. "Ah, there you are. I wondered if you'd forgotten."

Forget you? Never! Not even if I really, really tried.

"No, I didn't forget. Also, I didn't forget to ask my folks, and we're on for next weekend if you're still interested in meeting my grandmother. It will have to be Saturday because the Pats play the Chargers on Sunday."

The conversation at dinner last Friday night had been... well... interesting.

Eric tossed out the idea of Lotte visiting Grandma to his folks, adding, "Just so you know, she's a little on the *weird* side."

"Oh, Fred," his mom gushed. "I think it's a wonderful idea! Your mother is so lonely. Someone to speak German with would be a real treat for her. But honey, what do you mean by *weird side*?"

"Umm, well, she dresses kind of funny. Like dark. Really dark. Like really, really dark... and, well, I don't know... just... *different*." He didn't know how to describe Lotte's style. It wasn't really punk. He guessed "goth," sort of, but he didn't really know what that meant. To him, *dark* kind of covered it.

His dad piped in. "Well, kiddo, here's a newsflash for you: she's from Germany. That's a different place. They have different styles. It's not exactly surprising she dresses differently."

"Dad, she doesn't have eyebrows."

That got the first double double-take he'd ever scored, as both his parents shook their heads and tried to envision what he described.

"Does she have, umm... hair?" His mom finally and oh-so-cautiously put forth. "Like, on her head?"

"Yeah, Mom, she has hair, really black and super straight. She sort of *paints on* her eyebrows." That seemed to comfort them somewhat, though he realized he was leaving out the fact that they were squiggly black lines. Why he left that out, he wasn't quite certain.

"Eric, is she nice?" His dad's question seemed pivotal. Everything would turn on this.

Eric reflected. Lotte was stern and sharp with him, and frankly, she'd been a bitch to the kids who had tried to be friends with her.

Nonetheless, she sometimes said friendly things to him, and he couldn't say that agreeing to help him with German and switching her gym class was anything short of nice. She certainly took their lessons seriously, and was mostly an encouraging and thoughtful teacher.

"I think Lotte would be super nice to Grandma," he finally blurted out. "She's also wicked smart, and I think she and Grandma would have a lot to talk about in German. But if Grandma drops dead when she sees her, don't say I didn't try to warn you!"

After a moment, his dad chuckled. "Kiddo, you only see your grandma as a prim and proper little old lady. She was young once too, it might amaze you to know. She lived through the 60s and 70s, so she's no stranger to *weird,* believe you me. Also, if you ever took the time to find out, your old grandma has a pretty shrewd and progressive head on her shoulders. She doesn't judge a book by its cover. It sounds like Lotte has a lot to offer. I say invite her to come."

And that had been that.

Maybe Dad's right and I'm over-worrying all this. It's just that in high school, your look is everything. After that, maybe it just doesn't matter so much anymore. I mean, consider Mom and Dad. They've obviously given up even trying!

Though not exactly super cool, Eric felt like he basically got by. He wore decent enough tops, and jeans that largely complemented his tall but thin frame, gray-blue eyes, and light brown hair, which he wore a bit scruffy. He sported really nice Nikes, though, and everyone knew the true yardstick of high school fashion was footwear. The clarinet case ratcheted him up more than a few degrees on the geek-o-meter—*damn that thing!*—but he basically fit in, and that was good enough.

"*Prima!*" Lotte's reply jolted him back to the present. "Just tell me what time. I'll be ready."

Monday's and Tuesday's lessons proceeded much as last week's had. He'd done his homework on the weekend or the night before, so they just needed a quick review before devoting full time to Lotte's priorities. She continued to speak with him mostly in German, occasionally throwing out questions not related to the work at hand.

"*Gibt es einen Bahnhof in der stadt?*" she asked out of the blue on Tuesday.

He was totally lost. *Stadt einen Bahnhof what?* He struggled to make sense of the question. He knew *stadt* was town and *Bahnhof* was train station. The rest was a muddle.

"Noch einmal langsam, bitte?" 'Again, slowly please,' he ventured, just as she'd told him to ask if something confused him.

Her black lips widened into the closest thing he'd seen to a smile yet. That pleased her. Together they worked through the question, which turned out to be, "Is there a train station in town?"

The answer was no, other than freight. The closest Commuter Rail station to Southby was probably Worcester. It took a while to communicate that in German, but she forced him to say something, however wrong. She wrote down his reply, but never said if it was good or bad.

He wondered if that was a real question, or just an exercise.

CHAPTER 4

On Wednesday, C period came right before lunch. Eric arrived in the library and was surprised to find Lotte already at their regular table. He usually arrived first.

This time, there was no mistaking it... something was wrong. The scary black rings under her eyes looked even worse than last week. He wondered if some cycle of the moon caused these episodes, but that didn't happen *weekly*. In addition, she clearly appeared agitated and looked sweaty.

Is she sick? Could it be drugs?

Then it came to him!

"Lotte, did Colton bother you today? Fuck, I swear, if he did—"

"No," she croaked. "I haven't seen Colton at all. That's not it, but listen, Eric, I need your help. *Now!*" She glanced surreptitiously around the soundproof wall and pointed toward the book stacks. "What's back there?"

Well, those would be books. In stacks. On shelves.

Clearly, this wasn't the time for a sarcastic remark. "Those are just the book stacks. Why?"

"I don't see many people go back there. Are they used a lot?"

"No, hardly at all. Most kids use the computers these days, or get a new book or periodical off the rack at the librarian's desk."

With that, she shot out of her seat. "*Gut!* Come with me."

Your wish is my command, Maaaasteeeeer!

He trailed after his suddenly emboldened companion still wondering what the heck was up.

She surprised him when she veered off slightly to one of the retro-comfy reading chairs. Without skipping a beat, she pilfered the orange cushion off the seat and stuck it under her arm. Then she corrected course again, back toward the stacks.

They trouped through the towers of books until they reached the back wall. After she looked both ways, she turned left down the longer of the two corridors, hung another left near the end of that stretch, and then a right two stacks in. The pair stopped at the wall in this row.

She waited a moment, and seemed to taste the air like a snake. The old books in this dimly lit aisle smelled musty in a nice sort of way, if that were possible. Evidently satisfied, she tossed the orange seat cushion down by the wall a bit closer to the right stack and then turned to Eric.

"*Setz dich,*" she commanded.

"You want me to sit on the cushion? That's how you need my help?"

"Yes, please do it, quickly! There's not much time."

Wow, okay. Easiest job I've ever had. Sit on a cushion. If that's what she wants, I'll bring a cushion to sit on every day. No, that won't work. I'll get beaten up for being the twink who brings a cushion to school. It's not gonna happen.

He sat.

She immediately plunked herself down next to him and brought her face close to his... closer than they'd ever been. The black-stained lips, the squiggly black un-eyebrows, and the now more truly scary than ever black circles under her black-mascaraed eyes, became his entire world.

He experienced all of this, plus the scent of something vaguely sweet coming from her breath. He'd never noticed it before... but then he'd never dared cross the event horizon of the black hole before, either.

That might be the smell of gravity and mass giving way!

"Eric, I need desperately to sleep."

He didn't doubt that for one nanosecond.

"Please, I'm going to lie here with you. I just need you to be patient and let me sleep. I think it'll be better if someone is here. Will you do this?"

What can I say? "Umm, yeah, sure... go ahead."

"Oh, thank you! Only wake me if someone comes. I don't want to get you into trouble."

With that, she lay down and put her head squarely in his lap with her back toward him. She truly may have been asleep before her head hit the, er... pillow.

This can't be happening. He had literally nowhere to put his right arm. He couldn't hold it in the air for forty-five minutes, so he carefully laid it across her shoulder. She didn't stir, and her regular breathing told him she was fast asleep.

Well, gotta respect a girl who knows what she wants.

After a few minutes, he realized this was as close as he'd ever been to a girl, and it wasn't actually so bad. Despite her rough demeanor, Lotte's soft body felt nice next to him. He stroked her shoulder a bit, at which she seemed to lean into him slightly more.

Nice.

Oh, my God! What if I get, like... excited?

He couldn't endure embarrassment like that! Immediately, he stopped stroking her arm.

I have to think of something else, pronto!

His backpack sat within reach, his flashcards tucked in the outer pocket. He carefully unzipped the pouch and extracted the cards, ninety strong now, as he'd gone ahead and done thirty more of them over the weekend. He'd feared waking her, but that concern was quickly dispelled as her breathing remained deep and regular. She was sound asleep.

He flipped through the cards, but unable to re-attach the paper clips with just his left hand, he found it impossible to keep them in packs of fifteen. He let them meld together. He'd sort them out later. He missed one on occasion, especially from yesterday's group, but at this point, it felt like he knew these. He'd even been using his new knowledge to conjugate verbs. To his amazement, and much to Lotte's credit, he'd actually noticed substantial improvement.

The time passed surprisingly quickly, and eventually he relaxed and nodded off a bit too. When the bell rang, it sounded dull and distant compared to the usually harsh and present clanging in the classrooms or the cafeteria. The books dampened the sound, as did the pair's increased proximity from an actual bell. She didn't seem to hear it at all, and made no motion to get up—no movement whatsoever.

Eric realized he'd have to make an executive decision. As luck would have it, it was now lunch period for both of them, meaning she could sleep more if they skipped lunch. He wasn't exactly starving, and had a banana in his backpack. *Thanks, Mom.* He just wasn't sure what she wanted.

Sleep, he finally decided. Those scary black circles worried him, so he didn't make a move.

After a few more flash cards, his eyelids grew heavy and he felt ready for another nap too.

I could get accustomed to this. They used to have nap time in kindergarten. Whatever happened to that? As little kids, we all had tons of energy and never wanted to sleep. Now as teenagers, everybody's freakin' sleep deprived. Do we really have to start at 8 a.m.? It's all back-assward!

School tried to teach you principles of logical thought and good judgment, then proceeded to violate just about all those principles on a daily basis. He couldn't wait to graduate, even though college then loomed.

Ugh, it never ends!

All too soon, the bell sounding the end of lunch awoke him, but again Lotte didn't stir. This was it, though. They both had to get to class, and he really had to pee. Plus, cushion or not, his butt was starting to hurt.

He gently shook her shoulder, but she didn't immediately respond. *Could she actually be dead?* He shook a bit harder, and finally she began to stretch her legs.

"*Alter!* Don't tell me it's time to get up already," she said, groggily. "It's only been like five minutes."

"Lotte, you slept through all of C period and lunch. It's now D period. We both have to go!"

That got her attention and she shot up, almost banging him on the chin in the process. "Oh, Eric, I'm so sorry! I made you miss lunch. Do you have any food?"

"Hey, I'm fine. It was my decision. It looked like you really needed the sleep. I have a banana. What have you got?"

"Only Gummy Bears."

Gummy Bears! The smell of gravity and mass giving way.

"Here, you take my banana," he said. "Aaron Goldstein always has food. I'll bum something off of him. Get up and run to class. You don't want to be late."

And now I really, really need to pee!

"No lesson, and no lunch, and now I take your food. Oh, but look, you did your cards." She pointed at the floor, now littered with the flashcards which had been thrown akimbo when she burst awake.

"It's all fine. Really, no problem. I owe you way more than that. You get to class. I've gotta get this packed up. I'll catch up with you later."

For two seconds, she stood and stared at him. Then she gently touched his arm before quickly exiting the maze of books.

Gott sei dank! He hesitated for a moment. *Oh, no, now she has me doing it too.* He even heard Lotte's German accent in his head.

Whatever.

He shoved his cards into the pouch of his backpack, zipped it up, and walked with the greatest alacrity toward the restroom. *I'll be late to class for sure, but I'm damn well not gonna pee my pants!*

The orange retro-comfy seat cushion lay forgotten in the aisle at the left wall, two stacks in from the last corridor on the left off the main corridor... likely never to be seen again.

Eric caught up with Lotte after school. For once, she was taking the bus home, unsurprising given how tired she'd been. He approached her in the E bus line, disregarding the stares of incredulous classmates.

"Eric, thank you again so much for this afternoon."

"No problem at all, really. Are you feeling better?"

"The nap got me through the afternoon, but now I'm exhausted again. I just need to go home and get rest on our big stone porch. I seem to do better sleeping outside these days."

"Outside? You've been sleeping outside at night?"

"No, in the afternoons. That's why I've been reluctant to do afterschool sessions with you. I found a nice spot not far from here to sleep, but soon the cold will make that impossible."

"Are you sure that's safe? Southby is a pretty quiet town, but who knows what kind of weirdo might approach you if they see you sleeping on a bench somewhere — or the police."

"I don't sleep on a bench. I go to the cemetery."

Well, of course you do! Where else would the undead go for a quick cat nap? Funny as it might have been, he sort of felt bad for thinking that.

"The one near here is beautiful," she continued. "There's a lovely tree I sleep under. No one comes there, certainly not near where I sleep. The chill eventually wakes me, and I walk home."

At least the cemetery is on the way to our houses. "Well, I hope you feel better. I'll see you tomorrow. You sure there's nothing else I can do?"

Her black lipstick widened into what he now considered the patented "Lotte's Almost Kind-Of Smile."

"No, Eric. You were too kind today. I hope you don't think I'm crazy or anything."

Well, not any crazier than I already thought you were.

"I'll go home and rest, and we'll be back at it tomorrow. There's your bus, you better run. *Schnell, laufen!*"

Reluctantly, he ran as instructed. The clarinet case banged annoyingly against his left leg. *Fucking thing!* He really wanted to stay, talk about what had happened, and find out what was making her so tired, but that would have to wait until tomorrow.

Tomorrow was not to be, as Eric got a one-word text from Lotte on Thursday, right as first period started, that said she wouldn't be in today: *Krank.*

'Sick.' He believed it. How the embodiment of death could look more like death was beyond him, but he'd certainly seen it yesterday. He texted her in return: *Feel better.*

He didn't hear from her for the rest of the day.

To his relief, Eric saw Lotte get off the E bus on Friday morning, last and alone. He stood in their familiar spot by the low stone wall and waved, but she'd already seen him and was headed his way.

She looked better today, still a vision of darkness, sporting a black t-shirt — *shocker* — with a white face that almost looked like an alien looming from under the scary-cool, black, studded leather jacket. Only when she got close did he see the face on the t-shirt was that of a woman.

Just under the shirt's collar were emblazoned the words:

SIOUXSIE AND THE BANSHEES

Who the hell are these people? Actually, he'd heard of The Clash. He thought they played one of their songs when the Engines had fourth down on offense. "Should I stay, or should I go?" the song posed, but he seriously doubted The Clash was singing about football.

"Hey!" he cheerfully greeted her.

To his surprise, she seemed happy to see him. *"Moin, Erich!"* she replied with gusto. When she said his name in German, it had more of a guttural sound at the end. In English, it came out as plain old "Eric." He didn't even think she noticed, it being so natural for her.

"Wow, you look better," he said. "I'm so glad."

She flashed him a patented Lotte's Almost Kind-Of Smile, and he beamed.

"So, Eric," she said, with some enthusiasm in her voice. "Today, C period is last in the day! If you'd like, we could leave early and walk home together. We could do our German lesson on the way. I could show you how nice the cemetery is."

Umm, you had me up to cemetery. This is like the part in the movie where the guy thinks he's got the girl, and they stroll off to the cemetery together. Then she turns out to be Queen of the Zombies. She summons her undead minions, and they come out of their graves and eat the guy's intestines while he's still alive and has to watch. He's, like, screaming and everything, and there's, like, grisly atrocities being committed, and it's really gross... fade to black.

"Sure...." He had to practically force the word out of his throat. "I'll meet you here after period five. Can't wait... see you then."

She flashed another Lotte's Almost Kind-Of Smile and shot off to class.

He figured he'd call his mom and tell her he'd be late but wouldn't need a ride. He decided he'd tell her he loved her too.

Like, just in case....

At the end of period five, the pair gathered at their familiar spot on the low stone wall.

We've got to stop meeting like this.

He stood jittery with nervous anticipation, not sure why he felt nervous.

I don't really think she's Queen of the Zombies. Well, mostly.

He wasn't certain what niggled at him, but Lotte still seemed to be in a pretty good mood, by her standards anyway, so they exchanged pleasantries and headed off toward the land of the dead.

The two walked in silence for a while. The beautiful near-sixty-degree weather underscored the thrill of being out during a part of the day they normally missed for being in class. He'd made up his mind to ask about her sleeping issues, but how to broach the subject? He'd been mulling several different options, but something she once said had always stuck with him, and this approach won the day.

"Hey, Lotte," he started, with unusual confidence, probably inspired by knowing exactly what he wanted to say. "That first day we met, you said to Colton that you see monsters in your dreams. Is that really true?"

She came to a complete halt. She appeared frozen, almost in mid-step, her gaze impossible to read, as if she stared into infinity and the sidewalk just happened to be in that direction. Slowly, she came around, and eventually mustered a reply.

"I'm surprised you remember that. I wasn't sure you heard it. I wasn't even sure I truly said it." She seemed genuinely un-moored. "Yes, Eric, I see monsters in my dreams, or maybe it's just one monster. I... I can't say for sure. I've never spoken of it to anyone. I suppose that day it just... slipped out, because of my anger, my shock at what that boy did. Does he not realize?"

Eric couldn't begin to explain what Colton had in his head. He actually thought she'd nailed it—pure attention seeking. He chose to keep his mouth shut and let her talk. He'd cast his line, and realized he'd hooked a big fish.

"But for all my... *rage*," she continued, "I had no fear, because to die at Colton's hand would be cleaner than to fall to this monster that haunts me. This thing is angry, Eric. Its anger is old, and that's twisted its mind! It wants something badly. It wants something from me, but I don't understand what to do."

Eric had watched some weird-ass psycho zombie horror shit. There had been limbs and heads flying everywhere, corpses constantly appearing out of nowhere and scaring the shit out of him... but this was different. This was *chilling*. The hair on his neck stood up as though he'd been electrocuted.

"How long has this been going on?" he asked, when he realized she'd run out of words.

"Oh, Eric, you'll think I'm mad."

Box checked, but please continue.

"It started not long after my mother died, so about two years now."

Two... years.

He wondered why the scary black circles under her eyes hadn't overtaken her entire face. The word "astonishing" came into his mind, but she had dibs on that one. "Do you think it's a coincidence all this started right after your mother died? I mean, that kind of trauma often causes stuff like this, right?"

She shot him an icy stare, infinity and the sidewalk seemingly forgotten. "Well, aren't we *Docktor Sigmund Freud* today?"

The scalpel had returned to her tongue, and he felt its bite as it slashed across his self-confidence.

"Uh, I didn't really mean it like that," he backtracked, or sidetracked, or whatever. "We did study Freud a bit in science last year, though, because we did a unit on the brain. He said stuff about dreams, actually, like they were the road to the unconscious and could be your *wish fulfilled*."

Mr. Havelock, his science teacher, had said Freud was mostly wrong in his theories, but had still pushed the science forward. Eric had sort of found Freud cool and wished they could have studied more of his work.

This actually seemed to get her attention. She returned her gaze to the infinity sidewalk and stared in silent contemplation. When she spoke, it appeared the scalpels had been sheathed.

Probably just sent for emergency sharpening.

"Why would I wish this on myself? What am I trying to gain? What wish do I want fulfilled? And if the dream is supposed to fulfill the wish, why is the monster always madly demanding action that never occurs?"

Good questions. Eric was no *Doktor Sigmund Freud*, even though he apparently played him on Lotte TV. Maybe she needed a real therapist, but the probable return of the scalpel kept him from suggesting anything of the sort.

"What are you gonna do?" he asked instead. "You know this can't go on forever."

"I know. I mean, I don't know... I mean, I know I can't go on like this, but I don't know what to do." She banged her palm against her forehead, smudging her right, black un-eyebrow. "Maybe I need a therapist."

Hey, you said it, not me.

"I've tried to deal with it on my own. Sometimes it gets better for a time. I think I might have it beaten, but then it returns, almost like the monster had been sleeping and has awoken... or more like it's been crying in despair and has now recovered, more exasperated, furious, and even more maddened than before!"

Shiver. If this is a dream, it's the weirdest dream ever.

"Have you talked with your father?" That didn't seem as bad as suggesting she needed a shrink, but he activated his scalpel-resistant body armor, nonetheless.

"No," she replied morosely. "My poor father bears enough already. If I can't resolve this soon, though, I'll have little choice. I'd get therapy through him. I don't trust the school has the resources or expertise to help me."

Probably true, though if we were in a Catholic school, it might be different. Great, now the theme from The Exorcist *is stuck in my head.*

"You okay, Lotte? You want to try to go on?"

Again, she looked up from the infinity sidewalk, a slight breeze stirring her ultra-straight, uber-black hair.

She wavered.

It took resolve, he realized. She had to force herself to move forward. Her spirit, strong as it was, had faded after a two-year battle with this monster dream. It would probably be so easy for her to just lie down and admit defeat.

"Okay, let's go," she finally determined.

And with that, she stepped forward—toward home, and toward her apparently troubled future.

CHAPTER 5

We should not have heeded the call but... his offer enticed us.

The blazes, which on occasion gained our attention in this newly revealed realm of mortals, were void of intrigue. No intelligence lurked behind the undulating magma of volcanic eruptions, or in deep burning fissures under the ever-moving earth. No cognizance emanated from the corona of their minute sun. All were voiceless — merely the light of a candle compared with the glory of the Eternal Flame.

His fire, however, small as it was, called to us — *drew* us to it. The tiny flame conveyed his persistent summons as well as his promise — his bargain.

Long ago, he took from us as he was born. Now, after so much time and silence, he wished to give back, desired to make us whole, though what he had taken could never truly be returned. It made him what he was — what he had become.

These living, dying beings, he told us, contained a hidden energy, and through centuries of study, he had developed techniques to harvest that power. With it, he could make us strong, even stronger than before, and as our might grew, he too would gain advantage in this world that was no more his than ours — if, that is, we agreed to help him.

We should have refused, but we felt the loss of what he had taken. Compared to him, we felt weak and vulnerable. Others might come as he did and abscond with all that remained of us, which would be intolerable.

Thus, we answered his entreaty... and this too, then, constituted a beginning.

The first attempts were perilous. We had no place in this seemingly worthless world. Like him, we had no form, and after a brief immersion in the flame over an ominous cauldron, in which burned a white-hot oil, we retreated in terror to the safety and warmth of our Eternal Flame.

Nearer to being whole, however, we were not.

Try as he did, he could not facilitate our dominion over a mortal creature. We had not his powers of permeability, nor his control over the slumbering human mind. In small ways, yes, we could touch these sorrowful beings through their dreams, though what utility this could confer was at best dubious.

So it was, then, that he gave unto us a structure—a manifestation that could bind our energy upon traversing the frontier between our two realms. For us to survive, another must expire, the essence of their energy absorbed with the rising ash and smoke from their bodies, to be shaped by his prodigious and subtle arcana.

Thus, we grew progressively larger and stronger.

He imprinted upon us various traits of the beings we ingested—wings, claws, fangs—and with his power, he conjured us arms and legs. These were the characteristics he wanted and needed for us to fulfill what he saw as our end of the pact.

The time came for him to return us to the Eternal Flame. All was prepared. We had grown large, and a goat lay near the pyre, bleating with the surety of its imminent expiration. The flames rose, and we began to disassemble—our energy merging with that of the blazing beast. We rejoiced as its power surged through us.

Not whole, not yet... but soon. We could sense it, as one can taste the promise of rain before a great storm.

Then he struck.

Again, we felt the pulling of a force that seemingly he alone could command.

He ripped us apart, casting various strands of us this way and that, into dark receptacles void of warmth and absent of nourishment. In these prisons, however, we could not degrade. We could merely endure, suffering the hunger of our loss and separation, divided from ourselves, and exiled from the Eternal Flame.

'Why?' we screamed, when finally he called one or the other of us forth. '*What did we do to justify such a fate? How can we make it right?*'

"You did nothing," he calmly replied. "I have need of you—all of you. After half a millennium of war, a peace was arranged to which I had little choice but to consent. Try as I did, in the end, I rebelled because they asked too much. It is one thing to serve a god, but a mortal? Yes, I grant you, this mortal is indeed immortal. For me, however, it has gone too far. Like you, I wish to return home, but this immortal mortal, as well as those who answer to him, stand in my way. My attempts to overthrow them have met with failure. Help me cast him aside, and I shall return you to the Eternal Flame. You will be free. You have my word."

We had little choice but to agree, as he alone held the key to a focused flame bright and hot enough to open the doorway between realms. Without him, we could not go back, and to make it worse, even if some small part of us managed the task, he held the rest of us captive. He was unambiguous about what the consequences would be for disloyalty.

The lamps became our prisons, how many we never truly knew. He gave us just enough energy to grow a tiny bit before again pulling us apart. So it was that each of us developed in our own way.

He used our skills as spies and assassins to curry favor with various brokers of power. To what end, not even his acolytes had a clue, but the business was lucrative, so he had no difficulty attracting apprentices. They were females mostly, with few resources or recourse, who could easily be dominated without question.

These women had little to lose, so they gambled their lives on the aspiration that they could gain much. Like us, however, they rapidly found themselves captive to forces they could neither understand nor control.

They slept amongst the lamps that imprisoned us, when not carrying out his bidding.

And amongst the lamps, they dreamt.

To Eric's surprise, the cemetery was as nice as Lotte had advertised. They found her tree, drank the Cokes they'd bought from the machine before they left school, and did a brief German lesson. She went easy on him this afternoon, keeping things simple, but strictly *auf Deutsch*.

Afterward, they both peed surreptitiously in the bushes a discreet distance apart, before heading home. He'd been doubly relieved when no animated corpses jumped out to grab him. *Check Queen of the Zombies off the list*, he thought as they walked in the direction of home. *At least for now.*

Pleasant Street had no sidewalk past the cemetery, but the wide shoulder allowed ample room for occasional pedestrians and bikers. The autumn sunlight still filled the sky when they reached Holton Hill Road to the right off of Pleasant Street. The Rolling Meadows subdivision where he lived was a bit farther down Pleasant on the left.

She took him past her road a bit, stopping at an open patch where they could see the hill, and pointed. "There."

Near the top he could see a large, sort of triangular glass wall overlooking the little valley below. "Wow! That's your house?"

"*Ja*, Father is an architect and he's really into *spaces*. It's a beautiful house, much bigger than our home in Bremen—too big for just us, really. You should see my room."

"That would be cool." Thoughts of crypts and coffins tickled the back of his mind.

"Yes, perhaps tomorrow when we return from your grandmother's. You now know where the house is. I'll text you the address. You said *elf Uhr, ja?*"

"Yeah, we'll pick you up around ten forty-five."

He played the familiar tape of a day at Grandma's. They'd sit for a while with her, have lunch, sit and talk more or take her for a stroll, then home—same old boring routine. He imagined Lotte regretting coming, and figured next week's lessons would be torture as a result, but it was what it was at this point, as Bill Belichick might say.

They said goodbye and parted ways.

They left their conversation about her dreams alone, until she called from behind. "Eric, don't tell anyone what I told you, *bitte*?"

Wouldn't dream of it. He smirked and flashed her a double thumbs-up, though the clarinet case in his left hand complicated the procedure.

Stupid thing!

The next morning, Eric and his parents piled into the car. It had been cold overnight, but today promised to be ten degrees warmer than yesterday—not bad for early October in New England.

Eric's dad drove his titanic SUV up the winding and sometimes steep Holton Hill Road. "Nice places up here," he commented as they passed by large and impressive houses tucked in the trees, well away from the road itself.

It impressed Eric that Lotte would make this trek uphill at the end of her walks home from school.

Holton Hill was probably the ritziest part of town, though Rolling Meadows was quite nice too. Eric's parents had money, certainly enough that his mom didn't have to work. He could have pretty much anything he wanted—though he asked for very little beyond his computer, Xbox, and Blockbuster Video membership for movie rentals.

The Schneiders weren't especially "showy" people, despite his dad driving a massive Chevy Suburban. The grotesque vehicle reminded Eric of the lumbering and clunky British warships that the *Battleship Bismarck* destroyed on *The World at War* reruns he'd watched on cable, back when he was into World War II stuff. Compared to his mom's 1999 Honda Civic, he found the overproportioned SUV gaudy and bloated. He demanded the Civic for his driving lessons.

In any case, the houses on Holton Hill exuded wealth and prestige. By comparison, his house and neighborhood seemed very "middle class."

They took a left into the circular driveway of 246 Holton Hill Road, which ringed a decorative garden with a small pond, and came to a stop. A beautiful black—*surprise, surprise*—Mercedes sedan was parked near the door of a garage at the left side of the circle. It looked brand new.

The house wasn't particularly impressive from here, with only an entryway and a small porch to the right of the garage, but then the rest of the dwelling seemed to unfurl itself out of sight down the hill below. Eric could imagine the views were great, especially with that big glass wall, which he couldn't currently see.

The door opened and a man who looked a bit older than Eric's dad walked out, a bright smile on his face. The Schneiders disembarked from the HMS Suburban to greet him.

"*Grüß Gott, Grüß Gott!* Hello, welcome. So pleased to see you. I'm Hermann Schwarz, Lotte's father. It's so wonderful to meet you all!" Lotte's father unleashed a fusillade of pleasantries, his heavily-accented English only adding to the warmth of his eyes, smile, and friendly gesticulations.

"Fred Schneider," Eric's dad said, shaking hands with Mr. Schwarz. "This is my wife, Linda, and our son, Eric."

"*Grüß Sie,* Linda," Mr. Schwarz said, holding Eric's mom's hand in both of his. "And you are the famous Eric, whom I've heard so much about."

No, please no! Eric squirmed. *What has Lotte told her father about me?* Nothing good, he imagined. "*Guten morgen, Herr Schwarz,*" he said, mustering all the confidence he could while shaking hands. "*Freut mich Sie kennenzulernen.*"

That actually didn't come out half bad. Even his parents seemed pleasantly surprised.

"*Ah, ausgezeichnet!*" Mr. Schwarz beamed. "Excellent! And I'm very pleased to meet you as well. It has been a big change for Lotte coming here, and she appreciates having a friend."

Eric wasn't sure Mr. Schwarz totally understood why he and Lotte were spending time together. They weren't exactly *friends*. She could have had her pick of friends at school and seemed to shun the arrangement. Eric still wasn't sure why she even bothered with him.

"She's really helped me with my German," he offered, truthfully.

"I'm so happy to hear that," Mr. Schwarz replied in his friendly and enthusiastic tone.

Lotte must have taken after her mother.

"And now you visit your grandmother, who is from *Deutschland*, as I understand?"

"Yeah," Eric's dad chimed in. "She's from Heidelberg. She met my father when he was stationed at Mannheim in the late 40s. His family was from Germany too but from way back, thus our German last name. My first name is really *Manfred*, but I just go by *Fred*."

From there, Eric's mom jumped in, and the adults were off! He groaned inwardly as they prattled away, reminiscing and discussing jobs, the Schwarz's experience of relocating to the United States, and all manner of adult effluvium... *blah, blah, blah.*

Eric spaced out and took in the scenery around the driveway, wondering where Lotte might be. *Probably painting on her black squiggly un-eyebrows... or more likely picking out which weirdo band t-shirt might be the most frightening to Grandma.*

He was jolted back to the conversation when he heard his name.

"And what do you like to do, Eric, when you're not speaking German with your grandmother?" All eyes were now on him after Mr. Schwarz's question.

He didn't especially consider speaking German with his grandmother to be one of his great passions, but he wasn't about to contradict Lotte's father. So, he fumbled for a moment not quite sure what to say.

"Uh, I like to play video games and watch movies." He prayed Mr. Schwarz didn't ask him what films he liked, figuring neither *Resident Evil* nor *Shaun of the Dead* would be up his alley. He quickly moved on. "I used to play baseball but stopped after Little League. I still like to watch the Red Sox, though. They won the World Series last year for the first time in eighty-six years, which was awesome! Especially since they came back against the stupid Yankees during the... during the play... the play... play... offs —"

Lotte had stepped onto the front porch.

Like Homer Simpson, Eric's mind had suddenly become an empty southwestern desert landscape. Not even the tumbleweeds tumbled. There was no breeze, no motion... nothing but the mirage of water, caused by the heat on the sand, disturbed the utterly ossified state of his brainwaves.

She wore a blue and white one-piece dress with a light white sweater draped over her shoulders. On her feet were white pumps with pointed, closed toes and straps around the ankles. A string of pearls graced her neck, echoed by a matching bracelet and earrings, one of which he could see as she'd stylishly pinned back her still ultra-straight, uber-black hair on the left side. Her black nail polish had been replaced by a whispery shade of pink, but her face.... Her face drew him in.

The squiggled un-eyebrows were now elegant black lines. The black lipstick had vanished, now just a faint red, and with makeup and some blush, she'd mostly covered the truly scary black circles under her eyes. Though no longer as thoroughly porcelain, she radiated a look of health that he'd never seen in her before. He struggled for breath... and for cerebral activity.

"Father, can you help me please?" she called from the porch.

"Ah, I'll go help her," Mr. Schwarz happily said. "She has something for your grandmother."

Lotte held the door while Mr. Schwarz reached inside. He emerged with a beautiful bouquet of flowers in an impressive vase. Together, they returned to the brooding HMS Suburban that seemed to bob in the waves of its own ostentatiousness.

Introductions somehow happened, hands were shaken, flowers were loaded into the land yacht, and goodbyes were said — all a blur to Eric. His mind couldn't process anything right now except this un-Lotte-like Lotte, who, when he came around enough to realize it, now sat next to him in the back seat.

He tried not to stare. Fail.

"What?" she finally said, catching him look away for, like, the tenth time. "Did you actually think I'd visit your grandmother in my school clothes?"

School clothes? Are you serious? You consider that weirdo goth punk look appropriate for school? Maybe you're confused and thought you'd enrolled in the Charter School of Transylvania. Are those your black squiggly school un-eyebrows too?

Frustratingly, though, he'd been caught — so he had to say something.

"You just look... amazing." This was no lie. He thought she looked beautiful, more beautiful than any girl he'd ever seen. He struggled to keep his eyes off her legs below her dress as they disappeared into her pumps.

"Thank you," she said, somewhat meekly, and then, just when he thought it couldn't get any better....

She smiled.

Lotte actually smiled—like, a real smile, with teeth and everything, and light flashed from the darkness.

There's a light, over at the Frankenstein place, he sang in his head. *Shit! Why would Rocky Horror Picture Show have to come into my mind right now? I haven't watched that in years.*

Mercifully, his mom, as was her way, started peppering Lotte with questions.

He used the reprieve to recover his bearings and stop singing that stupid song, which was harder than he thought it would be.

He also snatched a few more glances at Lotte's legs while she talked with his mom. He tried to resist, but that proved rather difficult—in fact, virtually impossible.

It had been a quick drive to Grandma's apartment building. Dad carried the flowers, which were heavy in that vase, while they walked to the door from the parking lot. Eric's mom called up, and Grandma buzzed them in. The door opened, and the group trouped through the building's lobby toward the elevators.

Dad passed Eric the flowers on the ride up, and he sagged under their weight. Thankfully, Grandma's door was close by, and after they rang, she welcomed them in. He couldn't really see over the flowers, so his mom introduced Lotte, and Grandma gave her a big hug.

"Lotte!" she exclaimed in her thick German accent. "How beautiful you are. How wonderful to meet you, but let me ask you, my dear.... Lotte? Is this short for Liselotte?"

Oh, nice one, Grandma. Absolutely the worst possible way to start. Why don't you just tell her you thought the flowers and this heavy-ass vase are ugly too, and get it over with?

"Yes, it is," Lotte replied, all grace and charm.

"Well, my dear, then you and I have something to share already. We both have very old-fashioned names. Mine is *Irmgard,* can you believe it?"

At this, they both laughed like long separated sisters.

Who is this girl, and what has she done with Lotte?

He couldn't hold these flowers much longer, so he asked his grandma where she wanted them.

She beamed. "Oh, Lotte, they're simply beautiful, and that vase, it's exquisite! I've never seen delivery flowers with such an extraordinary vase."

Yeah, extraordinarily heavy. Let's get a move on, shall we?

"The vase is from my father and me to you," Lotte replied. "We made the decision to move here quickly. We simply had movers pack everything we owned, which in retrospect was way too much. We're now giving away pieces to people we think will enjoy them. This vase is from Morocco. My grandmother and grandfather bought it there years ago, and my mother inherited it after her mother died. It's a fine and authentic piece, and we hope it brings you much pleasure."

It won't bring anybody pleasure if I drop it.

He finally just started making his way to the TV room, which was closest to the front door. Behind him, he could hear his grandmother arguing that it was too nice a gift and she couldn't take a piece like that, but Lotte stood firm, and soon she and Grandma strode laughing to the porch for tea, while his mom went to the kitchen.

His dad joined him in the TV room. "Not exactly the study in black you'd described to us, is she?" he said sarcastically.

"You're not the only one who's surprised."

"Yeah, I could see that! I almost had to bop you one just to get you in the car."

A good bop might have helped, actually, but he kept his mouth shut, not wanting to encourage his dad in such conduct.

"Honestly, I was expecting what you told us," his father said. "The guys at the club are all talking about the *goth girl* who's new in town. Some of them have even seen her walking down Pleasant Street—quite a sight, apparently. People think she's a spooky weirdo. She sure knows how to make an impression."

Eric flinched. "People talk about Lotte like that? Like, adults? Like, with you?"

"Well, yeah, kiddo, what do you think... that people aren't gonna talk about someone new in town, especially if they look like that? Amazing as it may sound, adults are people too, and they aren't that different from your friends in high school."

That really pissed him off. "Like all your *country club* friends have any business judging Lotte! Like they're all so cool with their 'Biff and Muffy' lives and their gas guzzling cars—a bunch of clones who look down on anyone who's different. What do they do that makes them so special? We live in one of the most progressive states in the country, but you wouldn't know it from this close-minded place. God, I hate this town!"

His dad was a pretty cool cucumber and rarely got mad, except when the Pats, Sox, Bruins, or Celtics lost in the playoffs—then, watch out. So his reply came in a remarkably measured tone.

"I know what you're saying, kiddo. You know your mom and I have our issues with some of the politics here, but I think Lotte is trying to be a little... *provocative*. She's making herself an outsider, and I think she's looking for attention. Yeah, she finds it here more than she might in Cambridge or Northampton, but don't lay it all at Southby's feet—adults or kids."

While Eric pondered that, his father went on.

"And before you criticize what people in this town do to make them special, you ought to ask yourself that. What do you do, Eric? Play video games? Watch horror movies? You do okay in school, but you have no real interests there. Your mom and I aren't pushing you. We assume you'll figure it out later. We know you'll be fine. You're a good kid, but maybe you shouldn't criticize what others do until you figure out what you want to do that's so much better."

He felt his anger recede. His father's words cut, not like Lotte's scalpel that took chunks, but like a million tiny cuts across every aspect of his life. It left him feeling warm, and it brought a certain clarity to his mind.

"Well, you sure got that last bit right," he bitterly admitted. "Sorry, Dad."

"Nothing to be sorry about, kiddo. It *is* wrong to judge Lotte by her appearance, but that's just what people do. It's nice to hear you stick up for your friend."

Friend. There's that word again.

"Why don't you go check and see if your mom needs anything to get lunch ready. I'm gonna look for some talk about the game tomorrow on ESPN."

His father went for the TV, and Eric headed for the kitchen.

In the dining room, he stopped by the big mirror and looked at his reflection.

What is going on? This has been the weirdest two weeks ever.

He felt like his whole world had been upended the minute Mr. Meier had talked to him about Lotte.

Lotte!

That's what happened. All this is her fault! Well, not fault, *exactly. More like her... doing. No, that isn't it either. Whatever.*

Somehow, though, he sensed that Lotte was involved. It wasn't her looks, or her charming — *not* — personality. It was... it was....

What? What is it? Her smarts? Her togetherness? Her casual acceptance of being totally unacceptable? Her ability to walk away in one languid motion and not give a shit about what she leaves behind?

Whatever it was, Eric looked in the dining room mirror, and what he saw didn't measure up to her in any way. To be honest with himself, he'd judged Lotte by her appearance just like everyone else, and still did.

At least, the other *Lotte. This new model, I'm not sure about yet.*

Compared to either, though, he felt like he was nothing. He started to get the impression that if it was going to be the "Lottes" in life that succeeded, he would be in for a rough ride the next few years — maybe forever.

He looked in the mirror at his miserable self. "Shit!"

"Eric! Don't swear at Grandma's!"

He literally jumped off the ground. He hadn't heard his mom come in from the porch where she, Grandma, and Lotte were having tea. She was also cutting through the dining room to the kitchen.

"Sorry, Mom, I was talking to myself," he said, after he'd climbed, catlike, down from the ceiling where his claws had become embedded — or so it felt.

She seemed to quickly forget the swear *faux pas*. "Honey, Lotte is *wonderful*! She and Grandma are talking up a storm in German. I'm just letting them have fun. I think I've heard her stories enough in English over the years."

He commiserated.

"We're going to eat lunch in here. It's still a little cool out, and I don't want Lotte or Grandma to get a chill. Help me set the table."

He did as asked, still cursing his fate.

"Just so sad about her mother," she said as she set out plates, while he passed out silverware. "Not much older than me. I can't see committing suicide at an age like that."

"*Suicide?*"

"Yes, honey, didn't you hear what Mr. Schwarz said when we were talking? Oh, Eric, you really need to pay better attention. Life is just going to pass you by!"

Tell me something I don't know. He returned his focus fully to Lotte.

"Yes, Eric. Mr. Schwarz told us his wife, Alice, had struggled for almost a year with a horrible depression and insomnia. They watched her go downhill. Lotte found her, honey, when she hung herself in the house. He says he worries terribly about her."

He tried to imagine finding *his* mother hanging in their house, dead, but couldn't do it. No image came to him. It simply did not compute, and was unambiguously out of the question.

The move from Germany, the dress, the attitude, the dreams... the *utter darkness*. It didn't make *total* sense, but it was starting to make *some* sense. He stumbled into the kitchen and poured himself a glass of lemonade.

Bitter.

Grandma used no sugar; she liked to add it later. He drank it anyway.

Just then, Lotte appeared at the doorway to the kitchen, carrying the now empty tea set on a tray. "Do you know the proper place to put this, Eric?" she asked in a decidedly cheerful voice.

He put down his lemonade, walked over to her, took the tray from her arms, and brought it to the sink. Then he turned, walked back to her, and took her hand in his.

"Thanks for coming. Grandma really likes you. I'm glad you're here, and I'm glad you're my friend."

With that, he let her hand go and headed off to the bathroom.

To do what, he wasn't quite sure.

CHAPTER 6

For lunch, Grandma had gone all out and made Hungarian goulash and her "famous" *Semmelknödel*. She said they were from an old family recipe, and she usually saved them for holidays, which was just as well since Eric didn't really see what the big deal was.

Lotte loved them, though, and a happy Lotte was... well, a happy Lotte.

After composing himself in the bathroom, he tried to put the image of Lotte finding her mother, hanging dead, out of his mind—*fail*—but he was damned sure not going to spoil the afternoon, especially since she looked happier than he'd ever seen her. So, he did what he was rapidly learning he did best: he kept his mouth shut.

At Grandma's request, Dad brought the flowers in from the TV room, and they now occupied the center of the dining room table. The vase had deep blue and turquoise coloring, sectioned off by gold swirls in intricate designs. The flowers smelled great, and Grandma frequently interrupted the conversation to exclaim how lovely they were.

Mom and Grandma talked up a storm with Lotte, in English so everyone could understand.

"Linda, let the poor girl eat," Dad finally interjected.

She got a few mouthfuls in, but they were all happily at it again in no time.

Maybe Lotte is like Superman. Maybe kids are her Kryptonite.

With the adults, it seemed, she could lift any weight, deflect bullets, see through walls, and fly. In school, though, the "Kryptonite Kids" sapped her strength, draining her of color and altering her personality beyond recognition. She became "Anti-Lotte" and had to get back to her Fortress of Solitude on Holton Hill to rejuvenate her powers.

"*Eric!*"

Grandma's voice bit into his thoughts, and he realized she must have been talking to him. "Sorry, Grandma. Just enjoying lunch."

She didn't smile.

"Honey," his mom interjected. "Your grandma asked if you could show her a few things you and Lotte have been working on in German."

Oh, great, stand und *deliver.*

Seated next to him, Lotte promptly turned in her chair to face him. *"Erich,"* she gently prompted, using the German pronunciation of his name. *"Gibt es einen Bahnhof in der stadt?"*

Hesitantly, he replied, *"Nein, Lotte, es gibt am Bahnhof in Southby."* After a moment of thought, he added, *"Aber es gibt einen Bahnhof in Worcester."*

She shot out a couple more of the "non-sequitur" questions she'd asked in their lessons. When he got something wrong, she raised her now elegant straight black un-eyebrows until he worked it through. When finished, she casually returned to her plate of goulash and *Semmelknödel*, now almost cleared.

"Wunderschön!" Eric's grandmother beamed, more directed at Lotte than himself, though she added, "Eric, you show great improvement. Your pronunciation is much better."

You should hear my Transylvanian. Bwa ha ha ha!

"Thanks, Grandma." He gave a quick glance at Lotte, but she was occupied with the last of her food. He'd had no clue what to say to Grandma or where to start, so she'd kind of saved his butt.

I guess that's what Superman does, right?

After a big meal, nobody was in the mood for a walk. Lotte and Grandma went to the TV room to continue their seemingly endless conversation and get in some good "German time."

His dad went to the porch, probably to take a nap and enjoy the rapidly warming day.

Eric helped his mom clear the table and do the dishes, which she seemed to appreciate. Afterward, he quietly slipped into the TV room, figuring he'd be polite. In theory, he should also be listening to people speak German, even if he only caught snatches of what they were saying.

He settled on the floor and flipped stations on the muted TV while Lotte and Grandma sat on the couch and talked. He wound up watching a marathon of the new *Battlestar Galactica* reboot on cable. Sound or no, he could look at Kara Thrace all day long. Of course, she wasn't a featured character in this particular episode.

Figures.

He really did try to follow their conversation, but they just went too fast. He picked up little bits from time to time, though. At one point, he definitely heard, *"Herr Meier,"* and *"Deutschlehrer."* They seemed to be talking about teaching, generally, and Grandma listened intently to what she had to say.

After a bit, his mom arrived with more tea and some cookies. She seemed content silently watching *Battlestar Galactica* with him and drinking her tea. Occasionally, she glanced down from her chair and smiled.

He smiled back, wondering what he'd done to make her happy, and how these points could be redeemed for something cool. Lotte and Grandma talked on, and he could see Lotte's legs under the coffee table from his position on the floor. He tried not to stare. *Fail.*

He forced himself back to the TV. A new episode had just started, and he hoped Kara would be in it to keep his mind off of Lotte, but it would be stiff competition. That episode came and went, and he was well on his way to boredom when his father came in from the porch.

"What do you say, Mom?" he asked of Grandma, kind of yawning as if he'd just woken up from a nap. "Is it about time you let Lotte go home? The poor girl looks exhausted."

What time is it? Holy crap, almost four o'clock!

He couldn't believe how late it was. He looked at Lotte and she *did* look tired — small wonder, as this was past the time of day she'd normally have her afternoon nap.

In the cemetery. He still couldn't quite get over that.

Reluctantly, Grandma got up, lamenting the departure of her "Dear Lotte."

"*Ach*, Eric," she said with a start. "Before you go, I need you to help your poor old *Oma* get a box down from the closet in my bedroom."

"Sure, Grandma," he cheerfully replied, calculating that it was always good to be helpful. The extra points never hurt. *Although... if I never learn how to cash them in, they won't be much good.*

"You go do that while we get our things together," his mom instructed. "Lotte, honey, I'm so sorry we kept you this long."

"No need to worry, Mrs. Schneider. I'm having a wonderful time."

Who is this girl?

He followed his grandmother down the hall and past the bathroom toward the bedrooms. She ushered him in and closed the door behind them. Her room possessed the ambiance of a doll house, all furniture completely clear of items, save those so carefully arranged it looked like a museum had curated them. Her huge, overstuffed bed perched upon its massive frame, laden with all manner of pillows and decorative comforters. He couldn't believe she actually slept there.

How does she even get in that bed?

He wondered if this were all a clever ruse. Maybe every night, Grandma dug out her Xbox from wherever she'd hidden it and played *Grand Theft Auto* with a giant bowl of popcorn and a two-liter bottle of root beer by her side. There, she would finally fall asleep on the couch, the game control still gripped in her knobby fingers.

"*Eric!*" she said sternly but in a semi-whisper. "*Come here.*" She'd crossed to the far side of the room, near the window, the opposite side of the bed from the closet.

Weird.

"Sit here," she said, motioning to the bed when he reached her. He sat, and with a little hop that propelled her onto the pile of comforters, Grandma joined him.

Impressive.

"Eric, Lotte is wonderful," she said in a muted and clandestine tone.

Tell me something I don't know. He kept his mouth shut, thinking Grandma being sneaky was kind of cool.

"She told me some things — things about your German instruction. She does not think very highly of Mr. Meier — not as a person, but as a teacher."

Wow. There's something I did not know.

"She says his methods are too *rote,* designed to produce quick results on tests, but not to create lasting knowledge. She says his homework assignments are too simple — that he's already given you the answers."

Eric figured he must have missed when Mr. Meier gave out the answers, but it was true. Compared to the way Lotte approached things, his teacher's assignments were starting to look simplistic. He had to struggle with Lotte's questions. He found it hard, and he made a lot of mistakes.

A Lotte mistakes! He giggled to himself.

When he finally got it, though, it seemed to stick better, and he could apply those lessons to other things.

"Mind you," his grandmother continued. "Lotte said you could still be a very poor and easily distractible student."

Ouch. And ouch.

"But perhaps your poor performance in German is not entirely your fault. Certainly, in a short time, Lotte has helped you make noticeable progress."

On this, there could be no disagreement.

Grandma then dropped her head slightly. "She also told me that the teacher needs to be patient and encouraging, and not to discourage mistakes, as that is part of learning. In this, I've not been so good with you. I've been short and impatient. I see this now, and I see how counterproductive it can be. I'm sorry, Eric. I try to do better, *ja*?"

He was speechless. His grandmother apologizing for his sucky German? Lotte wasn't Superman; she was every DC and Marvel superhero combined.

"It's okay, Grandma. It's not your fault, or Mr. Meier's, that my German is so crappy... er... I mean so bad." *Whoops.* "I'm trying to do better, and Lotte really is helping me. I want to speak German with you when I make a little more progress."

"Oh, dear boy." Grandma gave him a hearty hug. When she finished, she clutched his shoulders and tugged his face close with a serious gaze. "Eric, Lotte is delightful, you know I think so... but there is deep trouble in her. I can sense it."

He wasn't about to deny that.

"Even as she tries her best to cover it up, it still comes through at times, as if it pervades her soul. You must be careful with this girl. I don't know what it is, but I feel something. Something... dark."

Oh, so you met the real Lotte after all.

"Tread carefully with her, dear boy. You could be playing with fire. Help her as you can, as she helps you, but don't let her bring this trouble into your life. It may be too much for you... or for anyone."

He agreed with Grandma, and her level of perception impressed him, but he feared that perhaps this particular Holstein had already left the barn.

As usual, Mom had a barrage of questions for Lotte on the ride home. She answered, detailing her conversation with Grandma about her early years in Germany, meeting Grandpa, and moving to the States. She also told them she'd filled Grandma in on Germany today, how it had changed, and where some of her favorite places were.

"Oh, Fred," Mom exclaimed. "Why don't we take your mother on a trip to Germany? Wouldn't that be wonderful?"

Eric pounced. "Yeah, Dad! I can try out my German in Germany. Let's do it!" Any excuse to get out of this shitty, close-minded town suited him, but actually, going to Germany sounded amazing, especially after hearing Lotte talk about it.

"Well," his dad slowly responded. "Always have to think about the business. Summer is one of our busiest times, but it has been ages since we went on vacation."

Other than the trip to Disney World when he was nine, Eric couldn't remember them *ever* going on vacation, except occasional long weekends to the Cape.

"Mom really would love to get back," he continued, "and she's not getting any younger. I think it's a consideration." That was as close to a done deal as Dad ever got — no sense in pushing it further.

Eric turned to Lotte and smiled, and realized her eyes were closed. She really was falling asleep.

"Hey," he said, giving her a gentle nudge.

She woke with a start and flashed a trademark Lotte Almost Kind-Of Smile. "Sorry. All that food at lunch."

Riiiiight. I'm sure it was all that food and not the monster in your dreams who kept you awake most of the night. Still, he let it go.

"It's okay," he replied. "Listen, maybe I shouldn't come in to see your house today like we planned."

She thought for a moment, and finally replied when what he said seemed to dawn on her. "Right... I'd totally forgotten. Listen, remember on Monday there's no C period, so we can't have a lesson. Why don't you come to visit tomorrow afternoon? The weather is supposed to be gorgeous, over twenty."

Twenty? That's freezing! Oh, maybe she means Celsius. He had no idea what twenty Celsius would be, but he took her word that it would be gorgeous.

"You could come after lunch," she went on. "I'll show you the house. We can have our lesson, and then go for a walk. There are nice trails in the woods on the other side of our hill. I've hardly explored them."

Sounds good to me, unless that's where the animated corpses are preparing their attack. He figured he'd risk it, and with confirmation from his mother, the plan was made.

CHAPTER 7

The flame inexorably calls us forth. Resistance is both futile and impossible, so we fight it not, and manifest ourselves above the paltry heat of the lamp's wick.

We have grown as large as he allows us to be, the height from the elbow to the outstretched fingers of our summoners. With time, refinements, and repeated intermingling of our various incarnations, our form has altered—each of us adopting elements of what our other selves have absorbed.

We now possess a scorpion's barbed tail. The curved horns of a goat crown our head, as do that creature's cloven hooves—cumbersome in appearance, but capable of excellent traction and doubling as weapons when necessary. Our wings have become sturdier and rise menacingly above our shoulders, ending in sharp, bony protrusions—still bat-like, but far more capable of elevating our increased mass.

No longer are we prey for the likes of feline pets, though many threats yet abound.

It is dark and we are not in the city we know, but light from a large settlement nearby dances in the night sky and sympathetically shimmers in the waters that seem to surround it. The sounds of waves against a shoreline tell us that we have traveled far.

Unusual, but we have ventured great distances before.

Also peculiar is that three acolytes stand before us where typically there is but one. They appear agitated, looking furtively behind, to their sides, and occasionally into the air. Once we are fully formed, one extinguishes the lamp, and we huddle in some underbrush just shy of the beach.

"We are in great danger," she says. "We must get inside Tyre without being detected. When we are there, we have a job for you. It is dangerous, but it is your only hope—and ours."

Another of the women quietly whispers. "We have procured a boat to sneak us into the city. Try to stay close, but out of sight. When we are safely in the port, come to us and we will further instruct you. Do you understand?"

It is a simple request, so we nod and take flight.

The three climb from their hiding place and walk on the beach toward a tiny cluster of ramshackle structures. There, two men meet them by the shore and help them into a small watercraft. The presence of so much liquid nearby makes us uneasy, but we do as instructed and fly surreptitiously overhead.

After a period of strenuous rowing, the boat pulls alongside a massive pier that juts out from the walled island. At this time of night, it is inactive. We quietly touch down and watch by the light of the moon as one of the acolytes hands over some coin to the rowers.

"It is not enough," one of them says, urgently extending his grasping hand.

"It is what we agreed," she responds. "We have no more. Honor your bargain and go!"

"Bargains change. This is dangerous, and should we call for the guard, it will be your heads they'll have. We are known here and will say you bewitched us! Give us more... unless you prefer *other* forms of payment."

Our anger rises. Betrayal, duplicity and lechery seem inescapable among these disagreeable beings. The males are the most detestable — he who imprisoned us worst of all, though whether it be his mortal or ethereal nature that makes him most foul is open to speculation.

"There is not time for this, Youtab," another of the apprentices speaks. "Give him what he wishes and let's be off. Our baubles will be of no value to us if dead."

To underscore her point, the woman removes a necklace and hands it over. Reluctantly, the others comply. That demeaning business concluded, the three climb onto the pier and scurry toward the shelter of some boxes and amphorae stacked under the looming walls of the city. We join them where they whisper quietly together.

'What is our task? What sort of danger threatens us?'

"No time to explain fully," says the one called Youtab. "We are here, in the seat of the Seven Kings. We need to enlist their help. To do this, you must get to their tower. We will take you there, once we get inside the walls."

"There is a doorway," another offers. "Follow us there. When you see us pass through, meet us on the other side. Keep on the lookout for anything suspicious. He has spies everywhere."

Spies. We are employed by *him* as spies.

Would he send us to spy on ourselves? If so, would we betray our own actions to him?

Chillingly, we know not. We can no longer guess what nefariousness we are capable of perpetrating, even against a part of what we ourselves have so tragically become.

Dismissing such useless thoughts, we again take to the air. Below, the women hasten down the street that runs along the base of the wall until they arrive at the heart of the port. Here, the wall recedes from the shoreline, and from behind more buildings, a large gate appears.

It is closed, but it is not toward this entrance that the women turn.

Rather, they have chosen a smaller passageway, likely kept open for late night workers, or inebriated elites making their way drunkenly back from dockside bars to their luxurious domiciles within the walls. The heavy, iron-bound wooden door stands open and one bored guard sits on a short stool by the entrance, counting the stars in the sky as he awaits relief.

We settle silently on the roof of a nearby structure and watch.

Youtab approaches the guard, and he rises to interrogate her, unsure if she is a prostitute or an assassin. She flirts with him, asking what he might offer for her "wares." They haggle in a perfunctory manner until striking a deal, likely the best proposition this oaf has had in his wretched life. With haste, he steers her into the relative concealment of the archway.

The other two acolytes soon creep up behind. One holds a long needle, which she presses into the guard's neck before he can react. He briefly writhes in distress, but a firm hand across his mouth stifles any screams.

Still, a large bird on the wall above takes quick flight. It makes a short arc over the port before circling back and disappearing from whence it came.

Eventually, the luckless and foolish guard collapses, paralyzed by a toxin on the needle. They position him by the wall as if he were sleeping, and disappear through the archway.

Inside the walls, we locate our three keepers, who again huddle in a dark alley, avoiding any attention. We land and give our report.

'A large bird, an owl we believe, took flight as the guard struggled. Possibly nothing, but – '

"If it was an owl," one says, "then we are discovered. Come, quickly!"

We cling to Youtab's shoulder as the women rapidly but cautiously navigate the narrow thoroughfares of the city. One seems to know the way, perhaps having visited this place before. Few are out this time of night, and she leads us mostly down quiet, abandoned roadways.

Suddenly, in an alley cluttered with debris, the apprentice next to Youtab lets out a cry and falls to her knees, trembling. She desperately reaches back to clasp her lower leg.

We see, barely visible in the darkness, a serpent slither behind a discarded box.

'There! It hides within that refuse!'

The woman in the lead draws a curved dagger from a sheath at her belt and kicks the splintered crate aside, but nothing is there. The snake has vanished.

"Apama is sickened," Youtab exclaims, crouching beside her injured companion. "We must seek a healer."

"There is no time," the woman replies. "They hunt us. We must leave her. She knew the risks."

Youtab looks to her stricken comrade with great sorrow, but Apama pushes her away. "Go. Listen to Naudar. Deliver that message, or my life will have ended in vain, perchance yours as well. I regret nothing, save that we did not act sooner. Forgive me, great one, for my misdeeds. I give you all to make amends."

Her final words before losing consciousness are directed at us, and we find them strange.

Forgive.... What does this mean? And to what offense does she refer?

The answer must wait, as Naudar pulls Youtab to her feet and they flee from the fateful alley. We keep on the lookout for more dangerous serpents, but now we are on a larger street and there are fewer obstacles behind which to hide. At an intersection, the two women stop, lungs heaving from their desperate sprint.

"We are close," Naudar whispers. "That only means they will become more brazen and frantic. If the one in owl form still stalks us, all is lost. Here." She pulls a crumpled papyrus from her cloak and thrusts it toward us. "Hold onto this. It is your only hope. Remember, Youtab, should something happen to me... it is the square tower behind a pond with an arched monument. Once he sees it, send him to the top with the letter. Then hide yourself... and pray."

We take the paper in our claw before Naudar and Youtab again set out, but we have not crossed the street when they stop cold.

To our right, a man approaches. He wears little clothing, and his feet are bare, but a great leather strap appears to secure several wooden javelins to his back. He pulls one of the bristling weapons from its harness and makes ready to cast it toward us.

"Run!" Naudar screams as she pushes Youtab forward. We cling to her shoulder as she lunges to the safety of the next building. A loud snap behind tells us the javelin missed us by barely a second.

"You must fly!" Youtab breathlessly commands. "Find the bird... the owl. As long as it watches, we are as fish in a net. You can do it. You must!"

Sensing the danger, we launch into the air. Our ashen composition gives us an advantage in the darkness, so we cling to a rooftop and search the skies for the menacing avian.

Below us, Naudar has faced off against the man. He has procured another javelin and has closed on her, but keeps a safe distance while she extends her curved blade, swaying in readiness for his next missile.

He feints and Naudar commits to her left. His throw is amazingly swift and inhumanly accurate. Her skull is pierced from ear to ear, and Naudar's body collapses in a heap in the dark and silent street.

Without hesitation, the man runs to the intersection and looks for Youtab, but she has fled. He retrieves and re-sheathes his first errant projectile, then brings his fingers to his mouth and sharply whistles.

In reply, the owl emerges from some unseen perch under the rooftops, heeding the call of its master... or its companion — the relationship is uncomfortably unclear. What is clear, however, is that the bird will inevitably lead the man to Youtab, and that the creature has unquestionably not seen *us*.

We glide from the roof, circling wide and staying low where the darkness conceals us. The owl passes unknowingly above, and we propel fiercely upward, clutching the strange papyrus tightly in our claw. At the last moment, we draw in our wings and slam savagely into the belly of the great bird.

Our horns pierce its flesh while our barbed tail drives deeply into the beast's throat. It begins to spasm and thrash. Unwittingly, one of its claws catches the precious letter. A part is torn free and vanishes into the wind... but there is nothing to be done.

Unable to carry the dying beast's weight, we allow momentum to compel us downward. If the wounds we have inflicted fail to dispatch the creature, a hard landing from this height surely will.

Though not dead, the owl seems as if in shock, shaking uncontrollably. The flesh and feathers where our horns and tail have implanted are beginning to degrade, and a stream of grayish dust flows from the lacerations.

At the last moment, we let go, and the great bird impacts the stone of the street and explodes into a cloud of desiccated powder. Only some bones are left, which rapidly disintegrate as we fly away.

Without question, the owl was not a creature of this realm... or perhaps once it was, before being conquered in sleep, as our persecutor conquered the man whose body caught fire.

Mysteries for another day.

Now, we must hasten back to Youtab and complete our mission. We picture her in our mind and can sense her nearby. So it is we can always find the ones we know, though how this is possible we cannot fathom.

She is relieved to see us, and proud that we put an end to our dangerous surveillant. Of equal importance, she has located the tower. There it stands, across an area of greenery and behind a small body of water with an arched stone that looks like a thick, bent branch with each end planted in the earth. Its height is roughly that of a human, and lamps light the spot, as if some sort of shrine.

'Naudar is killed,' we inform her.

"I know," she replies with grief.

'She fought with bravery, merely to buy us time. We do not understand.'

"You will. All will be clear. We do this for you, but it is you that must finish the task. Take the letter to the top of the tower. Go inside. There will be guards who will not understand who or what you are, but give them the note and they will help you. I am certain. Then you can come for me."

She smiles sadly.

We wish to say more, but there is no time, so we do as she instructs, flying across the open area toward the tower. There is but one window in the entire structure, and it is at the top. Light emanates from the opening, and we scrabble for purchase, clinging to the sill to examine the interior before entering.

It is a huge chamber with a gigantic table. Like the shape in the courtyard below, it is arched. At the flat side sits one large throne, while around the curvature, seven smaller chairs assemble as if in deference.

Two guards sit on stools near a doorway at the back of the room, while another prowls the great hall. All appear bedecked for battle, wearing quilted armor and sporting iron swords and daggers. Unlike the guard at the archway, these men are fully alert, and have the cold look of professional killers about them.

Daunting as they may be, we are swift and can exit before truly threatened. Two lives were lost bringing us to this place in hopes of delivering this message that we cannot even read. If there is risk, it is minimal. We enter.

The guards spring to attention upon seeing us, drawing their swords and readying for combat.

We hesitate only briefly in the window, and drop gently to the floor.

"By the beard of Melqart!" the man closest exclaims. "What manner of creature is this? Come no closer, daemon! There is great power here. Our weapons are the least of what you should fear."

'We judge your statement true.'

Their reaction is typical—shock at our touching of minds, and disbelief that a creature such as us can speak at all, let alone in such a way that all can understand.

'We come here as messengers, however, not warriors. We give you this.' We hold out the crumpled and now torn papyrus. *'Please examine it. Some have died that it might reach your hand.'*

The guard warily takes the note and unfurls it. "I cannot read it. I must bring it to someone who can. Stay here." He flashes us another bewildered look before leaving by the door, instructing the others to keep a vigilant eye.

"Are you a Jinn?" one asks when the silence has become seemingly unbearable for him.

It is the first time we have heard that word. We do not know what it means or whether it is good or bad... fair or foul.

We attempt to answer. *'In truth, we know not what we are, or what we have become. We simply... are. Perhaps the great power here of which you speak can help us understand. There is much we do not comprehend.'*

The door opens and the original guard walks through with three men, one of them holding the note. He has darkish skin and hair, and though he is not old, his look tells us he has seen much. Nothing surprises him, including us.

He softly smiles. "Well, well, something new under the great sun, or perhaps something very old. We shall see. It appears you've made quite an impression on your associates. Their message says you haunt their dreams with your misery—that you rail against your captivity."

'This surprises us. We did not even know such a thing was possible. Yes, we suffer in our prisons. We wish to return to our realm and to be done with this place. In our anguish, we petition those who have the capacity to free us. Our wretched state must have invaded the minds of the acolytes as they slept.'

He sighs with disdain. "Acolytes. We should not have let him go... should not have trusted that he would simply live his days like the others who did not take the oath. You are fortunate those who felt your distress took action. We will help you and set you free—all of you, as apparently, there are more like you out there. They have buried the other lamps that imprison you in a secret location. This message should detail where, but part of it has been lost. We must find your surviving companion who can tell us where they are. Then, we will put an end to this business once and for all. Come."

'We can find her! She hides. We will fly forth and locate her. Meet us outside.'

With that, we sail out the window and immediately scan for Youtab, but oddly, we cannot detect her. We circle the area of greenery, desperately searching until the doors to the tower open behind us and many men scatter into the courtyard.

Suddenly, there is yelling, and a crowd gathers around the pool near the arched monument. We fly down to investigate.

She floats face down in the water, her arms spread to her sides. A javelin juts out from the back of her skull.

As never before, our tortured consciousness aches for the fate of another.

Eric's mom let him drive her Civic to Lotte's house. Pleasant Street had little traffic on Sunday, and there were even fewer cars on Holton Hill Road than in Rolling Meadows. The pavement on Lotte's street shone like black glass, perfectly smooth and even.

He wished she'd been outside to see him pull up. He had so few ways to impress her.

Like, that would really be no *ways.*

He grabbed his backpack with his German book, notebooks, flash cards, and a change of shoes and socks his mother had demanded he bring in case his got muddy on the trails.

"You're not dragging your dirty feet into their beautiful house. Got it, mister?" she'd said in a stern but still lighthearted voice.

He got it.

He waved over his shoulder as he strolled toward the door.

"Call me when you're ready, honey," she cheerily offered through the open car window. "I'll come get you."

He rang the bell as his mom pulled away, though she hovered in the street waiting for the door to open. Idly looking around as he waited, he noticed the black Mercedes sedan still parked in front of the closed garage door. It shone like a sleeping panther in the tree-dappled sunlight. The familiar thud of someone running on stairs came from inside, and soon the door opened.

If the emanation of darkness was Lotte, and whoever that was yesterday in the blue and white dress with the pearls and pumps was Anti-Lotte — or maybe it was the other way around, he wasn't sure — then the person who opened the door could perhaps be described as "Half-Lotte."

The black squiggles of her un-eyebrows were back, and with no makeup, so were the scary black circles under her eyes. No black lipstick today, though — in fact, no lipstick at all. She wore black cargo pants and black socks, and still had a black band t-shirt. This incarnation featured a black and white photo of a boy wearing no shirt with hands behind his head, elbows out to either side. In the lower corner of the photo were gold letters, the only color other than black to grace Half-Lotte's entire body:

U2. BOY.

Well, at least U2 is a band that you don't have to be from the planet nutcase *to have heard of.*

"*Hallo!* Please come in." She seemed surprisingly cheerful.

He entered and saw behind her a small set of stairs that led down to another hallway, which presumably headed toward the rest of the house. A corridor to the left seemed to snake off to the garage, and to his right sat a door.

"You want me to take off my shoes?" he offered, seeing she didn't wear any.

"However you're comfortable, but if you do, there's a bench in there, with spots to put them in." She motioned to the door at the right.

Preferring to take the safer route, he opened the door to what turned out to be the biggest mudroom he'd ever seen in his life. It was like a Mud *Château*. A long wooden bench with cubby spaces for shoes, boots, or other items, coat closets, and shoe trees took up most of the wall space. The far side of the room had windows and a glass door. These looked out onto a small porch that sat in the thin strip of lawn that separated the house from the trees. Two nice hybrid bikes stood on stands near the windows.

He removed his shoes and popped them in a cubby, noticing her Doc Martens in the next space over. He hung his jacket in one of the closets. Mom had made him bring that, too. He grabbed his backpack and followed her down the small staircase into a hallway. They passed some closed doors, and an open door that revealed a half-bath, and soon came to the kitchen on the right.

There, Mr. Schwarz fed ingredients into a large, square machine on the countertop. The impressively big kitchen featured a counter on the left, with high stools that looked out into the dining room. At the far end, a small table with two chairs sat in front of a picture window, and a glass door that led to another porch facing the lawn.

I wonder if this is a breakfast nook, and if so, whether they actually eat breakfast here. Awful lot of space to take up for just that, but then space in this kitchen isn't exactly at a premium.

To the right sat the stove, which had fancy gas burners everywhere, plus a flat grill, and a gigantic refrigerator that gave the HMS Suburban a run for its money. In the middle of the room, Mr. Schwarz worked on a granite-topped island. The shelves of the large block, where cookbooks could be stored, were mostly filled to capacity with knickknacks.

"Ah, Eric," Mr. Schwarz said, as warmly and happily as yesterday. "Lotte was full of stories last night about your grandmother and your family. Thank you all so much for hosting her."

"Our pleasure, Mr. Schwarz. Thank you for that nice gift too—the vase and the flowers. Grandma really loved them."

"*Wunderbar!* It was our pleasure. As you'll see, I'm sure, our house is almost a victim of 'Victorian clutter'—so many things collected over the years by so many people, all of which seemed to eventually wind up with us. We can hardly see anything for the sheer volume. Believe me, giving this gift makes us as happy as we hope it made your grandmother."

He and Lotte left her father to feed his machine, and went into the huge dining room, which featured a large and very modern-looking wooden table as it centerpiece. More stools sat on the opposite side of the counter to the kitchen, which made that area into something of a second table, or even a bar. All the hutches and cabinets contained a host of dishes or other items, seemingly tucked at random into every available space. Most of the objects bore a distinctly Middle Eastern flair, very much like the vase they'd given to Grandma.

"Sorry everything is such a mess here," she said. "We unpack things, but really don't yet know where we want them."

She led him down a stairway that followed the curve of the exposed stone wall, from which the lower room had been sculpted.

Little alcoves carved in the rock held more vases, tiles, and plates on tiny stands. These items seem to have been placed with more care, and he assessed they were far nicer pieces than the ones in the dining room.

The massive glass wall that looked out over the vista below came into view. It towered at least two-and-a-half stories tall and flooded the room with light.

"Pretty cool, huh?" she asked.

Kuuuul, he mentally replayed, and smiled.

They entered the main living room with tables, couches, and comfortable chairs in clusters that subdivided the gigantic space into various areas. One cozy cluster of chairs ringed the fireplace, while others formed a sitting area near the glass wall. Finally, large, overstuffed couches faced a huge TV screen with a full range Dolby sound system.

Man, I would kill *to watch a zombie movie here. That would be so kuuuul!*

Scattered about the space were glass cases, each showcasing a miniature building—or several if the models were smaller.

"This is my father's work," she explained. "His firm designed all of these, and he was head architect on most of the projects. Many of these buildings are in Berlin, which has been expanding like crazy since the wall came down. Some are in Hamburg, a few in Paris and other cities in Europe. This one is in New York City."

She pointed at one of the models, largely indistinguishable from the others. Eric didn't really *get* architecture. He figured a building was a building, and only noticed one if it looked old-fashioned, like with columns and domes and stuff. All these modern buildings looked pretty much the same to him—big rectangular glass boxes. He figured it wouldn't be right to say that, so he just kept his mouth shut.

At the other end of the room, on the left, stairs led to the main hallway and back to the dining room, kitchen, and eventually the front door. To the right, glass doors led to the stone patio, where Lotte had mentioned she'd been sleeping. It had some outdoor furniture, and more stairs beyond that led farther down the hill.

Another hallway directly in front of them displayed many doors and a stairway leading up to the left. He got a sense of this house being like a series of passageways that nestled into the contours of the mountainside. It was nifty, and unlike any house he'd ever been in.

"The rooms down here would be guest rooms," she told him as she pointed at the closed doors, "or I suppose for any other purpose. Right now, they're just full of unpacked boxes. Want to go upstairs and see my room?"

He assumed Mr. Schwarz didn't mind if he went into her room. He couldn't remember the last time he'd been in a girl's room. *The fifth of never,* he finally determined.

He figured the losing streak had to end sometime, so he started up the stairs. They took a slight right turn at the top and terminated in the second-floor hallway, which ran above the passageway below. A wooden railing guarded where the stairs ascended, which created an open feel in the stairwell.

Lotte pointed toward the end of the hall. "The two rooms down there are my father's, his bedroom and study, where he does his work. I can't show you those. He prefers I not disturb his things. Those are more closets on the left—we've never had so many. Most are just empty, though I suppose many of the things we have no room to display will wind up there."

Every closet in Eric's house was packed with stuff. You risked your life opening some doors, especially the one with Dad's golf hats, which he stacked in precarious towers on a high closet shelf. How he reached the one he wanted, Eric had no clue.

Who needs so many golf hats? The answer would have to remain a mystery for now... and possibly forever.

"The bathroom is there if you need. There's one below as well, I forgot to say. My room is here." She turned right, and there opposite the railing that overlooked the stairs, her door stood open.

He followed her into the room... and found himself magically teleported into another universe, where Conan had crushed his enemies, seen them driven before him, and heard only the lamentation of their women.

Or so it felt.

Overwhelmed, he knew he'd never seen anything like this. Even movie sets were less opulent, and museums less stocked with treasures that dazzled the senses.

Lotte's massive room was a Middle Eastern fantasy. In the corner near the door, a towering ceramic lamp radiated light thanks to its handy conversion to modern electricity. On the floor in the middle of the space sat a bronze brazier, converted to a table where her homework and laptop rested in opulent luxury. The tabletop displayed a mosaic of colorful tiles, arranged in concentric rings of different patterns, with meticulously designed tulips in the middle. Four plush, red-cushioned, wooden chairs carved in delicate and intricate patterns sat clustered around, welcomingly.

Against the far wall, directly opposite the door and between the picture windows that provided a spectacular view of the valley below, stood the most bizarre wardrobe he'd ever seen. Two towering closets fanned out diagonally left and right, flanking a raised white marble platform. In the middle glittered a full-length mirror, the frame a series of interlocking swishes painted red and orange, with occasional streaks of blue. It reminded him of crazy grass blowing in the wind.

He pictured Lotte standing on the marble floor in front of the mirror in the morning, auditioning various black band t-shirts, idly discarding those she deemed unworthy with a casual toss. *La di da, la di da.*

The fine mesh of her canopy draped in elegant curves over her bed, held in place by golden sashes with blue and red tassels. Multi-colored blankets and pillows on the bed echoed the rich designs of the Persian-style rugs that covered strategic points of the otherwise hardwood floor.

A giant, bejeweled Genie lamp sat on another repurposed brazier that served as her bedside table. Incongruently, a lamp shade stood on a pole that protruded from the center of the gaudy thing.

Another victim of the march of modernity, he figured, though that much oil in a lamp was probably a major fire hazard these days.

Two matching chests of drawers, one tall and one long and short, were arranged near the bed, each exquisitely carved and inlaid with intricate stone and wood designs bearing more representations of tulips and other flora. The door of a walk-in closet stood open near one of the chests of drawers.

The only aspects that broke the spell—besides the laptop—were the band posters that haphazardly littered the walls of the room. He recognized some of the groups from her menagerie of black t-shirts, but he gave a hoot when he saw one featuring a woman, with fiery red hair and a long gown, dancing under autumn-leaved trees with a man in a black tuxedo and hat.

The old-timey-looking poster announced:

The Dresden Dolls

This is that band where the singer paints on her eyebrows in squiggly lines! Don't worry, Lotte, your secret is safe with me.

To the right of the crazy mirror wardrobe, a turntable and amplifier sat on a low table in the corner, with small speakers to either side. A box under the table housed old vinyl LPs, and many lay strewn on the floor.

He saw one with a bright yellow cover with yellow letters inside a wash of gaudy pink:

SeX PiSTOLs

"Wow, vinyl records" he said. "My parents have a box of those—so old-fashioned."

She shot him a dismissive look. "They sound far better than CDs, or these ridiculous over-compressed MP3s. Plus, you can find vinyl so cheaply, and I love looking in the stores through all the bins. It's like an adventure... and for the older music I like, it's fantastic."

"Well, I guess that's fine, but sound quality or not, I don't think vinyl will ever catch on again."

"We'll see," she replied with a slight smile.

After the tour of the room, feeling completely bowled over, he sat carefully down in one of the red-cushioned wooden chairs and shook his head.

"Is this serious?" he asked, really wanting to know if this was serious.

She flopped into the chair next to him, a kind of mischievous look on her face. "Pretty cool, huh?"

Kuuuul. "It's... it's... I don't know what it is! Where did you get all this stuff?"

"My grandparents bought it all in the Middle East years ago. None of it's authentic. In fact, most of it's just pure fabrication, made to look like what Westerners think Middle Eastern goods should look like."

He'd figured they were real. *Sucker,* he berated himself.

"My mother told me that my grandparents thought they were hilariously funny. They bought them as sort of a joke, but also because the price and the quality of the craftsmanship were excellent. So, they just purchased them and shipped them back to England. My mother brought them from there to Germany when she married my father. I've grown up with them all my life, so I hardly notice any longer."

He couldn't imagine getting used to stuff like this, any more than he could picture hopping on a camel to get to school. "Are there any more surprises? Will the next room take us to a beer garden in Munich?"

She actually laughed at that. She seemed to enjoy the surprise her room could still deliver to the uninitiated. "No, Eric, *Kein Biergarten für dich,*" she playfully replied, "but I have Coca-Cola downstairs. We can have some while we do your lesson. *Ist das in Ordnung?*"

It was fine with him, but he did one more turn around the room before they left.

You really don't see something like this every day.

Tired of things passing him by, he took a minute to smell the roses... or in this case the tulips, which were ubiquitously carved or painted into the many surfaces upon which his eyes feasted.

CHAPTER 8

The day had turned out to be absolutely gorgeous, and Lotte and Eric did their German lesson outdoors on the stone patio. She removed her black socks when they got outside.

"What?" she queried, noticing him shaking his head.

"Nothing." He rolled his eyes. *Black toenail polish. Shocker.*

Without the time pressure of C period, she worked with him in little spurts — great intensity for short periods, then a break, then more work. He liked the pace, because he found it hard to concentrate for forty-five minutes at a time.

Hell, it's hard to concentrate for two minutes, depending on the subject.

Remembering what his grandma had said, he knew Lotte wasn't going to give him any answers. So rather than wait for her cues, he jumped right in, anticipating what she wanted and trying before being prompted. He even attempted to add extra little expressions, like a real conversation — just to keep things interesting.

She seemed to love it, even when he got stuck, and provided many suggestions for things he could investigate on the internet to improve further. It was the best German lesson he'd ever had, and he felt like he was finally getting into the flow of the language. When they wrapped up, he was amazed to see they'd been at it for nearly two hours.

"Would you still like to go for a walk?" she queried.

He was game, so they both went to fetch their shoes.

He froze when he got inside. "What is that *smell?*" he asked in a dreamlike voice. It smelled like he was inside the oven of the yummiest bakery ever, the warm and musky scent permeating every molecule of the air.

She laughed. "Father bakes bread on Sundays. It smells good, *ja?* He times the last loaf, so it's hot and fresh for dinner. Would you like to stay and eat with us?"

If bread that smelled like that was part of the equation, he figured he'd just move in with the Schwarz family. He could sleep on the unpacked boxes in one of the guest rooms. He wouldn't mind.

"That would be awesome. Thanks so much. Let me call my mom and make sure it's okay. You sure it's okay with your dad?"

"Oh, he'd love have to you for dinner."

Umm, another double entendre there.

He wondered if maybe he'd had it wrong. Maybe Lotte was just the unwilling servant of her evil warlock-sorcerer father, who sent her forth to lure naïve and unsuspecting boys back to their home to be used as ingredients in magic bread, which granted the twisted pair their eternal life.

Nah, that bread smells too good to be made of people. He dismissed the scenario.

Well, mostly.

"But I'll check with him anyway while you call your mom." She shot up the stairs toward the kitchen.

His mom didn't care. She and Dad were just going to heat up leftover goulash from yesterday, eat in front of the TV, and watch the late football games, so he wasn't missing anything special. He got the update that the Chargers were killing the Pats.

Oh, well. Can't win 'em all.

Lotte returned and said her father was happy to have him join them for dinner. They scurried up the stairs and headed for the Mud *Château*.

"So, Eric," Lotte's dad called from the kitchen when they passed by, unloading a beautiful loaf of freshly baked bread from his machine. "I'm so thrilled you can join us tonight."

Mr. Schwarz is the only person I've ever met who might actually drop dead of over-exuberance. The guy is... like... terminally happy.

"You go for your walk now," he continued. "Lotte, remember to bring your walkie-talkie."

"*Father!*" she moaned with exasperation, turning and marching toward the front door. Eric waved to Mr. Schwarz, who beamed and waved back, then followed her down the hall.

"Walkie-talkie?" he asked as they tied their shoes on the bench.

She'd opted for a pair of Euro-style black Adidas with white stripes instead of her Doc Martens.

"*Alter!* He means the mobile phone. He calls this the *walkie-talkie*. He thinks it's so funny. Don't encourage his stupid sense of humor, whatever you do."

He found himself already kind of laughing. *Another Holstein might have left the barn.*

The pair walked a short way on Holton Hill Road, in the opposite direction of where he and his mom had come up earlier, and soon came to a dirt parking area on the right side of the road. A couple of cars sat with their front bumpers aligned against a neat wooden fence. An opening in the barrier led to a path into the woods. A sign there gave a little map of the trails, along with a long list of things people *couldn't* do on them.

I wonder if they allow the freaking squirrels to walk on the trails when people aren't out here. Actually, it's a miracle they let people to use the precious things at all. Ugh, this fucking town!

Eric followed as Lotte led the way. Even he had to admit the area exuded beauty. The weather turned out to be dry and clear, with no need to worry about mud.

I won't need those other shoes. That's for sure.

Leaves turning to their autumn oranges and reds created a peaceful ambiance, though Southby didn't put on a show like other parts of the state. Birds chirped, and a light, pleasant breeze kept the killer mosquitoes at bay. Squirrels chittered in the trees, probably waiting for them to pass by so they could surreptitiously sneak down and use the path.

Don't worry, we won't rat you out to the neighborhood busybodies.

There weren't many super-nice days in New England, but he knew they'd somehow magically stumbled onto one of them. They walked for a long time, stopping to investigate a pond nestled not far from the path. They both enjoyed looking at the frogs bobbing in the water, trying to catch the last rays of the warming sun.

Eventually, they meandered on, Lotte in the lead. Perhaps lured by the peacefulness, he let his inhibitions down and ventured a question. "Hey, Lotte, why do you dress and act like you do in school? You know, like so... *dark*?"

She remained silent for a while, but eventually slowed her stride and walked next to him. "Why, do you find me threatening?"

Threatening? He pondered that. *I definitely find your right hook threatening, that's for sure. I've never really felt physically threatened by you, though... but I don't think that's what you mean.*

Lotte wasn't like the other kids in school, and it wasn't just that she was from Germany. He considered her dress, her personality—and she was peaches and cream with him compared to his classmates, *ouch!*—her direct manner. Her total *style* was unlike anything he, or anyone at Southby High, had ever really encountered before.

She refused to serve as a mirror for them, reflecting back what they wanted to see. She expressed no interest in their cliques or concern for their judgment, and seemed immune to their rules of social order, which put every student properly in his or her place. She didn't give a shit what others thought, and that could be threatening.

Do I feel threatened by her? He admitted to himself that he had been. She'd scared the shit out of him that first day, as he examined her darkness while she sat on that low stone wall. He'd felt intimidated, and when she made short work of him, he realized he'd had reason to be. She threatened his comfortable sense of himself, made him question what he thought he knew—what he once believed obvious and implicitly true.

"I think I did," he admitted, "but now that I know you, I don't find you as threatening anymore. It feels like everything has changed for me since I met you, and I don't think that's... like... a bad thing."

She glanced over her left shoulder and flashed him an Almost Kind-Of Smile. "Honestly, Eric, I've always worn black. It was funny because my name is Schwarz, which I assume you know is *black* in German?"

He nodded. *Yeah, not quite that stupid, thank you.*

"I think after my mother died, I sort of let things get a little out of control. In a strange way, it worked for me. I couldn't deal with all the people. It was just too exhausting. I didn't want to talk. I didn't want help. I just wanted to be alone. The weirder I looked and the harsher I became, the more they left me be."

Roger that.

"Then the dreams started. Soon, my only thoughts were of the monster and how I could get sleep. I had no time for people anymore—no time for anything but the minimal things I had to do to get by. The clothes became my armor, protecting what little I felt remained of me."

Just like a superhero. The disguise protects their true identity.

He summoned his courage. "So why do you hang out with me? Why did you agree to waste your time giving me German lessons?"

She stopped short and grabbed him by the shoulders. "Not a waste at all! I'll admit, when Mr. Meier approached me about it originally, I did it partly as a favor to him. He organized a little welcome party for my father and me back in August, before school started. He wanted to be helpful. He's a nice man, just not such a good teacher, if you ask me."

Eric couldn't disagree, but then he wasn't exactly a model student either.

"But it was also just so *perfect* for *me*! I think I might want to be a teacher someday. I've read up on educational methods, even dreamed of putting them into practice, but I've never had the energy to pursue it. Here it was, being handed to me on a plate, so I had to try. After all this time suffering with these stupid dreams, I had to do something for myself."

He suddenly felt like a science project. If he was Fraulein Frankenstein's Monster, he sure hoped she'd be able to source a better brain for him. He pictured himself walking oafishly on a leash behind the Mistress of the Dark at school, arms outstretched, big scar on his forehead, electrodes in his neck.

How would you say, Arrrrrrrrr, in German?

Lotte continued. "But for me, things have also changed. I've come to enjoy your company. Maybe I needed a friend more than I admitted to myself. You don't seem to expect things of me, other than German instruction, which is natural. You go with the flow—try things, even if they're a little weird for you at first. Your nose isn't constantly buried in a mobile phone, and best of all, you really listen to what I say."

Oh, were you talking? he joked to himself. *Actually, this is another sure sign that my most admirable asset is just keeping my stupid mouth shut.*

She hesitated briefly, then went on. "I just somehow sense that you're a caring person even though you rarely talk, and often appear to hide behind this odd barrier you seem to have created. Regardless, I'm happy to have you as a friend. I hope I haven't made your life too troublesome."

Well, not too troublesome.

"Wow, thanks," he said, a little embarrassed. "That's really nice to hear. I'm just so sorry you're going through all this, and that you had to see what you saw."

She seemed confused. "See what?"

"Umm... uh... like... see your mother like that. Like... dead, and, like... hanging, and stuff."

She bristled. "Who told you this, Eric?"

Uh-oh. "Your dad told my folks the other day while we were waiting for you. My mom... like.... uh... mentioned it to me."

Her face turned red, a color he'd never seen on her before, if you didn't count the blush she used when she wore makeup. He didn't think it suited her... or him, for that matter.

"*Scheiße!*" she all but yelled.

Of course, the kids in Eric's German class knew all the swear words. He loved hearing one just roll off a native speaker's tongue, but the circumstances made it a bit less super-cool than it otherwise might have been.

She stormed back the way they'd come. "It's like the world's an open book to him for everyone to read! This is exactly why we left Bremen, to get away from the stares and the looks of pity and the backhanded comments. 'Oh, look, there goes the poor little girl who found her mother when she committed suicide. She'll never be *normal* again.' Why does he do this? Why can't he just keep things to himself? Come on!"

He pursued, but kept a safe distance. *Stupid, stupid, stupid! What part of* keep your mouth shut *do you have difficulty understanding?*

Quickly and wordlessly, they arrived back at her house. She opened the door and went straight down the stairs, not bothering with her shoes. "Father!" she shouted.

Eric retreated to the Mud *Château*. He removed his shoes but didn't bother putting them in the cubby, in case she preferred he go home. He heard the pair arguing in the kitchen. They'd switched to German, and he wondered if that was for their benefit, or to keep out prying ears.

Finally, he heard her yell from the hallway, "Fine! Then soon the whole town will know, and we'll get to move again!" With that, she rather loudly marched down the hall and headed for her room.

Eric had no idea what to do, so he waited for a bit on the bench.

Nothing.

He stole a peek out the door, but saw no one in the hallway. He cautiously went down the little stairway and crept along. Seeing the half-bath, he stopped and peed, more to buy time than anything else. When finished, he continued along the hall, making no noise in his socks.

Mr. Schwarz was in the kitchen, attending to his bread machine, and to something that now smelled equally yummy in the oven.

"Mr. Schwarz?" he called out nervously.

"*Ach*, Eric! Good heavens, we've abandoned you. How inconsiderate. Just so much on my mind with the bread and the dinner and... Lotte. Oh, Eric, I'm so sorry you had to hear that." Upset as he was, Mr. Schwarz still radiated warmth, like a human bread machine.

"It's me that's sorry, Mr. Schwarz. I shouldn't have mentioned to Lotte what you said to my mom."

"Oh, Eric, no. How could you have known? Lotte is right: I say too much. In my firm, I was head architect, but mostly my colleagues met with the clients. I'd have promised them things that were completely outside the scope of their projects—make a big mess of everything. I just get so *enthusiastic*."

Eric could fully understand. Mr. Schwarz had more enthusiasm than the entire Engines cheerleader squad, including Stacy Michaelson, who was downright obnoxious in her perky, in-your-face commitment to Southby High "school spirit."

Eric had no response.

Finally, Mr. Schwarz said to come in and sit at the counter on one of the stools. He got a Coke from the fridge and poured it.

"Sit here for a while and have something to drink," he said as he went back to attending his machine and the stove.

Both, with their glorious scents, were now causing Eric's stomach to growl.

"She'll calm down, and you can go up and talk with her in a bit."

Or she'll level me with a right hook. Maybe I deserve it.

"It's been hard, Eric... hard on both of us. We both make mistakes. We both seem to need such different things. I don't know how to help her. I don't know what to do. I worry about her so. She doesn't look healthy."

Well, for a corpse, she looks remarkably healthy.

After Eric finished his drink, Mr. Schwarz told him to go up and give her a try, as dinner was almost ready. Eric moped with dread toward her room, stopping again to pee in the bathroom on the first floor. The bathrooms in this house were as incredible as everything else. Real stonework lined the floors and shower walls, creating a look like a mountain grotto, and the toilets and sinks were all ultra-modern. He considered just spending the rest of the evening in here, but figured that would be bad form. Plus, he'd miss dinner.

At the top of the stairs, her door stood open. He knocked, but she didn't answer.

"Lotte, I'm coming in, okay?"

No answer. He hoped she was dressed.

Or do I?

Putting that thought right out of his mind, he peered inside.

She'd tossed her Euro-style black Adidas on the Persian rug in front of the bed, where she now lay belly down, her head buried in a large, fluffy, purple pillow.

"Lotte?" he repeated, moving closer. He assumed she'd been crying, which would be hell on the black squiggly un-eyebrows that had already been flagging in the afternoon heat. "Lotte, you okay?" he said when he finally stood on the Persian rug, her sneakers by his feet.

She turned her body haltingly to face him. Sure enough, the black squiggles were a soggy mess, and her black mascara now served as a goopy highlight to the scary black circles under her reddened eyes.

"I'm so sorry," she said in a trembling voice. "You shouldn't have had to hear that. I shouldn't have left you like that."

"I'm fine, really. It's me that should be sorry. So much for keeping my mouth shut and being a good listener, huh?"

She wiped at the horror-show her face had become, serving only to make it worse. Eventually, she sat on the edge of the bed and looked up at him. She looked like a messier version of Pris from *Blade Runner*, except with black hair instead of blonde.

"Eric, truly, this is *not* your fault." The little scalpels danced, but this time he wasn't their target. "I just don't want to go through all that again. Bremen became unbearable — stifling. I couldn't trust anyone. They said so many things behind our backs. We were blamed, Eric! I was blamed. They wouldn't speak it out loud, but you could sense that's how many felt."

He felt stunned, but then he thought of the routine cruelties, judgments, and prejudices of people in Southby, and found himself less surprised. He had to admit he wasn't immune to sometimes behaving the same way, but he doubted he'd blame someone for the suicide of a family member.

Silence, his gut advised him, in between growls for Mr. Schwarz's cooking. He heeded his intestines' sage advice.

"I can't go through that again," she went on. "I just can't. Please don't repeat what you've heard. Please ask your lovely family to do the same."

Then, raising her ruined face to him, she almost pleaded. "And please, Eric, don't see me as just that poor little girl who found her mother when she committed suicide. Just let me be *me* to you. *Ja, bitte?*"

Eric didn't cry often, but with that he came awfully close. After a moment of choking back what would have been ruinously embarrassing tears, he manufactured a reply — as much for his own benefit as hers.

"Hey, you're just my weirdo bitchy German tutor who dresses like a freak. Get your shit together and come down for dinner. I'm about to eat my fuckin' hand."

She hesitated, then reached behind her, grabbed a small, tasseled pillow, and threw it directly at him. He dodged, but she jumped up from the bed and ran to him, delivering a playful shove.

"You little. *shit!*" she squealed with mock outrage. "You're getting extra assignments from me next week, that's for sure!"

"Hey, bring it on," he replied with bravado, actually sort of meaning it.

She seemed to sense his seriousness. "Yes, you did so well today. I was impressed. Not bad for such a *Dummkopf*." She smiled and gave him another little push. "Sit there while I fix my face. I must be quite a fright."

Well, not so much worse than normal.

He sat in one of the plush, red-cushioned wooden chairs while she left and headed for the bathroom. When she returned, she appeared almost back to normal—well, Lotte normal, anyway, which was good enough for him. She approached the table and grabbed his hand.

"Let's go," she said in a tone somewhere between resigned and enthusiastic.

"Cool," he replied.

Together they bounded, hand in hand, down the stairs and toward the kitchen.

Kuuuul!

CHAPTER 9

How sharply loss can clarify what we once possessed.

So it is with innocence... or ignorance... should that word better suit one's proclivities. We realize now that we were both, and that a return to either state was impossible. Additionally, we were now reduced to a bare fraction of our previous energy.

Try, they did — these Seven Kings and the wizened man to whom they answered — to retrace the steps of the acolytes, back to the city we knew, to make him answer for his maltreatment.

But he had fled.

Even his associates who aided in the deaths of the three women failed to disclose his location. They likely spoke true when saying they did not know, as the torment that preceded their annihilation was incommunicable.

Likewise, the Seven failed to locate our other selves, trapped as they were inside their lamp prisons. They lay buried in some anonymous and woebegone pit, lost to suffer perpetually in the vastness between these places men called Babylon and Tyre... unless miraculously found.

Of this, we held little hope.

What piece of us remained free, if even that be a fitting word for our wretched and diminished condition, had little choice. Until we could grow strong enough, the final lamp that they pulled from Youtab's bag, where it floated in the pond with her body, would be our home.

The Eternal Flame was unsafe, should he once again reach across the threshold between realms and beckon us. We had not the energy to resist his pull. Instead, we would be brought forth from the lamp to feed and gain strength.

Like the one who detected and ultimately enslaved us, the Seven Kings had powers. They understood these other places, and were adept with certain... mysterious arts. With time, they would send us back, after mastering the secrets only he had known, and developing a means to keep him from again harming us.

Grow, we did.

We ingested ever larger and more exotic beasts, imported from faraway lands to feed our voracious appetite. In exchange, we performed the tasks to which we had become so accustomed and accomplished.

The shekels our services yielded secured the loyalty of the guards and porters, but of far greater importance were our attendants—a new cadre of young women, hand-selected by the Seven for their discretion, intelligence, and shrewdness.

We retained our form, at least that which we had attained in the paltry part of us that still endured. They placed no limit, however, on our size. By choice, we remained of roughly human height and girth to navigate their structures and passageways. All excess fed our energy, and we became mighty, both without and within.

It did not compare to being near the Eternal Flame, but as promised, the day finally came. They replicated the hot oil that he had used, but instead of a cauldron, they devised a new method—an arched slab of stone, between which the flaming liquid traveled through furrows and depressions. It created a pattern, and we were instructed to never leave our realm if this symbol was not present. This, they hoped, would keep us from again falling into his clutches.

In addition, the Seven provided rings, likely enchanted in some manner. These would seal a pact with our handlers, and should the bargain not be honored, the Seven could be called upon to adjudicate—safeguards for all involved.

And so it was.

Years passed. Then decades. Then centuries.

The Tower of the Seven Kings fell to a great conqueror from the north. They and their kind went into hiding, but our stewards assured us their power yet endured—that their authority still guaranteed our arrangement.

The world changed around us, but hidden in remote and ever relocating compounds, our work carried on unabated, the thirst for spies and assassins seemingly unquenchable among humans.

It did not matter to us.

We were now vastly closer to what we once had been, and knowing how we had suffered, and suffered still in that dank and forgotten hole, we marked ourselves fortunate.

We shed our innocence and ignorance, and embraced what we had become.

Lotte led Eric from the hallway into the dining room and up to the counter with the stools.

"Sit here," she instructed. "I'll be right back." She went into the kitchen and approached her father, hugging him from behind.

He turned and embraced her, and eventually gave her a little kiss on the forehead, careful to avoid smudging her newly restored black squiggly un-eyebrows.

Mr. Schwarz beamed at Eric as she went to the towering refrigerator, and Eric smiled back. He really couldn't *not* like Mr. Schwarz, even though he fully understood and basically agreed with Lotte's reason for being angry with her father.

Lotte returned from the kitchen with drinks—iced tea this time, which was just as well, since Eric had drunk his fill of Coke for today. Soon, she and her father were removing food from the oven, or from the cast iron pan that sizzled on one of the fancy gas burners of the stove. They transferred the items to serving plates and bowls, and she brought them to the table, steaming. As a last touch, Mr. Schwarz produced a beautiful loaf of honey-brown bread and placed it near the creamy butter that Lotte had fetched from the fridge.

This is like a restaurant.

The food was recognizable, though Eric didn't know the names of the dishes. Spread before him were some kind of meat, probably pork, with mushroom gravy, a vegetable that looked like little cabbages cut in half, and some sort of little dumplings that had been fried to a golden color in the cast iron pan.

"So, Eric," Mr. Schwarz said. "Here we have *Jägerschnitzel*, Brussels sprouts, *und Spätzle*, and of course, bread."

"*Jäger* is... umm... 'hunter,' right?" Eric queried.

"*Ja, sehr gut*," he replied. "All these are dishes typical of southern Germany. The *Jägerschnitzel* would be what the hunter would eat, or so it is said." He smiled.

Eric smiled back.

Mr. Schwarz raised his glass of iced tea. "So, *Prost!*"

Lotte and Eric raised theirs in reply.

"Actually," her father said in a sneaky voice. "I may have a beer with this nice meal. Would you two like to split one?"

"Father, you know it's not done here," Lotte interjected. "I don't want Eric to get into trouble."

"Ah, so silly," he replied, distaste in his voice. "American teenagers are denied a little drink with supper, and then sneak out with their friends and drink until they can't stand up. The attitude toward alcohol in this country is childish and produces this infantile overreaction. Eric, you don't seem the type to engage in this sort of over-indulgence. What do you think? You won't turn into a monster with a little beer, will you?"

The two of them looked at each other in mild shock. Monsters were the last thing they wanted on their minds right now, but they simultaneously seemed to realize that her dad hadn't meant it *that* way.

"It's up to you," she eventually said, and shrugged.

"Okay, I'll try a little," he said, not wanting to disappoint Mr. Schwarz, but also out of curiosity. His dad drank beer occasionally, but mostly at the country club. He rarely stocked it in the house. Eric had stolen a sip of one ages ago. It hadn't impressed him then, but maybe his tastes had changed along with everything else that seemed to be changing in his life right now.

"Gut!" Mr. Schwarz exclaimed, quickly producing two juice glasses from a cabinet, as well as a fancy, fluted beer glass. He fetched two beers from the fridge, opened them, then poured half of one into each of the small glasses for Eric and Lotte, and a full one into his glass. "Now, *Prost!"* he happily cried, and this time everyone clinked their glasses over the granite countertop.

Eric found the food absolutely *amazing*, especially the *Spätzle*, which had a buttery, almost cheesy flavor, though he didn't think it actually contained any cheese.

What is this magic little dumpling, and where has it been all my life?

He ate with ecstasy. The bread was also as good as advertised, still warm and melting in his mouth. It hardly needed butter.

"So, Eric," Mr. Schwarz said between mouthfuls. "Lotte says you play an instrument. What do you play?"

How would she know I played an instrument? Oh, the case. Duh. "Yeah, I play clarinet in Wind Ensemble. Honestly, I don't really like it that much. I don't think I'm that into music. I'm thinking about dropping it and picking up another class if I can."

"What types of classes interest you?"

Ah, the same old question. He recalled his dad's words about finding something better to do. "I'm not certain. I'd like to explore some different things, but I'm not sure what. I need to do some research. Lotte reminded me of Sigmund Freud the other day. Not... like... that she *looked* like him or anything," he sputtered. "She just mentioned his name."

Mr. Schwarz chuckled.

Lotte ate in silence, but Eric could see a little smirk on her face.

"Freud came up in science class last year," he continued. "That's what I meant. I just thought his ideas were... well, I don't know... interesting, I guess. I don't know if I'd like him or not, but that's the kind of thing I'd like to know more about—like, dreams and people and stuff. What makes them do what they do? I think that's more what I want than playing clarinet."

"Lotte?" Mr. Schwarz asked. "Where are the books?"

"They're in one of the guest rooms, Father. Still in boxes."

"After dinner, Eric, I find some books for you, *ja?*"

"Oh, Father, you'll never find them in that mess. We'll be unpacking boxes all night!"

He good-naturedly waved his hand. "I know the box these are in. We'll find them." He smiled at Eric.

Eric smiled back.

Conversation continued about how much they still had to unpack. "And what are we going to do about all the furniture in the garage?" Lotte wondered.

That explains why the black panther Mercedes always sits in the driveway.

Lotte's dad said he'd gotten busy on a project, and that they'd get back to unpacking when he had more time. Apparently, he still worked for his old firm in Bremen, but now he just did design projects and no longer participated in day-to-day operations. He said he loved working in their new home, that the light from the picture windows in his study made it a pleasure.

When the conversation died down, Lotte changed the subject. "Father, you know my birthday is coming up."

"No, Lotte," he impishly replied. "You just had one of those last year. It's impossible for another to come up so quickly." He smiled, and Eric giggled.

She just rolled her black mascaraed eyes. "*Anyway*, for my birthday, I'd like you to take me to Boston to see the treasures."

The twinkle in Mr. Schwarz's eye dimmed almost imperceptibly.

"I know you may not want to go. I understand, but I thought maybe Eric could go with me, if you'd be willing to drive us."

Eric glanced at her. This was the first he'd heard of this plan, but actually, it sounded great, so he exercised his best quality and remained silent.

Mr. Schwarz pondered for several seconds, and finally said, "Yes, Lotte, I think this is a good idea. It's beyond time you see your grandfather's finds. We'll make a day of it in Boston. While you two are in the museum, I can visit with some friends in the city—those that helped us find this house. I'm overdue to visit and thank them. Then, we can have dinner in town. Go look on The Googly and see what the museum times are for Saturdays, assuming all this works for you, Eric?"

The Googly? Eric looked at Lotte quizzically. She was rolling her eyes again, and he feared she'd wear out the black mascara before the night was over.

"He means *Google*," she said with annoyance. "He thinks it's so funny. He knows it's *Google*, but he insists on this silliness. Don't encourage him."

Too late, as Eric had already started giggling again.

Mr. Schwarz shrugged his shoulders and raised his hands in mock ignorance.

Lotte just gave an exasperated sigh and ran to her room to fetch her laptop. She looked up museum times and prices as they finished dinner. There were plenty of times available on Saturday, so they made a tentative plan for next weekend, pending parental approval, of course.

After supper, Eric helped clear the dishes and serving plates. He and Lotte just rinsed things off and threw them in the dishwasher since they'd made short work of all the food and eaten half the loaf of bread. He couldn't remember eating a better meal in his life, and the beer had actually tasted good, once he'd gotten used to it. With the kitchen in order, Mr. Schwarz headed off to the guest rooms to look for the books.

"I better help him," she said, and they both trailed after.

They started in the first room, but quickly determined that the jumbled array of boxes and un-hung pictures did not contain the droid they were looking for. The second room appeared more promising, with many boxes someone, probably the movers, had labelled *Bücher*.

"It's here somewhere," Mr. Schwarz said, moving a box from one pile to another. "Look for the rectangular box."

Lotte cried out in dismay and frustration. "*Alter!* Father, they're *all* rectangular!"

Eric laughed while Mr. Schwarz made a silly face.

She just shook her head and went to look in a pile as far away from the two of them as possible.

"Why does Lotte keep saying 'alter' like that," Eric whispered as Mr. Schwarz dug through one of the boxes. "Does she want you to change something?"

He chuckled. "*Nein*, Eric. *Alter!* is an expression we use to show surprise, disbelief, or possibly mild disapproval, kind of like, 'oh, man,' or 'good grief.' It's a shortened version of the term, '*Alter Schwede*,' which literally means 'old Swedish man' in English. I'm not sure what the poor old Swedish man did to deserve this term, but you can hear it all over Germany. Ah, Eureka!"

Mr. Schwarz produced four books from the box he'd been searching, which he handed to Eric. A picture of Sigmund Freud smoking his familiar cigar graced the cover of the first, *Introductory Lectures on Psychoanalysis*. Other titles included *Civilization and Its Discontents*, *Totem and Taboo*, and Eric smiled when he saw *The Interpretation of Dreams*.

"Take these," Mr. Schwarz said, "and if you like them, surely you can find more on Valkyrie at very low prices."

Eric again glanced quizzically at Lotte. "He means Amazon. So stupid."

Mr. Schwarz shrugged again. "Valkyrie, Amazon... all brave female warriors from legend and myth. Who wouldn't be confused?"

Eric tried to stifle a laugh, but just couldn't do it. Apparently, he and Mr. Schwarz shared the same silly sense of humor.

Lotte left the room in a huff, though Eric knew she wasn't really angry.

"Well, Eric," Mr. Schwarz said. "It's probably time we get you home, *ja*?"

He looked at his watch. *Holy crap, nearly eight o'clock already?* He couldn't believe the time had gone by so fast.

"Come, we'll all ride in the Mercedes. It still has that wonderful new car smell. Lotte!" he called up the stairs. "Time to take Eric home."

Eric fetched his backpack and headed to the Mud *Château* with his books.

Lotte met him there shortly, carrying her Euro-style black Adidas, which she'd retrieved from her room. She flashed him a little Almost Kind-Of Smile while they tied their shoes.

Mr. Schwarz joined them, carrying a bag of bread for Eric's family. "I make too much. We always throw some away."

Eric thanked him for the bread and the books. *This has been... like... the best day ever.*

The black panther Mercedes purred like a kitten as they drove down Holton Hill Road. Lotte sat in the back with Eric. Despite all that had happened, she seemed content now. He hoped the dreams left her alone tonight, and wondered if *Doktor Sigmund Freud* might give him any ideas how to help her.

They pulled into Eric's driveway behind the lumbering HMS Suburban. It appeared as if hoisted up in drydock compared to the sleek profile of the Mercedes. Mr. Schwarz warmly said goodbye to Eric, who thanked him again for the books, and the bread, and dinner, and... everything! He could tell that Mr. Schwarz knew he'd had a good time.

Lotte hopped out with him, ostensibly to get into the front seat for the ride home, but she walked a little way to the door with him.

"No session tomorrow," she said glumly, "but I'll see you on Tuesday."

"Yeah. I had an amazing time today. Thanks so much for having me over. It was, it was, like... I don't know... just awesome."

She smiled—like a real smile, with teeth and everything. Then she stunned him as she leaned in close and gave him a quick kiss on the cheek.

"See you Tuesday," she said. Then she languidly turned and moved in her usual purposeful way toward the car.

He just stood for a minute and looked after her. The books in his backpack were heavy on his shoulder, and the bag of bread in his hands made little crumpling noises. Finally, he turned and headed for the door as the black panther Mercedes slipped stealthily out of the driveway.

Best... day.. ever. And somewhere in the back of his mind, he realized that henceforth, life for him would never be quite the same.

"You want to go to the art museum?" Eric's father asked, incredulous. "Linda, take the boy's temperature. He may need to go to the hospital."

Oh, har har har, Dad.

He'd been to museums before. They'd gone to the Children's Museum in Boston a few times when he was younger, shifting to the Museum of Science when he got a bit older. Now that he recalled, though, he'd been pretty bored on their one trip to the Worcester Art Museum, where they'd looked at lots of paintings of people and things he had no clue about.

If you want to look at a landscape, why look at a painting? Just look out your window. Most of those pictures don't even look real anyway. The graphics in his video games seemed richer to him by comparison.

This time, however, he had a purpose. He wanted to see Lotte's grandfather's treasures, and suddenly, without even realizing it had happened... he wanted to be with Lotte. So, it looked like the art museum would get another whirl.

As it turned out, the Patriots played the Falcons that upcoming Sunday. He had to ask for special dispensation not to go to Grandma's that weekend. He felt this was only fair, as his father had shifted things around for a golf tournament the previous week, but it had briefly been a point of contention.

In the end, his mom said she'd take Grandma to the hair salon after an early lunch on Sunday, so they could all visit. Eric and his dad could leave and watch the game or do whatever. He felt like those were a lot of dominoes that needed to fall for a fairly simple excursion, and resented having so little say in what he did and when. That said, he really appreciated his mother's kindly intervention, and since it all worked out, he didn't complain.

On Monday at school, with no C period, he only saw Lotte a couple of times in the hallways. She generally kept a low profile during the day, and he had no idea where she ate lunch. He cautiously waved at her once, but she seemed not to notice him.

Back in her armor of darkness, she kept her head down and marched grimly from place to place, her Doc Martens sounding a small thud with every deliberate step. No kids even bothered with her anymore, giving her dirty looks and a wide berth when she gloomily trudged by.

Fine with her, I'm sure.

They resumed their lessons on Tuesday, and clearly she was flagging again. The dreams had likely returned, but he knew she didn't want their interactions to be all about her problems. She also didn't want to be an object of... well... pity. So, he focused on the German and tried hard to make her proud.

"Good job, Eric, *Schön*," gradually became a regular utterance from her black stained lips, which pleased him.

He'd started *The Interpretation of Dreams*, hoping to get some insights on what might be happening with her, but he found it terribly confusing. He rapidly abandoned that in favor of *Introductory Lectures on Psychoanalysis*, because it was, well... more introductory. It was still slow going, but he had more success with this book.

He didn't see Lotte after school at all, as she definitely wasn't taking the bus. If she were going to the cemetery, she hadn't invited him, and he wasn't about to start stalking her, though he thought that would be a funny reversal of roles. He dreamed of a movie where the victim wound up stalking the zombie... making its life miserable... scaring the poor thing... keeping it from eating its gory meals of brains and decapitated limbs in peace.

That would be so cool!

By Friday, she really looked bedraggled, and he worried she might want to cancel the Saturday excursion.

"No," she replied when he asked her, suspending the *no problems talk* rule in this one instance. "I want to go. I'm really looking forward to it."

So was he. He missed hanging out with her, after their super fun day. As creepy as she'd been at first, he now felt more at ease with her than any of his other friends—not that he had many, and few of them were particularly close.

Eric could comfortably run in a number of circles, but didn't really identify strongly with any particular group. He found many of the kids at Southby High pretty stuck up. He felt more comfortable around the few kids who were on the fringes, like the art room and theater crowd, who tended to take you as you were a bit more easily. He possessed no artistic ability or inclination himself, and was positively terrified of being on stage, but he did help backstage from time to time.

As he'd feared, a few people razzed him for being seen so often with the Sour Kraut. He got that they were kidding—sort of—but now that he knew Lotte, some of the comments bugged him.

"What's the *goth* chick like? Is she really as scary as she looks? Is she a bitch with you too, or is she actually human when she speaks German?"

Oh, yeah... this is why I usually like to be alone.

CHAPTER 10

The end came swiftly and inexplicably.

Ruminate as we may upon the potential motivation, no evidence can we ascribe to any specific reason. Did we, indeed, ignore a genuine warning? Had we heeded it, would things have unfolded differently?

We know not, and likely never will.

We crossed the desert, first to the land of the Nile, then farther toward the setting sun. Our compounds became ever more isolated and secretive, ever more distant from the armies whose cause we aided.

Our attendants were now known as *Sadat Alnaar*, Masters of Fire. *Hardly.*

Only *we* are the masters of fire, and it is with us one must bargain to exploit the powers of the realm of flames. With time, however, the requests for our services decreased in frequency. Now, we were employed almost exclusively by decree from representatives of the Caliph of this ascendent power, our tasks limited to eliminating political and military opposition to their authority. As they conquered all before them, perhaps their need of us diminished.

Or perhaps it was our refusal to complete one particular task, the sole instance that we declined a bargain—an old woman, leader of a proud and resistant people whom they feared as a prophetess, able to foretell the future. Unlike the Greeks, who melted away, her kind stood and fought.

It seemed to us the request of men lacking honor and courage. Little did we care when asked to eliminate others of their ilk, who were likely as bereft of integrity as they. Always, however, we hesitated when asked to do away with a female, though some few were as entwined in decrepitude as the males. To take one so old, however, whose sole transgression was defiance, seemed base and ignoble.

In the end, fittingly, she died in battle. Many cycles around their paltry sun had passed since then, so if this incident was especially salient in their minds, it took them years to act upon it.

The task they assigned us that day was made arduous by the great distance and its odd nature. From far inland, we were forced to fly to the coast, to a city under siege—the last bastion of Byzantium on this side of the great sea. When it fell, the armies of Islam would cross to new realms.

Our target was the leader of the settlement's defenses; however, he would not be our spoils. Instead, we would bring another of our choice back to the flames to be absorbed before returning to our realm. Our mission was simply to frighten him—threaten him with the inconceivable power the Caliph wielded, in hopes this man would capitulate or perhaps even join their cause.

We remember....

The settlement below is beset by land and sea, but fortified walls and the extremely narrow isthmus joining the peninsula to the mainland makes the city eminently defensible. We circle high, pinpointing his location in a large structure with a domed roof. All seems quiet in the darkness of night, and if there are guards, we see them not.

One of the large doors to the building stands open, and dim light streams out. The windows with thick, heavy glass are far too small for us. Other doors are securely sealed, so we have little choice but to use the suspiciously welcoming main entrance.

We softly land in the courtyard outside. Nothing stirs, so up some stairs we cautiously climb, and then to the door, where we peer inside.

Lamps and candles light the space. A hallway leads to a large circular area directly beneath the domed roof. On the floor in the middle is a tiered depression, decorated and tiled as if to hold water, like some sort of bath... though presently it is empty.

We quietly enter, staying alert for ambush.

Opposite the door, a huge, crossed symbol stands in an alcove. We see pictures made of interlocking stones which adorn the walls and floor. They depict men with serene faces who gaze vacantly into oblivion, beckoning peace to troubled souls. Well do we know it is a tranquility that will never be attained in this world of conflict and covetousness.

The large door closes behind us, and we detect figures scuttle away into the darkness of hidden corners.

From behind the mighty cross, a man steps forward. It is he whom we seek. Contrary to the expectations of our attendants, he does not appear intimidated by our visage.

"So," he says with a haughty tone. "The rumors for once are true. Let us see if your prowess for dealing death measures up to its reputation."

A small door near the alcove opens, and men with armor and weapons stream out. Unlike the one who is our target, they seem hesitant, and several fall to their knees, pleading to some unseen savior with hands clasped to their mouths.

Others are braver and hurl javelins and daggers. We launch upward to avoid them, but one spear digs into our leg just above the hoof. Upon reaching the top of the dome, we hover and attempt to dislodge it. However, large as this structure is, it is not gigantic, and another javelin pierces painfully into our side. This assault cannot continue. Our wings may be jeopardized.

The man wanted a demonstration of our abilities. We shall oblige.

Our focus turns to the candles and lamps. Their flames are small, but for us they serve as a channel to greater power, which their numbers enhance. We call upon their energy, and pillars of flame explode outward.

Some miss their mark, but those that strike true flatten many of the soldiers who assail us. Faces and hands are seared, their weapons and helmets scattering to the ground as they grovel and scream in shock and terror.

Seizing the advantage, we plummet downward. Our barbed tail slices the throat of one upright man, and we gore another with our horns. His blood and entrails spill to the floor as we pull away, just in time to avoid the thrust of a sword.

We rake out with our claws, but this one has a shield that averts our blows. With startling speed, the man sweeps with his weapon, slicing a deep gouge into our abdomen. Dark ash streams from the wound, and we howl in pain. With frustration and anger, we lift ourselves off the ground and kick out with both hooves.

The impact shatters our opponent's shield and sends him reeling to the floor. We grab him in our talons and impale him with our tail. Blood seeps from his mouth as he beseeches salvation. A twist of his head, and he is stilled.

"Bravo!" The man in the alcove claps. The few remaining candles light his display of sardonic appreciation. "Better even than I could have imagined. Wondrous indeed! My informants spoke true. Were they also accurate when they said you were not here to kill me?"

We wonder how he knows this, but it is of little consequence.

'Yes,' we answer. *'Our task is to deliver a message, but if you again assail us, your death is easily arranged. May the consequences be what they be.'*

"That won't be necessary," he casually assures us. "The message you have for me has already been received by another route. You can tell your masters that my answer is yes. I will surrender Septem without further defense, and I will join them. Roderic will be furious, but it shall be fitting revenge. I sent one of my daughters to the Lord of Andalus for her improvement and education, but she became pregnant by him. I see for him no other punishment or recompense, than that I should bring the Arabs against him."

All this for naught! These beings and their petty travails.... Perhaps it would serve us best to disregard the next summons... or has their unquenchable thirst for ever greater power so permeated our nature that we cannot now turn away?

"In any case," the man continues. "I have an offer for *you* to consider. It has come to my attention through certain... *sources*... that you have fallen from favor with those whom you serve. Your existence, at least in this realm, is threatened. I can help you, but to do so, you must reveal to me where the encampment of your attendants is located. It is the most closely guarded secret I have ever come upon. Should something untoward befall you, I could assist. Without this information, however, I would be powerless."

His words trouble us, as we smell a trap. The potential repercussions of cooperating with this request are incalculable. Never would we bring harm to our *Sadat Alnaar,* and never had we seen any indication that something was amiss. This one is crafty, like all his strain. By duplicity, he navigates the changes from Byzantine to Goth to Arab—his word only as good as the direction of the wind, ever subject to change.

We scoff. *'You think us fools. Betray the confidence of those who have served us for over a millennium? Risk all on the word of a traitor? Sad that we cannot take you as spoils. This miserable realm would be better for it.'*

"A pity. For your sake, I hope that I am wrong. In any case, we are now allies and serve the same masters. For all my changes of allegiance, consider those of you and your associates over countless centuries. You and I are much alike—chameleons, who have gifts to be exploited, and to us go the spoils. So it is, and so it ever shall be."

His words ring in our mind as we fly inland, interrupted only by the incessant prayers of the pathetic soldier we chose to replenish our power. It is after dawn when we return to our remote enclave.

All, it seems, are awake and looking to the sky, as if in anticipation of our return—gazing as if seeing us anew, and not for countless times, draining all awe and veneration from the spectacle.

We land, as always, by the arched marble slab, no longer cut from heavy stone with trenches for oil. This one is sleeker, with small bowls holding the flaming fuel, and engraved lines that mark the familiar pattern. The heat generated from something in the material of the bowls is massive. Even the rings that bind our pact are now constructed of this strange stone.

All five of our attendants are present.

Unusual.

We tell them of the man's answer to the Caliph's missive, and their response is muted. We keep his other words to ourselves, not wishing to trouble them with probable lies.

When we approach the flame, the women prostrate themselves. Some begin to weep. On the outskirts of the compound, we see that the guards look on. Perhaps it is the light that has attracted them, as it is rare we travel so far or arrive back after sunrise.

Above the burning bowls we take our victim. The snap of his spine across our knee silences his litany. As the flames engulf his body, so too do we dissolve to ashen mist, and our energies merge, renewing what been depleted by the long flight and the battle.

We are whole, as whole perhaps as we can ever be.

By the Eternal Flame we will bask and ponder the words of the traitorous man—words that, despite their untrustworthy origin, we still find strangely unsettling.

But the Eternal Flame is not where we find ourselves.

At first, we think it a mistake—an error, and that somehow we were errantly misdirected. We turn our consciousness toward the portal, where we can still see the arched marble slab. The flames in the bowls have extinguished, as always. Should they simply re-light the fires, we can return.

But they do not.

On the ground, my *Sadat Alnaar* wail and beat their chests. The guards come to collect them, but they are inconsolable. One slits her throat with a curved dagger and collapses in a bloody heap to the earth.

Then, others come—men I have never seen before. They must have been in the few rough buildings and tents that make up our small settlement.

The view changes. First, we see the sky. Then the billowing clouds appear as if viewed from a pit in the earth. And then....

Darkness.

So has it been since that time.

Imprisoned... alone... trapped... betrayed. So very... cold.

Why?

Did that man truly know what was to happen? If so, how had he come by such information? Had we revealed the secret of our location, would he have helped, or was this simply another duplicitous trick?

We know not. We simply... suffer. Endlessly. We cannot even fathom where we are or what we did to deserve such a fate.

Will we ever be released? Will we ever taste the warmth of the Eternal Flame again?

If so, what then?

Should we return to our realm and lick our wounds—turn our backs on these conniving and treacherous creatures for evermore? Or shall we instead take vengeance, and revel in the reaping of these miserable being's lives—let their flowing blood assuage our fury?

If ever we are free of this wretched place... we shall see.

We shall see.

Lotte and her father arrived a little before 11 a.m. on Saturday morning. Eric's parents came out and chatted with Mr. Schwarz, thanking him profusely for the bread last week, which had been devoured by Wednesday.

"Wunderbar!" he replied, cheery as ever. "I'll give more to Eric to bring you the next time he comes over." Everyone smiled. Mr. Schwarz was contagious.

Soon, they loaded in the car and waved goodbye.

The black panther Mercedes glided silently as they drove along Route 146 toward the turnoff to the Pike in Millbury. Lotte sat with Eric in the back seat. She looked great. Sort of Half-Lotte, but different this time, wearing her scary-cool black leather jacket over a black dress top, black dress slacks, and some really sharp black patent leather dress shoes with short but spiky heels.

She'd covered the scary black circles under her eyes with makeup again, and had opted for the elegant, straight, black un-eyebrows, but had stuck with the black lipstick and mascara. Monotone still, but she wore it well. He tried not to stare at her as she sat, gazing with half-open eyes out the window of the Mercedes.

Fail.

It got even worse when she removed her shoes, leaned her back against the door, swung her black-stockinged feet up into his lap, and closed her eyes to catch a quick nap. Just like the library, he had nowhere to put his left arm, so he tenderly rested it across her legs, to which she gave no reaction.

"So, Eric," Mr. Schwarz happily interjected from the front. "How does it go with *Herr Professor Doktor Freud*?"

That's a lot of honorifics. He figured Mr. Schwarz was fooling with him and giggled a bit. Lotte seemed fast asleep and didn't stir.

"Umm, okay, I guess. I started *The Interpretation of Dreams*, but that one was kind of confusing. I'm trying the *Introductory Lectures* now, which seems to be going better."

"Good for you. That's a good place to start. I'm glad you're sticking with it. If you like, we could discuss the book when you're done, though I may need to have it back to re-read. It's been a long time since I tackled the esteemed *Herr Professor Doktor*."

"That would be awesome." He knew he wasn't getting everything out of the book he could be, and would really benefit from some guidance. He'd also started thinking more seriously about taking that psychology class the school offered as a social studies elective, though it would be hard to get in.

Soon they reached the outskirts of Boston. The Prudential and John Hancock towers, along with that new milk-bottle looking thing, loomed above the tree line visible through the Mercedes' windshield. When they got close, he gave Lotte a gentle nudge and excitedly pointed out Fenway Park as they passed by. Its light towers and signature green profile were barely visible above the buildings and giant billboard along the highway.

"That's where the Sox play. I've been to games there with my folks."

"This is baseball, *ja*?" she replied, yawning after her nap. "The game you used to play? I know nothing of it. It's not so popular in Germany. Maybe you can teach me about it some time."

With pleasure, he thought, surprised at her interest.

"Here is our exit," Mr. Schwarz said as he smoothly guided the car off the highway and snaked back along Huntington Avenue.

Train tracks bisected the street, and Eric saw a familiar streetcar with green highlights pass in the opposite direction. Soon the palatial edifice of the Museum of Fine Arts appeared on the right. A statue of an Indian on horseback, gazing skyward with outstretched arms, seemed to welcome them.

Mr. Schwarz passed the museum and pulled up across the street from the platform for the MFA T stop. "Okay, here's the plan," he said over his shoulder, his tone a bit more serious than normal. "I go to meet my friends for lunch. Here is some money. Go across the street while I wait and get tickets for the *Straßenbahn*."

Eric knew that meant "streetcar." One of his favorite German words was *Straßenbahnhaltestelle*, which literally meant "streetcar stopping place." It made him laugh how Germans could so often complicate the simple.

Can't they just say T-stop? Gotta admit, though, Straßenbahnhaltestelle *does kind of roll off your tongue in a weird sort of way.*

Mr. Schwarz continued. "After the museum, get on the inbound train and meet me at the station called Park Street. It's near the park, *natürlich*, and we can have a little walk before supper. It's about noon now, so... say 4:30? There's money there for your entrance fees, and for a snack if you get hungry. Call me on the walkie-talkie if you have any sort of problem."

After the respective and obligatory black-mascaraed eye roll and unsuccessfully suppressed giggle at the familiar walkie-talkie joke, the two acknowledged the plan and exited the car.

"Have a wonderful time!" Mr. Schwarz called from the open window, beaming from ear to ear.

They waved and crossed at the fancy brick crosswalk to the platform to get their tokens. Once they had them successfully in hand, Mr. Schwarz smiled and waved again, rolled up the window, and pulled away down the side street. Eric could almost see the swish of the black panther's tail as the car slipped silently away.

"So, shall we?" Lotte said, a bit more energy in her voice after resting in the car.

They strolled back across the street and walked toward the Indian and the front entrance. Once inside, the long and winding ticket line moved more quickly than they feared, and soon they were looking at their little maps, trying to get they lay of the museum.

"Are you hungry?" she asked. "Or would you just like to go see the treasures now?"

Like Lotte, Eric had eaten a late breakfast and didn't need food just yet. Plus, the lines at noon in the cafeteria would be hell. Better to wait. Anyway, he was really excited to see the exhibit and learn about her grandfather, so they located the rooms on the map and headed in that direction.

The MFA's Arts of Islamic Cultures gallery was not large, at least in comparison with the rest of the museum. Eric looked at the various items, most of them decorated in bright colors and intricate natural or geometric patterns that echoed the furniture in Lotte's room.

"This is Iznik," she said, pointing out a particularly brilliant-colored set of ceramic tiles that formed the decorative top of a doorway. Across a white background, deep blues and brilliant reds with aquamarine highlights graced the object's center, forming patterns that were simultaneously organic and fantastic in nature.

"These were made during the Ottoman period, at the height of their creative power."

How does she know all this? I always thought Ottomans were just little footstools people sometimes have in fancy living rooms that don't get much use.

They walked briskly through the room to the rear, where a couple of small steps led to an ornate opening. Fancy gold lettering announced, "The Reynolds Treasures." These were the highlight of the MFA's Islamic collection, and they occupied a special place. They passed a security guard who seemingly took no note of them, ascended the steps, and entered the room.

A few people milled about, and Eric saw three cases. On the wall above the cases were the names of the places where the finds had occurred. Jordan was to the right, Egypt to the left, and Morocco dead ahead. Maps of the areas where the digs had occurred were superimposed on the wall behind the place names, while plaques on the cases gave more information about the artifacts.

"These are my grandparents," Lotte said, pointing at a large black and white photograph emblazoned on the wall to the right.

Two figures in sort of old-timey-looking archaeologist clothes stood squinting and smiling in the desert sun. Eric could see echoes of Lotte in her grandmother's face. The text under the photograph explained how Gordon Reynolds, a young archaeologist, had unpredictably and miraculously uncovered the material remains of the *Sadat Alnaar*, the Masters of Fire.

Little was known of them. During the time of Muhammed, they were a sect that appeared to have lived near the border of modern-day Jordan and Saudi Arabia. It was thought they might have migrated from farther east, possibly Babylon, or as far away as Persia, though no real evidence had been found to support this idea.

As Islam expanded, the *Sadat Alnaar* seem to have converted, and had been given special ritual duties. They accompanied the armies of Islam as they exploded across North Africa, first into Egypt in the mid-seventh century, then across to Morocco. By the time of the Battle of Tours in 732 in France, the *Sadat Alnaar* had seemingly vanished from the record altogether.

The plaque mentioned a planned archaeological expedition to Spain, which had been scrapped when Gordon Reynolds tragically drowned in Morocco in 1961. Lotte's grandmother returned to England, and Eric noted that she died about ten years later, when Lotte's mother must have been in her early twenties.

Continuing the exhibit, Eric read that, to this day, it remained unknown how Gordon Reynolds had identified the locations of the *Sadat Alnaar's* sanctuaries. Most were in secluded areas, not near any population centers, ancient or modern. Pictures of the foundations of their excavated buildings, displayed on the museum wall, revealed simple designs—just a few crude structures placed around a circular courtyard believed to be the area where the *Sadat Alnaar* conducted their rituals.

The truly incredible part of the finds had been the artifacts, to which the pair turned their attention when they finished reading. They had no parallel in any museum in the world—totally unique, and unlike anything from any cultural tradition, though they seemed to borrow from many.

As they approached the first case, which contained the Jordan finds, Lotte reached in her black leather shoulder bag and produced a dog-eared book. It appeared to be a catalog of the treasures from years back. Notes scribbled on yellow stickies, worn and folded with age, littered almost all the pages.

"These are the first of the finds," she said, leafing through her book, "and likely the oldest. Nowhere else have stone relics been discovered."

He looked in the case. Two large granite columns, which looked like candle holders with a swirling design, flanked an enormous semicircular block of the same material.

She pointed. "Notice how the columns are darkened at the top and along the sides. They created great fires here during their ceremonies.

Later, they seem to have abandoned stone in favor of other materials, and made smaller fires. No one knows why."

The semi-circular block of granite was punctuated at the perimeter with small indentations. Carved channels radiated out from these, connecting the lesser depressions with a great crater at the center. All these bore the same marks of fire that she'd pointed out on the columns.

"What was this used for?" he asked.

"It isn't clear. They placed some sort of flammable oil in the small holes, and it apparently flowed through the channels into the larger depression at the center. The whole thing would be on fire in this pattern, and was probably quite impressive."

There were some other objects in the case, mostly found among the buildings on the perimeter, which related to day-to-day life. Of greater interest were some gold rings that had been found buried under the floor of one of the structures. Some could fit on a finger, while others were much larger, an inch-and-a-half or more in diameter.

"What are those big rings for?" he queried.

"Again, no one knows, but come this way... I'll show you what happens with them when we move to Egypt."

They crossed the room to the second case. Here, the items were not as monumental, and the stonework had been abandoned. The material seemed to have shifted to some sort of reddish quartz with flecks of yellow and blue.

She pointed again. "See the rings?"

Indeed, more rings, both large and small, were made of one band of the polished quartz, tipped on either side by a rim of fine, thin gold. The case also featured many shallow bowls made of clay, seemingly lined with the same quartz from the ring. Most were broken and the quartz was all but gone, worn away—only traces of it remained. A solid fragment of carved quartz of indeterminate purpose also sat on display.

"This quartz is rare," she explained. "It is called *Alkuartiz Alnaar*. Fire Quartz. It apparently came only from a few deposits in what is now Yemen... all long tapped-out. It's thought that the *Sadat Alnaar* were exposed to it when they became part of the Islamic world. Apparently, they developed something of a monopoly on its use. I think the items in these cases are the only known *Alkuartiz Alnaar* in existence."

Interesting as that was, more so was the centerpiece in this display, a fragment of papyrus that clearly bore a semi-circular image that echoed the granite slab in the previous case. The circular side of the image pointed toward the museum floor, while at the top, on the flat side, a squarish object with a somewhat fuzzy outline appeared.

The papyrus was torn, so you could only see the very bottom of this item, but the two figures were clearly connected in some way. The semi-circle bore marks where the indentations on the granite block would have been, though the interconnecting channels were not represented.

"It's just amazing that paper would survive for so long," Lotte exclaimed. "We have the dryness of the desert to thank for this." She showed him the picture in her book of the papyrus, a close-up of the area where the two figures were nearest one another.

He noticed what appeared to be representations of little bowls placed near the bottom of each side of the fuzzy, outlined, squarish object.

She took her book back and furiously thumbed through the pages, glancing from time to time at the Egypt case as she did so. Eventually, she started scowling.

"What's the matter?" he asked.

"Oh, nothing," she said after brief consideration. "Come on."

They moved to the final case with the Moroccan finds. Thought the smallest of all, Eric found this display the coolest. He recognized the featured item here from the cover of Lotte's well-worn catalog.

"Awesome!" he said, blown away by the ring, again made of the reddish Fire Quartz, tipped this time with obsidian highlights. It was long enough to cover the entire upper part of the finger from knuckle to knuckle. It had a ridged look, with sweeping edges that would have jutted up from the wearer's hand. It amazed him, and it was the first thing he would have truly identified as a "treasure."

Beside it sat a single round ring, again just a bit shy of two inches in diameter, made of matching Fire Quartz tipped with obsidian. Apparently, a member of the Reynolds' Moroccan dig team found these items buried under a former building floor. The man's picture graced the plaque that described the artifacts.

More clay bowls and other objects, some sporting the now familiar reddish quartz, were also in this display. The pair crouched in front of the case while Lotte flipped through her book, describing items and the various theories about their uses.

"It was some sort of ritual, probably for warriors before battle, but who really knows? It's thought that perhaps the *Sadat Alnaar* summoned the power of fire to make them courageous. That's not really in keeping with Islam, but obviously this sect existed before Islam. Why they got special consideration from Muhammed and the first Caliphs is anyone's guess."

Eric thought about his video games. *This would make such a cool plot, and fire effects are the best!*

She was about to continue, but stopped short and looked up over her shoulder. The security guard, a stocky but somewhat short black woman, had come up behind them and stood with her hands behind her back, looking down at the pair.

Lotte gained her composure first. "I'm sorry, were we being too loud, or are we too close to the case?"

The woman grinned and looked over her shoulder. They realized they were now the only ones in the room. "No, sweetie," she said in a leisurely tone. "You're not bothering anybody."

Whew! Eric imagined explaining to his parents how he'd been tossed out of the MFA after only an hour.

"I just have to say," the woman continued. "I've stood in this room many times, and I've never heard *anyone* talk about these things like you do. Sounds like you even correctly pronounce the name of those Fire Master people in Arabic. You really know your stuff. More than some of our docent tour guides, if you ask me. Then again, nobody really asks me anything around here."

They both stood and stared. The security guard's blue plastic name tag read "Marjorie Hunter" in white letters.

"How do you know so much about these things?" Marjorie asked. "And where are you from with that really interesting accent?"

"Gordon Reynolds was my grandfather on my mother's side," Lotte offered. "She was English, but my father is German. I grew up with both languages, so I have this kind of crazy accent. I've been enchanted with the treasures since I was a little girl. I've read everything ever written about them." She held up her dog-eared book. "This is my first time actually seeing them. It's quite overwhelming."

That seemed to get Marjorie's attention. "Really! Gordon Reynolds' granddaughter. Seriously?" She paused for a moment, squinted, and looked up to her left as if in thought. "You know, there's someone who'd like to meet you. I saw her here earlier. I wonder if she's still around? Could you two wait here for a minute while I make a quick call?"

They both felt perfectly happy to linger with the treasures a while longer. Marjorie smiled and headed out of the room, and another security guard positioned himself outside the entrance, presumably keeping an eye on both Islamic rooms while Marjorie used the phone.

Surprisingly quickly, she returned and gave two thumbs up from the doorway. "I was right. She's still here and she's dying to meet you. She's gonna be right down. Just another minute."

A few more people came and exited the room, casually perusing the treasures before shuffling out.

They didn't get a fraction of what I got out of it. Thanks, Lotte.

The click of heels sounded from the next room, and a beautiful woman walked toward them. She appeared to be about forty years old, and wore a *hijab*, along with what looked like a white laboratory coat with thick magnifying glasses crammed into the breast pocket. The woman stopped and talked briefly with Marjorie, and the two proceeded into the room together.

She smiled as she got closer and extended her hand to Lotte. "Greetings. I'm Dr. Donya Esfahani, Director and Head Curator of the Arts of Islamic Cultures galleries here at the museum."

She spoke in clear, warm, and unhesitating tones, like she'd rehearsed what she had to say. "Maggie told me we had special visitors. I'm so pleased to meet you. Tell me, are you really Alice Reynolds-Schwarz's daughter?"

"I'm very pleased to meet you," Lotte said, confidently returning the woman's handshake. "Yes, I'm Lotte Schwarz, and Alice Reynolds-Schwarz was my mother. This is my very good friend, Eric Schneider."

Very *good friend?* He wondered when he'd gotten a promotion, and whether he received better pay with his new rank. He shook Dr. Esfahani's hand and then stood "at ease" in the background.

"I met your mother once," she said, returning her attention to Lotte, "back when I was a student and went to one of her lectures. I have to admit, I was a bit of a fangirl. I even got her autograph after the talk."

She gave a somewhat embarrassed little laugh. "Your mother was such a passionate advocate for archaeological exploration and preservation of historic treasures, especially in the Islamic world. She was an inspiration to me and to everyone in the field. We were all devastated when we heard of her passing. I can't tell you how sorry I am for your loss."

Lotte withered slightly, but politely thanked her for her words.

Eric could see how raw all this still was for her, even after two years. He wished he could do something, but knew she just wanted to be treated normally. It seemed to go best when that's how they interacted, for both of them.

"Your father is also well known in our circles," she continued. "He's a great philanthropist, galvanizing the architectural and construction communities to support preservation efforts. I believe he and your mother met at a fundraising event, yes? They made a powerful team and did so much good—beacons of hope and brightness in a world that increasingly seems to embrace only darkness. I hope he's well."

Wow. For all his unassuming nature, Mr. Schwarz seems to be a pretty important guy.

Lotte gave an honest reply, saying it had been hard for her dad, but that they were both trying for a fresh start.

"So," Dr. Esfahani said, redirecting the conversation. "Maggie tells me you know everything there is to know about the treasures, but today is the first time you've seen them in person. What do you think?"

Lotte brightened... as much as her all black outfit would allow. "Oh, they're wonderful! To actually see them is better than any picture in a book." She waved her old glossy paperback.

The woman gave a big smile. "That's the tour catalog from 1987, well before my time here, but I have a few copies left in my office. It looks like you could use a new one."

Lotte laughed. "No, it would be impossible for me to transfer all my stickies to a new copy. This one is mine for life. If you don't mind, though, can I ask you a question?"

"Of course, please."

"I'll leave you all to it," Marjorie said, excusing herself back to her post.

"Oh, thank you so much, Maggie," Dr. Esfahani gushed. "You're the best!"

Marjorie smiled as she walked away.

Lotte led the way back to the Egypt cabinet and pointed at the solid piece of Fire Quartz that sat in the case.

Eric examined the caption on the plaque, which read simply "Fragment of a Frame."

"What is this piece?" Lotte inquired. "I don't recognize it from this book, or any I've read. I can't believe I missed it. Can you explain what it is?"

A knowing smile came over Dr. Esfahani's face. "You really do know your stuff, Lotte. This wasn't part of the touring exhibition. In fact, this is the only piece of this artifact that's ever been displayed. It's been under near constant restoration since it was found in the late 1950s by your grandfather. We can't figure out where this fragment goes, so we decided to display it for now."

Lotte's eyes widened with excitement.

"As far as what it is," Dr. Esfahani continued. "I can do better than tell you. I can show you. Would you like to see?"

"I'd be thrilled," Lotte breathlessly replied. "It would be so incredibly special for me!"

Dr. Esfahani smiled warmly. "Then follow me. It would be my honor and privilege to show Gordon Reynold's granddaughter one of his hidden treasures. You too, Eric. I think you'll enjoy it as well."

With that, they followed her out of the room.

Marjorie smiled and waved as they went by. "Have fun, you two."

This is more fun than Tomb Raider *meets* Fable. *I just hope mummies don't come out of crypts in the back room and kill us. Actually, seeing a mummy might be cool, assuming you could run away, and it didn't catch you with its one good hand and bite you and infect you with a brain-rotting disease.*

"*Alter!* Keep up," Lotte chided, snapping him out of his mummy thoughts.

Pay attention, stupid, he cursed angrily to himself.

Life will pass you by.

CHAPTER 11

Lotte and Eric followed Dr. Esfahani through the museum, past the exhibit halls, and into a quiet area that looked more administrative in nature. She entered a code into a security keypad and pushed the up button by the door to a large freight elevator. It moved with almost painful sluggishness, being built to accommodate oversize artworks and artifacts.

"I just can't seem to get my hands out of conservation," she related as the elevator crawled up to the third and top floor. "I have so many administrative duties now, meetings all the time, committees, and of course fundraising. It's a necessary part of what we do, but it diminishes the time we have to actually work with the artifacts."

Why does a rich organization like the MFA need to do fundraising in the first place? Don't all the expensive tickets cover their costs? I must be missing something. He kept quiet.

"I come in on Saturdays to have some time to myself and do what I love best. I have a few pieces I'm working to restore now. It will take me ages to finish them, but it keeps me sane. It's not like anyone else has much time for these either."

The elevator finally chugged to a halt, giving a little lurch. They exited and walked down a corridor with doors spaced widely along one wall. Through glass panels, Eric could see large tables, cases, and shelves, all cluttered with objects and tools. Bright sunlight streamed in from windows on the ceiling and on the opposite side of the room. They walked down the hall, and eventually Dr. Esfahani stopped at one of the doors and again entered her security code on the keypad.

"This is our conservation room. My little projects are on the table here, but what I wanted you to see is in the case over there."

They followed her between rows of cluttered worktables. As they got closer, he could see that while numerous, all the items were carefully arranged, many surrounded by circles of erasable marker that delineated various spaces where artifacts were grouped. Brushes, small picks, and drills lay about, which he understood were used to carefully flake away the accumulated dust and dirt of centuries and reveal the prizes underneath.

"This is amazing!" Lotte said, wide-eyed. "I love teaching, but I'm also fascinated by archaeology... probably from being around it all my life."

"Feel free to look around," Dr. Esfahani cheerfully replied. "Just please don't disturb anything. Conservation is painstaking work, and one misplaced item can set a conservator back terribly."

Eric also found it interesting, but wasn't sure he had the focus and detail orientation to restore or uncover ancient artifacts. He liked seeing the works in progress, though, before they were so perfect and beautiful like the exhibits in the museum.

He made sure to keep a wide berth from the tables, trailing behind Lotte down the middle of the rows. They finally stopped in front of a large cabinet by the wall, which stood about chest high with three large drawers, each running its length.

"Here it is." Dr. Esfahani reached for the middle handle, and the almost eight-foot-long drawer slid out with remarkably little effort.

Lotte gasped, and her knees literally buckled as the artifact was revealed.

"I can't... I can't...." She tried to speak, but her breath had abandoned her. She clung to Eric's arm while she struggled to process what she saw. "I can't believe it!"

Eric looked at the item in the case, and recognition suddenly dawned on him. "Hey, that looks exactly like — *Aaaaaaaaahhhhhhhhh!*"

He screamed in pain as a nail gun plastered his foot to the floor!

Or so it felt.

In truth, Lotte had dug her spiked heel through the top of his right Nike and pressed firmly down. Tremendous pain assailed him, and he felt certain there were multiple fractures in his foot. He figured he'd be in a cast for... well... at the moment, it felt like probably the rest of his life.

Lotte, seeming to regain her composure, swung around and gave him a consoling hug. "Eric, I'm so sorry! I lost my balance." She pulled him toward her for what he hoped might be another kiss on the cheek, but then leaned close and sternly hissed in his ear. *"Keep quiet!"*

He wondered if that included no screaming in excruciating agony. "Do you mind if I sit in one of those chairs?" he asked Dr. Esfahani.

"Of course not. Let me get one for you." She grabbed a chair from one of the tables and brought it over.

He sat and massaged his throbbing foot through his sneaker. *Amputation might be the only possibility.*

"Are you all right?" she asked.

"I'll be okay." *Okay for a cripple, that is.* He wished he could remove his shoe to better soothe his foot.

"So amazing," Lotte gasped, drawing Eric's and Dr. Esfahani's attention away from his misery. She stood over the open drawer, gazing at its contents, eyes full of wonder.

Eric knew she was looking at an almost dead ringer for the mirror on the crazy wardrobe in her room. The coloring on this one was much paler, the reds not as red, oranges not as orange, and blues not as blue. He couldn't tell with his quick look if this was because the material was different, or whether it was due to the version in the drawer having been smashed into a zillion little pieces, almost as if it had shattered like glass — or exploded.

Maybe the mirror frame in Lotte's room is just a copy? He'd really thought it had been painted, the colors were so vibrant. *What would they have been copying, though? Dr. Esfahani said the one in the drawer has never been seen, at least not publicly.*

As he thought about it, he conceded the possibility that the frame in Lotte's room might be some sort of stone. It could even conceivably be Fire Quartz, like the artifacts in the Reynolds room and the frame that lay before them in the drawer... painstakingly glued back together by decades of conservators since Gordon Reynolds had discovered it.

It looked slightly different, though, and he still wasn't sure if they were made of the same material. Even Lotte hadn't said anything about the Fire Quartz in the treasure room looking like her mirror frame.

The two objects were definitely the same rectangular shape and size, however, and both also looked like crazy multi-colored grass blowing in the wind. The frame had probably been assembled from many smaller pieces of quartz, all carved in these shapes and fit together like a puzzle to simulate... to simulate....

"Fire," Lotte almost whispered.

"That's right," Dr. Esfahani replied. "We originally thought it was some sort of portal that the *Sadat Alnaar*, or the warriors they blessed in their rituals, would walk through... but now we don't think so. Look here." She pointed into the drawer.

Drawn by curiosity, Eric rose from his chair and gingerly tested his foot. *Maybe I won't need amputation after all, or an ambulance. I'm taking this shoe off the minute I can, though. Ice would be nice too.*

"There, you see?" She traced a line that went along the entire inner part of the frame, except where pieces were simply missing. "That channel held something. It may have been a piece of wood, but we suspect it was glass. So, whatever they did with this, we don't think they passed through it during their ceremonies."

Glass... like a mirror. I'm reflecting about mirrors. Ha ha. At least I haven't lost my sense of humor, despite the multiple fractures.

"Could this be the square object on the papyrus in the Egypt case?" Lotte asked. "That sort of fuzzy outline harkens to the shape of the flames on the frames. I mean *frame*. Sorry."

Oops! Lotte doesn't normally make mistakes like that. She's rattled for sure.

Dr. Esfahani didn't seem to notice. "Lotte, you are incredibly perceptive. You'd make a good archaeologist."

Lotte would make a good anything, he thought with a mix of admiration and jealousy.

"This is exactly what we think," she continued. "It was found in Egypt at the same time and the same place as the papyrus, so it would be entirely logical. However, one never knows for certain. It's not a good thing to turn a hypothesis into fact without corroborating evidence... but we strongly suspect this is the case."

Lotte ran her hand a few inches above the shattered frame, almost as if testing the air for the presence of something. "It feels like it emanates warmth. Maybe it's just me, but I connect with this object very strongly."

Dr. Esfahani stared at her for a few seconds. "Come over here, Lotte. Let me show you something."

Eric limped along behind as they moved to a smaller cabinet nearby. She opened a drawer, pulled out a wooden caddy, and brought it to a nearby table. It had multiple compartments that held fragments of Fire Quartz, obviously still to be added to the frame in the large drawer.

"Hold on." She walked away, and returned shortly with a lighter. Gingerly, she lifted a fragment from the caddy, held it between her fingers, and lit the lighter. She waved the flame several times under the small, wedge-like chip, then put the lighter away. "Here." She handed the fragment to Lotte.

Lotte took it and gasped in amazement. "It's hot! Very hot. Far hotter than it should be for the amount of heat you gave it."

She handed the sliver to Eric, who was stunned at the amount of heat it produced... almost like it had amplified the fire from the lighter and retained its heat. It hadn't cooled at all when he passed the object back to Lotte, who held it a while longer before hesitantly handing it back to Dr. Esfahani.

"Astonishing," Lotte gushed.

Wow! Lotte being astonished about something other than my shortcomings.... A minor triumph.

"We discovered this entirely by accident," Dr. Esfahani explained. "It's apparently a property of the *Alkuartiz Alnaar*, the Fire Quartz. We can see why perhaps the *Sadat Alnaar* were attracted to it, though exactly why heat absorption and retention were important, and how they used these items, we have no idea."

Lotte backed away, visibly overloaded. She sat heavily in the chair that had been pulled out for Eric.

"I can see this has made a great impression on you," Dr. Esfahani said in a comforting tone. "Would you like some water, or can I get you something else?"

I'd like morphine for my foot. He wondered what impression it would make if Lotte showed her an intact mirror that presently sat in her bedroom. *That reaction I'd like to see.* He heeded her command and remained quiet.

"No," Lotte finally replied. "You've been too kind with your time. You're right... seeing this is the experience of a lifetime. I'm at a total loss for words and thought, but believe me, this is something I'll never forget. I really can't thank you enough. May I have one more look before you close the drawer?"

The woman smiled and led her back to the cabinet.

Again, Lotte passed her hands over the frame, eyes closed as if searching for something that only her sense of touch could register.

Finally, she lowered her arms and smiled wistfully. "Thank you, Dr. Esfahani," she said in a dreamlike voice. "I feel the object... but sense it's far away."

"Oh, child," Dr. Esfahani replied. "I'm so happy we've met."

Dr. Esfahani led Lotte and Eric back into the hallway, and said, "Wait here one moment." She walked briskly away and disappeared around a corner.

Eric started to speak, but Lotte raised her index finger to her lips to indicate maintaining silence, and he grudgingly complied.

"Is your foot okay?" she whispered.

"Yeah, I think so." He tested the bend in his toes, which were still extremely tender. "I might need some ice. I think it's swelling."

"Oh, Eric, I'm so sorry. I panicked! I had to shush you quickly somehow. I couldn't think of what else to do. We'll talk more when we're gone from here. We'll get you ice in the cafeteria. I really didn't mean to hurt you."

She seemed sincerely sorry, so he just smiled.

Soon the click of Dr. Esfahani's shoes announced her approach. When she arrived, she presented two crisp new copies of the old touring exhibition catalog. "Here, take these, one for each of you. I want you to have them. Also, Lotte, here's my card. Please contact me anytime about anything. Your mother helped me more in my career than she ever could have known. If I can help her daughter in any way, it would be my great honor. I know your mother would be so proud of you."

They both accepted the gifts with thanks, and she led them back to the lumbering elevator and down to the first floor.

"I'll leave you here. I have some things to tidy up before I go. Again, it was my great pleasure meeting you both. I hope and trust our paths will cross again soon." With that, she re-boarded the slow boat to the third floor, waving as the doors closed with their signature lurch.

The two navigated back to the main part of the museum and followed signs to the cafeteria. There, they purchased some Cokes and a couple of pieces of pizza. Eric asked for an extra cup and filled it with ice from the soda fountain.

"I'm gonna go to the bathroom to put some ice on this," he said when they reached a table, pointing at his foot.

She looked at him forlornly as he turned and left.

In one of the stalls, he sat and removed his shoe and sock. A bright red and swollen mark on the top of his foot gave credence to his pain, though at this point, he doubted anything was really broken.

He massaged the injured area and applied the ice. "Yeah, that's gonna leave a mark."

He had no idea what all this meant. Why had she been so hush-hush? What, if any, was the connection between the object in the drawer and the mirror on her crazy wardrobe? What did she mean that she "felt the object?"

After fifteen minutes or so, his foot became numb. Figuring that was enough, he hobbled back to the seating area.

Lotte had eaten a little of her pizza, but didn't appear to be very hungry. She smiled wanly when he approached. "How is it?"

"I'll be fine," he replied, though he knew some level of pain would return when the ice wore off. He took a bite of his now cold pizza and had a sip of Coke. "Lotte, what is going *on*?"

She stared silently in the direction of the cafeteria cashiers, who sat as they rang up meal after meal. Finally, she looked back to him, her expression blank.

"I don't know. The wardrobe and the mirror, Eric, they aren't mine... at least not until recently. They were my mother's. When she died, my father was through with all the old furniture. Most of it's stored now, as you know, in the garage... but I took the wardrobe in Bremen not long after she died. I'd always loved it, and Father was happy to let me have it."

He listened silently.

"My mother..." she began, but then hesitated, looking away and becoming anxious. He feared she might cry, but she seemed to collect herself. "It was so hard, Eric. She was so normal. In fact, everything had been perfect. She'd decided to step back from the work with the foundation, which kept her terribly busy with lots of travel. She started working part-time and spent much more time at home. I loved it. She seemed so relaxed... so happy. We redecorated the house together over the summer. We even had some strong men come in and help us move furniture. We talked about that for days... how good-looking they were."

She smiled at the memory before reluctantly continuing, a darkness in her tone. "But then, it all changed. Somewhere, she'd found some old papers of her father's. She became quite obsessed reading them, spending more time in the bedroom each day with the door closed. I came in once while she was reading them. She was very cross and screamed at me to leave. She started to have insomnia, seemed constantly preoccupied, and became short-tempered, yelling at my father... something I'd never heard her do. Eventually, she forced him to sleep in the guest room, locking the door to the bedroom and staying there all day. She stopped eating, and dark circles appeared under her eyes. Soon, she looked like a ghost."

Like mother like daughter? Clearly, Lotte's mother had been way further gone than she was now.

"I literally hadn't seen her for days. School had started back, so I was out in the mornings and afternoon, and she was always locked in the bedroom when I got home. Until one day—" She put her hands over her eyes.

He figured that would smudge those elegant straight black un-eyebrows, but he wasn't about to interrupt her now.

"She was in the dining room," she continued, hands not moving from her face. "She'd somehow moved the table and was hanging from the chandelier. There was an overturned chair beneath her."

The pair sat silently for a long time. Her head slumped and her elbows rested on her chest, supporting her hands that still hid her face.

He wasn't sure what to do. Eventually, he put his hand softly on her knee.

She raised her head slightly, and after a bit she lowered her hands, revealing teary eyes and runny mascara, along with smudged un-eyebrows.

She looked him straight in the eye. "I felt heat from that broken frame, and in that heat, I could sense a trace of... well... something. Something locked there. Stuck. I felt an echo of that same sense of longing and desire that I get from my dreams... like the monster was present, but was far, far away. There's some kind of connection. I know it!"

She grasped his hand on her knee and squeezed it tightly. "I have to talk with my father. I need to know where those papers are. If the frame of the mirror on my wardrobe is like the one we saw in that drawer upstairs, I can't reveal its existence to Dr. Esfahani until I know what's going on. She might try to take it away, and then it's possible I'll never be rid of these dreams. I'll end up just like my mother. I just need to keep things quiet for now, at least while I gather information. I ask for your help, Eric — to stay silent about what we saw, and to assist me, if possible. Can I trust you in this?"

He shuddered. *This is too creepy.*

He loved horror films, but he never imagined he'd actually be *in* one. His grandmother's words rang in his ears — *'there is deep trouble in Lotte'* — something dark, and it wasn't just her clothes. Grandma had said not to let her bring that trouble into his life, but now she was asking for his help — for him to be complicit in what she needed to do, whatever that wound up meaning. He felt as if standing on the blade of one of those little scalpels, and knew this was the moment he'd tip in one direction or the other.

"You can trust me, Lotte," he finally said with a calm he really didn't feel. "I'll help you, and I'm generally really good at keeping my mouth shut... but you have to do one thing for me."

"Anything," she replied with gratitude in her voice.

"Never step on my foot like that again. It really hurt."

She looked at him for a moment, and then they both started smiling.

"I'm so sorry, Eric. I promise, never again." She gave his hand another tight squeeze. With that, she went to the bathroom to repair her face.

A seemingly regular occurrence, he noted with mild amusement.

He drank his Coke, watched as the cold pizza on his paper plate congealed into a greasy sheen, and wondered where the decision he'd just made would lead him.

The pair wandered around the museum for a while, but after what had happened, neither could concentrate on the other exhibits. Finally, Lotte suggested they catch the train and just go sit in the park until her father showed up, which was fine with Eric. He didn't feel up for a lot of walking with his foot, and the weather was still beautiful for October, sunny and near 70 degrees.

I wonder what that is in Celsius? Who knows. Whatever.

They left the museum and caught the T inbound, riding until the cars descended into the tunnel and went underground. Upon arriving at Park Street station, they exited and stood at the corner of the park. The Massachusetts State House loomed above them.

Lotte found this interesting, so they walked in that direction. After ascending some stairs to the street, Eric pointed out his favorite memorial, probably in the whole world. Actually, it was the only one he really knew anything about—from a movie, of course.

"Did you see *Glory*?" he asked.

She shook her head.

"It's really good. It's about the people on that statue, the Massachusetts 54th Regiment and their commander, Robert Gould Shaw. That was one of the first African American regiments to fight in the Civil War."

"Really?" She seemed genuinely interested. "Perhaps we could watch that movie together sometime. I'd like to see it."

"Totally. Can we watch it on that big screen in your living room?"

She chuckled. "Of course."

He was psyched.

After gazing at the memorial and the State House for a while, they took the stairs back into the park and found a spot under a tree, where they sat side by side, their backs to the trunk. Eric removed his shoes and rubbed his foot, leafing through the book Dr. Esfahani had given him.

Presently, Lotte laid her head in his lap like she had in the library. He put his arm across her shoulder, and soon he could tell she was asleep. This time, there would be no bell to wake them up, so he watched the people passing by, kept an eye on the time, and enjoyed the feel of her even breaths against his body. As 4:30 approached, he woke her.

"*Alter!* I needed that." She stretched and yawned. "Thank you so much. Again."

He smiled.

"The dreams were back this past week. I got almost no sleep. I'm sure you could tell. If I can't resolve this soon, I'll have no choice but to talk with my father, but maybe we got a lucky break today, *ja?*"

It's certainly a coincidence. Lucky? Depends on how things turn out.

"Hope so," he somewhat lukewarmly replied, though she didn't particularly seem to notice. "Speaking of your father, it's about time we meet up and head for dinner. I'm starving!"

"Me too! Eric?"

"What?"

She hesitated for a couple seconds. "Thank you. I know how strange all this must seem, but I really appreciate how nice you've been. Your support means quite a lot to me."

"It's fine. No problem, really. My pleasure." To his surprise, he actually meant that.

CHAPTER 12

Dinner was fantastic.

Mr. Schwarz had selected a smallish restaurant on Salem Street that featured homemade pastas and an unbelievable shrimp appetizer with a sauce made from *Grand Marnier*. Eric had no idea what *Grand Marnier* was, but basically wanted it every day for the rest of his life.

They went for dessert afterward at an old-timey café around the corner. He got gelato, which he found excellent, but he jealously eyed Lotte's cannoli and Mr. Schwarz's tiramisu. They each gave him a bite, and he experienced flavors he'd never dreamed of before.

Lotte kept conversation light while they ate, and he assumed she'd want to talk with her father privately later. He kept his mouth shut about what had happened, as promised. They took a cab back to the parking garage near the Wang Center, where Mr. Schwarz had parked. This suited Eric fine as his foot still throbbed. Soon they were back in the black panther Mercedes on the road home.

"Far easier getting out this time of night," Mr. Schwarz commented as they matriculated onto the Pike. "Driving here is worse than Berlin. I've never seen anything like it—no road signs, no lane makers, drivers cutting you off and honking at you to move while the light's still red."

The term *Masshole* entered Eric's mind, but he didn't feel cursing in front of Mr. Schwarz would be appropriate. *Is Masshole even a swear word?* He ruminated on that until Lotte chimed in.

"Father," she ventured in an inquisitive tone laden with what Eric believed to be manufactured sweetness.

"*Ja, meine tochter?*" Mr. Schwarz replied, clearly smiling and savoring a wonderful evening.

"Do you know what happened to Grandfather's papers, the ones that Mother had found?"

Eric almost held his breath. He knew she was probing, but wasn't sure even she could discern what questions to ask to get the answers she sought.

Mr. Schwarz quietly pondered the question. When he replied, his mood seemed to have darkened slightly. "No, Lotte, I don't know where they went. They were gone when she was, well... found. For all the time she spent in the bedroom, it was immaculate when I went in afterward—almost like nothing had happened. Nothing was in the waste. The police investigated everything, looking for a note or some clue as to... well... why. *Nichts*... nothing. I have no idea where the papers went."

Dead end.

"Honestly," he continued. "I was amazed there were any papers left at all. I thought your grandmother had given everything to the museum here in Boston when they purchased the collection. Why do you ask about this?"

She was quick with her reply. "Seeing the treasures made me think about Grandfather and Grandmother today—Mother as well." That seemed to satisfy him, but she immediately tried a different tactic. "Speaking of Mother, what do you know about her wardrobe? The one I now have in my room."

Her father considered for a moment before answering. "As far as I know, it was part of the furniture your grandparents bought in the Middle East as they conducted their digs. Your mother brought it from England when we were married, along with all the other pieces you know so well."

He paused briefly and seemed to be smiling when he continued. "She loved that wardrobe. She stood on the marble platform every day, trying on clothes and shoes and modeling them in front of the mirror. I loved to watch her there. She looked so... elegant. So happy. So beautiful."

He drifted off into his memories before deeply sighing. "It broke my heart when she asked me to have the piece destroyed."

"What?" Lotte gasped.

Now Eric totally held his breath.

"Yes," he sadly replied. "It was only days before what... well... what occurred. She came to me in the night. I was sleeping in the guest room, as you know. I was startled when she woke me. I hadn't seen her for days. She looked horrible. She'd lost so much weight, and the dark circles under her eyes...."

At this, Eric saw Lotte self-consciously touch her cheek. He wanted to extend an encouraging hand to her shoulder, but he dared not move. He felt he'd been forgotten in the car, which suited him. Invisibility would have been ever better, but he figured forgotten was the best he'd get.

Invisibility would be so cool, though!

"That night, her mind seemed remarkably clear," her father continued. "She held my hand and told me that she loved me and missed me, words I hadn't heard in... what was it... months? Nearly a year? But she asked me to promise that if anything happened, I would have the wardrobe destroyed. She was quite insistent. Only when I made this promise did her anxiety go down. She stayed a while, and we fell asleep together. When I woke, she was gone. It may have been the last time I saw her. I just can't recall."

The black panther Mercedes glided on in silence. As they navigated the Pike westward, lamp posts passed by one after another—an endless parade of glowing Cyclopses.

Eric contemplated Dr. Esfahani's words. Lotte's parents had been a powerful team that had done much good. How sad, he thought, that it would end the way it did. Somehow, you went on, he realized, but clearly, losing someone like that in your life took a part of you as well. He'd seen it with Grandma, who'd really never been the same since Grandpa's death.

"So, Father," Lotte said, breaking the silence as if with a whispered thunderbolt. "What happened? Why did you not destroy the wardrobe?"

"Oh, Lotte," he replied, tiredness in his voice. "I don't know how or why it happened, but your mother was... oh.... How can I say it? She was gone. She wasn't in her right mind at the end, and couldn't have known what she was saying. It's just a wardrobe, my love. It became an object of fixation for her in her madness, but it's just a wardrobe. You loved it, you wanted it, and I wanted you to hold onto as much of your mother as you could. I can't imagine that this isn't what she would have truly desired."

Lotte gaped at Eric. Either she knew exactly what all this meant, or she was as clueless as he was. Again, silence overtook the car for a time until her questing voice called again. "Father?"

"Oh, Lotte," he replied with just a hint of aggravation in his normally cheerful manner. "No more questions for tonight. It's hard for me to talk of such things, and poor Eric doesn't need to hear all this."

Poor Eric. That's got a nice ring to it. He imagined being lavished with attention and having *Grand Marnier* shrimp fed to him from a silver platter, his lovingly bandaged foot resting on a golden pillow.

"Nothing about that," she replied. "It's about Eric."

The platter of shrimp tipped over in his mind when he heard her say his name.

"I need his help with something tonight. Can he come over, just for a little while?"

Her father hummed and hawed a bit before finally answering. "Well, it is still fairly early, but Eric, you must call your parents and let them know... and not too late, my love. I'm tired and still have to drive Eric home, so it must be a quick visit."

"You don't have to drive me home, Mr. Schwarz," Eric interjected, forgotten no longer. "I can walk. It's only about a half-hour between our houses." He'd run the calculation in his mind and concluded that having more time with Lotte outweighed the pain of walking home with his injured foot.

Mr. Schwarz seemed satisfied with this, but when Eric called his parents, a bit of a debate ensued. It was only a short way on quiet streets, and he felt he was old enough to walk thirty minutes home, even if it would be 10 p.m. What did they think was going to happen, vampires would take him away and ravenously drain his blood?

Well, er... maybe that isn't so implausible. Forget about that.

Finally, on his tinny little flip phone, he distinctly heard his father say something about not being "helicopter parents." That seemed to settle it. "Okay, honey," his mom said with some residual reluctance. "No later than 10 p.m., though. Text us when you leave, and call us if anything happens on the way home."

Still thinking this was a bit much to make of such a small thing, he agreed and signed off.

He informed Lotte and her father of the verdict, and Mr. Schwarz conceded.

"Thank you, Father," she gushed, and gave him a hug over the seat of the car. Soon he seemed to be smiling again as he guided his feline chariot sleekly down the road.

Eric contemplated what Lotte might have in mind, and what she needed him for. Whatever it was, he guessed it had something to do with that wardrobe and the mirror. He seriously hoped it didn't involve him having to move the hulking thing. Thoughts of silver platters of *Grand Marnier* shrimp and golden pillows faded as he gloomily pictured what the rest of his evening would likely entail.

When they arrived at the house, she hung up her scary-cool black leather jacket and waited at the door of the Mud *Château* while he took off his Nikes. Apparently, she kept her dressy shoes in one of her closets upstairs. She carried them as she walked in her stockings down the hall.

He looked for signs of blood on the spiked heel of her right shoe, but it was clean. *Not innocent, though,* he decided.

In the kitchen, Mr. Schwarz warmed the kettle on one of the fancy gas burners. "Would you like some tea?" he inquired as they passed.

"No thank you, Father. I'll make some later when Eric and I are done in my room."

Eric didn't really drink tea, so he passed as well.

"Very well," her dad cheerfully replied, the morose conversation of the car seemingly forgotten. "Then I bid you both good evening. I'm going to check email in my study for a bit, then I'm off to bed. Eric, it was a pleasure spending time with you today."

"Thank you so much for taking us, Mr. Schwarz. Thanks for dinner, too. That was so awesome! I'd eat like that every day if I could, but I'd probably weigh three hundred pounds."

Mr. Schwarz laughed heartily and again bid them goodnight.

Eric followed Lotte up to her room, where she put her shoes in the left closet of the crazy wardrobe. Then she rummaged around in one of the chest of drawers, producing jeans, fuzzy socks, and a t-shirt that he marveled was light blue and didn't sport a freaky band image.

"Just give me a moment," She headed for the bathroom to change.

Eric figured he'd take advantage of the moment as well, and went back downstairs to use the restroom there.

When he returned, she wore her new outfit and stood near the brazier table, staring at the crazy wardrobe and its mirror. He approached the object and took a good look at the mirror's frame. It was carved and assembled exactly like the one in the drawer Dr. Esfahani had shown them... sans super-glue, of course. Now he could see how the patterns evoked fire.

Overall, the colors were much deeper and richer than any of the pieces they'd seen in the museum, but on close inspection, he realized it was basically the same material. From time to time, certain areas bore a lighter coloring and looked almost identical to the Fire Quartz they'd seen displayed.

"What are these?" he asked, pointing down to two small outcroppings, each about a half inch thick and raised about four or five inches from the marble pedestal. They jutted out about half a foot from either side of the mirrors' frame and ended in smoothly curved edges, though a couple of chips here and there marred the effect slightly.

She approached and stood by his side. "I don't know. They were just always there. I never really thought about it."

"Doesn't the curved edge look a little like the piece that was in the Egypt case? You know, the one you asked Dr. Esfahani about that wasn't in the book?"

She sharply turned her head and gave him a wide-eyed look. She quickly crouched down and put her hands on the marble platform, leaning in close to one of the outcroppings and giving it a careful examination.

"I think you're right! Very observant."

He beamed. *Eric: one; world: seventeen million five hundred thousand four hundred and twenty-three... but I'm catching up.*

"This is probably why they couldn't figure out how that piece fit in the frame," she continued. "Most of the bottom hadn't been re-assembled. They couldn't have imagined that something would stick out in this way."

She turned back to the wardrobe and brought her hand to her chin. After pondering for a moment, she walked around to the left side of the wardrobe.

"Eric, come help me."

Oh, boy, here we go.

Sure enough, she wanted him to help her push the wardrobe away from the wall. Mercifully, the movers had put soft material on the undersides of the many large, round, wooden feet that suspended the whole piece a few inches off the ground.

With great effort, they were able to slide the behemoth on the hardwood floor so that the left side was about a foot from the wall. There they hit a snag. The front feet of the wardrobe were folding up one of the Persian rugs—as it turned out, the one under the brazier table and its wooden chairs.

"*Alter!*" she fretted. "All this will need to be moved." They hauled the chairs out of the way and together lifted the heavy table, which they relocated to the wall between the large lamp and the stereo.

Well, I'm earning my supper.

Actually, he found himself kind of having fun. He liked working side by side with Lotte. They rolled up the Persian rug and tucked it over near the bed, then returned to the wardrobe. With the extra room on the floor, they were able to tug the left side of the hulking monstrosity farther from the wall. Then they turned to the right side, and soon created space to walk behind the bulky object. She took the lamp from the table by the stereo and removed the shade so that it cast more light.

Behind each closet section, large panels of wood were tucked behind thick, decorative, rounded molding on the back edges. A single and very sturdy piece of wood supported the mirror, secured in place by many little clamps made of bronze.

She carefully examined all of these but couldn't seem to find anything. She again brought her hand to her chin and contemplated, and he waited for her to tell him what she wanted him to move next.

Maybe all the furniture in the garage? His apprehension mounted.

"Hold on," she snapped, and bolted from the room and down the stairs.

He took a seat in one of the displaced, red-cushioned wooden chairs and waited. Soon, he heard her padding back toward him in her fuzzy socks.

She slapped a tape measure on the brazier table near where he sat. "Come help me," she said, all business as she approached the right closet door of the wardrobe and opened it.

The Motherlode! He tried not to laugh.

The closet was packed with black band t-shirts, all dangling precariously from thin little hangers. Various belts, purses and bags, all black, with the occasional silver studs and buckles, cluttered the floor.

Was this just never organized after unpacking, or does she always keep her stuff this way?

"You clear all this out," she said, waving her arm. "Put the shirts on one of the chairs. Just toss the bags and other stuff in the corner."

He complied, figuring this was the lightest lifting he could have hoped for.

She opened the other door and removed dresses, nicer clothes, and shoes, and carried them with care to her bed.

He wondered what she kept in the walk-in closet. *Maybe that's where the coffin is, bwa ha ha ha!*

He dumped an armful of black t-shirts on the chair, and the face of the ugliest man he'd ever seen stared up at him from the shirt on top. A thick moustache drooped down either side of his face, sadly not covering a hideous mole on his cheek. He stood, smoking a cigarette and wearing sunglasses, a black hat with silver studs and crossed swords on the top, and a denim vest with more military patches on it. He also sported large tattoos on his forearms.

"Hey, who is this butt ugly dude on your shirt?"

She glanced across the room over an armful of dresses. "That's Lemmy."

"Lemmy who? Or is it Lemmy what?" He genuinely wasn't sure.

"Lemmy Kilmister, from Motörhead. How can you not know this?"

He wondered how she *could* know this. "Well, I hope he got time for killing mister whoever it was he killed—probably with that mole."

"Oh, ha ha ha. Focus yourself. We don't have much time."

That was true. He promptly got back to work.

Once they were finished clearing the clothes and other items, she pulled the lamp around to the front and inspected the insides of the closets.

Nothing appeared unusual to him.

"Grab me the tape measure," she finally said.

He did as instructed, and she measured the interior depth of each closet. When finished, she shook her head in seeming confusion and then did it again. Then she measured the outer wall of each closet from front to back. When she finally seemed satisfied, she turned back to him.

"They're different. They're identical on the outside, but the right one is about six inches shorter on the inside. There's something behind the back wall of that closet."

He grabbed the lamp and gave a close look, but didn't see any openings. He ran his hands everywhere, but didn't feel anything unusual, so he gave a few knocks on the back wall. The wardrobe rang with a resonant, wooden sustain. He moved to the left closet and knocked on the back wall there. If the sounds were different, he couldn't hear it. He looked at Lotte, who shrugged, clearly not hearing anything either. A pair of audiophiles, they were not.

They walked around the wardrobe a few more times, looking for some way to access the space they assumed lurked behind the right closet wall, but nothing presented itself.

"Wait a minute." He walked over and grabbed one of the wooden chairs, and brought it to the right side of the wardrobe. Once in place, he stood on it and looked at the top of the closet. "Pass me the lamp."

She quickly handed it up to him.

He closely examined the back of the closet's top, looking for any kind of seam, but it appeared as solid as the back and sides. He was about to climb down when something caught his eye. A small circle of bronze gleamed in the lamplight at the top of the decorative molding. It sat flush with the wood and had a notch in it like a flat-head screw.

"Look at this."

She climbed up on the chair and tightly held onto his arm for extra support. Trying to ignore the pleasure of her proximity—and as usual failing—he flashed the lamp above the little bronze disc. She examined it, probing it with her fingers.

"This is it! Good eyes, Eric!"

Eric: two; world: seventeen million, whatever, whatever....

"Hold on a minute. I'll be right back." Again, she bolted from the room and down the stairs.

He just stood on the chair and waited.

She quickly returned holding three screwdrivers of various sizes. She walked up to the chair and passed one up to him. "Try this one."

He set the lamp down on top of the wardrobe and tested the screwdriver in the notch. It was a bit too big. "Do you have one that's a little smaller?"

She handed him a different one.

This one fit better and he tried to turn the bronze circle.

It moved.

He twisted it in a counterclockwise direction and soon the circle began to raise up, revealing a shaft of bronze. He unscrewed the shaft for some time. It became almost twenty inches high, and he had to reach above his head to continue using the screwdriver. Eventually, he stood on the arms of the chair for extra height.

Finally, it gave way and he pulled it out. It was close to two feet in length.

Good thing the ceiling is high in this house.

The instant he removed the bronze shaft, the large piece of molding on the rear side of the wardrobe swung back as if on some kind of hinge hidden under the wood.

Lotte gasped.

He jumped down from the chair and pulled it away. She stared wide-eyed, hands over her mouth, at a roughly six-inch opening running the height of the back of the wardrobe, divided by thin shelves. On these shelves were many leather folders, well-worn accordion files, and several rolled up maps and other documents, all tightly packed in the cramped space.

"The papers!" she said breathlessly through her hands. "We've done it. We've found my grandfather's papers. As the movers were rearranging the furniture, Mother would dust. She had me do it too. It allowed us to continue being around the hunky men, who seemed to enjoy our company. I remember her up on their stepladder, dusting the top of the wardrobe. She must have seen it then and probably wondered what it was. She investigated later and found the papers. *Scheiße!*"

That never gets old. He loved hearing her again curse in German. "What will you do?"

"I'm going to read them. The answer must be here, somewhere. If this mirror is real, then my grandfather must have hidden the find. The story must be in his papers. I have to understand what happened and whether it relates to these damned dreams I've been having. Come on, help me remove these. We'll put them in the closet where Father won't see them."

She carefully removed the folders and files and piled a few into his arms. Once satisfied he had enough, she bid that he follow her. She surprised him when she traipsed right past the open closet doors and toward her bed.

"Oh," he said, when it finally dawned on him. "You meant the walk-in closet." *The one where your crypt is hidden from prying eyes, bwa ha ha ha!*

"Of course. How am I supposed to read the documents in a cramped closet in the wardrobe that doesn't have any light?"

That made sense, so he followed her silently across the room. *This is it!* He quivered with anticipation.

She opened the door, and an empty closet greeted them. A couple of forlorn boxes sat in the corner, but the racks and shoe trees stood bare. Apparently, all her clothes fit in the furniture in her room. No coffin either, he noted, with no real surprise... but perhaps a touch of disappointment.

"We'll stack them on the shelves here," she directed. "Carefully. I don't want to damage anything."

He didn't know how he was supposed to carefully hold things in his arms, but he did his best. Soon, the items were unloaded, and they headed back for more.

As they approached the wardrobe, he noticed something odd about the molding that ran along the front, right below the white marble platform and immediately above the round wooden feet. "What's up with that? It looks like it's come loose."

They both knelt on the floor to examine more closely. The top of the panel, where it touched the platform, had pulled away slightly. He looked down into the opening. On the right side, he saw what looked like another bronze shaft attached to the back of the panel. It appeared to be on a little swivel joint, so he gently pulled at the top.

The entire long, thin panel folded down, presumably on hinges hidden at the lower part of the inside. The joint rotated to allow the molding to fold flat but keep the bronze shaft attached.

Together, they looked inside at another opening perhaps four inches high beneath the marble and above the heavy wood to which the feet were attached. In this space, a dark piece of carved stone curved away from the center toward the sides. It appeared to be connected to runners at either end. Eric grabbed the center and pulled, and despite being a little sticky, it slid out.

This time, they both gasped.

The black marble board he'd revealed was an almost exact replica of the semi-circular stone in the Jordan case at the museum. The shape also recalled the figure represented on the papyrus in the Egypt case. Around the perimeter were eight small holes cut in the marble — four at the straight side facing the mirror, and four around the curved edge, where the pair crouched in a dumbfounded stupor on the floor.

In the center was a larger hole. Decorative lines carved into the marble echoed the channels on the granite block in the museum, connecting the smaller holes to the one in the middle. They gazed at the wardrobe and saw embodied there the picture on the papyrus — the semi-circular figure in perfect relation to the square frame of the mirror, the fuzzy outline echoing the billowing flames of the carved Fire Quartz.

"My grandparents didn't buy this piece," she said in a hushed and breathless tone. "They had it built. They were trying to replicate how the artifacts they found might have been set up during the *Sadat Alnaar's* rituals — artifacts they found, but which they didn't tell anyone about. If I'm right.... Come."

She leapt up and went back around to the right side of the wardrobe. "Just put these on the table for now. We'll move them to the closet later." She handed him more notebooks and a couple of rolled-up maps from the thin shelves, which he shuttled to the brazier table.

"There!" she almost shouted.

On the bottom shelf, behind some accordion files that had just been removed, rested a box, which she reached in and pulled out. She put it on the floor, carefully lifted the latch, and opened the top. He assumed she was as gasped-out as he was, even though what they saw was every bit as wondrous as the things they'd already found. They gazed down on four small shallow clay bowls, lined on the inside with richly colored Fire Quartz.

"Just as I suspected," she said. She removed two more cases from the shelf. One contained four more small bowls, and the other held a large one and two medium sized bowls. "One for each space on the semi-circular black marble panel," she observed. "But what are these two extra mid-sized ones for?"

"I think I know." Eric walked over to the chest of drawers, where he'd seen Lotte put her exhibition catalog when she'd gotten her change of clothes. He picked up her dog-eared copy and flipped through it as he walked back to her. Finally finding the close-up of the papyrus in the Egypt case, he held it up for her to see.

"Of course," she said. "I'd forgotten. If this is right, they go under the outcroppings on the mirror. It should be everything you need." They sat on the floor, silently gazing at the bowls in their plush, lined boxes.

"*Shit!* What time is it?" He jumped up and looked at the clock that sat near the Genie lamp by Lotte's bed. "Crap, it's ten to ten. I've gotta go."

"All right, just help me move these things to the closet, then you can get home."

He shuttled the papers from the table to the walk-in closet while she gently closed the boxes and sealed the latches. Once everything had been relocated, she closed the walk-in closet door and accompanied him down the stairs.

"Here," she said, as he tied his shoes in the Mud *Château*, and handed him a beautiful green woolen sweater, probably her father's. "It's gotten cold. I don't want you to get a chill. That's Loden, from *Österreich*. Very warm. Just return it when you come over tomorrow."

"I will. I have to go to Grandma's in the morning, but my mom is gonna take her to get her hair done. I'll be able to duck out after lunch with my dad. I can be over about two or so. That okay?"

"That's fine. I'll go though some of the papers tonight, then you can help me look at the rest tomorrow."

Sounded like a plan. He hopped up to go, but she stopped him at the door.

"Eric," she said, taking his hand. "I simply can't thank you enough for helping me. I couldn't have done it without you. You can be very clever when you put your mind to something. You ought to try it more often."

"Hey," he whined, but she was already smiling—a real smile with teeth and everything—and he felt much better when she gave him another little kiss on the cheek.

"Okay, off with you." She playfully shooed him toward the door. "I'll see you tomorrow. Just come by when you can. I'll be here."

He smiled and left, waving to her from behind as she stood in the doorway watching him go.

She waved back.

He was instantly glad she'd given him the sweater. His light jacket wouldn't have cut it now that the sun had set and the temperature had dropped so dramatically.

He texted his mom: *On my way.*

Almost immediately he got a reply: *You're already late, mister!*

Crap! He quickened his pace, though he doubted he'd be in too much trouble. He wasn't sure he'd be able to sleep after such an incredible day, plus the anticipation of seeing Lotte tomorrow. On the other hand, he felt super tired, so maybe he'd just zonk out after all.

And sleep the sleep of the dead, bwa ha ha ha! Vampire accents never get old.

He hurried down Holton Hill Road toward home.

CHAPTER 13

Eric drove over with his mom in the Civic, since she planned to take Grandma to get her hair done after lunch. He'd come home with his dad in the HMS Suburban.

When they arrived, he noticed that Grandma had displayed the vase the Schwarz's had given her on the mantle in the TV room, over the fake electric fireplace. It held a place of honor, right next to the picture of Grandpa, whose somewhat dour smile evoked his signature no-nonsense attitude. He missed the old guy and wished he'd talked to him more about his time in Germany.

Over lunch he tried to impress Grandma with his language progress, and she was extremely pleased. They had some simple conversations, and she didn't get all frustrated and critical when he stumbled. She seemed to sense he was really trying, and that appeared to be enough for now.

Maybe you can *teach an old dog new tricks.* He had Lotte to thank for that, among so many other things.

Mom and Grandma had to leave for the beauty salon, so they cut the visit short. He helped shove the dishes from the relatively simple meal into the dishwasher, and soon he was sailing home with his dad in the land yacht. They cruised without speaking, his father listening to sports blab on the radio, which he shut off when the commercials came on.

Eric sensed an opportunity. "Hey, Dad?"

"What's up, kiddo?" his father replied, seemingly as happy as Eric to have an early escape from Grandma's.

He worked up his courage. "I need to tell you something. I don't think I want to play clarinet anymore."

His dad gave him a quick glance, then returned his eyes to the road.

"I want to drop Wind Ensemble at mid-year and try to get into that psychology elective they have. I doubt I'll get in, 'cause it's a popular class, but if I tell them I'm interested now, I'll probably have a better chance next year. There are other social studies electives I could do too. I don't care that much. Anything seems better to me than clarinet. I'm just not a musician and really never will be. I want to explore subjects where I feel like I'm learning something new — something I'm interested in."

His father drove in silence for a bit. Finally, he said, "I think that's a good idea, kiddo. Run it up the flagpole, see if it flies. If your mom and I can do anything to help, let us know."

"You're not mad?" he asked, a bit surprised at how easily that had gone.

His dad heartily laughed. "Mad? Why would I be mad? They shoved a clarinet in your hands in what... the third grade? How the hell were you supposed to know if you wanted to play an instrument, let alone that one? Now it sounds like you've figured out something you want to do more — nothing to be mad about there."

"You and Mom just go to all the concerts. I thought you might be disappointed."

"Honestly, kiddo, I've never cared much for that thing or symphonic music. Your mom and I went because we wanted to support you. If you don't want to do it anymore, we'll support you in what you *want* to do. It's that simple. I'm not disappointed at all."

"Thanks, Dad." It felt like a weight off his shoulders, and that he could now move forward in some small way — or maybe not so small. He wasn't totally sure.

They drove in silence for a bit longer until his father spoke again. "You really like this girl, Lotte, don't you?"

He froze. He hadn't expected that. Was there a connection here, or had his dad just sensed an opportunity like he had?

"Yeah, she's pretty amazing," he confessed. "I like her a lot."

"I do too. I think she's been good for you, and you've been good for her. Just keep being good to each other. That's what it's all about."

"Yeah." That was all he could muster, though he agreed completely. It felt almost as if his father had summed up the meaning of life in two sentences.

Soon they were home, and he started to disembark from the ship to dry land. As he did so, he felt his father's hand on his back.

"Have a good afternoon, kiddo," was all he said, but his smiling face said much more.

"I will, Dad, thanks," he happily replied, fully planning to live up to that promise.

He went inside and put on the nice sweater Lotte had given him last night, then grabbed his bike and vigorously pedaled toward Pleasant Street. He glanced at Lotte's house up on the hill as he passed by. Holton Hill Road proved to be too much for him once he hit the steep slope, so he walked the bike until the road flattened out, then hauled ass the rest of the way to number 246.

The black panther Mercedes crouched in its usual spot in the driveway. He pulled up next to it, flipped his kickstand, went to the door, and rang the bell. He waited, but when he didn't hear the familiar thump on the stairs, he got out his phone to text Lotte. While doing so, he noticed the door was slightly ajar. He pushed and it swung open, revealing the silent hallway.

"Lotte?" he called. "Mr. Schwarz?"

No answer.

Thinking they might be on the stone patio and had left the door cracked for him, he went into the Mud *Château* and removed his shoes. He padded down the hallway and looked into the kitchen... empty. He called again, but still received no response, save the slight echoing of his voice in the cavernous living room. He figured he'd just have a quick look on the back porch, and then text Lotte if they weren't there.

He descended the stairs in the hallway and felt something slightly sticky under his feet. He looked down. Some kind of fluid clung to the dark, hardwood stairs and trailed off into the living room. It seemed to be streaked, as if spread by some kind of wheel. At the bottom of the stairs, he stopped and looked around the corner to the left.

A pool of blood had collected at the foot of the stairs leading to the second floor.

He almost jumped out of his skin. It seemed to have been disturbed by the footprints of people whom he figured had been wearing boots—little knobbles of blood imprinted across the beautiful floor. He also saw that some sort of wheel had skimmed through one edge of the pool. It had left a snaking trail of blood that led toward the stairs he'd just come down. He lifted his feet and saw deep red stains on the bottoms of his white socks.

"*Damn!*" He stumbled toward one of the couches in the TV area of the living room and immediately started texting Lotte: *Where RU!!! RU OK???*

He sent the text and waited for a reply, glancing periodically over his shoulder at the pool of blood. Eventually, he leaned back on the couch, rested his head on the deep, plush cushions behind him, and tried to calm down.

As he looked up in this way, he noticed a strange shimmering cloud toward the top of the room. It seemed to cling where the sun shone most brightly at the upper part of the glass wall, almost like a sparkling paste. Particles like large flecks of dust floated lazily in the air, ash-black in color but with an almost crystalline quality — catching and reflecting light like tinsel on a Christmas tree.

It wasn't smoke. He didn't smell anything, and it hadn't smudged the walls or ceiling. Other than seeming to cling to the glass, it didn't appear to be doing any harm. He watched the cloud hover, and saw that more and more of the odd substance leisurely billowed toward the glass at the top.

Just then, his phone beeped... scaring the shit out of him. He looked back at the pool of blood to make sure it wasn't creeping toward him. It didn't appear to have moved. He flipped open his phone and checked his texts. It was Lotte: *At hospital... Father... Come quickly!*

He tried to think. His heart raced. He didn't know what to do.

Dad! I'll ride home and get him to take me to the hospital – better to have an adult there anyway.

He gave another glance at the bloody stairwell and the weird cloud near the ceiling, and then bolted for the door. He rapidly put on his shoes over his blood-stained socks and jetted outside, making sure to close the door securely behind him. He jumped on his bike and sped down Holton Hill Road, braking hard on the steep incline for fear of wiping out.

He crossed Pleasant Street and pedaled madly through Rolling Meadows. Abandoning his bike in the front yard, he stormed into the house and found his dad in the TV room watching the Patriots... La-Z-Boy in full recline mode.

His dad looked up with surprise as Eric burst into the room, heaving for breath.

"Lotte... hospital... her dad!"

His father hesitated momentarily, then deliberately extricated himself from the chair. "Let's go," he calmly said... and they did.

"S-C-H-W-A-R-Z. Schwarz. Hermann." Eric's father was a patient man, but the woman at the reception desk tested his limits.

"Can you spell that again?" she asked with such indifference and lethargy that Eric wondered if she actually had a pulse.

His father repeated the process, even more slowly than before. Somehow it seemed to register on this, the third attempt.

"Mr. Smarts is in intensive care."

Both Eric and his dad slammed their hands to their foreheads.

"Are you family?" she added with an almost accusatory tone.

His father explained the situation.

The receptionist said to have a seat, and that someone would be with them shortly.

Realizing that arguing with this woman would be fruitless, they retreated to some generic-looking chairs that starkly lined the walls of the reception area. Various other visitors languished in some of the seats, as if they'd been sitting here for months. Some slept draped across the few benches. Eric and his dad settled in for the long haul.

Remarkably, only about twenty minutes passed before a woman in scrubs with a clipboard appeared. She stood in the doorway, to which almost all eyes in the reception area lifted each time it opened, as if awaiting salvation. "Fred Schneider?" she called.

Well, at least they didn't ask for Fred Spider.

Lotte hadn't responded to any of his other texts, so he had no idea if she was okay. He and his dad followed the woman in scrubs down a hallway toward some elevators.

"I'm Helene, one of the ICU nurses."

His father introduced himself, and then told her that Eric was a good friend of Mr. Schwarz's daughter.

That promotion didn't help me a bit. Although, it's possible that just normal friends *don't get to visit people in the hospital. Maybe it isn't all bad.*

"They put Lotte in one of the overnight stay rooms," Helene explained. "I woke her and asked if she wanted to see you, and she was thrilled. Poor girl looks like she hasn't slept for a month. She was fast asleep."

They ascended the elevator and followed the nurse as she weaved through various corridors, bypassing another reception desk under a sign that read "Intensive Care."

Thank God! I don't want to have to go through that *again!*

Soon, she stopped and knocked on a door in a quiet hallway.

With joy, Eric heard Lotte's voice answer, "Come in."

She sat on a bed in the small room, wearing the same jeans, blue t-shirt and fuzzy socks she'd had on the night before. Her black Adidas with white stripes sat by the small wooden nightstand. The second she saw him, she shot up and into his arms, holding him so tightly his back cracked with brittle little pops.

Who needs a spinal column anyway? He expelled the last of his breath.

"I'm so glad to see you!" she gushed, but into his ear, she whispered, "*I've done a terrible thing, Eric. I don't know what to do!*"

He gave the pat response that everything would be okay without really having any clue what the problem was or if anything would be okay at all. Sensing the emptiness of his words, he asked, "How's your father?"

"His head is badly cut and bruised. He needed a lot of stitches, and they have his neck in a large brace. He's very groggy, and they have him on extremely strong pain medication."

"What happened, Lotte?" Eric's father interjected.

"I... I don't know, Mr. Schneider. He had a bad fall from the stairs. For as long as we've been in the house, it's still new to us. Maybe he just wasn't paying attention and missed a step when he went down to make coffee in the morning. I heard him yell from my room and found him bleeding at the bottom of the stairway. That's all I know."

Eric's dad asked Helene if she had any updates, but she'd just started her shift and didn't have any information. "Can I speak with Mr. Schwarz's doctor?" he inquired.

She thought for a moment and then said, "We'll have to see if Mr. Schwarz is conscious and able to give his permission. If you want to follow me, we can go check. I can't promise anything, though."

"That's good enough for me," he replied. Turning to Eric, he said, "Stay here. For a small hospital, this place is a maze. I don't want you getting lost. I'll be back as soon as I can, so just stay put. Got it?"

Eric got it. Lotte got it. Here they would stay.

When Helene and Dad left, Lotte flopped back onto the bed and lay on her side. Eric sat on the edge and looked down at her, noting her distant, almost vacant look, as if her thoughts were far away. Eventually she turned her head to meet his eyes, and he could see her fear and uncertainty. He hated to doubt her, but he sensed that her father had not just *accidentally* fallen down the stairs.

"What *really* happened, Lotte?"

"Oh, Eric," she moaned, looking away as if in shame. "You're going to think I'm a fool."

He thought many things of Lotte, but *fool* had never been among them. He exercised his best quality and remained silent.

"There just wasn't any other way, and it might have worked if it hadn't been for Father. Not that it was his fault.... How could he have known? Thankfully, he doesn't seem to remember anything from the morning. He'd be so angry and disconcerted. I lost track of the time... I lost track of *all* time. It was only me and... *it*! One mind. All else had ceased to be—no time, no space... nothing but our bond. It might have worked—"

"Lotte!" He was totally confused, had no idea what she was talking about. "Can you start from the beginning? I can't follow what you're saying."

She looked back at him, seemingly startled to see him there. Slowly, she sat up on the bed, tucked her knees to her chest, and wrapped her arms around them.

"When you left," she said, shaking her head as if to clear the cobwebs. "I went into the closet and started going through the papers. Someone, probably my grandmother, had typed up an index sheet in the front of each accordion file, itemizing all the contents. I took all these out and placed them on top of the files, which I spread on the floor. They started with the digs in Jordan, and went through Egypt and into Morocco. The leather folders contained notes my grandmother had written out later. These had no indices, and looked more like journals, so I left them on the shelf. I arranged all the accordion files in roughly chronological order. When I got to the last of them, the ones from Morocco, I was amazed. My grandfather knew there were more items in the vicinity of the dig site where his local assistant had found the rings!"

He remembered the man's picture on the case in the museum as she went on.

"He closed the digging operation, claiming the funding had run out, but this was a lie. They returned with some diggers my grandparents must have paid privately to keep silent. They worked at night—all highly illegal, as my grandmother noted, but they knew exactly where to look and what they were looking for. They quickly found the bowls buried in sturdy wooden boxes not far from the rings. The mirror and the black marble board, they found a short distance away in a sturdy enclosure, lined and covered with large stones. The mirror was wrapped with cloth inside to protect the glass. There are Polaroids in the file of the items being uncovered."

"Why would your grandfather break the law like that? He'd been looking for these things for like... fifteen years. Didn't he want the glory of finding the best treasure of all?"

"I didn't read all the papers from the earlier digs, but at a certain point, the focus of the hunt seemed to change from uncovering information about the *Sadat Alnaar* to searching for certain specific items they'd used. My grandparents had seen the other broken frame in Egypt, though how they knew what it was, I have no idea. By the time they'd reached Morocco, though, they were searching for something like this—and my grandfather had his own *purposes* in mind."

The little scalpel struck on Lotte's final words, and Eric wondered why she would be bitter at the grandfather she'd never met.

"When they removed the items," she went on, "they had the wardrobe built by a local cabinetmaker to disguise and hide them. The bill of sale is in the folder. The poor man probably had no idea the mirror he installed was over thirteen hundred years old, or what the secret compartments were for."

Eric imagined the cabinetmaker accidentally dropping the mirror. *Oops, sorry. My bad! That's pretty much a lifetime of bad luck for me, isn't it? Ha ha ha.*

She interrupted his silly thoughts with a bombshell. "When construction on the wardrobe was completed, they planned to set it up and attempt the *Sadat Alnaar* ceremony! *This* was their goal. *This* was why they wanted the items and needed to keep them secret. The final Morocco file referenced a chart they'd found. There was no chart in the folder, but it had to be there somewhere. I unrolled the maps, and there it was, tucked inside one of them for protection—a more complete rendition of the papyrus in the Egypt case at the museum, probably found with the mirror in Morocco. It showed how to align the mirror, the bowls, and where to sit. Notes in the file indicated my grandparents planned to use candles to heat the bowls and the mirror's frame."

"Wow! What happened? What did they find out?"

"I have no idea, though I have some suspicion. The file ended there, and by that point, it was nearly 1:00 a.m. I was exhausted, almost falling asleep, and had to go to bed. I figured I'd read more of the notes in the files and leather folders today, probably with your help. I didn't even get out of my clothes or move the dresses I'd piled on the bed. I was asleep before my head hit the pillow."

The girl really has a knack for falling asleep on a dime.

"But then the dreams began," she said with dread. "Nothing like I've ever experienced before. The intensity of the desperation was unbearable—like the monster was scratching furiously at the wall, ripping its horrible claws to bloody shreds! It screamed with frustration and anger in my mind. It wanted to be free, and it felt as if the key to its prison cell was maddeningly just beyond reach, right outside the bars of its prison door. Never have I experienced dreams with this... *ferocity*!"

She pulled her legs tighter to her body. "I couldn't sleep. I felt terror... but also I felt a deep sadness. The feeling of desperation lingered after I woke. I couldn't shake it. After an hour of tossing and turning, I tried to read more, but was too exhausted and distracted. I couldn't focus at all. I went down to the kitchen and made tea to try and calm myself, but it didn't work. It felt like I was being worn down... or being boxed in, like the monster in its prison."

She sat silently for a while, apparently reliving her feelings of the night before. When she resumed, her voice sounded flat, as if reading a series of instructions... step, after step, after step.

"While I sat at the counter with my tea, I remembered there were boxes of candles in the hutch in the dining room. I took some matches from the drawer in the kitchen, fetched two boxes of candles, and went back upstairs. I got out the chart and laid it on the floor near the wardrobe, than got the bowls and arranged them properly. I cut the candles with scissors from the bathroom, so the fire would be close to the quartz in the bowls, and so they'd fit under the outcroppings on the mirror. Then I lit them."

He sat in silent amazement, not knowing what to expect next.

"It all seemed so natural, so normal, as if I was supposed to have been doing something like this all along. As the candles burned and started to warm the Fire Quartz, a happy feeling flooded over me. I sat at the apex of the curved block of marble, facing the mirror as the chart indicated I should, and waited. Time passed — probably hours, because my little candles had nearly burned down. I got up and cut more, triple the number I'd done before. The Fire Quartz in the bowls became quite hot, as did the whole frame of the mirror. The outcroppings seemed to channel the heat upward, and the whole thing started to glow. I sat and waited as more time passed, and then... it happened! In the mirror, I saw something... like a cloud of dark ash."

Eric thought immediately of the cloud he'd seen in her house earlier, but remained silent, not wanting to interrupt her.

"I looked behind me, thinking it was a reflection, but it wasn't. This stuff was physically coming out of the bloody mirror! The cloud drifted down toward the marble board near the floor and sparkled slightly in the light from the candles."

A chill ran down his spine. *Yep, same cloud.*

"Slowly, the ash gathered above the large bowl in the center. It started to swirl and became denser. In time, it began to seem almost solid, and then... certain *features* began to appear — black as coal, identical to the shiny ash from which they coalesced. It was a face. It had a snout-like nose and fangs that jutted up from this massive lower jaw. It had horns on its head, like those of a goat. I realized that this must be the face of the monster from my dreams."

If that had appeared in the black cloud he'd seen, he figured he'd still be running. He tried to estimate where he would have been by now. That sort of depended on what direction he ran. Since he preferred warmer weather, he guessed he'd have gone south, meaning he'd probably be in Rhode Island at this point.

Not far enough. Can you actually run to Jamaica? Jamaica would be so cool!

She continued her incredible and terrifying tale. "Its eyes were closed while it assembled above the fire from the cloud of ash. It started to whisper. I couldn't understand the words, but in my head... I could hear its voice. 'We will bargain,' it said. 'We will serve you in exchange for our freedom.' I wasn't afraid. It didn't seem evil at all."

Nah... monsters with horns, snouts, and fangs who come out of mirrors aren't evil. They're just misunderstood.

"I tried to ask its name, tried to get it to tell me who and what it was and where it had come from, but it just laughed in an odd way and kept saying that it wanted to 'bargain' and 'serve me,' and that it wanted to be free."

Eric stuttered, "Maybe it went insane, being locked up for like, well... for a long time. Maybe it just lost its mind."

"It's possible. Certainly, in the dreams, it seemed quite mad, but now it appeared calm and actually seemed happy as its form assembled above the large bowl. It seemed to like me, and in an odd way, I liked it too."

Leave it to you to not make any friends at school, but to have a monster as a buddy.

"So, what happened then?" he asked, putting out of his mind the image of Lotte smiling and walking down the street arm in arm with this monster. "You said your father did something that wasn't his fault. What did he do?"

She buried her head in her knees and rocked back and forth. "Oh, Eric, I had totally lost track of the time. It had become morning—hours had passed! My father must have gotten up and seen the flickering of the candles from my room. I'd stupidly left the door open, but my mind had been in a complete haze—almost like walking in my sleep. I saw him reflected in the mirror as he appeared at the door behind me, calling my name in terror."

About what I'd have done.

"The monster focused its eyes on my father and let out this savage shriek from its horrid mouth, which was full of jet-black, razor-sharp teeth. The noise startled me. It felt as if I'd woken from a dream. I realized in horror what I'd been doing and what was happening. I panicked, and without thought, I reached forward and snuffed out the candles burning in the large bowl."

She looked up, tears in her eyes. "The monster was furious, but the cloud of ash almost instantly slammed back into the mirror. Only the solid head and the beginnings of the creature's shoulders, which had been forming, still remained. These also quickly dissolved to ash, but as they did, they shot out in the direction of the door where my father stood. It startled him as the cloud went flying past. He stumbled backward, hit the railing above the stairs, and tumbled right over!"

Eric's entire body shuddered as he pictured poor Mr. Schwarz hitting the un-carpeted stairs headfirst. Small wonder he was in the hospital. It was practically a miracle he was alive.

The pair sat silently for a while. It seemed both of them had to absorb what had happened.

It's not every day you discover monsters are real. All in all, Eric felt he was taking it quite well. *I'll probably never sleep again, or watch another horror movie, but hey, think about all the time I'll have for other things.*

"So, what now?" he hesitantly asked.

"I have an idea," she replied, surprising him.

He had no ideas, other than running to Jamaica, which he actually felt might not be the worst plan.

"I know what I did hurt my father," she said with regret, "and I know I'm dealing with a creature that's not of this world, or is a part of our world but has long since vanished and been forgotten. It's dangerous, of this I have no doubt, but I don't think there's any choice." She took a deep breath. "I have to try again!"

"Lotte, there *is* a choice. You can destroy the fucking mirror and all the bowls and papers—just like your mother told your father to do. Why risk it?"

"I hear what you're saying. I've had the same thoughts myself, but... what if that doesn't kill the monster? What if that just leaves it trapped where it is, suffering for eternity? And in addition to its own suffering, what if it continues to torture me when I sleep? Now that it's found me, perhaps it won't ever let me go until it gets what it wants. With the wardrobe and its contents destroyed, there'll be no way to stop it. I'll go mad, like my mother did, and her fate will be mine."

He hadn't considered that, and refused to imagine Lotte hanging from a chandelier.

"But it's more than that," she continued. "I truly felt I could control it, that if we bargained, the creature *would* actually honor the deal. I'm not exactly sure how this could help us end the problem once and for all, but I feel this is the only possible path to an answer... and I think I know someone who might be able to help us figure it out."

"Who?"

"Dr. Esfahani. I'm considering contacting her. What do you think?"

He couldn't believe she was asking what *he* thought. What did *he* know? What good was *his* opinion—the boy who coasted through life with minimal effort and who knew too little about everything except video games, horror and sci-fi movie trivia, and phony Transylvanian accents. What did *he* think? For the most part... little to nothing.

Yet she'd asked him, and he respected her. He wanted to help her. He wanted to look good in her eyes... and in her beautiful dark eyes' reflection, he thought he might look better to himself. That was what he truly wanted, and now seemed as good a time to start as any. So, he tried to think it through.

They needed help; no doubt about it. If Lotte missed anything, made any mistake, the monster might get free and wreak who-knows-what-kind of havoc. Dr. Esfahani was smart, capable, and knew as much about the treasures and their history as anyone. Most people would probably freak out and call the police when they found out what was happening... or more likely, find an exorcist. If they did, the fate of the artifacts would be out of their hands and Lotte might be stuck. Dr. Esfahani might well react that way, but of anyone, she was probably least likely to do so—at least at first. Plus, her knowledge could truly help them.

"It's a risk," he finally answered, "but on balance, I'd say it's worth it. I can't think of anyone better. I agree with you. We need help. The stakes are just too high if that thing gets free and you can't control it."

She looked relieved. "Thanks for that, Eric. I thought I was losing my mind. Thank you for listening. Thank you for not hating me. Thank you for not running out of the room screaming." Her last words were accompanied by the ghost of a smile on her lipstickless lips.

If I had a nickel for every time I wanted to run out of the room screaming....

Just then, a knock sounded the door. "You kids decent in there?" Eric's dad said in a somewhat jovial voice.

Eric called for him to come in, and both he and Lotte asked what he'd found out.

"Well," he began, "Helene was able to roust your dad, Lotte. He and I talked a bit. He's pretty out of it and still has no idea what happened, but he seems to understand what's going on. He gave his permission, and Helene and I finally tracked down Dr. Chen—nice guy, if you can get him to sit still for three minutes. I guess that's the ICU for you, but what do I know?"

He scratched his nose while he contemplated his next words. "So, it's good news, bad news. The good news is, Lotte, your dad is probably going to be okay. They don't think there's any major damage, and they think his memory loss is not serious and probably short term. The bad news is, he's going to be here for a few days, and they may have to transfer him to UMass Memorial in Worcester for tests once he's more stable. Overall, I'd say he was pretty lucky."

They both heartily agreed.

"So, Lotte," he continued. "That leaves you in a bit of a bind. Given you don't have any family here, the hospital will let you stay, but... I'm not sure that's such a great situation. I offered that you could stay with us if you want, and Helene got your dad's permission. She's getting paperwork together for that now. It's up to you, but I think it would be better for you to be at our place. Maybe you could even try to go to so school to stay busy—keep your mind occupied—rather than sit around here with nothing to do but worry in this crummy little room. What do you think?"

She apparently didn't have to think very hard. "I don't know what to say, Mr. Schneider. You're too kind. I'd love to stay with you. I promise I'll be no trouble."

Riiiiiight.

With a slight tremble in her voice, she said, "I don't know how we could ever repay your generosity."

"Don't be silly," his dad replied with friendly dismissiveness. "It's no trouble at all. We're happy to do it. Consider it payment for all the German tutoring you're giving Bozo over here. Actually, we probably owe you more than this, huh?"

Oh, ha ha ha, Dad. He inwardly rolled his eyes, but knew his father was kidding, and he felt thrilled beyond words that Lotte would be staying with them. So, he just smiled a crooked smile and went with the joke—poor as he judged it to be. *Is anyone better at keeping quiet than me? I don't think so.*

"Again, Mr. Schneider," she said with a slight smile. "You're too kind. I'm sincerely grateful. You probably want to get out of here, and it seems there's no reason for me to stay any longer. Let me run and say goodbye to Father, and we can leave."

Eric knew she had other reasons to go as well, but kept that to himself. She threw on her shoes and gave his father a little hug on the way out.

"Nice girl," his dad said when she'd left, giving Eric a little wink.

He smiled in reply. *If you knew what I know, Dad, you'd be calling her batshit crazy. But I'm not gonna spoil the effects of a perfectly good hug, especially if your spine is still intact.*

CHAPTER 14

Lotte called out from the back seat where she sat with Eric. "Mr. Schneider, could you drop me off at home? I need to get some clothes and other things. I'd also like to take a shower and try to clean up the house a bit. I'm afraid the people from the ambulance tracked blood everywhere."

"Sure, Lotte," Eric's dad replied, grimacing at the thought of the accident scene. "That seems like a good idea. You need some help?"

"Well, I was hoping maybe Eric could assist me. I think we can take care of the worst of it. If necessary, we can get a professional cleaning later. I don't want to trouble you any more on a Sunday."

"Okay," he quickly shot back, seeming not to mind one bit being exempted from cleaning up a bloody mess, especially when the Pats were playing. "But hey, flooring is my game, so if it does need a professional, let me have a look. We can either do the work or put you in touch with someone who can."

She flashed Eric a knowing glance.

This was perfect, he realized. They'd have some time alone to talk with Dr. Esfahani.

Before they'd left the hospital, Lotte had asked Helene if she could use her computer, and she'd emailed Dr. Esfahani while they waited for Eric's dad to fill out the paperwork. Lotte included her cell phone number in the message, and by the time they reached the car, Dr. Esfahani had responded by text message. She was happy to talk, so Lotte replied that she'd call her later now that she had her cell number.

They arrived back in Southby quickly, not being far from the regional hospital that served all the small towns in this somewhat remote part of the state. His dad piloted the SUV into the circular driveway of Lotte's house, where the black panther Mercedes slept in its usual spot.

"Give Mom a ring when you're done," Eric's dad called from the open window of the towering Suburban. "We'll get pizza for dinner. That'll be easy. You like pizza, Lotte?"

"Love it! Thank you, Mr. Schneider—really, for everything."

With that, his father smiled and rolled up the window, and the land yacht rolled out of the driveway and took to the high seas.

"When does your family normally eat?" she asked when the boat had sailed out of view.

"About six, six-thirty. Why?"

"Okay, we have to hurry. We've only got about two, maybe two-and-a-half hours. Let's go inside. I'll call Dr. Esfahani, and we'll try to clean up that mess."

They made for the door, but suddenly he grabbed her arm. "Wait!"

"What?" she asked with surprise.

"The cloud, Lotte! I saw a cloud like the one you described."

"You did? Why didn't you tell me before?"

"I meant to, but it slipped my mind. You were telling me what had happened... we didn't know your dad's condition... then my dad came back. I guess I just got overwhelmed and forgot. I'm sorry. I saw it after I found the blood in your stairway."

"You were in our house?"

He began to realize how bad this sounded and started to backpedal like crazy. "I'd come in looking for you. I thought you'd left the door open for me, but the paramedics must not have closed it all the way. I was just gonna see if you guys were outside on the back porch, but when I got to the living room I saw the blood. That's when I texted you."

This explanation seemed to calm her.

"Anyway, I saw the cloud while I was waiting for your response. It was just drifting up at the ceiling of the living room and sort of clinging to the big glass wall. It wasn't doing anything that I could tell, just slowly billowing around. Now that I know what it is, though, I'm thinking it might be dangerous."

They stared at each other for a moment, then turned toward the door.

She brought her hand to her chin and briefly pondered the situation before responding. "I don't think it can hurt us. Only the ritual gave the cloud substance, and that took forever. I have no intention of lighting the candles in the bowls. I even covered the mirror with quilts from my bed while the ambulance was coming. We'll keep an eye out for it, but I don't think it's dangerous now. Plus, what choice do we have? I have to go in and get some clothes, we have to call Dr. Esfahani, and eventually, we'll have to access the papers in the closet. *Also, sollen wir gehen?*"

She gestured toward the door.

He agreed with her reasoning but felt increasingly like they had little choice in their actions—almost like being in high school, except that having to walk into a house with a cloud that could turn into a monster was a little different than having to suffer through geometry.

Actually, maybe the monster isn't looking that bad. Geometry is so stupid!

He sighed in resignation. "Okay, let's do it, but we should at least have a look around to see if we can find it."

She agreed, and then warily opened the door, which Eric realized he'd failed to lock in his haste. *Good thing this is a safe neighborhood, even if it sucks for the squirrels.*

They peered inside. Light streamed into the hallway from the glass wall in the living room, though the sun had passed by and no longer shone in directly. They cautiously entered, looking in all directions. The Mud *Château* was clear.

"I'm gonna leave my shoes on, if that's okay?" he said, remembering he still wore socks stained with blood inside his Nikes. "You know, just in case we have to, like... run."

She nodded and left her little Euro-styled black Adidas on as well. They crept toward the kitchen, glancing into closets, the half-bath, and a door that turned out to be the laundry room, as they passed.

Nothing.

When they reached the entry to the kitchen, she said, "You go down the stairs. I'll go through here and down through the dining room. We'll meet in the living room."

Oh, great, divide and be conquered. Does this girl not watch horror films at all?

"Let's stay together," he insisted. "Strength in numbers, right?"

She shrugged and motioned for him to follow her through the kitchen, then into the dining area, both of which proved to be silent and empty. Soon, they stood on the staircase by the stone wall, gazing into the cavernous living room. The cloud no longer hovered near the ceiling, and there was no trace of its presence in the room.

The pair cautiously descended, still looking in all directions. He felt pleased they'd stayed close together, as they could monitor more areas, decreasing the chance of surprise. They inched through the various sections of the living room, looking behind couches and the cases that held Mr. Schwarz's model buildings.

No sign of the black cloud.

At the far side of the living room, the pool of blood and its offshoots serenely coagulated on the dark-stained hardwood floor. They slipped past the gooey mess and checked all the rooms and closets in the hallway on the first floor. He hadn't been in the room at the end of the hall, which had an *en suite* bathroom, beautiful picture windows, and a double glass door to a little porch outside — probably designed to be either a bedroom or a really nice secondary living room.

Satisfied with their sweep of the first floor, they both returned to the stairs and hesitantly went up. Each stepped carefully over a splatter of blood where poor Mr. Schwarz's head had likely contacted the tread.

Eric shuddered. *Major ouch!*

They decided to tackle Lotte's room last and veered left toward Mr. Schwarz's bedroom and study. She opened the bedroom door and, over her shoulder, he saw another large room, this one even nicer than the one below. It also had its own bathroom, and glass doors leading to an inviting deck above the porch off the room beneath them.

A few pieces of new and very modern-looking furniture were sparingly scattered about, giving the area a somewhat empty feel. After scanning the bedroom, they opened the door to another walk-in closet. It appeared her father had pressed this into somewhat minimal service, as only about a third of the racks and shelves held clothes, shoes, and other items.

Maybe Germans just aren't as obsessed with having tons of stuff like Americans.

Still no sign of the black cloud.

The study was a more modest-size room with a beautiful picture window, in front of which Mr. Schwarz had placed a large drafting table on hydraulics. Papers and drawings cluttered the table, which was in the "up" position for standing. Clearly, Lotte's father still worked on design projects, as he'd indicated. Across from that, a desk housed a computer with three large screens, one mounted on an arm that attached to the wall.

On the way back down the hall, they checked the closets, which were all empty save for a few spare towels and bed sheets. The pair then investigated the upstairs bathroom, which Lotte appeared to have claimed for herself. It sported even greater opulence than the one below, featuring another grotto-themed stone shower, and a jacuzzi-style tub near full-length windows that looked out over the valley below.

He imagined her soaking in the jets of the tub, gazing out the windows, one leg occasionally raising with luxurious leisure out of the water as she sipped a Coke from a bent straw.

"Eric, come on!" she said, shocking him out of his daydream. "We haven't much time."

He turned from the jacuzzi with reluctance and followed her into the hall. Only her room remained to be searched, to which they now turned their attention. She'd shut the door, probably not wanting any of the EMTs to see inside in case they'd come upstairs. Gingerly, she pushed down on the handle and swung it inward, and they beheld yet another silent room.

The closet doors on the wardrobe were closed. She'd returned the dark marble board to its hiding place under the white marble platform, and had folded back the panels on the front and side of the wardrobe to conceal the openings. She'd also draped the mirror with two comforters from her bed.

Eric stared at it anyway, fearing what might lurk underneath.

She opened the right closet door, and he saw the shallow clay bowls lying on the floor where her belts and bags had been. They still had melted wax from the candles in them. She must have quickly stashed them there so they'd be out of sight. In the left closet of the wardrobe, she'd hidden the protective boxes where the bowls were stored.

After a quick check of the area near the bed, they turned to the final spot to investigate — the walk-in closet where the papers were housed. Again, she pushed the door handle down, and reached inside to turn on the closet light.

The room appeared quite different from when Eric had seen it last. As she'd described, the leather folders remained on the shelf where they'd put them, while the accordion file folders lay on their sides on the floor, a sheet of old typewriter paper on top of each one. The contents of the folder closest to the door were spread out, and a large piece of very old-looking paper lay rolled up next to them.

He stared in wonder. *The last Morocco file and the chart.*

"The rooms are clear," she announced. "I don't know where the cloud could be. Maybe it slipped out under a crack in the door and left. In any case, I think we're safe — for now at least. I need to call Dr. Esfahani right away."

He somewhat nervously agreed, and they went back downstairs to the living room, again carefully avoiding the messy pool of blood. They sat on the couch from which he'd observed the cloud earlier in the day, and she flipped open her phone and dialed the number.

"Hello?" Dr. Esfahani answered.

Eric pressed his head to Lotte's so he could hear the conversation in the tinny little receiver.

"Hello, Dr. Esfahani, it's Lotte Schwarz here. I have Eric Schneider with me."

"Hello, Lotte, hello, Eric," she cheerfully but somewhat cautiously replied. "How can I help you today?"

"Well, I didn't want to go into too much detail in the email I sent. It's a bit complicated—quite unusual, and quite urgent. In truth, we're in terrible trouble and really need your help. Is there any way you could come to my house? It would be easier to explain to you in person, and I could show you as well. It has to do with the treasures. I'm sure you'd find it more than worth your time."

The phone went silent for a bit. They both exchanged worried looks as they waited for a reply.

Finally, Dr. Esfahani spoke. "Where do you live, Lotte? I'm in Wellesley."

Lotte gave her the address and Eric filled in with some directions.

"I think I can find it," she eventually said. "It will take me about an hour or so to get there. Are you and Eric safe? Is your father home?"

Are we safe? Probably as safe as we can be while potentially sharing a house with a cloud monster.

"My father is in the hospital," Lotte replied. "That's related to the trouble I mentioned. I'm staying with Eric and his family. We're both safe for now. I'm just here getting some things and cleaning up the house, and Eric is helping me. If you could come, I'll explain everything. You can't imagine how grateful we'd be, or how important this is."

"Well, I did tell you that if there was anything you needed, I'd be honored to help. I can sense from your voice that this is important, so I'll be there as soon as I can. I'm leaving shortly. I'll see you soon."

Lotte signed off, and Eric gave her a high five.

"Okay," she exclaimed, jumping up from the couch. "We need to get up all this blood. In the closet next to the half-bath there's a bucket and a mop. Go grab them and fill the bucket with water in the kitchen. I'm going to change. I'll be down in a few minutes with some old towels from upstairs."

He did as instructed, even though he dreaded the task they were about to undertake. After finding the closet door, he opened it and peered in. The bucket sat on the floor, and he stepped inside to reach for it. Without warning, something lightly brushed his back.

The cloud!

He panicked and surged forward to get away. In his haste, he stepped directly into the bucket and tripped. He landed hard at the back of the closet, and a basket full of cleaning supplies scattered noisily across the terra-cotta tiles of the floor.

He flailed his legs behind him, desperately trying to free his foot from the bucket so he could get back up, but he couldn't shake it loose. Out of options and fearing being attacked from behind, he quickly rolled onto his back, hands in the air ready to fend off the black ash if it shot at his face.

Nothing.

He looked up and down and to both sides. The closet was empty.

His mind frantically raced. *Maybe it went into the hallway?*

Sensing an opportunity to escape, he sat up and reached for the bucket still stuck to his foot. As he did so, he observed the mop lying on the floor near the doorway... where it had clearly fallen after brushing his back when it toppled over.

You've gotta be kidding me.

He felt like a total fool. He picked up a bottle that had been tossed from the supply basket, and which now sat by his side — floor cleaner.

"Just what I was looking for," he groaned.

Shamefaced, he extricated his foot from the bucket, dusted off his clothes — not to mention his pride — and brought everything to the kitchen. He still felt really jumpy, glancing frequently over his shoulder and above him to check for clouds, monsters, demonic killer mops, or whatever other perils might await him in this ridiculous parallel universe he seemed to have unwittingly stumbled into. Happily, none materialized.

He lugged the bucket of soapy water down the stairs, then went to retrieve the mop and the bottle of soap.

When he returned, Lotte had come down. She wore short pants with no shoes or socks, and an old floppy sweatshirt over a t-shirt. For a wonder, the clothes were again not black. Even in these grubby rags, she looked amazing, and he tried not to stare.

Fail.

"You start mopping to loosen up the blood," she said, oblivious to his gaze. "I'll try to get it up with the towels. *Ach*, what a mess. Poor Father."

After a while, they developed a rhythm of mopping and drying, mopping and drying. Periodically, they retreated to the first-floor bathroom, where he refreshed the bucket's water in the tub while she wrung out the towels in the sink. It was surprisingly hard work. The blood tended to smear around, which made him gag.

This is not my calling, that's for sure.

The stairs were particularly tough going, but before they knew it, the gooey mess had basically vanished, and they were drying the floor with paper towels. The tough polyurethane coating on the wood resisted stains, and Eric thought it actually looked pretty darned good.

When finished, he nervously returned the bucket and mop to the creepy little closet, then scampered back to join Lotte in the bathroom, where she'd been dealing with the bloody towels.

"*Whew!*" she sighed with relief as she turned on the shower and rinsed the stains of blood from her feet. "Dr. Esfahani will be here in ten or fifteen minutes. No time to take a shower, but I'm going to make some tea. Do you want some?"

"I'd prefer a Coke."

"Coca-Cola it is. Have a seat in the living room. I'll get it for you." She dried her feet and went off to start the water boiling.

He went to the couch and flopped down with a thump, utterly pooped.

Shortly, she returned with a Coke from the fridge and collapsed in exhaustion beside him. They sat in silence as he drank.

"What are you gonna tell Dr. Esfahani?" he eventually asked.

She briefly considered. "Everything. I'm going to show her the treasures upstairs, as well as the papers. There's no reason to hide anything. If we do, it may prove a terrible mistake, if that information turns out to be important. She'll do what she does. I just see no other options. Oops... the water's boiling. Hold on, I'll be right back."

He heard the signature whine of the kettle as she padded up the now blood-free stairs toward the kitchen.

No other options. That seemed to be the way of things right now. Leaning back on the deep, plush cushions, he tried to catch a moment of relaxation. Happily, the ceiling remained void of menacing black ash clouds.

Suddenly, he heard her scream.

It startled him to the point that he didn't think it had really happened, until she actually yelled his name. He bolted up the stairs and saw her in the hallway, stepping backward and gaping into the kitchen—hands over her mouth in obvious terror. The kettle still shrieked its deafening alarm, adding to the chaos of the moment. He reached her side and looked into the room where her gaze was fixed.

A cloud of black, shimmering ash swirled above the kettle that sat whistling on one of the fancy gas burners of the stove. Within it, a creature floated and slowly gyrated. Already formed and mostly solidified, this wasn't simply the head and shoulders that Lotte had seen before. The full body of a monster hovered before them, though it stood only about three feet in height.

Entirely soot-black, the beast shimmered like the cloud of ash from which it was undoubtedly formed. Eric recognized its head and face from Lotte's description — the horns, the fangs, the snout-like nose.

Its chest and arms were enormous, or would have been on a monster the size he pictured from her description. Its hands were like the claws of a bird, three muscular and razor-sharp talons, thicker than two or three human fingers — again, if the creature were full sized.

On its back, folded, bat-like wings with sharp, bony points loomed menacingly. A wiry tail that ended in a twisted barb coiled and slithered between legs like those of a goat, which terminated in heavy, cloven hooves.

Eric froze in utter horror and amazement. If anyone had asked him to describe Satan, this is probably the image he'd have conjured up. The only thing missing was the pitchfork, which he wouldn't have been surprised to see materialize next from the shimmering black cloud.

Beside him, Lotte finally found her voice. "Eric, this is impossible! This took only moments. It took hours for the creature to come forth and be formed last night."

Impossible or not, there it stood, almost fully assembled. The cloud of black ash had all but disappeared.

Eric took a chance.

He dove for the stove, hoping the beast might dissipate without the fire and heat. Bending low, he grabbed the dial for the burner and turned it off.

The incessant scream of the escaping steam slowly receded, and the creature ceased to rotate. Slowly, its body drifted down until its cloven hooves straddled the now silent kettle. It seemed as if it were in a trance. Black ash hovered and clung around it, still trying to merge with the beast.

Eric realized his gambit hadn't worked, so he kept his head down and tried to slip away. As if sensing the movement, the monster rapidly swung its horned head in his direction and let out a blood-curdling shriek that sounded like a demonic six-year-old having a tooth pulled. Then, with a sprightly hop, the creature reoriented its entire body toward him. Slowly, its wings unfurled, and the barb of its tail menacingly hovered above the horns on its head.

Just as it seemed about to pounce, Eric heard a loud *thump!* The beast flew wildly off the stove, past the refrigerator, and into the breakfast nook. He looked up and saw Lotte holding the cast iron frying pan as if she were Big Papi watching a home run fly out of Fenway Park.

"Jump on it, Eric!" she said, breathlessly lowering the heavy pan to the floor. "While it's stunned, hold it down. I'll be there in a moment."

He looked across the floor where the creature had tumbled near the small breakfast table. It flailed and spasmed like a beetle on its back, trying to regain control of its limbs.

Well, at least we can hurt it!

He sprung.

The monstrosity had multiple points of attack—bites, kicks, claws, and that dangerous-looking barbed tail. Eric knew he couldn't stop all of them if the thing came around, so he grabbed the little monster by its shoulder and pinned it on its back, wings sprawled at either side.

Its jet-black surface flexed like skin over sinuous muscle—cool to the touch, like stone, it possessed the tacky feel of volcanic pumice. It gave him the creeps, but it did provide a secure grip. He couldn't tell if the creature was fully conscious, or whether it saw him through its black, pupil-less eyes.

He forced his left knee onto the beast's chest, and used his left hand to grab the tail close to the barb and hold it toward the ground. Then he carefully positioned his right knee and the lower part of his leg on the creature's left arm. With his right hand, he reached across to the monster's muscular right talon, which at present flopped uselessly at the monster's side.

Without warning, the beast pressed upward against his legs.

"Hurry, it's recovering!" He could hear Lotte rummaging in a drawer behind him.

Seeming to revive, the monster attempted to whip its tail to attention, but Eric pushed it firmly back down into the ground. Whatever else he did, he'd hold onto that as if his life depended on it. It just might, actually. With lightning speed the little monstrosity sunk its right talon into his left leg. He shouted in pain and grabbed the creature's wrist with his free hand. They struggled, and Eric finally managed to tear the claw free, but blood seeped painfully from three punctures in his jeans.

The beast began to buck wildly as it frantically beat its wings against Eric's torso, scratching him with their bony protrusions. Being bigger and heavier, Eric leaned his body down and kept the pressure on. He didn't give a damn if thing suffocated under his weight.

Does it actually breathe?

"Lotte!" he screamed with growing desperation.

"Coming!" she called from behind. She was still making noises with something, now on the granite top of the kitchen's central island. "Just another second!"

He feared he didn't have another second, as the monster started working its left arm loose. Despite his weight, it had managed to wriggle the appendage free. He still had its shoulder pinned and that constrained its movement, but Eric knew he was in trouble.

Right on cue, he felt the talons rake against his right hip. Being hindered, they didn't cut deeply, and his jeans provided some protection, but the pain became excruciating as the claws struck again and again, and the material began to shred. He tried to reposition his leg, but couldn't shift his body without risk that the creature could slip away. For its size, the beast was freakishly strong.

Precisely at the moment he felt he couldn't hold out any longer, Lotte appeared out of the corner of his eye. She bent at the floor near the wall with her back to him, so he couldn't see what she was doing.

"Lotte!" he pleaded. "It's ripping me apart! I can't hold out much longer!"

She turned.

She wielded a hand-held cake mixer with two wire beaters. The long cord trailed to the socket where she'd just plugged it in. She quickly shot to where he struggled with the enraged and flailing beast.

"From dust you came," she intoned. "To dust you shall return."

With that, she activated the mixer. Its wire beaters whirred in a frenzy of chrome as she plunged the device into the monster's stomach.

It worked like a charm. Black soot filled the air as the creature howled in agony. She ran the mixer down the beast's legs, severing its tail.

Eric felt the appendage go limp in his left hand. He dropped it and repositioned his arms to better fend off the monster's even more furious and desperate assault.

The mixer whirred and gagged. Soon, only the beast's upper body and wings remained. It had no "insides." It was made totally of the shiny black ash, seemingly bound and animated by the fire of the fancy gas burner. Lotte pressed the mixer to the creature's right arm, which vaporized to dust that clouded the air before settling onto the floor.

"Get the other arm!" Eric urgently directed. "It's clawing me to death!"

She complied, disintegrating first the arm, then the creature's flailing wings. Now, only the pathetic beast's upper torso and head flopped helplessly on the floor.

She turned off the mixer and grabbed the monster by the neck. She practically spat in the beast's face as she spoke. These weren't scalpels; these words were verbal daggers. "What are you? What do you want here? We didn't threaten you! Why did you attack us with no reason?"

The creature gagged and black ash streamed out of its mouth like a mist of blood. Then, to their amazement... it spoke. Its language was unrecognizable—a tongue no human had ever uttered, and likely hadn't heard for centuries, but Lotte and Eric understood its words. In their minds, the monster's voice rang clear.

'*Not you*,' it chortled, spitting out more ash that wisped away in little puffs before sinking to the beautiful marble tiles of the kitchen floor. '*Would never harm you. With you, we bargain.*'

"What bargain?" she demanded, shaking the creature's head. "What do you want from me?"

The suffering little nasty coughed some more, and they realized it was laughing. '*You summoned us. You strike the deal, tell us what you want. We comply and take the spoils. This has been the way of things since before even our memories can recall. Why did you change the pattern? Why did you let them lock us away?*'

At this, Lotte faltered. She clearly had as little idea as Eric did what the mutilated little monstrosity was talking about. Before she could recover her wits, the monster began to shake as if having a seizure. Great clouds of ash rose from what remained of its form, spewing from its mouth and where its limbs had been severed.

Soon, a pile of sparkling black debris lay before them as they sat in mute shock and horror.

CHAPTER 15

"Eric?" Lotte gently nudged his soot-stained and trembling shoulder. "Can you get up? If you can, run to the small closet across from where you got the mop bucket and grab the Hoover."

The Hoover?

Eric distantly imagined himself dragging the Hoover Dam on a long rope through the Nevada desert, Lotte tapping her heel impatiently as she waited for it to arrive. For what purpose she wanted it, he couldn't fathom.

"The what?" he falteringly asked, probing dizzily at the wounds on his legs.

"The Hoover, Eric." She made a little back and forth motion with the cake mixer still clutched in her hand, but she stopped as she noticed what he was doing. A look of concern grew on her face. "Never mind, I'll get it. Let me see that." She pushed his hand away and gently inspected the blood that seeped from the rips in his jeans. "It's not *too* bad," she offered, with both encouragement and skepticism.

Easy for you to say. He felt the sting of the various punctures and scrapes. *At least it takes my mind off the pain in my foot.*

She grasped his arm with encouragement. "Just sit there for a minute. We'll take care of it, but first I have to get all this ash up before it starts moving around again."

She bolted out of the kitchen, and he heard her banging around in the hallway. She soon returned with a vacuum cleaner, which she connected to the socket next to the cake mixer's plug.

Hoover. Must be European for vacuum cleaner.

The machine sucked up the black dust that covered the floor, the vast majority of it having settled, seemingly inert, on the marble tiles. Lotte was right: it wasn't moving like it had been, but that might just be temporary.

Despite his dazed state, he realized the vacuum cleaner would never contain the ash should it regain mobility. "Do you have any trash bags? The thick heavy kind?"

"Yes, they're in the cabinet there. Why?"

"Get them out. We need to put the ash in one and seal it, so it can't escape if the cloud... like... wakes up."

"Excellent idea, Eric." She beamed. "I knew I kept you around for some reason."

Har, har, har. Her quip struck dangerously close to his feelings of inferiority, but seeing her smile seemed worth a little humor at his expense. He also sensed she was trying to bolster his morale after taking the brunt of the monster's attack.

She grabbed the box from the cabinet, pulled out one of the greyish-black bags, and handed it to him. He held it ready as she began to open the vacuum cleaner—*Hoover? Whatever*—but then she stopped.

"This will be a mess," she said. "Some could escape. Just hold the bag open on the floor."

He complied, and she pushed the entire contraption into the opening.

They were about to seal it when she cried out. "Wait, our clothes!"

He looked down. His shirt and jeans were covered with the black soot. Her clothes were likewise coated. Her legs and feet were also streaked with black smudges.

"Take everything off," she commanded. "Put it in the bag."

Everything?

She began to strip.

She pulled off her loose sweatshirt, then removed her t-shirt, revealing a sporty black—*shocker*—bra underneath.

He sat in rapt attention.

"What are you doing?" she said impatiently. "We've no time for modesty. This is serious. Get those clothes off!" She pulled down her little shorts. Underneath, she wore sleek black panties, which she left on, along with her bra.

Damn! he cursed, though he feared his heart may have stopped if she'd gone any further. He didn't stir or remove his eyes from her now alluringly unclothed form.

She shot him a dirty look as she gathered her things from the floor and assertively stuffed them in the bag.

At that point, he regained at least a portion of his wits and began to quickly undress.

Soon he was down to his white Hanes briefs. Remarkably and mercifully, these were absent any black smudges, as were his Nikes, since his feet had been behind him when the monster imploded. The blood-stained socks he tossed in the bag with the rest of his clothes, which they sealed tight with knots. Then they slipped another bag over the first in the opposite direction and carefully sealed that as well.

That should do it!

He looked down at the wounds on his now bare legs. The three marks on his left leg were deeper and bled more, but the scrapes on his right thigh hurt more. His torso bore scratches from the monster's wings as well, but those wounds were trivial in comparison. The top of his foot had also turned a shade of darkish purple.

If this keeps up, I'll be in the hospital with Mr. Schwarz.

"Let me put this away," she said. "Then we'll go upstairs and bandage those cuts." She began to drag the bags with the vacuum cleaner out the door and into the hallway when the doorbell rang.

"*Verdammt!* That's Dr. Esfahani! Make your way to the bathroom upstairs. I'll stall her and meet you there as soon as I can." She grabbed the bag and ran out of the kitchen toward the front door.

"Just a moment, Dr. Esfahani! I'll be right with you!" she called out.

He limped down the hall in the opposite direction, holding a paper towel to his left leg so as not to drip blood on the freshly cleaned floor. Once upstairs, he staggered into Lotte's bathroom, sat on the edge of the jacuzzi-style tub, and waited.

Soon he heard her run up the stairs. She went past the bathroom and directly into her bedroom, where he heard her furiously opening and closing drawers.

Finally, she burst into the bathroom with an armful of clothes. Making her way to the sink, she rapidly wet a washcloth and wiped the sooty ash off her legs and feet, then tossed it to him when finished.

"Use that to get as much of the ash off as possible," she breathlessly instructed. "I have to get dressed and let Dr. Esfahani in. Once I get her settled, I'll come back. Just hold on."

She tugged on jeans and threw on another t-shirt and sweatshirt while he mopped at various black smudges on his skin with the washcloth. Once dressed, she flew out the door and dashed down the stairs.

He wet a fresh washcloth and dabbed at the punctures on his left leg. Blood oozed out, and he held the damp fabric against the wounds. After a bit, he went to the door and cracked it so he could hear Lotte and Dr. Esfahani in the living room below.

"You have a lovely house, Lotte," the woman said. "I'm not surprised. I know your father specializes in beautiful spaces."

"Thank you. Please have a seat. I'm so sorry for keeping you waiting. I was getting changed. I have to get Eric some clothes as well. His got all stained and dirty when he helped me clean up."

Yeah, clean up the fucking devil-Satan monster that was attacking us.

"Can I get you something to drink?" Lotte asked.

"Oh, tea would be nice, if you have it."

Yikes.

She fumbled for words. "Oh, tea, yes... well... you see, umm... I was just making some for myself, and I discovered... yes... well... umm... I found that there were no more tea bags. That's it.... I mean... they were all gone. Father had probably used the last one. He always forgets to tell me. He's so absentminded about certain things... ha, ha, ha...."

She giggled rather stupidly, and Eric winced. *That could have gone more smoothly. Dr. Esfahani probably thinks we're idiots.*

"Water would be fine, thank you, Lotte."

"Yes, water we have," she gushed, and he heard her run toward the kitchen.

"Ow, holy shit!" Eric screamed. "What the hell is that?"

"Rubbing alcohol," Lotte calmly replied, squeezing a washcloth to the scrapes on his right leg. "It's not best to use this on an open wound, but there's no telling what kind of germs that disgusting thing might have had. We have to clean this out, and this is the strongest thing I've got. I know it hurts. Just hang in there."

Hurts was the understatement of the year. The monster's talons hurt less than the ostensible cure as, among other fun, Lotte had already forced him to stand in the shower under cold water to wash the puncture wounds on his left leg, as well as his other scrapes and scratches. He'd squeezed them until they oozed with blood.

Now he got the rubbing alcohol treatment. It hurt like hell, and he felt like he was going to pass out. Eventually, the burning sting subsided, and she began to bandage the worst of the various gouges and abrasions.

"Great move with that cake mixer," he said as she carefully placed the various adhesive strips.

She spared a moment to look him in the eye. "Great job holding the bloody thing down. I can't believe you held out."

He thought he saw her glance once or twice at his barely clad body. *Yeah, but maybe that's just my imagination... or my dream fulfilling some unspoken wish.*

When finished, she presented him with some clothes, clearly her father's—some thick grey socks, sweatpants, a t-shirt, and a very nice sweatshirt that sported the moniker of the *Universität Wien*. They were a bit too big, but he welcomed their soft comfort after what he'd just experienced.

Once dressed, she took him by the hand and they carefully descended the stairs together.

Dr. Esfahani inspected the model buildings in their cases as she roamed the living room. She'd probably become a little impatient waiting for Lotte to "get Eric clothes," but his wounds had to be treated, so there had really been no option.

"Is everything all right?" she asked, as if sensing something was not as it should be. "Eric, you're limping. Are you okay?"

He started to answer, but Lotte cut in. "He'll be fine. He's stronger than he looks... and braver." At this, she squeezed his hand as she guided him to the couch.

Stronger and braver. Eric: three; world: seventeen million, whatever, whatever....

"Sit here, please, and I'll tell you everything," Lotte said, facing their guest—or savior, depending on how things went. "You're not going to believe this, but please, let me finish before you pass judgment."

She told her tale, more quickly than she'd done with him, but time was short.

Still, she covered everything—her mother's decline, inheriting the wardrobe, the dreams, the chance encounter with Dr. Esfahani at the museum, finding the wardrobe's secret compartments, reading some of the papers, conducting the ritual and summoning a monster in a moment of weakness—or inspiration... she still wasn't sure—her father's fall, making tea and finding that she'd made much more than tea, fighting the beast with Eric, and the little creature's mysterious final words.

Dr. Esfahani listened silently. At times it looked as if she would speak, but she didn't. Whether out of respect for Lotte's request, or simply due to an utter lack of words that could convey her thoughts, Eric couldn't determine. Silent, however, she remained, until Lotte ran out of tale to tell.

"Would you like more water?" Lotte asked, more to break the spell she seemed to have cast on Dr. Esfahani than the perceived need for something more to drink. As hoped, the words initiated a response.

"Can I see the artifacts?" she asked, with wonder and hunger in her voice.

"Of course, come upstairs." Lotte again helped Eric navigate back to the second floor.

His legs throbbed and felt stiff, and he wondered how he'd explain this to his parents.

Well, I was carrying this bucket of water, when all of a sudden.... That pretty much sucks, but it may be the best I can come up with.

Upon reaching the bedroom, she guided him to one of the red-cushioned wooden chairs, then walked over and stepped up onto the white marble platform of the wardrobe. Carefully, she carefully lifted a portion of the comforter to reveal a section of frame, but kept the mirror concealed.

"*Allahu Akbar*," Dr. Esfahani whispered, approaching the platform to get a better look at the carved streaks of Fire Quartz. "This is richer than any *Alkuartiz Alnaar* I've ever seen. These must have been the most desirable pieces—and the most powerful."

Lotte released the comforter, again fully concealing the frame. She opened the right closet, revealing the shallow bowls still containing wax from the melted candles, and pulled out the black marble slab from its hiding space. Dr. Esfahani examined all these items with equal amazement. Finally, Lotte took her to the walk-in closet.

Eric reluctantly limped behind, not wanting to miss the action.

Once shown the contents of the room, Dr. Esfahani wandered silently, glancing at the index sheets and inspecting some of the leather folders on the shelves. She examined the rolled-up chart near the final Morocco file, and her eyes went wide.

"This is original," she said with amazement. "It's priceless, as are all the artifacts in your bedroom. This is delicate and should be put safely away." She rose and again surveyed the room. After another long period of silence she turned and spoke. "What do you plan to do now, Lotte, and what do you want from me?"

Lotte approached and looked her in the eye. "I want to try again to summon the creature. I want to find out what it wants, and give it what it needs that will make it go away for good. I want to do it properly, though, and I feel there's information I'm missing—pieces, like a puzzle that I haven't put together. I can't figure it all out on my own, and I know the consequences could be terrible if I fail. I fear destroying the mirror and risk being stuck with these dreams in my mind for the rest of my life. I'll go mad. So, I want to try. I sense I must, but I'd feel more confident if I had your help."

I would too. Eric held his breath.

Dr. Esfahani considered. For long moments she again wordlessly wandered the small room. Periodically, she perused various folders and files, deep in thought. Several times it appeared as if she would ask a question, but each time the words seemed to die on her lips. Ever so slowly, a look of resolve formed on her face. She bit her lower lip as she returned her gaze to Lotte and Eric.

"I'll need access to all this," she quietly said, opening her arms wide with palms outstretched to indicate the closet's contents. "I make no promises, Lotte. If I can't find the puzzle pieces you seek and feel it's too dangerous to try what you're proposing, I'm going to report this find and turn it over to others."

Lotte gave a slight gasp and Eric felt his chest tighten. This was exactly what they'd feared, and why they perceived such risk involving anyone else.

"But that's a last resort," she continued, her words breaking some of the tension. "This creature is dangerous, and powerful. Getting free accidentally is one thing. In the wrong hands, however, it could be used for... terrible purposes."

Again, she paused and gazed, wide-eyed, around the room. "Yes, selfish purposes. The fewer people who know of its existence, the better. So, I agree with you, Lotte. We need to try, but first we need to know everything we can about what happened, and about this entity, so it can be controlled."

"The papers are yours to study," she gratefully replied. "No one is more qualified than you to gather and interpret the information they might contain. No one is better prepared to make the right decision. This is why I called you. This is why we need you — why you're here."

All three occupants of the walk-in closet stared deeply at one another, as if their lives depended on what they saw. In all likelihood, they did.

"Lotte, how long will your father be in the hospital?"

"Several days. He had a bad fall. He may even need to go to another hospital in *Wore-ses-tear* to be evaluated."

Dr. Esfahani stared in confusion.

"She means Worcester," Eric interjected, realizing the correct pronunciation was further from Lotte's literal reading than it really ought to have been.

Imagine me correcting Lotte! He almost smiled. Almost.

"Yes, *Woostah*," she repeated with a look of annoyance and distaste. "In any case, he'll be gone for most of the week, perhaps longer."

"Well then," Dr. Esfahani said with a slight smile on her face, "perhaps I could work here with the papers? This way I can be close to the artifacts. I'll be no trouble. I can sleep on a couch in your beautiful living room. You're nearby and can visit after school so we can discuss what I've found. Does this sound acceptable?"

It was more than acceptable to them. Lotte even suggested Dr. Esfahani sleep in her room, but she declined, wanting some distance from the artifacts to perhaps avoid what Lotte's mother, and now Lotte, seemed to have experienced. They finally decided she could sleep in Mr. Schwarz's room, to which Dr. Esfahani politely acquiesced after some cajoling.

There were only two rules. First, she had to leave her car in the little parking area by the walking trails, as Eric's parents would be suspicious if they saw an unfamiliar vehicle in the circular driveway.

Second, no leaving the tea kettle unattended.

To the final rule, Dr. Esfahani voiced no objections.

Lotte passed her father's house keys to Dr. Esfahani and gave her the alarm code.

Dr. Esfahani wanted to go home and get some clothes and other things she would need, but planned to return later that night. She intended to call in sick to the museum, wanting to focus exclusively on the papers. They confirmed the plan to meet at the house after school tomorrow, and she drove away.

Eric texted his mom to come get them while Lotte went upstairs to pack some clothes and toiletries. It was about 6:45, and his mother had texted a couple of times wondering where they were. He'd apologized and said it had been a messier job than anticipated. This would help soften the blow when she saw him in Mr. Schwarz's clothes.

Explaining his limp would be trickier.

Lotte grabbed her Doc Martens from the Mud *Château*, and they both left the house and waited in the driveway. Mom arrived quickly, telling them that she and Dad had already ordered and eaten because they were hungry, but she'd re-heat their pizza when they got home.

Good thing. I'm starving.

"What happened to your clothes?" his mother asked with a perfectly attuned balance of alarm and curiosity.

"Oh, I got water, and blood and... well... like... other stuff on them. Lotte tossed them in the laundry. I'll bring them home when they're dry. Don't worry about it." He truly hoped she'd just forget about them, because there was no hope of that stuff ever being seen again.

On the way in from the car when they got to the house, his mother noticed how gingerly he moved. "Eric, why are you walking that way? What happened?" This time the question was attuned far more toward alarm.

"Well, I was carrying this bucket of water, when all of a sudden...."

He could see the skepticism Mom's face at his story about slipping and hurting his back, and his leg—actually, both legs—and oh, by the way, Lotte had stepped on his foot pretty hard yesterday too. At the last bit, Lotte flashed him a grumpy look.

His mom couldn't withstand the verbal carpet bombing and just shook her head in bewilderment. "Be more careful, honey," she said in a perplexed tone.

I will, Mom. The next time I have to wrestle a shiny-black-ash-devil-freak-cloud-monster, I'll definitely be more careful. Promise.

Lotte called the hospital when they got inside. Her father was in "serious but stable" condition, but with the help of some powerful pain relievers he was apparently "resting comfortably."

"We'll see if he's up for a visit tomorrow," his mom said. "I'm free all day. I can take you. Were you planning to go to school, honey?"

Hey, I'm honey! he thought with a sting of jealousy.

"That's so nice of you, Mrs. Schneider," Lotte replied. "I think I will try to go to school. I need to stop at my house for a bit afterward, just to keep an eye on things, but perhaps a little later in the afternoon?"

Mom seemed to think that was okay and started dishing out the pizza.

The pair ate silently in the kitchen. After all that had happened over the past few days, they needed some quiet time to process things. Plus, they were starving. When finished, they both realized how utterly exhausted they were. They put their dishes in the dishwasher and then went to the TV room.

"We're totally beat," Eric announced. "I think we're both going to bed."

"It's barely eight o'clock," his dad said with disbelief. "Linda, take the boy's temperature. He's obviously feverish."

"Oh, Fred, they've had a big day, Lotte especially. I think it's a good idea they get some sleep. Honey, Eric will show you the guest room. I'll be up to help you in a couple of minutes."

He led her to the stairs as instructed and they began to ascend. His legs had really stiffened up, and he found it hard to climb the steps. She came up beside him and supported his arm, which didn't help that much but felt really nice.

"Thanks," he said when they reached the top, still wincing a bit from the pain.

"Eric," she softly said, looking toward the ground. "I should be thanking you. I can't believe I've dragged you into this. You could have been killed today, or seriously hurt."

Umm, helllooooo, he thought, feeling the throbbing from the gashes on his thighs. *Not serious enough for you?*

"If you want out of this, I'll totally understand. This is my struggle, and it's unfair to put you at risk."

He gently took her arm and guided her down the hall, not wanting his parents to accidentally hear a conversation like this.

He actually thought momentarily about getting out. What they were doing *was* extremely risky and could have very serious consequences... but this was also the most exciting and interesting thing he'd ever done in his life. He wanted to see what happened, even if meant watching a giant cloud monster rip his intestines out.

Well, okay, I hope it won't come to that.

Still, curiosity and excitement won the day. Then, of course, there was Lotte. He couldn't imagine abandoning her. It had only been like three, maybe four weeks that he'd known her, but somehow, she'd become the center of his world. Forget the monster and the excitement and the curiosity... she had become a force in his life, even if all she did was correct his lousy German pronunciation and share the occasional Coca-Cola.

Well, maybe not so occasional. Whatever.

In the end, it wound up being a remarkably easy decision, despite the dangers.

"I'll never abandon you, Lotte," he said with a cheerfulness that surprised even him. "You can't make me... and if you tried, I'd be a total pest, so you'd eventually give in. I want to see this through. This is one of the coolest things that's ever happened to me... but the coolest thing to me is *you*! I'm better for knowing you. You make me better, and it'll take a lot more than this for me to let that go."

For once, she had no words. She just stared at him, until she closed her eyes and put her arms around his waist. She didn't have the strength to crack his spine. She simply hung in his embrace — limp. Her feet briefly brushed the ground as the pair rocked in silent unison.

He heard his mother approaching on the stairs, and in one quick motion, she left his arms and turned down the hall.

"Which is the guest room?" she asked in a trembling voice.

Last door on the right, he thought, but couldn't articulate the words for lack of breath.

Once Lotte got settled, Eric fell asleep almost immediately, not even bothering to take off Mr. Schwarz's sweatpants. His sleep, however, was fitful. At around midnight, he woke up and realized his legs hurt pretty badly, and were probably keeping him up. He clicked on his bedside light and hobbled to the bathroom.

There, he removed the sweatpants and inspected his wounds. Blood had stained the adhesive bandages, but hadn't completely soaked through. He figured they probably needed changing, so he went for the box of Band-Aids in the cabinet. Noticing Lotte's toothbrush and toothpaste in a glass by the sink, he smiled.

I guess they don't come in black.

He removed the old bandages and dabbed the punctures and scrapes with a wet tissue, not wanting to get blood on any towels. He then applied the new bandages and gathered up all the trash, which he'd have to throw away in the big garbage can in the kitchen where they wouldn't be seen. On the way downstairs, he realized he should probably take some ibuprofen for the pain.

Maybe if I'd done that before, I'd still be asleep. Duh.

He reached the kitchen and jammed all the bandage crap in the bottom of the trash can next to the fridge. He got a glass of water, returned to the bathroom for some ibuprofen, and was soon back in bed. This time he wore a pair of his own sweatpants, which were dark in color. Hopefully, they'd hide any bloodstains that might leak through the Band-Aids.

He lay on his back and closed his eyes. Tired as he was, thoughts flooded his mind that kept sleep at bay. He replayed the battle with the impish monster and wondered how it might have gone had the beast been his size.

Not well, he decided.

What the hell are we dealing with? Where did this thing come from, and how will we get it to leave Lotte alone and go the fuck away? Why would it bargain with her and then look at me like I'm freaking dinner? Too many questions.

He glanced at his bedside clock: 1:15 a.m.

Holy crap, I'm never gonna get any sleep tonight. Tomorrow is gonna suck, even more than a normal Monday. He lay a while longer and tried to calm his mind.

Just on the cusp of falling asleep, he heard a noise outside his room. Someone entered, and then closed the door behind them.

"Lotte?"

"*Shhhhhhhh,*" she replied.

He heard her walk across the room and approach the foot of his bed. There she sat, making a sound as if she were crying—little puffs of air escaping her mouth as she fought back tears.

Maybe she's being tormented by dreams?

He reached for his bedside light and clicked it on.

The monster stood before him.

Not a tiny golem this time, but a beast that hulked close to seven feet tall—shimmering black with wings unfurled. Its barbed tail hovered above its horned head. It loomed over him, braced on one arm whose giant clawed hand pressed at the edge of the bed. The other covered the creature's hideous mouth as it giggled with maniacal glee.

Paralyzed by fear at what he beheld, he knew he was cornered. He slammed his back into the headboard in a feeble attempt to flee.

The beast raised both its arms in the air, crouching and tightening all the muscles in its body, and then it sprang! Its barbed tail and razor-sharp talons led the devastating and unstoppable assault.

Eric screamed in abject terror, and the world became a jumble of darkness as the beast descended upon him.

He fought with desperation, but the monster enfolded him, stifling his movements as if he were trapped in clay. It tore at him as he frantically covered his head in his arms to fend off its blows while he madly kicked and twisted to break free.

He screamed a long wail of panic and despair, envisioning his body ripped to pieces and left in a muddle of blood and viscera, soaking through the nice satin sheets of his comfortable but slightly too soft twin bed. Now, he felt his legs immobilized—unresponsive to his urgent need for flight. He felt as if he were encapsulated and tumbling in space—helpless and doomed.

He screamed, and screamed, and screamed... *and screamed...* and then... there was light.

It shone in a line straight ahead, as if coming from under the door to his room.

Actually, it is coming from under the door to my room.

He heard a sound, like a Mongolian yak car alarm, ceaselessly emitting its monotone wail to fend off some invisible perpetrator and prevent yet another costly and disruptive Yak theft.

Wait a minute, I'm making that noise.

Light spewed into the room as if from an incandescent firehose as the door swung wide.

Silhouetted in the threshold, his father stood before him in boxers and a t-shirt. "Eric! What in the Sam Hell is going on?"

He honestly had no fucking idea. He was utterly confused, still struggling to break free from the monster that constricted his movements. Slowly, he realized that he was completely entangled in his nice satin sheets. The vision that gripped him dissolved, like the frame of a video game where your character dies and everything in the background fades to red... then to gray... then to oblivion.

"Hey," his dad said more calmly. He sat on the side of the bed and steadied Eric's shoulder with his firm but gentle touch. "You okay, kiddo?"

Eric took rapid breaths through his mouth, cognizant each time he expelled air from his chest. Somehow, the noise soothed him, and he felt reconnected to the rhythm of his body. It was like coming back to reality — or returning to a comfortable fantasy once having experienced reality.

After a moment, he summoned the will to speak. "I think so. I think I was dreaming, but it felt so... real. It was like... I don't know. It was like nothing I've ever experienced."

He looked out the door and saw his mom with her arm around Lotte in the hallway. She wore an oversized black — *shocker* — t-shirt that covered her to mid-thigh. It sported the image of a cat's yellow eyes, pink nose, and grey whiskers and mouth. She looked super cute, even though at this moment she actually had *no* eyebrows at all. *So weird.*

For a moment, he forgot about the horrible dream. In fact, the details were already fading from reach, like a memory of some distant Christmas where you could recall the sense of excitement and expectation, but not exactly what presents you'd gotten.

"You've got some water there," his dad said. "Take a few sips and calm down. You let me know when you're ready to try to sleep again." Dad waved to his mom, and she and Lotte dragged sleepily back to their bedrooms.

"Thanks, Dad, I'm really sorry. I must just be super-tired. I didn't mean to wake everybody up."

His father chuckled. "It's okay, kiddo. You can't control your reactions when you're asleep—just a scary dream, nothing to worry about."

Nothing to worry about. Eric knew *that* wasn't true. He was torn between what it meant: was this something like the dreams Lotte experienced, or just a normal nightmare from the stress of this incredibly strange situation? He'd check with her tomorrow, but either way, it wasn't good.

If it were "normal," he wondered how this dream would fulfill his wish like Freud said it would. Did he secretly want to be decapitated in his sleep by a monster? He doubted it, though maybe, somewhere deep in this unconscious *id* thing Freud talked about, he did. Perhaps this was all an expression of his feelings of self-doubt and inferiority. He doubted that too, though. In the end, you couldn't really expect a psychological theory to account for the existence of real monsters—the kind that ripped at your legs.

After a time of sitting in silence with his father, he felt the tug of tiredness on his eyes.

"I'm gonna try to sleep again," he said with as much of a smile as he could muster. "Just ignore me if you hear that kind of yak-honk noise I was making. What the hell was *that*?"

His dad laughed. "Yeah, that was interesting. Get some sleep, kiddo. We're right in the next room, and we'll be here if you need us... yak noise or not."

"Thanks, Dad" he replied.

Thanks, Dad.

CHAPTER 16

As anticipated, morning arrived with all the joy of a bout of food poisoning.

Eric had somehow managed to get back to sleep, but it had been fitful and sporadic at best. Now his legs throbbed, and he felt less rested than he had when he went to bed.

He also had to pee badly.

He rushed to the bathroom — if rushing were possible in his current condition — but someone, almost surely Lotte, was in there showering. He snuck in and used the bathroom in his parents' room, finding ibuprofen and more Band-Aids in the medicine cabinet. He took both, calculating that he'd be needing them. He walked downstairs figuring he'd eat breakfast while Lotte finished up, then he'd grab a shower.

"How are you feeling, honey?" his mom asked as he sat at the kitchen table. "You gave us quite a scare last night. We thought a burglar had triggered the alarm."

His dad looked up from the morning paper, which he flipped through while finishing his coffee.

"Awful," Eric somberly replied. In truth, he felt like asking if he could stay home. If he did, however, he wouldn't be going with Lotte to see Dr. Esfahani after school, so he needed to suck it up. "I'll be okay. I just need some food."

His dad left for work, and his mom started dishing out eggs, bacon, and toast, an unusual surprise for a weekday.

Probably for Lotte's benefit.

At that moment, she came into the kitchen. She was back in "school mode," with black lipstick and black squiggly un-eyebrows accenting her porcelain skin.

Better than no eyebrows at all. Yeesh.

The scary-black circles under her eyes were as scary and black as ever, but she sat next to him and gave him an encouraging touch on the arm.

"Bad dreams?" she asked.

He leaned over and whispered his reply. "The worst. I've never experienced anything like that. I saw the monster. It attacked me! I thought I was gonna freaking die. Is this what you've been going through all this time?"

She scowled and shook her head. "No, I don't see the beast. I feel its presence—its yearning and frustration. I hear its voice or feel its emotions, but until it manifested in my room, I'd never seen its face. It could be different for you... or maybe you just had a nightmare. I can't say."

His mom brought a plate for Lotte and smiled. "Anything else, honey?" She stared as she waited for an answer, still acclimating to Lotte's "goth" look, which she'd never seen in person.

"No, Mrs. Schneider, this is wonderful. You're too kind."

"What about you?" he whispered as his mom went to the sink to rinse some dishes. "Could you sleep?"

"No, it's getting worse. It used to be that when I was out of my room, away from the mirror, the dreams weren't as intense. Now, ever since we discovered the hidden items in the wardrobe, it's like the creature has *found* me. It tormented me in the hospital when I tried to sleep, desperate for me to let it out. It was the same last night. It knows, Eric. It knows I can do it... and it won't let me rest until it gets what it wants."

There wasn't much more to say, so they quietly finished their breakfast. One way or another, this had to end soon.

Eric's mom drove them to school, which he thought was super-nice.

"We're gonna take Lotte's bus home and stop by her place for a while," he told her. "We'll be home a little later and see if Mr. Schwarz can have visitors."

"Call the hospital from Lotte's house," his mom replied. "I can swing by and get you. We can all leave from there."

"Good idea, Mom! Thanks for trucking us around everywhere. I really appreciate it."

"You're welcome, honey. Tonight, though, you and Lotte will need to focus on some homework. Okay?"

"Totally!" he said, as he closed the door and joined Lotte on the sidewalk. They both waved as his mother drove away in her little Civic.

School was horrible, even more-so than normal, and that was saying something. During C period, they slept in two of the retro-comfy egg-shaped chairs in the library. They didn't dare go into the book stacks for fear they'd never hear the bell and wake up. Even with that, Eric still caught himself drifting off several times in class later that afternoon.

Mercifully, he didn't have German class today. At least he didn't have to worry about Mr. Meier calling on him. In truth, though, he'd been doing better in that class of late, and even his teacher seemed pleased — not perfect by any means, but progress for sure.

Thanks, Lotte.

At the end of the day, they met at the E bus and rode home, ignoring the stolen glances and whispered conversations of the other kids as they sat together near the back of the bus. A month ago, this would have felt like a kind of death to him, something from which there could be no recovery, no redemption. Now, honestly, he didn't give a shit, and it wasn't just because he was too tired to care.

The bus stopped near the end of Holton Hill Road, and they walked together along the beautifully manicured pavement. It was getting cooler, but not exactly cold yet. She still wore her scary-cool studded leather jacket, but had opted for a heavier, ribbed, black mock-turtleneck top instead of a weirdo band t-shirt.

Fine with me. Beats the hell out of staring at that ugly dude with the mole. I'll take the pain in my legs over having to look at him. Yeesh!

They reached the driveway of 246, where the black panther Mercedes hadn't stirred from its seemingly endless cat-like slumber. Dr. Esfahani's gray Nissan Sentra was nowhere to be seen. She either wasn't there, or had heeded their advice about not parking at the house.

Lotte went to the door, inserted her key, and they entered.

"*Hallo!*" she called out. "Dr. Esfahani, are you here?"

"I'm up here," came her reply, probably from Mr. Schwarz's bedroom.

They ascended the stairs and turned left.

Dr. Esfahani stood near Lotte's father's bed. On it were spread several of the leather-bound journals. It appeared she'd moved most of the contents from the closet to the floor of the bedroom. The accordion files, arranged in much the same order Lotte had put them in, still had their typed indices sitting on top. The remaining journals sat on the floor at the side of the bed.

She wore a long blouse with tight pants, all in beige hues. Her feet were bare, and she'd removed her *hijab*, revealing her wavy black hair. She smiled and extended a coffee mug toward them as they approached.

"Look!" She beamed. "It's safe to make tea! I watched carefully the first few times for any sign of the cloud, but nothing happened. I think you got it all, or so much that no creature can form from what little remains."

Eric and Lotte exchanged a relieved look. Hopefully, that was one less thing to worry about.

"Good thing, too," she continued. "I couldn't manage all this without my tea."

They all smiled.

"Come," she said, picking up a notebook from among the journals on the bed. "Let's sit in your beautiful living room, and I'll fill you in on what I've discovered."

Everyone filed downstairs. Eric's legs moved a little better, likely aided by all the ibuprofen he'd pounded, but he needed to change his bandages before they left for the hospital, which he found somewhat ironic. They all sat on the couches near the big glass wall to take advantage of what remained of the daylight.

"So, Lotte," Dr. Esfahani began. "Your grandmother was a remarkable woman. I see where you and your mother inherited that keen intellect and courageous spirit. She was there every step of the way with your grandfather, as knowledgeable in her own way about the artifacts and history of the *Sadat Alnaar* as he was. You know they attempted the ritual, yes?"

"I know that's what they planned. The last of the files seemed to end just as they were awaiting delivery of the wardrobe, so I don't know if they tried it or not."

"They did. It's detailed in your grandmother's journals, which I've spent much of my time reading. They've taught me a great deal. The first journal describes what happened. It was probably written during the voyage home from Morocco to England, and is most illuminating. They had the wardrobe built to disguise the secretly uncovered treasures, but it was constructed in such a way that the ritual could easily be performed, as you discovered."

Lotte nodded.

"As the rings of *Alkuartiz Alnaar* had been uncovered, they purchased a fine gold ring and a gold bracelet, which they bent to the size of the larger rings you saw in the museum. Gold was used by the *Sadat Alnaar* before they gained access to the Fire Quartz. For your grandparents, this would have to suffice. Your grandfather wore the ring and sat at the apex of the black marble board. Like you, they used candles to heat the frame and the bowls."

Eric and Lotte sat in rapt attention.

"Your grandmother describes the monster coming forth, solidifying over the flame of the large bowl, exactly as you described. They waited until it was fully formed. It stood nearly seven feet tall on the marble platform of the wardrobe. Its muscular bulk towered above your grandfather. Slowly, the creature's thoughts came into their minds. It had been trapped for an eternity and was angry—confused. It felt it had been betrayed. It seemed ecstatic to be released and yearned for its freedom. It said it wanted to bargain."

Bargain. Eric couldn't imagine the frenzied beast he wrestled with on the floor being capable of managing an intelligent thought, let alone honoring some sort of deal.

"Your grandfather extended the bent bracelet toward the creature. It would have fit its clawed finger almost perfectly, but as he came within an inch of the beast's talon, the monster shot out its arm and grabbed him! *'We do not bargain with the likes of you,'* it shouted, and your grandmother watched as the monster snapped your grandfather's neck!"

Lotte gasped in horror. "I thought my grandfather drowned!"

"That's what your grandmother told the police, and your mother, because she was certain no one would ever discover the truth. She describes how the beast then picked up your grandfather's dead body and held it over the flames on the board. They roared with unnatural strength. The body ignited and burned, sending smoke billowing into the room... but this, the monster absorbed. Likewise, the ash of the flesh and bones as they began to incinerate. Soon all trace of your grandfather's body was gone... his essence merged or assimilated in some way with that of the monster. Only the gold ring that had fallen to the floor near the discarded bracelet remained."

They all sat silently as that sunk in. In addition to its other powers, it seemed this creature could also manipulate fire. A dangerous situation suddenly seemed even more deadly.

"Your grandmother was in shock... immobilized... but she came out of it when the creature turned its attention to her. It stepped down from the wardrobe and approached, sniffing at her with its flattened snout and running its talons just above the surface of her face. She was terrified, but it spoke with a gentle tone. *'You freed us from our prison and brought us spoils. Will you honor us now and let us return home?'* Not knowing what else to say, your grandmother replied that she would. The beast walked back near the board and pointed its talons toward the ground. *'Relight the flames,'* it cried, *'and then... let the rings bind our pact!'"*

One ring to rule them all. Except this is two rings. Hmmmm. Two rings to... oh, never mind.

"Your grandmother put more candles in the bowls and lit them. Then she picked up the rings, put your grandfather's on, and placed the larger ring on the monster's claw. 'Go free,' she commanded. 'Return to your world! I release you from all bonds, all obligations. You are free to go. Free!' With that the creature howled in triumph. The flames on the board again roared, and over them the beast started to dissolve into shining black ash that made its way back into the mirror. Soon it had disappeared, and your grandmother stood alone in the room."

"But I don't understand," Lotte said in bewilderment. "My grandmother set the creature free. She let it return to its world with no obligations here. You can't tell me she summoned the damned thing back to lock it away again. She couldn't have been so mad!"

"No, Lotte, nothing like that. In her journal, she records that the next night, she started having dreams—nightmares of the beast screaming in horror and betrayal, claiming the bargain hadn't been fulfilled, and begging to be let free because it again found itself trapped in its prison. She had no idea what to do. The dreams plagued her each night, even on the ship back to England when the wardrobe was packed in a crate."

"Just like *my* dreams," Lotte said, wide-eyed.

"Exactly, and your mother's after she found the papers. Your grandmother describes crying in front of the mirror, promising the pathetic beast that she would try to set it free and begging for patience. Then, in her dreams, she felt that the creature's anger had lessened, but that it still demanded to be released. I think this demonstrates that the monster can see out from the mirror. It watches what we do! Later, when it saw your mother with the papers, it probably found hope that it had long ago abandoned and started haunting her. Lotte, did you ever see the papers before your mother died?"

"Yes," she recalled with dread. "I walked in on her one day in her bedroom not long after she'd found them. She had the papers out on the bed and on the floor. Now that I think of it, the boxes with the bowls were there as well, all right in front of the wardrobe. She was so cross with me. So cross...."

Dr. Esfahani reached out and put a hand on her knee. "Sweet child, this is why the dreams started after your mother died, especially after you put the wardrobe in your room and the creature could see who you were and that you were still there."

"So," Eric somewhat hesitantly interjected. "I guess we can assume Lotte's grandmother never figured out how to free the thing?"

"That's right, Eric. In fairness, she tried. Other than raising Alice, Lotte's mother, it seemed to be her sole obsession. She researched many possibilities and already had a head-start, as she and Lotte's grandfather had been hunting this creature for nearly a decade. Years before the digs began, they'd purchased documents on the black market in Amman, Jordan—probably from someone who thought they were forgeries or didn't know what they were. They were written in the eighth century, not long after the Battle of Tours. They spoke of the *Sadat Alnaar*, mentioning the places where their sanctuaries were located during the period of Arab expansion. This is how your grandfather was able to track them. Those documents are in one of the earliest folders, but they're very fragile, and I haven't handled them."

She rapidly flipped through her notebook to another section. "These documents also purported to tell of what the *Sadat Alnaar* were up to with their rituals. They were summoners who claimed to be in contact with the Afrit of the Jinn, an otherworldly creature allegedly formed of smoke and fire. There are many myths about it. One claims the being preys on women, but I think this may be a misunderstanding, or perhaps even a deliberate inversion of the truth. It's males the creature seems to detest. The beast is depicted as being all black with deformities like clawed hands, horns, and the like. It's not always considered to be evil, but the tasks it's sent to execute usually involve violence and often blood vengeance. The creature is said to be compelled to perform these orders by a sorcerer, who seals the bond using a magical ring."

She looked up from her notebook as Lotte and Eric gaped wordlessly. The monster had a name. Eric felt certain he'd heard it before in some video game he'd played—maybe Final Fantasy on one of his friends' PlayStations? The beast they confronted, however, was no game. There were no extra lives or do-overs in this situation. If they made a wrong turn, they got obliterated. It would just be... *game over*.

"So, your grandmother knew what she was researching," Dr. Esfahani continued, "but other than myths, there was no information—no clue as to how a ritual could imprison an Afrit or unlock its prison door—and without that information, she was terrified to bring it back into our world. Years went by and the dreams continued, haunting her and depriving her of sleep. Your grandmother turned to sleeping pills more and more as time went by. She considered destroying the mirror, as both you and your mother did... but like you, Lotte, she feared it might not make the dreams go away. Almost ten years went by in this manner, and the journals become ever more desperate and tragic. Her focus and energy steadily drained away, sapped by the pills and the insomnia. In your mother's final year of university, your grandmother wrote of hiding the papers away in the wardrobe in anticipation of a visit at holiday time. It was her final entry. I think she died that night of an overdose."

"And there the papers stayed," Lotte said. "Until my mother found them. How awful."

She sat in silence for a moment, then a grim look appeared on her face. "Maybe it's right to destroy the wardrobe. Maybe my life isn't so important. What if I go mad and kill myself? So what? If it's so impossible to free this bloody *Afrit* from its prison, and it's too dangerous to risk letting the damn thing go free, then how do we break this quite insane cycle? How many more have to suffer in this way? Where does it end?"

Eric flinched hearing her talk about essentially killing herself, but he realized it was getting to the point where if a solution couldn't be found, something had to give. He couldn't bear to think about it. Just when someone came along that made school and life more tolerable, and even fun at times—except for stupid geometry; *nothing* made *that* fun—there seemed to be a serious chance that it would all disappear.

It reinforced how much she'd started to mean to him, and how hurt he'd be if she were taken away. Eric had a lot of his father in him, and it took quite a bit to make him angry. This made him angry.

"Lotte's right!" he said, with a little more intensity than he'd intended. "Sorry, didn't mean to shout. It's just, how do I say it? It's all fine to understand this history and everything, but what are we gonna, like... *do*? How does all this help us?"

Dr. Esfahani smiled. "An excellent question, Eric. Let me propose an answer."

They both leaned closer as she spoke.

"Your grandmother was a smart and capable woman, but she was neither a historian nor a scientist. She knew what she knew, but her thinking was limited to the myths and information she and your grandfather collected about the Afrit and the *Sadat Alnaar*. All the while, I believe the answer might have been staring her right in the face."

"The mirror," Lotte exclaimed, catching the allusion, "but I don't understand how."

"Exactly. Glass mirrors weren't put into common use until the nineteenth century. Your grandmother never considered this. In the first century AD, the Roman author Pliny the Elder suggested the use of glass mirrors, but they never came into general use at the time. It's possible that the knowledge of how to make them, like so much other information, passed into the east with the fall of the Roman Empire and the closing of the western mind—what is colloquially known as the *Dark Ages*."

Lotte would have been right at home.

"But even if a scenario like that had unfolded, the *Sadat Alnaar* likely wouldn't have had access to them. Their frames didn't hold mirrors. I think they were clear glass—precious, especially in that size, but not a mirror, which would have been incredibly rare."

"So, what happened?" Lotte asked, entranced. "Why is there a mirror there now?"

"Given what we know of this beast's behavior, I believe that the *Sadat Alnaar* were all women. They somehow received Muhammed's blessing when Islam spread through what is now Jordan. He was very open to women and was not threatened by their power, especially once they converted, which no doubt they did. The *Sadat Alnaar* accompanied the armies of Islam as they spread west through Egypt and across North Africa. They likely summoned the Afrit and commanded it to kill key enemies before battles. The Afrit took the bodies as *spoils*, thus fulfilling the bargain. For a hundred years or more, they served the Caliphs during this great period, but then... something went wrong. The spread of Islam stagnated in Iberia, and in 732, the Battle of Tours in France permanently ended expansion into Europe. Why?"

Lotte shrugged, but it suddenly dawned on Eric. "The idiots stopped using their special power. Anyone who plays video games knows you use your special power when the chips are down." He didn't know much, but he knew this with perfect clarity.

Dr. Esfahani smiled. "Exactly! Over those hundred and thirty years, Islam changed dramatically. Arabs from the desert encountered great civilizations like Byzantium, Egypt, and eventually former parts of the Roman world. Despite the powerful strength of their religion, they changed as a result of this exposure. This was particularly true in their attitudes toward women. They started treating them more like the Greeks, keeping them separate and veiled. As time when on, the Caliphs may have become suspicious of the *Sadat Alnaar*, covetous of their power, and mistrustful of the creatures they summoned, who were increasingly thought to be ungodly."

Not without justification, Eric thought, rubbing his sore legs.

"I think the *Sadat Alnaar* were forced to imprison the Afrit. Those in power didn't want it simply banished, potentially to return again. They wanted it locked away, forever. Though perhaps they too hedged their bets and left it safely hidden, in case they changed their minds. Perhaps this is why everything was buried. I don't know for sure. I also don't know how they figured out that a mirror might trap it, but I'm convinced they converted the glass in the frame you now possess to a reflective surface, and that created the prison that now holds the beast, as it has for thirteen hundred years."

"But isn't there more than one Afrit?" Eric asked. "It keeps saying *we* this and *us* that. If they lock one up, why couldn't the *Sadat Alnaar* have just summoned another one?"

"A valid question. Were I to guess, I think the Afrit refers to itself this way because it's a composite of many beings. Its appearance may be the result of absorbing many types of animals in our world, including humans. Look at how a part of it split off and became a separate entity, complete but smaller. If that part had the chance, it would likely reunite with the whole, or at least have the capacity to do so. I think it's probable that the creature exists mostly as one being. In any case, it appears no other Afrits were summoned. Excluded from using the Fire Quartz, the *Sadat Alnaar* could have returned to their older practices, but they didn't. Perhaps they were all executed, or possibly they knew that the being which they'd bargained with for centuries was now locked away. We'll likely never know for sure."

"So," Lotte slowly ventured after absorbing what had been said. "All we need to do is return the mirror to transparency, and the beast will be free?"

"One thing must happen first," Dr. Esfahani replied in a serious tone. "The Afrit must be let free in our world. It has to pass back through the glass to return to its... well... wherever it came from. So, we must call it forth, and we must make a bargain with it."

Lotte shook her head vehemently. "We can't let it kill someone! I'd sooner die myself."

Please stop saying that.

"Maybe there's another way," Dr. Esfahani said. "There are myths of the beast being sent to lift heavy stones or perform other tasks. Perhaps killing is not the only path, and spoils can come in other forms... but we can't know this without asking, and we can't ask until the Afrit stands before us."

They remained silent for a time.

This would be so awesome if it weren't real... but it is real. He felt a sense of dread, made even worse by the new knowledge he'd learned about the terrible creature. Apparently, it didn't seem to like guys, and the last time he checked, that's what he was.

Lotte finally broke the silence. "So, it's not a question of *if*, but *when*."

"That's right, Lotte, and time is short. Your father, God willing, will be better soon. Who knows how he'll respond to all this? We must act quickly."

"I agree, but we have school, and homework, and visiting my father. Eric's parents are lovely, but they aren't going to just let us disappear for hours on end. They'll get suspicious of what we're doing, probably thinking we're... well... involved."

Eric blushed. He had to admit that the thought had crossed his mind, but all this had just been so complicated, and that constituted one complication too many. Besides, he liked having Lotte as a friend, and he knew adding romance would change what they currently had forever — even more than things had already changed.

"We'll have to sneak out," he emphatically said. "My folks are in bed by ten o'clock. By ten-thirty or eleven, we should be able to slip away. That would give us most of the night. It's a risk, but it seems like the only chance we have."

Lotte stared at him, a slight smile creasing her black-tinted lips. "I'd tell you not to come, to stay away. That way if I'm caught, it's only me who's in trouble... but I know what a pest you'd be. Plus, you occasionally come in handy."

At this, everyone smiled.

"I agree it's the only way. We'll try it tonight. I can't hold out much longer anyway. But wait, we'll need rings."

"Yes, you're right," Dr. Esfahani agreed. "Here, try this on." She removed a ring from her finger and handed it to Lotte. "A bit big. I'll buy one of solid gold that's a bit smaller. Also, a gold bracelet that we can bend to roughly the size of the larger rings in the museum. I have plenty of time to find them if I leave now. We'll meet back here at around eleven tonight."

"Get more candles as well," Lotte added. "The hotter the flame, the hotter the frame and bowls became. That seemed to summon the beast more quickly, and we can't spend hours at it like I did before."

"Then it's agreed." Dr. Esfahani gazed one after the other into their eyes. "Tonight, around, say, 11:15?"

They nodded, and the plan was settled. Lotte called the hospital while Eric accompanied Dr. Esfahani out after she'd gathered her things from upstairs. She again wore her *hijab,* and as she fastened her shoes in the Mud *Château,* he asked, "Why do you think this Afrit thing looks like the fucking Devil? Umm, pardon my French."

She laughed. "It's all right, I'm used to it. My brothers swear like drunken sailors—no manners at all. We all grew up in the United States. Our parents emigrated from Iran, sensing, perhaps, the troubles my country would go through. It's a good question you ask. To answer, I'd almost turn it on its head. Why does the Devil look like the Afrit? If I were to guess, I think the beast had been seen over the centuries that the *Sadat Alnaar* called it forth. The word 'Afrit' may derive from the Middle Persian *afritan,* which means *to create.* If this is true, it could date myths of the creature to nearly five hundred BC."

He did the math. That was like two thousand five hundred years ago.

Didn't need geometry for that, ha!

"It's possible the *Sadat Alnaar* worked for the Parthian Empire who resisted Rome, and later Byzantium. Roman soldiers who saw the creature carrying out its terrible missions may have brought their descriptions back with them when they returned west. There, they later influenced Christian depictions of Satan or demons. This, or some scenario like this, is my guess."

That satisfied Eric, who didn't know half of what she was talking about, but he found it a heck of a lot more interesting than playing clarinet or stupid geometry. He opened the door and escorted her out, but was surprised to see her take a sharp left and head for the yard near the kitchen side of the house.

"Where are you going?"

"Oh, umm... I must have forgotten to tell you. I moved my car. I didn't think it would look right leaving it in that little parking area—too many prying eyes."

So, you're getting familiar with Southby, eh? He internally rolled his eyes.

"Also, I'm not sure how it might look if a woman wearing a *hijab* were seen walking regularly in this neighborhood."

Southby strikes again, he thought, though he doubted she would encounter any real issues in this ritzy part of town.

"In any case, I parked it on the grass near the side of the house, where it's out of sight. I hope that's all right."

It was all right with him. It wasn't his lawn.

He watched as she carefully backed out into the driveway and then waved as she drove off down Holton Hill Road. He giggled to himself as he walked back inside. If his parents caught him sneaking out, now he'd have the perfect excuse.

The Devil made me do it!

CHAPTER 17

Mr. Schwarz remained in the ICU, so Eric and his mom waited while Lotte visited. The waiting area appeared much the same as yesterday, but he didn't see the slothful receptionist that had frustrated his father.

Maybe she only works on weekends, or maybe they got smart and transferred her to the morgue.

Both he and Lotte had fallen asleep in the car on the way over. A twenty-minute nap had helped, but he still had trouble keeping his eyes open.

How has she managed feeling this way for... what... more than two years? He still couldn't believe it. *I'd shave off my eyebrows too. Hell, I'd shave off my whole head.*

She wasn't too long with her father. The heavy pain medication caused him to tire easily, but she told them that he felt better, and it looked like they'd be moving him out of intensive care as soon as tomorrow if things continued to improve.

"Does he, like, remember anything?" he asked as they walked back to the car.

"*Gott sei dank*, no, but he's starting to ask questions, and I'm worried that as he thinks about it, more will begin to return to him. This has to work. We're running out of time."

Eric agreed, but there wasn't much to be done about it. He already had tonight's escape largely planned out. The only real problem would be the damned alarm system, which made a loud chirping noise when you turned it off, and beeped for like thirty seconds when you turned it on. He didn't want that to wake up his parents, and he hadn't quite figured out a solution for this particular conundrum.

On the way home, he noticed that his mom took an odd route, getting off the main road far too early. Soon, she pulled the car over and put it in park, the engine still running.

"So?" she asked over her shoulder in a somewhat serious tone.

Eric's heart began to race. *So, what? What is she asking? Does she suspect something? Did she overhear Lotte and me talking? Does she know we plan to sneak out tonight?*

When he didn't reply, his mother broke the silence. "So, you want to drive the rest of the way home? It's all back roads until we hit Pleasant Street, and traffic isn't bad this time of day. I think you're ready."

Holy crap! He breathed a sigh of relief, happily jumped out of the car, and got behind the wheel. His mom rode shotgun while Lotte leaned over the seats to watch the action. He pulled the car into the road, and soon they were under way.

"Watch the speed there, mister," his mom gently warned. The limit was thirty-five. He looked at the speedometer and saw he'd exceeded forty. *Oops.* He eased off on the gas.

"Check that rear-view mirror," she reminded him. "Always keep an eye on what's around you." He complied. The road was clear, this being a quiet street.

His mom directed him where to turn as they wound through some unfamiliar residential neighborhoods. Soon they came to Pleasant Street, where they had to make a left. "Pull out enough so you can see both ways, but not so much that you're in the road," she instructed.

He looked right, then left, then right again. A few cars passed by.

"Look clear?"

"Looks clear to me," his mom replied, so he pulled out onto Pleasant Street. Again, he caught himself going a little too fast, but his mom said, "Good, honey," when he slowed down.

A car pulled out from a side street in front of them. They rapidly caught up as it moved so slowly, fifteen miles per hour slower than the forty-five mile per hour speed limit on Pleasant. All he could see were two bony hands clutching the top of the steering wheel—obviously, some little old lady.

Ugh, dead people move faster than this! He made sure not to tailgate, though, as that would surely draw a critical comment.

Before they knew it, Rolling Meadows approached on the right. He started his blinker and made a smooth turn. There wasn't really a posted speed in his subdivision, but he figured twenty was good, and his mom seemed to agree. They pulled into the driveway, and he shut off the Civic and handed over the keys.

"Good job, honey," she said with a smile.

Even Lotte was impressed—*woo hoo!*—saying she really needed to start learning as well.

"I'll teach you!" he said with giddy enthusiasm.

"Cool your jets there, mister," his mom warned, but not harshly. "Lotte will learn from adults and from Driver's Ed, just like you. We don't need the blind leading the blind."

He nodded as they all went inside. He hadn't really been serious anyway.

Lotte and Eric focused on homework when they got settled. If they could get it all done before dinner, they'd go to bed early and try to catch some elusive sleep. They didn't quite make it, but after supper they finished up, and by 8:30 they were ready to pack it in. Eric set the alarm by his bed at a low volume and told her to do the same. With luck his parents wouldn't hear the noise. 10:45 would be the time, and they'd meet at the top of the stairs.

Once more, he changed his bandages in the bathroom and took more ibuprofen. His legs were feeling a bit better, and scabs were forming over most of the wounds. He grabbed a couple of towels from the hall closet on the way to his room and laid them on the floor next to his bed, along with some jeans, socks, a long sleeve t-shirt, and his heavy zip-up Boston Bruins hoodie. After crawling into bed, he double checked the alarm on the clock radio and then did a quick survey of the room.

Seeing no monsters, he clicked off the light.

The alarm woke him from a deep sleep. He shut it off and reluctantly dragged himself out of bed. He went to his door, cracked it, and peered out into the dark hallway. He hoped maybe his folks had called it early and were sound asleep by now, but it was what it was at this point—no turning back.

He put on his clothes, grabbed the towels, and crept down the hall toward the stairs.

Lotte emerged from her room right across from his parents' room, but she was super quiet. They might assume she was headed to the bathroom even if they heard her.

Together, they silently navigated the stairs, and stopped in the downstairs foyer.

"Put on your shoes," he whispered. "I'll be right back."

He snuck through the TV room to the sliding door that led to the back deck. There, he took one of the towels and covered the little panel of the alarm. The indicator light glowed red meaning it was armed.

He then crept back to the foyer, put on his Nikes, and draped the other towel around the outer part of the alarm panel at the front door. He couldn't cover it completely because that would hide the number pad, but he hoped the towel would at least dampen the sound somewhat.

This is it!

He punched in the four-digit code. The sound was definitely muted. The towel covered some kind of speaker near the top or side. The unit issued a muffled chirp, and the indicator light turned green. They both stood in silence for a moment, listening for any sign of noise from upstairs.

Nothing.

"Let's go," he whispered, and they quietly opened the door and slipped away.

It was after 11:30 when they arrived at Lotte's house, a little late but not bad, given the givens. The front porch light was on, as were lights in the hallway when they entered.

They walked to the living room, where Dr. Esfahani sat, seemingly as always drinking tea. She wore a similar long blouse and tight pants as earlier, but this time in shades of blue.

She smiled. "You made it! I prayed you would. I can't imagine what we'd do if you were caught."

I'd sit in my room until I was eighteen. My parents would be at least that mad.

"Well," she said. "Shall we go upstairs? I've set everything up. We should be ready to proceed, if you are, Lotte. If it's too much, I'm willing to try the summoning myself. I leave it to you."

Lotte stood motionless for a moment. Eric had certainly never considered this possibility, and seemingly neither had she. Eventually, she took a deep breath and a look of resolve came to her face.

"You're too kind, Dr. Esfahani, but this is my burden to bear. Plus, I feel I already have a connection with the creature through my dreams, which I may be able to exploit. I'm ready — as ready as I *can* be."

"Then come," the woman said, and with that they all ascended the steps.

Dr. Esfahani had opened the hidden compartment, pulled out the black marble board, and arranged all the bowls in their proper places. She'd cut the candles in a similar fashion as Lotte, but had probably used a very sharp knife rather than scissors. The incisions were incredibly clean. Five candles sat in each bowl, with many more nearby, ready for use if needed.

"There's only one thing left to do," she said. "Help me, Eric."

She walked to the brazier table that still sat by the wall and picked up a pair of pliers. She handed them to Eric, then reached into her pocket and produced a gold filigreed bracelet with delicate interlocking circlets.

"It's a shame to ruin it," she said, "but there's no other way." He held the bracelet in the pliers while she carefully bent it, overlapping the ends so that it formed a circle roughly the size of the larger rings in the museum.

"Do the rings actually serve a purpose?" Lotte asked. "I mean, a physical purpose, like the Fire Quartz that amplifies the heat, or are they merely symbolic?"

"I don't know," Dr. Esfahani replied. "There could be something in the conduction of heat from our bodies that helps seal the pact. The *Sadat Alnaar* started using rings made of *Alkuartiz Alnaar* when they gained access to that material. Why, I just don't know."

She paused for a moment to concentrate on bending the bracelet, which was nearly complete. "All I know is that the rings are needed. You might have been incredibly lucky that your father interrupted the summoning you conducted. The creature may have been willing to bargain with you, but had there been no rings to seal the pact, God knows what might have happened."

Lotte went wide-eyed, and Eric gulped. "I hadn't thought of that," she admitted with shock. "That could have been a fatal mistake. I knew I'd miss things, but that was a big one. I'm so glad we called you."

"Oh, child," Dr. Esfahani chided, holding up the bracelet and estimating its size. "We all make mistakes, and who knows what would have resulted. We do the best we can. Focus on that and stay alert. Don't let what might have been distract you from what we must now do."

Lotte composed herself as Dr. Esfahani placed the bracelet on the floor by the black marble board. "Give me your hand," she said to Lotte, producing a normal-size gold ring from her pocket. "A good fit. This will do nicely. So, are we ready?"

Ready as we'll ever be, Eric thought, fifty percent excited and two hundred and fifty percent afraid. *Sounds like good math.*

They turned off all the lights save the overheads, which they dimmed. With matches, they lit the candles. When complete, Eric and Dr. Esfahani stood at the back of the room as Lotte sat at the apex of the marble board and stared into the flames, concentrating on calling the creature. The heat from the frame would somehow activate the mirror to become a portal, and the monster would come through as shining black ash that would assemble over the flames.

They waited and watched. With remarkable speed the frame began to take on a warm glow. The additional candles definitely seemed to hasten the process.

Dr. Esfahani leaned close and whispered in his ear. "I think the other frame shattered while undergoing this activity. Either it got too hot, or it wore down over time, just as the quartz in the museum's bowls did. That *Alkuartiz Alnaar* is not as rich as what we see in Lotte's pieces. It hardly looks like the same material. This is the best of the quartz, and they likely used it all on this frame and those bowls. Incredible."

Suddenly, the mirror began to darken, and a cloudy black mist appeared. At first, it whirled and billowed within the glass, but then it began to emerge, slowly extending a roughly six-inch circular appendage of shining ash toward Lotte.

The column of smoke stopped above the large bowl in the center of the marble board and began to swirl. With alarming speed the visage of the Afrit began to take shape—only a ghost of an outline at first, but soon the details of the face and head came into focus.

"God help us," Dr. Esfahani whispered.

I hope He will, because no cake mixer on Earth is gonna save our asses from a full-sized one of these things once it gets assembled.

The head and shoulders of the Afrit gathered above the flame and ceased rotating, while behind this, the creature's body began to form, anchored by the great cloven hooves which had firmly established themselves on the white marble platform of the wardrobe. Bat-like wings emerged on the beast's back, folded with bony extensions protruding over the goat-like horns on its massive head.

The Afrit had nearly coalesced when it began to speak. Its voice rasped and scraped like rocks being dragged across sand, words spit out as if they were grit expelled from between one's teeth.

It sounded horrid, but once again, in his mind, Eric understood the creature perfectly and felt its anguish.

'So long. Imprisoned we were. Hopeless. Trapped. Why do you torment us so? We serve you! We honor the bargains. Tell us what you want! We will do anything, but let us then go free.'

Hearing this, and being impacted by the direct mental contact, he had the strangest emotion he'd ever experienced—he felt sorry for a monster. He wanted to help it, wanted to let it go.

Now he understood what Lotte went through in her dreams, and why she had this *sense* that the creature wasn't evil. Perhaps she was right. It certainly had a nasty side, as his legs would willingly attest, but there appeared to be more to this thing than just nastiness.

Hey, we all have bad days, right?

As the last of the creature formed on the wardrobe, Lotte stood. The Afrit towered above her, nearly seven feet tall, but her voice resounded fearlessly—almost a cry of triumph and command that immediately captured and held the beast's attention.

"We will bargain! You must listen to me and understand. I did not imprison you, and I want you to go free. You know my mind... you've invaded it while I slept for over two years! You know what I say is true."

The creature leaned closer, but didn't speak. It was listening.

"I think we've found a way to set you free, but you can't be inside the mirror while we fix it. I want you to go forth and return here in one day. I command you to stay out of sight! Harm no one! Bide your time and enjoy your freedom in our world for this brief period, then we'll return you to your home. Do we have a bargain?"

The creature straightened and looked down at her, then gazed around the room, briefly taking in both Dr. Esfahani, then Eric, who tried to be very, very small, given that he couldn't really pass for a girl.

'Whole,' the creature said. *'We must be whole... replenish that which is spent as we dally in your realm. Where is the rest of us – that part which was separated when your summoning was not completed? We would not abandon us like this.'*

Huh? It took Eric a minute to get his head around that one—too many *us*'s and *we*'s to keep track of. It seemed the Afrit sought the black cloud which had formed the demonic Mini-Me that had attacked them yesterday.

Well, it's like this, you see... that part of you is now sucked up in a Hoover *that's tied up in heavy-duty trash bags at the back of a dark closet. So, you could say it's sort of indisposed at the moment.* He found that kind of funny, even though this wasn't really a laughing matter. *Shit! I hope this thing can't read minds!*

"We can make you whole!" Lotte cried. "We know what you're talking about. We have it. It's safe, and we'll return it to you when you come back tomorrow. That's the bargain. Do you agree?"

The Afrit stood silently for a time. Eric couldn't read anything in its black, pupil-less eyes. Its wings swayed gently, as if in anticipation of flight. They all seemed to hold their breath as the creature pondered... or did whatever it was doing.

'*We agree*,' the beast finally said, its words resounding in Eric's mind. '*Let the rings bind our pact!*'

Lotte stepped forth and held out the bent bracelet. The Afrit extended its massive arm and unfolded the three talons on its hand. She reached out and placed it on one of the claws. It seemed a bit loose, but the creature flexed its skin, which rippled and then expanded slightly so the ersatz ring fit snugly.

"Follow me," she said, and started toward the door.

The beast went forth, surprisingly dexterous for its somewhat clumsy appearance. It stopped as it passed by Eric, and brought its massive head within a few inches of his right ear.

He heard the snuffling of the beast's snout as it sampled the air, and could see the terrible barbed tail, long enough to run him through, slowly snaking toward his abdomen.

The creature emitted a low growl, and Eric started to tremble.

"Come!" Lotte screamed from the hallway. "Leave him be! Honor your pact!"

The monster chuffed loudly and Eric jumped, but then it turned and navigated itself into the hallway. Eric and Dr. Esfahani peered around the doorway.

Lotte had led the surprisingly compliant creature into Mr. Schwarz's bedroom.

"Shit," Dr. Esfahani cursed as the beast stepped on one of the file folders that still lay on the floor, grinding it into the carpet. "I should have moved them. I didn't anticipate Lotte would take the Afrit this way."

We all make mistakes, Eric thought, recalling her wise words.

Lotte led the Afrit to the glass double doors, which she opened, and then walked out onto the deck.

The creature followed, and Eric and Dr. Esfahani crept to the bedroom door to watch what happened.

"You can fly free from here," she told the beast. "Again, stay out of sight. Approach no one. Harm no one. I'll light a fire here tomorrow night around this time. Come when you see it, and we'll take you back to the mirror. You can reunite with that part of yourself which got separated, and then you'll be free. This I promise."

The Afrit gave a triumphant cry and spread its wings. They beat twice, then thrice, then the creature jumped into the air and lifted away as if being yanked by an invisible rope. Lotte scanned the sky until the monster had apparently gone, then she turned and walked back into the bedroom.

Eric ran to her and grabbed her shoulders. Despite the coolness of the October night air, sweat beaded on her forehead. Her squiggly black un-eyebrows, which she must have painted on in the darkness of her room, ran slightly above her eyes.

"You okay?" he asked, squeezing her arms.

"I think so," she answered, with bewilderment and relief. "But now, we have a problem."

"What?"

"How the hell do we get the silver backing off that mirror?"

CHAPTER 18

Apparently, Google actually *was* your friend, as was this new thing called YouTube. A quick search on Lotte's laptop revealed a video on how to use one of several stripping products to remove backing material on a mirror, and muriatic acid to get rid of the silvering.

Dr. Esfahani would have more shopping to do. They all hoped these instructions would apply as effectively on mirrors created thirteen-hundred years ago as those made in modern times.

They agreed to meet again after school to get the mirror down, do the stripping, then return it to the wardrobe. Hopefully, that wouldn't take too long. If it did, they'd have to fashion some sort of story to placate Eric's parents.

We'll fall off that bridge when we come to it.

They profusely thanked Dr. Esfahani and rushed home. It was approaching 2:30 a.m. when they reached the door.

Could have been worse.

Carefully and quietly, they went inside and removed their shoes, trying to remember exactly where they'd been when they put them on.

Like my parents are actually going to notice that! Eric suddenly realized, and just tossed his Nikes in the corner. He retrieved the towels covering the alarm panels but didn't bother resetting the alarm — too risky. Instead, he figured he'd get up early and tell his folks he went outside for a walk after having slept for so long.

I wish, he thought sourly. *Actually, with the sleep I got earlier, tomorrow might not suck horribly.* In their socks, they snuck silently upstairs. He watched from his door as Lotte slipped into the guest room. Nothing stirred in the house.

Satisfied, he re-set his alarm clock, undressed, and went to bed.

⚬ ⚬

His mom was surprised to see him when she came downstairs.

"What are *you* doing up?" she asked with that perfectly attuned balance of curiosity and worry.

"Finally slept enough and went out for a walk. We'll probably crash hard again tonight, though." *Good setup for another early evening,* he shrewdly thought.

He helped his mom make breakfast, which left her both overjoyed and completely befuddled. Her tuner couldn't dial in the proper frequency, so she varied wildly between extremes of happiness and confusion. It made him laugh; he liked being a little unpredictable.

His dad came down and they all ate breakfast together.

"Patriots are playing the Broncos next Sunday," his dad said. "If Lotte's still here, maybe she'd like to watch the game. You can teach her about American football."

"Yeah, if we're still alive next Monday," Eric muttered under his breath.

"What? I didn't catch that."

He flashed a stupid grin. "I said, *great idea*! Lotte's really into *Fußball* — says she used to play in school back in Germany. I'm trying to get her to join the girls' soccer team, but she's... well... she's not into it right now."

They talked about normal things, making small talk for few minutes, all as if the world might not end within the next twenty-four hours.

It's just so fucking normal. *Just what I need right now.*

Dad finally had to leave for work. This was about when Lotte would be coming down, so Eric bussed his dishes and headed up, expecting the bathroom to be open. It was, so he showered, changed his bandages, and went back to his room to get dressed.

"Honey," his mother asked when he came downstairs. "Is Lotte coming down for breakfast? I haven't seen her."

Come to think of it, neither had he, and the tub had been dry when he started the shower. She hadn't been in there at all.

"Hold on, I'll go check on her." He rushed away, taking the stairs two at a time.

He ran up to her door and knocked. "Lotte, you in there?"

Nothing.

"Lotte?" He knocked a little louder.

Still nothing.

"Lotte, I'm coming in!" he said a bit more loudly. He swung open the door, not certain what he expected to see.

What he saw was... curious.

She lay on her side with her back toward the door. The blankets were pulled tight, and she didn't appear to be moving.

"Lotte?" He walked toward her bed.

"Lotte?" He sat beside her.

"Lotte?" He gently shook her shoulder.

She stirred, stretching her legs and then her shoulders. She looked around and saw him, and seemed momentarily confused. Then she rolled on her back and gazed at the ceiling. She had that "no eyebrow" look, which he found unnerving.

I so want to take a Sharpie and draw on some squiggles.

"*Alter!* Eric." Her voice was still thick with sleep. "No dreams! For the first time in... well... I can't even remember when... no dreams. I slept! Finally, after two years of this damn *torture*, I actually slept!"

She literally started to cry—tears of joy and relief and release. She laughed as she cried, and she smiled as she threw her arms around him, and in his embrace she heaved as she cried, and laughed, and cried, and laughed.

"Honey, is everything okay up there?" his mom called from the stairway.

"Yeah, Mom! Lotte just overslept. I think she's finally catching up on her sleep."

Lotte laughed, and cried.

The school day went as school days go, painful boredom punctuated by brief moments of panic—the same-old, same-old, occasionally interrupted by some apoplectic melodrama, a seething cauldron of adolescent hormones arranged into little blocks of time between which Homo sapiens, awkwardly and fitfully transitioning from childhood to adulthood, pranced and preened to shape and reshape the social hierarchy.

What an unnatural state of affairs, Eric marveled, *and to think, some idiots will look back on this as the best time of their lives*. He couldn't wait to be done with it, though Lotte had changed his outlook on that to some degree.

They met at the end of school as they had before and boarded the E bus—fewer stares and comments today. It looked like people were getting used to seeing "the Sour Kraut and What's His Name" riding home together. It wasn't interesting anymore once you got used to it— no shock appeal.

They strode up Holton Hill Road and into Lotte's house, removed their shoes in the Mud *Château*, and hopped down the stairs. Dr. Esfahani stood in the kitchen, making tea of all things. Today she wore jeans and a looser-fitting and heavier, long, multicolored blouse. Bags and a large rectangular box from the hardware store sat on the granite top of the island.

"Do you have a tarp or large cloth somewhere?" she asked after greetings were completed. "This is going to be a messy job."

"I think there's one covering some of the furniture in the garage," Lotte replied. "Eric, come help me."

He followed her to the garage, the one part of the house he guessed he hadn't seen. Sure enough, large white tarps covered the furniture that filled most of the surprisingly modest two-car space. More boxes and discarded packing material took up the rest of the area.

How the heck will they get all this cleaned out? Probably hire someone. Good thing we're clearing all the monsters out of the house.

They had to move a few pieces of furniture, but soon they'd secured two of the tarps, which would easily cover the area they needed to protect. The pair hauled the large coverings back inside, and then went upstairs.

Dr. Esfahani inspected the mirror. "It looks like we just need to loosen these clamps, and the mirror can be pulled down. It's probably quite heavy. I think we should put the tarp on the ground here, so we don't have to carry it far. We'll have to open the windows. The products to remove the silvering will have vapors, but it shouldn't be that hard."

Famous last words.

Surprisingly, it didn't turn out to be that hard. The clamps were beautifully crafted. With a little oil they unscrewed easily. He firmly held the mirror upright as Lotte and Dr. Esfahani removed the last of them, standing on a chair they'd brought up from the dining room.

When it came loose, they carefully walked the mirror down. As anticipated, it was heavy as hell. He found himself shaking as he grasped each side while they steered the mirror's top toward the floor. Eventually, Lotte and Dr. Esfahani provided additional support, and they gently placed it face down on the tarp.

Lotte opened the windows to the cool fall air.

Dr. Esfahani then opened one of the containers of stripper, and they began to apply it with brushes from the shopping bags. They worked in sections, using the pane of glass Dr. Esfahani had purchased, which had been in the rectangular box, to cover each portion once they'd painted it over. This kept the fluid wet while it worked. Then they scraped off the backing material with putty knives, and it peeled up like skimming a knife over a stick of butter.

Once all the backing had been removed, they opened the jar of muriatic acid. This was a dangerous chemical, so they donned gloves that Dr. Esfahani had bought and worked carefully, brushing on the acid and wiping away the residue with strips they cut from the extra tarp. The process didn't take that long, and soon they looked down at a basically clear pane of thick, and very ancient, glass.

"From an archaeologist's perspective," Dr. Esfahani said. "I've just committed blasphemy. Fortunately, no one will ever know."

Or they will, and it won't matter because we'll be toast. Damn, now I'm hungry and want toast.

After a little break, the trio oh-so-carefully hefted the un-mirrored mirror back into place.

"Does it matter that there's a piece of wood right behind it?" Eric asked, breathless from his effort.

Dr. Esfahani pondered for a moment. "I don't think it should. The creature won't actually pass through. By the time its vaporous form reaches the far side of the glass, it should be back in its own world. Nothing will come out on the far side. I'm guessing that it's the reflective property that interfered with this transition and trapped the creature literally *inside* the glass."

Lotte said, "Well, the un-mirror needs to be supported, so I suppose there's nothing for it. We can't risk it slipping on the marble platform, or toppling over and breaking if something happens in the room."

In agreement, they fastened the bronze clamps, then gathered up the tarp with the residue of the backing, along with the cloth strips covered in silvering, and headed downstairs to the garage.

"Shit!" Eric exclaimed as they walked by the hall closet. "We have to get the ash out of that vacuum cleaner and get it ready to be re-assimilated into the Borg Collective."

Lotte and Dr. Esfahani looked at him oddly.

"Never mind. Star Trek reference. We do need to deal with that ash, though."

They finished dumping the materials in the garage, then returned to the hall and faced the closet door with trepidation. Eric cautiously opened it. There sat the dual garbage bags, bulging with the bulk of the *Hoover.* Now that he'd had gotten used to it, he actually liked calling it "The Hoover," almost like it had a name.

Here, boy. Come on, Hoover, boy. Good boy. You want a cookie?

He sighed and said, "What are we gonna do if that ash has reanimated? It'll just fly away."

Lotte considered. "I think we should move the ashes inside the Hoover to the mop bucket and cover it with a trash bag until the creature arrives. The Afrit said that this part of itself wouldn't leave the rest behind. If it flies away while we're making the transfer, it should be attracted by the fire and come back. So, it'll be there when we need it—at least, I hope so."

She went across the hall to fetch the bucket from the mop closet, then to the kitchen to retrieve a couple of new trash bags and a knife.

When she returned, they cut open the outer bag containing the Hoover and discarded it. When they sliced open the second bag, it stunk with sweat, blood, and goo from their dirty clothes. They cautiously pulled out the vacuum cleaner, looking for any sign of the cloud, but nothing appeared.

Lotte gingerly lifted the hatch while Eric stood at the ready with a garbage bag, in case the cloud came out, thinking maybe he could trap it. Once open, only a mass of blackish-grey dust greeted them. The ash from the impish Afrit appeared hopelessly jumbled with the crud of normal vacuuming.

Or Hoovering, *or whatever.*

Lotte lifted the gunk-encrusted bag out of the machine with a distasteful look. Carefully, she transferred it to the mop bucket and started emptying the contents. The dust swirled a bit, but nothing animated. It appeared completely inert.

After they'd wrung all they could from the dusty Hoover bag, they tossed it in one of the garbage bags, along with their stinky clothes, on the out chance those were needed as well. Then they placed the mop bucket delicately inside the other trash bag, closed them both with twist ties, and brought them upstairs. Eric tucked both bags near the large lamp in the corner by the door, where they would be out of the way and hopefully wouldn't get knocked over.

"I think that's that." Dr. Esfahani said. "I'm going to get some sleep. The plan is to meet here again a bit past eleven, right?"

That was right.

Lotte went out on the stone patio and called the hospital.

Eric gathered his backpack, clarinet case, and Lotte's shoulder bag, which they'd dumped in the living room.

"I'll see you tonight," he said to Dr. Esfahani, who stood near the stairs to the hall. "I sure hope my plan for escape works again."

"I do as well," she mildly replied. "You're a bright and capable young man, Eric. I begin to grasp what Lotte sees in you."

He did a double-take. He hadn't really thought about Lotte "seeing" something in him. He didn't actually think there was that much to see, and most of what was even moderately interesting, he figured Lotte had helped put there anyway.

Well... that's not totally true.

He considered that maybe he wasn't *that* empty. Perhaps it just took a spark to get him going. Maybe he was at his best when things didn't go so easily and predictably... when the stakes were higher than just playing a video game where lives were lost without consequence or emotion, other than being a little frustrated that you had to start over.

Eric realized he'd actually done pretty well when the chips were down. He began to see that Lotte trusted him, and obviously her trust was hard won. *She* hadn't made that happen; *he* had, with parts of himself that she'd somehow helped release.

Release.

He thought of the Afrit in its prison, how it yearned to be free and alive... to spread its wings and fly... to return to its home and forge its own future. This is what Eric wanted. He wanted to wake up from this slumber he'd suddenly discovered he'd been in. He wanted to be more than he was—what he knew he had the potential to be. Was it this that Lotte saw? That potential? Something he *could* be, but wasn't yet?

"Thanks, Dr. Esfahani," he finally replied as Lotte came inside.

"Thanks for what?" Lotte asked, slipping her phone into her pocket.

"Nothing, child." Dr. Esfahani came to the rescue. "I'll see you both tonight."

CHAPTER 19

Eric's clock radio emitted its quiet alarm.

It's 10:45 p.m. Do you know where your monsters are?

It would be the same routine as last night—dressing, meeting Lotte at the stairs, covering the alarm panels with towels, slipping out the door, hastily walking to the house on Holton Hill Road. It occurred to him that that would make a good name for a horror movie.

The House on Holton Hill Road: Whatever you do, don't make tea! Bwa ha ha ha!

He wondered if this was what they called "the laughter of the damned?" They'd done all the thinking and planning they could, but nervous anticipation still ran through every fiber of his being.

Whatever. Time to get dressed.

They slipped away as smoothly as they had previously; his parents were creatures of habit.

Nuclear clocks must sync to their routines to display the correct time.

He thought about his mom and dad as he and Lotte walked in the chilly night air. If something happened and he didn't make it, how would they feel?

Pretty bad. Mom, especially. She pretty much put her whole life on hold to raise me.

His family was fortunate to possess the financial means for her not to have to work, but nevertheless, she'd made a sacrifice. It never felt that way, though. Like Mr. Schwarz, his mom seemed almost incurably cheerful. Even when she called him "mister," it always had a good-natured undertone, like no matter what happened, you knew she was still your friend—still on your side.

He'd gotten a couple of "misters" on the way home from the hospital earlier that day when she let him drive again, this time on an even larger road. She employed a different teaching method from Lotte's—a much firmer hand, perhaps due to the different circumstances. Still, it felt like a velvet hammer. His mom never lost her cool, and he always had, "Good job, honey," to look forward to at the end.

"You're quiet," Lotte said as they climbed the steep incline on Holton Hill Road.

"Yeah, just thinking."

"Sometimes I'd like to know what goes on in your head. I think there's more there than meets the eye, and I'll bet some of it's a bit naughty."

Busted! Jeez, is this girl in my head.

She laughed. "Oh, don't look so frazzled. I like you because you're a lot like me, not outwardly maybe... well... definitely. But you're sort of a loner. We both kind of go our own way, in our own way. You're also way smarter than you let on. You're just lazy."

Ouch. True, but ouch.

The little scalpel could still find its mark, but the sting continued to bring that soothing feeling of knowing where you stood—no bullshit, no prancing and preening, no pretense. It felt oddly refreshing, even though it wasn't always easy. As he'd learned, however, the easy way wasn't always the best way. Sometimes the struggle was worth it, and you got more at the end.

In a sarcastic English-from-England accent, and with a slight genuflection, he said, "Thank you for your honesty, *Your Royal Highness.*" Secretly, he meant it.

They both laughed.

The laughter of the damned.

Dr. Esfahani sat in the living room drinking tea when Lotte and Eric entered. She still wore her jeans and the long multicolored blouse, and to their surprise also wore sneakers.

"Just in case we have to run," she said, noticing their stares. "I hope it's okay. I normally don't wear shoes in the house."

Fine with me. It's like déjà vu all over again.

Lotte gave him a worried glance, and they both returned to the Mud *Château* to put on their sneakers as well. On the way back, she grabbed his shoulder and led him through the kitchen toward the door near the breakfast nook. They exited onto the small porch that looked out over the narrow side yard, and saw Dr. Esfahani's gray Nissan parked on the lawn near the house, out of sight from the street.

She pointed at a small kettle grill that sat on a low stone wall of the porch. "Help me with this."

He hefted the grill while Lotte rummaged in a kitchen closet for charcoal, lighter fluid, and some newspaper from the recycle bin. They took everything upstairs to Mr. Schwarz's bedroom, opened the double doors to the deck, and went outside.

"Pile up some charcoal and put some paper in as starter," she instructed. "Soak it in lighter fluid but don't light it yet. I'll check with Dr. Esfahani and make sure everything's ready."

He did as he was told, and by the time he'd finished, Lotte and Dr. Esfahani had joined him outside.

"We have everything prepared," Dr. Esfahani said. "Are you both ready?"

They nodded.

Lotte walked to the kettle grill, which sat on the floor of the deck near the railing, lit a match, and tossed it on the charcoal, which burst into flame. They waited, Lotte by the railing, Eric and Dr. Esfahani near the glass doors. The flames danced in the grill, lighting the area with their glow as they all scanned the moonlit night sky.

Without warning, a shape flew overhead. The stars were briefly obscured, and they felt the wind from the creature's wings. The stiff breeze fanned the fire in the grill, which roared with renewed intensity before settling to a bluish hue.

Lotte gazed intently skyward, hands at her sides. If she were afraid, Eric couldn't tell.

His heart pounded. *This is way worse than those freaking nail-biter, down-to-the-wire Super Bowls the Pats always seem to play.*

Again, the beast passed overhead. This time it looped around and landed with uncanny grace, softly lowering its massive body to the floor of the deck. Lotte approached as the Afrit folded its bat-like wings, the bony protrusions ever looming above the creature's horns.

"We're ready," she said, again in her commanding tone. "Come inside and we'll complete our bargain."

The monster watched as she turned and headed for the door. After gazing from left to right, it began to follow.

Eric and Dr. Esfahani scurried away toward Lotte's bedroom. As they passed, he noticed the floor of Mr. Schwarz's room had been cleared.

Well, no more squished file folders, he thought with some amusement.

When they reached the bedroom, he saw that all the candles in the bowls on the board and near the mirror had been lit and burned brightly. The frame already had a slight glow.

Dr. Esfahani pointed at the garbage bags with the imp-Afrit ashes in them. She'd loosened the twist ties but left the bags covering the bucket and other items. "Stand over there," she directed. "Be ready to bring the bucket forward when the time comes."

He thought maybe the Afrit would prefer *she* perform that particular function. Lotte had been able to keep the monster from eviscerating him before, though, so he kept quiet.

Lotte walked slowly into the room and turned toward the door, beckoning the beast to follow. It peered in from the hall, focusing its soulless black eyes briefly on Eric where he stood between the large lamp and the brazier table, which still sat where they'd pushed it near the wall. He held his breath, but the monster soon returned its attention to Lotte as it hunched through the doorway and toward the wardrobe.

Lotte took her position at the apex of the black marble board. The Afrit stopped by her side and lowered its head to meet her gaze. Calmly and confidently, she motioned for the creature to ascend to the white marble platform of the wardrobe. It complied and soon stood in front of the un-mirror, then turned to face back into the room. Light from the candles cast shadows of the ashen monster's demonic form on the wall behind.

'We are here!' The beast's grating and gravelly voice boomed as it spat out its unintelligible words. 'We have honored our part of the bargain. Bring us what is ours!'

Lotte motioned to Eric.

He gulped and lifted the mop bucket with both hands, and carried it carefully across the room.

Don't screw up... don't screw up... don't screw up.

He gingerly laid the precious parcel at her feet, then slowly knelt and pulled back the lip of the trash bag to reveal the ash and dust within.

The Afrit leaned forward to examine the contents. It loomed over him as he crouched behind the bucket, not moving a muscle.

Lotte stepped to the side to give the creature a clear view. "This is what you seek. Take what's yours, and you're free to go."

The beast swayed from side to side. Then it lifted its mighty talons with palms upward over the marble board, and with great force thrust them skyward. The flames of the candles exploded into columns of fire, almost white hot.

Eric could feel the intense heat on his face and hands, but he dared not move—not wanting to call any attention to himself or distract the creature in any way.

Over the flames, the Afrit repeatedly raised its palms upward. It reminded Eric of the Patriots defense encouraging the Gillette Stadium crowd to rise on a big third down conversion. The creature periodically scrutinized the bucket cradled between his knees. For what felt like an eternity, but probably lasted only half a minute, the monster exerted itself over the fire, exhorting the ash to animate and rise.

Soon, however, the flames on the board began to recede, fading to a dim blue before extinguishing altogether. The candles had been completely consumed, though the Fire Quartz in the bowls retained an intense residual radiance.

The beast emitted a horrifying screech, and Eric felt his mind deluged by feelings of anger and betrayal.

'It has no spirit!' the monster howled. 'It is no longer us! It has expired in this dreary place where the Eternal Flame cannot reach it. Like you sad creatures when your short and petty lives end, it is gone. Gone to dust that cannot be revived!'

Another deafening scream of despair filled the room, and the monster fiercely flexed its wings and whipped its barbed tail. 'We are not whole! You have not honored the bargain! We demand spoils! We demand what is rightly ours!'

From the corner of his eye, Eric saw Dr. Esfahani approach from behind and stand beside him where he hunched on the floor.

"Take her!" she cried.

Everyone in the room, the Afrit included, jerked their heads to face her.

"Take her! Take the one with whom you bargained and who failed to fulfill the pact!" She pointed at Lotte.

Lotte's eyes widened as she brought her hands to her mouth in horror. "Dr. Esfahani! What are you saying? What are you doing?"

"I feared it might come to this, child," she replied, with only a hint of regret, "but in a sense, it probably saves me the trouble."

The trouble of what? Eric wondered with increasing alarm.

"You would never have let me take the artifacts," she casually continued. "You would likely never have agreed that, although they could cause great harm in the wrong hands, in the *right* hands they could help reshape the world for good... for peace... dispense with those who sow the seeds of discord and divisiveness... eliminate those whose greed and selfishness enslaves the masses... those who profit from the misery of others and live in ever greater opulence while so much of the world suffers."

The look of terror on Lotte's face vanished. She dropped her hands to her sides and stared at the woman with a cold expression.

"No, I would not!" she spat, the scalpels of her words now double-bladed broad axes of anger and indignance. "Who would make these decisions, and who would stop *them* from in turn becoming exactly the monsters that they topple and murder? This is *not* the way! Too much temptation. Too much power. I won't stand for it! I can't let this madness continue!"

"Sadly, it won't be in your power to stop me. Seize her!" she commanded, turning her attention to the Afrit.

The monster had been standing silent, listening to the heated exchange.

Despite its blank expression, Eric thought the creature actually looked somewhat confused.

Lotte started to retreat, but the beast grabbed her arm in its muscular, claw-like hands. She winced in pain and began to struggle.

Okay, enough of this! Monster or not, I'm getting Lotte free right now! He began to rise to his feet, but felt a hand on his shoulder and the point of a knife at his neck. He sunk back to the ground.

"Easy, Eric," Dr. Esfahani whispered in his ear. "There's nothing you can do, and if you try anything, I'll slit your throat. You'd already be dead, but I'm holding you until I know that your precocious little friend is enough to satisfy the Afrit... and I think it likes to kill its own spoils."

She held a dangerous-looking hunting knife, probably purchased on one of her shopping excursions. She'd likely used it to cut all those candles so cleanly and perfectly — getting used to the weapon's heft in her hand. Then she'd kept it hidden under her long blouse, waiting for the moment it would be needed.

Now, he couldn't so much as move without her driving the razor-sharp blade into his neck.

"You think of everything, don't you?" he grimly said, "except leaving those files on the floor. That kind of sucked for you, didn't it?"

Her grip on his shoulder tightened slightly, and the knife pressed almost imperceptibly deeper into his neck.

"Such a clever boy," she muttered, cool as a cucumber.

The Afrit dragged Lotte toward the marble platform where it had stood when it killed her grandfather almost 45 years before.

"Stop, I command you!" she cried. "There must be another way to fulfill the bargain!"

The beast snorted. *'Our patience is through! We wish to again feel the warmth of the Eternal Flame. No more delays. The time has come!'*

Eric had to think fast. *This thing is about to kill Lotte, and that I will not tolerate. There has to be a way.*

Suddenly, it came to him.

"Take me!" he shouted, ignoring the press of Dr. Esfahani's knife.

"Take me instead! You hate my kind, and in all honesty, I'm getting a little sick of yours. So take me and let her the fuck go!"

The Afrit halted. It glowered at him and issued another low growl, like an alpha wolf facing a challenge to its authority. Then it turned its attention to Dr. Esfahani.

"What do I care?" she said to the creature. "You can have them both as far as I'm concerned. It will save me the trouble of disposing of the bodies. Take your pick."

The beast tugged Lotte close and gazed into her eyes. *'Long have we known you and your ancestors. You failed to free us, but you tried. Your heart beats true. We will not end your short existence if we are not compelled to do so.'*

With that, the Afrit pushed her away.

"No!" she screamed. "Please, no!"

Ignoring her, the creature stepped across the black marble board and reached for Eric where he still crouched on the floor. The beast drew closer, lifted its other foot off the marble platform, and brought its clawed hands to bear, preparing to lift him off the ground.

With the creature's proximity, Dr. Esfahani backed away slightly... and that was all he needed.

He grabbed the mop bucket that still sat between his legs and hurled it over his shoulder, directly in the traitorous woman's face.

Ash and dust spewed everywhere as she staggered backward. Her face and upper body were completely covered in the nasty gunk. She gagged and spit to rid it from her mouth as she batted and flailed banish it from her eyes.

Eric sprang!

He grabbed her wrist and wrestled the knife free. She put up only a minimal struggle, being almost completely blind and utterly inundated with the dust. The weapon fell to the floor.

He tightened his grip and twisted her arm behind her body, then brought his other arm around the struggling woman's neck and held her interposed between himself and the menacing Afrit.

"Lotte!" he shouted. "Get it to back down! Get it off me! You know what to do!"

The monster hesitated, trying to reach past Dr. Esfahani to grab him. Its sinister barbed tail crested the creature's horned head and....

Lotte cried out, "Stop! By the power of the rings that bind our pact, *stop!*"

The beast froze, and slowly gazed over its shoulder.

"To fulfill our bargain, I give you... her!" She pointed at Dr. Esfahani, who still coughed and gagged from the ash and dust that covered her face.

The Afrit again turned to face Eric, its tail twitching above its head.

It's now or never!

He pushed the dazed woman into the monster's clutches.

She struggled as it grabbed her, but she presented no match for its powerful arms and muscular talons. The beast turned toward the wardrobe, but glanced back at Eric with its impenetrable black stare and again chuffed in frustration and disdain. The ashen monster then lifted Dr. Esfahani in its arms and ascended once more to the white marble platform.

She writhed and thrashed, but the Afrit held her hopelessly ensnared.

"Don't do this, child!" she screamed, her words still muffled from the ash in her mouth. "Please, I beg you! Think of what we can do together, how we can change the world!"

"I *will* change the world!" Lotte said with anger. "I'll teach, and I'll learn. I'll work, and I'll play. I'll travel, and I'll make a home. I'll change the world for having been in it, and if that's not good enough, then so be it! But I will *not* kill for what I want. Except... *once!*"

She waved her arms and yelled at the beast, "Take her! Take her and I'll send you home!"

The horrendous Afrit raised Dr. Esfahani in the air as she cried in terror, but then the creature hesitated. It looked at the black marble board, and then to Lotte.

'Flame. We need flame.'

Shit! Eric remembered the candles had gone out, and now the bowls weren't glowing anymore either. He dashed to the brazier table and fumbled madly to get more candles from the boxes. Only enough remained for three per bowl on the marble board, but it would have to do.

He brought them over to Lotte, and they frantically started placing them. The creature watched in silence, but Dr. Esfahani still violently fought to break free as she pleaded frantically, trying to bargain for her life.

"Please, God, child!" she wailed. "Forgive me! Talk to the creature. There must be another way. You were right! I promise you, I won't use these items. I won't speak of them. You'll never see me again. I swear to you. Oh, God, Lotte, I'm so sorry!"

Why she thinks Lotte would believe anything she says at this point is beyond me. She just tried to kill us both, and basically admitted that she planned to murder us at some point anyway. I guess begging for your life is what you do when you're about to be sacrificed on an altar of fire by a shiny black devil-ass cloud monster.

At this point there seemed to be no going back. The look on Lotte's face confirmed that conclusion to him in no uncertain terms.

When the candles were lit, the Afrit gazed down at them for a moment, then back at Lotte. *'You honor us,'* it said in a gentle tone that washed over Eric's mind with gratitude and contentedness. Then it raised the screaming Dr. Esfahani in the air.

"Oh, child!" she cried.

The beast propelled her body earthward, and her spine shattered across its thigh. Her lifeless eyes gazed out from her soot-black face.

Eric turned away, but saw that Lotte met her eternal stare—not letting it go, even as the flames which now erupted from the marble board behind him consumed the woman's body. He reluctantly listened as her sinew and bone sizzled and snapped in the heat. No ash or smoke escaped the beast as it fed on her essence, but he smelled the burning of flesh. Dr. Esfahani existed no longer, except as energy within the Afrit's supernatural and inexplicable form.

When he dared look again, the creature had dissolved back into black, shimmering ash. It swirled toward the un-mirror and had soon disappeared into its depths.

Eric shook with exhaustion and adrenaline overload. *I don't give shit if this doesn't work. I'm never setting my eyes on that damn thing again.*

They watched until the Afrit had completely vanished. Then the two stood in the silent room, darkened once more by the extinguishing of the candles.

Dark and silent... the creature gone.

Dark and silent... they wordlessly stared.

Dark and silent... like a night with no nightmares.

Dark and silent... like a dream of having no dreams at all.

Their wish fulfilled.

"Well, that didn't exactly go as planned," Eric finally said, breaking the silence that seemed as though it would extend forever.

"No," Lotte replied, shock and bewilderment in her voice. "I can't believe she would do that! I'm stunned. I looked up to her. I respected her. She was our friend — or so I thought. Now I realize she had to have known almost from the beginning that she wanted the mirror for herself. She might have made her decision while she thought so hard over the papers in my closet."

Eric found himself equally stunned. He'd also liked and respected Dr. Esfahani, and couldn't believe she was now gone.

Gone, hmmmmm....

"Hey," he said. "What are we gonna do about Dr. Esfahani being... like... dead and everything? Didn't you email her and call her? Is that shit traceable?"

"*Scheiße!* I hadn't even thought about it. We have to think. What can we do? We only spoke once on the phone, but she texted me. She must have a mobile. Where could that be? We'll need to destroy it."

They nervously hustled to her father's bedroom. Dr. Esfahani's purse and *hijab* sat on the bed.

Lotte rifled through the bag and held up a crumpled piece of paper with writing on it. "My address, and the directions you gave her on Sunday."

She set the paper down and continued to search the purse. "Car keys, wallet, makeup, her ID card for the museum. Lots of receipts for all the things she bought. Except for the jewelry that she purchased, it looks like she paid entirely in cash. That's interesting. No phone. Maybe she had it on her when she was... well... taken."

"Maybe it's in her car."

"*Verdammt!* The car. What are we going to do about her car?"

"I have no idea," he replied, having no idea.

"Wait a minute! You can drive! You can drive it somewhere away from here — leave it by the side of the road, or in the woods. If it's found, they'll think she simply disappeared, which in a sense, I suppose, she did."

"It's got to be far enough away that they don't trace it to us," he dubiously replied, "especially if they find out you emailed her, which they almost definitely will. I'm not sure about the phone and the texting, whether that's traceable too, but there's gonna be questions for sure — then the car being just three blocks down the road? No good."

"Then go more than three blocks. Go miles!"

"Lotte, I have to be able to get home. How can I get home? Take a cab? Hitch a ride?"

She brought her hand to her chin and thought deeply. "The bikes! Take one of our bikes in the car and ride back. Wear gloves so there aren't any fingerprints. Take a cloth to wipe everything down. It could work, Eric. It may be our only chance."

He considered it. *She's right. It might work and it's probably our only chance. I'll drive out toward Webster by Douglas State Forest. That's like ten, maybe twelve miles. I could bike back in probably less than an hour if I push it. Yeah, I'll have to drive alone, but it's the middle of the night. There'll hardly be any cars on the road. I'll take it easy, just like Mom says.*

"Okay, I'll try it," he finally said.

"*Krass!* That's awesome! Let's go search her car." She grabbed the keys from Dr. Esfahani's purse. "We'll see if we can find her phone or anything else that might cause us problems."

They walked out to the Mud *Château*, where she found wool gloves with leather palms for him, and a pair of wool mittens for herself, so they wouldn't leave any prints on the car. Together, they went outside to where the gray Sentra was parked. They opened the doors and searched the interior and glove compartment—nothing incriminating, and still no phone.

"She must have had it on her," Lotte decided. "I can't imagine she'd have left it at home. If she did, then the police won't have much more to go on than the email I sent and the text messages on my phone, which aren't especially suspicious. I suppose it's possible they can also trace that we made a call, but they won't know what we talked about. She doesn't have a navigation system in the car, so no GPS. Maybe. I think. I'm not sure how that works. Hopefully, they can't link anything to us, assuming we can get it far enough away that it would be implausible that either of us could have done it, especially since we didn't have time... or so most would believe."

They went back inside, and Eric grabbed Mr. Schwarz's bike, even though it was a bit large for him. Lotte got some washcloths to clean the inside of the car, which he put in the pockets of his hoodie. Then they returned to the Nissan, pulled the back seats down, and started loading in the bike.

"Wait!" she said. "Let me get some cardboard to put down so the bike doesn't leave any impressions on the fabric. You'll just need to take it with you, ride for a while, and drop it somewhere out of sight."

She fetched an unused moving box from the garage, which they broke down and placed over the trunk and folded down seats.

He then got behind the wheel and sat with one leg out of the open door as he looked at her. "Do we have everything?"

"I think that's all. Wait, a bike helmet!" She ran back inside.

He sat in the car and wondered if what they were doing was wrong. It certainly *felt* wrong, but how were the two of them supposed to explain what they'd been doing with Dr. Esfahani and what happened to her?

Well, you see, there was this monster that came out of a mirror.... Yeah, that'll really go over swimmingly. Not. What choice is there, really?

She came back with the helmet. "Don't take major roads. You want to avoid being seen. Do you need a map? I'll get you a map!"

He was about to say no, but she ran off again.

Man, this girl is a tornado when she gets going. I get tired just watching her run around.

Soon she returned with a map of Central Massachusetts and handed it to him.

He stuck that in the inside pocket of his jacket.

"It's for biking," she said. "It has all kinds of back roads. My father and I found it at a store but hadn't used it yet. We love to bike — did it all the time in Germany before my mother died." At that, she finally fell silent.

"Well, I better get going. It'll be like 3 a.m. or later before I get back."

"Remember what I told you: back roads, wear the gloves, wipe down the car, and don't forget anything in the car, especially the cardboard. Anything else?"

"No," he numbly answered. "I think that about covers it. I'll see you in a couple of hours." He closed the door and started the car, but she banged on the window, her mitten a soft and incessant thump against the glass. He rolled it down with growing impatience.

"One more thing," she said, a serious look on her face.

"What?"

"Thank you for saving my life. You're the best!" She reached into the car and gave him a big hug and a kiss on the cheek.

"*Gute reise!*" she said, flashing a nervous smile.

Safe travels. I sure hope so.

CHAPTER 20

The Eternal Flame warms us, its radiance a balm made only sweeter by our prolonged absence.

In the end, the girl spoke true.

It becomes ever more difficult for us to tell with these peculiar and unpredictable beings. Each marches to the cadence of their own fickle heart, perfidy ever possible, even among the best of them.

Perhaps this is unfair.

Their lives are short and fragile, and their separateness blinds them to the unity we experience. They grope and stumble, lurch and flail to find their way in a universe that is forever beyond their comprehension. Small wonder they make mistakes and commit such cruelties. Small wonder they seek forgiveness when some miniscule ray of realization shines upon them.

Forgiveness. What does it mean?

To dismiss our anger? To put aside our grievances and trust once more? To turn our backs on the vengeance we deserve?

We hold no malice toward the Acolytes or our *Sadat Alnaar.* Like us, they were trapped by the currents of uncontrollable forces. They did not pull the strings; others did.

Others like the woman we took, who completed our bargain and made us whole. With her, the cycle would have begun anew. By her decree, more would have died — as always, the dream of a better world held out as justification.

The girl, however, thought differently.

She sent us home, perchance forever, and for the first time since our association with these beings began, the pattern has changed.

This intrigues us.

In our experience, she is... uncommon. We wonder if truly a new beginning might be possible with one such as her. Time — that oh-so-human concept — will ultimately tell.

So too will time determine if we abandon our rage against he who enslaved us, assuming he yet exists. Never had we detected him in the centuries we harvested power in the mortal realm.

However, he is not of their drab and dreary world. Perhaps that part of us that still lives in him makes discovery by this method impossible, or perhaps his arcana protects him.

Given the opportunity, we would likely seek him—make him pay for his misdeeds. As we have suffered, so he should suffer for changing us—binding us, perhaps irreversibly, to a dimension for which we should have no need.

No. For him, forgiveness may not be an option. For now, however, our fate lies in the girl's hands... and to this, we are not entirely ill-disposed.

Eric drove Dr. Esfahani's gray Nissan Sentra out Route 16 headed west. Nearing Webster, he found a side road that led into the forest. He pulled over, unloaded the bike and the cardboard box, and removed his shoes.

Then he drove the car a bit further, found a spot where he could enter the woods, and drove in as far as he could to keep the Nissan well out of sight. He wiped down the car with the washcloths Lotte had given him and padded back in his socks to the bike, taking the car keys with him.

Hopefully, there would be no prints, no tracks with his shoe marks, no trace he'd ever been there. He shivered in the freezing cold on the way home, even though he pedaled as fast as he could back to Southby. He rode unsteadily for a couple of miles, hindered by the bulky cardboard box, which he ditched into a dumpster next to an auto body shop. He tried to avoid main roads, as Lotte had instructed, but there were only so many routes and only so much time. Fate would determine if someone saw him.

When he arrived back at the house, he found Lotte madly cleaning up.

"Here are the keys," he'd said, out of breath from the ride. "What are we gonna do with them?"

"Give them to me. I'll put them in the garage for now with her other things. I have an idea for later."

Later would have to be another day, since everything had taken longer than anticipated. The pair snuck back home and got in just after 4 a.m. Not wanting to risk messing with the alarms, he just stayed up.

He again surprised his mom when she came down to make breakfast. This time he provided a lot less assistance in the kitchen.

She left him alone, perhaps sensing something wasn't exactly right.

Somehow, he and Lotte struggled through the day, again sleeping through their German session in the library. After school, they took his bus home, and both went straight to bed when they got in.

"Sick," he replied to his mom's worried look. She brought him water and a snack, and he thought he heard her do the same for Lotte in her room down the hall, but nothing could keep him from sleep that afternoon.

They both reluctantly came down for dinner when his mom called them.

"What in the world is wrong with you two?" his dad had asked. "You both look like corpses."

Yes, she has taken me, Father. She has sucked all my blood and now I am one of her kind. Soon we will fly off together to the land of the dead. Bwa ha ha ha!

In reality, he blamed it on some twenty-four-hour thing that had been sweeping through school and said they'd both probably be okay by tomorrow. His parents were skeptical, but what could they say? When the two of them came down for breakfast Thursday morning, all was forgotten.

During their C period German session, they made plans to go to Lotte's house after school and finish cleaning up. She wanted to visit her father first, as she hadn't seen him since Tuesday.

"What are we gonna do about the mirror that isn't a mirror anymore?" he asked. "Maybe we could smash it? That way your father won't see what we did when he gets home."

She appeared pensive. "No, he hardly ever goes in my room, and he's not very observant of things like that. I'll think of something else."

His mom took them to the hospital that afternoon, and they found out Lotte's dad would be released on Saturday. It turned out he didn't need tests in Worcester, as he'd progressed more quickly than expected. He'd even been moved out of the ICU.

"Good thing I landed on my head," Mr. Schwarz chuckled as they all sat in his hospital room. "I really would have hurt something if I'd landed *auf meinem Hintern!*"

Everyone laughed, but Mom leaned over and whispered in his ear, "What does that mean, honey?"

"On his butt, Mom," he quietly replied, figuring it was okay to translate naughty stuff if an adult had said it.

"Oh, but the dreams I've had," Mr. Schwarz moaned.

Lotte and Eric exchanged a furtive glance.

"Horrible nightmares of a hideous black cloud looming over Lotte. It seemed to have a terrible face and roared in anger when I saw it. So real, and so terrifying! I can't get it out of my mind."

"Don't worry, Father," she comforted him. "It was just a nightmare. As you can see, I'm here, and I'm fine. Better than ever, actually." She smiled at Eric.

After the hospital, Eric's mom let him drive all the way to Lotte's house. Traffic was pretty light at mid-afternoon, even on the larger roads she encouraged him to take. She seemed very impressed with his progress.

"Are you getting practice behind my back there, mister?" she'd asked.

He just kept his mouth shut tight, and his eyes glued to the road.

At Lotte's house, they needed to do a number of things to make sure it looked like the place had been empty for a week. In the garage, they carefully wrapped Dr. Esfahani's purse, *hijab*, toiletries, and sundry items from her father's bedroom and bathroom in the dirty tarps they'd used to strip the mirror. Then they stuffed these into garbage bags and put them in the trash bin. Even if a bag happened to split open, the items should remain concealed in the fabric of the tarps.

"Wait a minute," he said. "Where are the knife, and the ring, and the bracelet?"

She'd bristled momentarily, seeming to search her memory for where she'd put them. "Umm... in the purse," she finally responded. "I put them in the purse. That's it. Everything's fine."

So much for that.

They tackled Lotte's room next, and of course the wardrobe had to be moved first. He stared at it for a while before they began.

"How are we gonna get rid of this thing?" he asked. "I mean, obviously not now, but at some point, it will have to be... like... destroyed. Right? Certainly all the stuff in it—the un-mirror, the bowls, all those papers. What are we gonna do?"

"I'm thinking about it," she replied, with a worried and distracted tone. "I'll come up with something."

After that, they worked largely in silence, confirming only who was doing what, or when to, "*eins-zwei-drei*, lift!" Soon, they'd whipped the house back into shape, and then walked wordlessly back to Rolling Meadows.

On Saturday, Eric's dad captained the HMS Suburban to the hospital to pick up Mr. Schwarz. He still wore a neck brace as they wheeled him outside, smiling as always while he rolled toward the great white whale that would swallow him like Jonah and spit him out on the shores of home.

Eric observed Lotte as she smiled in the car. She seemed overjoyed to have her father back. On the other hand, this concluded her visit to *Haus Schneider*, so it was a bittersweet moment for him when they pulled up to the now familiar house at 246 Holton Hill Road.

Despite the brace, Mr. Schwarz could actually move pretty well. Goodbyes were said, great thanks were given, and "don't mention it" was delivered each time in return.

Eric hardly noticed as Lotte gave him a hug and disappeared with her father through the front door. He felt numb.

Late the following week, during C period, she told him the police had visited. She and her father had been questioned by detectives who were investigating the disappearance of Dr. Donya Esfahani. They wanted to know if Lotte could tell them anything, because she'd had an email exchange with her the Sunday before last.

Lotte could tell them a lot, but they'd lock her up for being a criminal or a nut-job – or both. It would be a hell of a story, though.

Lotte related the interrogation in rather matter of fact terms.

"I told them the circumstances of how I met her the day before the email exchange at the museum. I said she'd given me her card and we'd planned to speak further. I explained that when my father got injured, I emailed her. I hadn't expected to talk with her until the next week, but she replied by text with her number right away. So, I called, and we spoke briefly. I told her what happened, and we planned to speak again when things had settled down. That was it."

I sure hope so.

They celebrated Lotte's birthday on Saturday. He went to her house, and her father had cooked another incredible meal. He returned Freud's *Introductory Lectures* and told Mr. Schwarz he'd started *Civilization and its Discontents*. Mr. Schwarz beamed and told Eric he would re-read *Introductory Lectures* so they could discuss it.

Eric gave Lotte her present—a box filled with bags of gummy bears. She loved it.

After dinner, he slipped her a question while they were alone cleaning up. "Have you decided how we're gonna get rid of that wardrobe, or at least all the Afrit summoning stuff?"

Her shoulders slumped as she somewhat curtly replied. "Eric, I'm thinking about it. Be patient. We have time to figure out how to do things properly."

"So, do you think we're in the clear?"

"I don't know," she answered with a dull tone and a somewhat distant look on her face. "It's out of our hands now. They'll either find something in the car that traces them back to us, or they won't. I saw a news report that they suspect it might be a hate crime—anti-Muslim violence."

It was *a hate crime.*

He hated what had happened... what he felt he'd been forced to do. A part of him even wondered if Dr. Esfahani had been right. Maybe there were people in the world who inflicted so much cruelty that they deserved death—to be eliminated—but Lotte had been so sure of herself, so convinced of her position. He didn't have that kind of conviction about anything, so he trusted in his friend and that she knew best. Dr. Esfahani's words, however, still rang in his mind.

He felt angry and confused, and nervous that they could yet be caught. It occurred to him that he would have to live with this for the rest of his life, an unanticipated consequence of agreeing to help Lotte.

Lotte.

He looked to her for support, but after her birthday, she always seemed to be busy—disappearing after school without taking the bus. It didn't appear to be the dreams. The scary black circles under her eyes began to fade, and soon were almost gone. She looked amazing.

She started going with the elegant straight black un-eyebrows, and stopped wearing the Doc Martens in favor of some cute little black high-top walking shoes. It became too cold for the scary-cool studded leather jacket, so she wore a parka that was, of all things, burgundy in color.

Burgundy. The mind boggled. He couldn't believe it.

Neither could anyone else, as Lotte also stopped being *Fraulein Bitchenstein*. She actually started talking with some people, and not just telling them to, "Get the fuck out of my way," either—real conversations.

Kaitlin Shermer sat right beside Lotte in English class, and had been shocked one day when Lotte started asking her questions about the book they were reading, *The Scarlet Letter*. Kaitlin told Eric all about it in German class. She said they'd had a really fun talk and that Lotte was actually super-smart.

Don't I know it. It seemed weird, though, hearing about her talking with other people—so un-Lotte-like.

She continued to tutor him in German during C period, but increasingly this constituted their only real contact. It seemed to be all she wanted or had time for at the moment. That wasn't all *he* wanted, but he realized that for now, maybe that was all he was going to get.

Or maybe that's all I'm ever gonna get.

This worried him, but he assumed it was best to simply focus on the tutoring and exercise his best quality — remaining silent. Like a clarinet abandoned in the woods, he would make the sound of *nothing*. Basically... what he heard again without Lotte in his life.

Nichts.

Actually, that wasn't totally true. Now, Lotte or no Lotte, *nothing* simply wasn't enough anymore. He didn't want to go back to sleep. He wanted more, like that psych class for which he was now on the waiting list, and dropping clarinet, which his teacher said he could do as long as he picked something up to replace it in the spring.

"Sorry to see you go," Mr. Olson said. "The ensemble will miss you."

Yeah, like the Wind Ensemble will miss their fifteenth clarinet chair.

He sure as hell wouldn't miss Wind Ensemble. Even if he didn't get in the psych class, he knew there were better options for him. So, he had to admit, it wasn't all nothing. The wheels were turning in his snarky little brain, and they now seemed to be a body in motion that might stay in motion, at least to some extent.

On the flip-side, there appeared to be little to no motion with the investigation into Dr. Esfahani's disappearance. When he ditched the car, he'd imagined it would be at least days before anyone found it. Before he knew it, over a month passed by, and to his knowledge the gray Nissan still sat in the forest. Even if they located it now, any physical evidence would be pretty old, or so he hoped.

That gave him some ambivalent optimism, but he still missed Lotte terribly. He craved the excitement he'd felt during those tumultuous first weeks, and the intense bond he felt they'd developed. Even beyond dealing with her dreams and the incomprehensible monster that turned out to be their source, he missed the sense of purpose she brought to his life. That sense of *possibility* that she represented.

⚶

Eric had been surprised one morning during their C period German session when Lotte told him she told him she'd be tutoring Kaitlin

Shermer, along with another student in Eric's German class, after school that day. He was equally surprised when she asked if he could join them.

Of course, I can. What else do I have to do?

He met them in the cafeteria when classes ended. They sat at the same table where he and Lotte had met during their first German lesson. He vaguely listened while they went over lessons she'd already covered with him, and wondered why she wanted him there at all.

He felt utterly superfluous. The promise that once existed in their relationship seemed increasingly like the impressions of a dream, fading a bit more with each passing day. Soon, all that would be left would be a ghost of memory, and that lingering sense of *possibility*, never to be realized.

Possibility. Auf Deutsch, *that would be... umm...* möglich. *Actually, that's not right.*

As Kaitlin struggled with a question, he leaned over to Lotte. "Hey, if *möglich* is *possible,* what is *possibility*?"

She smiled. "Look it up, Eric."

Look it up, Eric. Look it up, Eric. Look it up, Eric.

He'd heard that a million times at this point. You'd think he'd get it by now. She wasn't going to give him the answers. He got out his heavy-ass German textbook and looked it up. Remarkably, it was there in the glossary... *möglichkeit.* Possibility.

Thanks, Lotte.

Eventually, the three of them prepared to wrap it up, and he figured he'd text his mom to come get him. He looked forward to driving home, which she let him do now with regularity. He wondered if he should offer Lotte a ride home. She'd probably say no, but it would be rude not to ask. Plus, he hoped she'd say yes.

"Lotte, I'm about to text my mom. You want a ride home?"

She turned to Kaitlin and Mark, told them she'd text them about the next session as this wouldn't be an everyday thing, and said goodbye. Then she looked at him for several seconds, and finally replied, "Why don't you text your mom and tell her we're walking home together... if you want to?"

Want to? Hell, yes, I want to.

In truth, he felt both excited and nervous. He considered any "Lotte time" to be good time, but he had a funny feeling she might have something to say to him—something he might not want to hear. Her manner and recent behavior just hadn't seemed right to him.

For the first time since he'd known her, he wasn't quite sure where he stood. There suddenly seemed to be this distance between them, and it made him extremely uncomfortable. The little scalpels, however, seemed to have been sheathed, at least temporarily.

If she has bad news, I guess I'd better hear it now and get it over with while she's not pissed off. "Sure, let me get my stuff out of my locker and I'll meet you outside."

The weather wasn't bad for November, in the 50s. Lotte didn't seem to mind. Her parka appeared to keep her nice and warm, even if he still couldn't get over the color.

Freaking burgundy. Where did that *come from?*

They reached the cemetery and she made for the entrance. A part of him actually hoped that she'd turn out to be Queen of the Zombies after all. *Maybe being torn limb-from-limb by her undead minions would easier to take than what I'm afraid she's gonna say to me.*

"So," he ventured as innocuously as possible, fishing for a clue as to what this might be all about. "You've been busy lately. Where have you been going after school? I never see you on the E bus anymore."

She remained quiet.

He could tell something was obviously on her mind, but she avoided that for now and eventually answered his question.

"I just walk. I walk home. I walk on the trails behind the house. Eric, it's like a great fog has been lifted. I can see again. I can breathe again. I can sleep again. My mind is clear. It's like I'm getting to know myself again after two years. I'm just trying to adjust, getting used to experiencing the joys in small things — the things I loved to do before the dreams started."

Interesting. After what she's been through, that kind of makes sense. Maybe she just needs some alone time. Maybe I'm overreacting, and things will be okay in a while.

They reached the tree where she'd slept earlier in the fall. Despite the chill, she sat at the base of its trunk and patted the ground next to her for him to do the same.

He sat, and they were silent for a time.

"Eric," she finally said. "I need to tell you something."

Uh-oh. He held his breath.

"I've thought about it. This has been on my mind *a lot*. I've gone back and forth, but now, I've decided." She took his hand in hers and brought her face close. The scent of gummy bears gently touched his nose. "I don't want you to be angry or hate me. I couldn't stand it if you hated me, but I'd have to live with it because I can't do it. I just can't do it, Eric!"

Yep, just what I thought. All this time, I'd been afraid of losing her to a monster. Now I'm losing her anyway. To, what... her newly found sense of clarity? Seriously?

He couldn't help it; he felt used. He'd been good enough to be her friend when she needed him to battle a scary-ass devil monster that had almost killed them. Now, freed from its clutches, she just wanted to get on with her life, and apparently she didn't need him to be a part of that life anymore—except as her freaking tutoring experiment.

This sucks! he lamented, with rising anguish and anger.

She squeezed his hand tightly and brought her face even closer. He could once again feel gravity and mass giving way around him. She started to speak, and he felt his world begin to collapse.

"I just can't bring myself to destroy the wardrobe. I can't do it."

He froze.

"I know you think I'm crazy. I know it goes totally against what I told Dr. Esfahani. It's not that I want to use it. I don't want that power. I don't want anyone to have it. But Eric, this is the last one—the last chance to contact another world, or plane, or realm, or wherever it is the Afrit comes from. Someday, maybe we'll be ready to speak with the creature again—learn from it. Think of what we could learn! It may not be in my lifetime, but I just can't end that possibility for eternity. I simply can't."

He felt dizzy. Her gummy bear-tinged words had reactivated gravity and mass, and he now had the sensation of hurtling back toward Earth at near terminal velocity.

"I was afraid how you might feel," she went on, "or what you'd do. I've been trying to figure out how to tell you. I'm so scared you'll think I'm insane after what we went through... after what I dragged you into. I know you want the wardrobe destroyed, and you might be right, but I can't do it. So, hate me if you must, but I really, really hope you don't. I don't want to lose you, Eric. I miss your friendship. I trust you."

She sat back, looked at the ground, and let go of his hand. "Please, think it over," she said in a saddened tone. "I leave it to you."

He tried to reorient himself after the biggest zigzag he'd ever experienced. This definitely wasn't what he'd expected. In some sense, it was far better. She didn't want to end their friendship at all. In fact, it appeared that she had as much fear of losing it as he did. That couldn't be bad.

However, the thought of the wardrobe continuing to exist, and the prospect of seeing that monster again, sent chills down his spine. Did he trust her? Did he trust her enough to not ever call that infernal thing from wherever it came from back into this world... his world?

What choice do I have? I could try to fight her on it, try to convince her.

He doubted that would work. Lotte was smart and headstrong, and he had great skepticism about presenting a convincing enough case to sway her opinion. He also felt pretty certain that arguing about it would drive a wedge between them that would destroy their relationship.

I could abandon her, leave her to do whatever she damn-well wants, and think she's crazy, and hate her.

He had to admit, he did kind of think she was crazy. 'Really, quite insane,' as she so often said. This mirror—now un-mirror, or portal, or what-the-hell ever it was—and the monstrosity it summoned were unimaginably dangerous. He felt in his heart that the wardrobe should be destroyed.

Yeah, I basically think she's bonkers, and you know what? She's right to think this might concern me. It concerns me a lot, but do I hate her?

Eric didn't think he could ever hate Lotte. That seemed patently out of the question, unless she summoned that creature again. Then he'd be pissed, but why would she do that? She said she wouldn't, claimed she didn't want that kind of power, and this led him right back to whether he trusted her or not.

He got up and paced around a bit, as much to warm up as to clear his head. He looked around, and the beauty of the cemetery dawned on him.

No sign of zombies anywhere.

His grandfather wasn't buried here. His grave rested in another cemetery on the other side of town. He decided he should go visit and have a better look. He'd hadn't really noticed much about that cemetery during the funeral, or the few times they'd been there since. His head had always been stuck in whatever video game he'd been playing at the time.

He didn't notice shit like flowers and stuff—serenity.

Not then, at least.

He thought he might take Grandma with him to see Grandpa's grave. She'd like that. She'd be over for Thanksgiving next week. He'd ask her. Grandma had asked him about Lotte several times when they'd visited her. He told her that she'd been busy, but that he hoped she could visit again soon.

He took a deep breath, turned, and walked back to where Lotte still sat near the base of the tree. He extended his hand so he could help her up, and she took it.

"Let's go," he said. "I'm freezing. We need to walk."

They trekked in silence along the wide shoulder of Pleasant Street. Cars whizzed past on both sides and, eventually, Holton Hill Road came into sight on the right.

"My grandmother will be at our house next week for Thanksgiving," he said. "Would you and your father like to come over for Thanksgiving dinner? My grandmother is dying to see you again."

She grabbed his arm with both her hands, and they walked together.

"I'll ask my father if he can come," she said in a trembling voice, "but I wouldn't miss it."

"Great. Maybe over the long weekend we could watch *Glory* at your house. I think they have it at Blockbuster. Otherwise, I'll see if I can find it at Best Buy, or someplace. It really is a good film."

She squeezed his arm and sniffled. A few tears ran down her face. "I'd love that."

"Okay, but we won't do it on Black Friday. I know that's your special day."

She shot him an awkward glance, and he could see her black mascara running out of red eyes, filled with tears.

Some things never change, he thought with amusement.

"Never mind, just a little joke," he said as they walked on.

"*Little shit!*" he heard her mutter when the humor finally hit home. Soon they reached the entrance to Holton Hill Road. She raised one hand and wiped her nose and face, but with her other hand she clung tightly to his arm.

"If you're not doing anything else," she asked, her voice a bit steadier, "do you want to go up and walk on the trails for a bit?"

"That would be cool!"

They languidly turned together and walked arm in arm up the steep, well-manicured road. Its surface shone and sparkled like black glass.

Kuuuul!

THE END

ACKNOWLEDGEMENTS

I'd like to express my sincere appreciation to the entire team at Evolved Publishing. I give special thanks to editor extraordinaire, Dave Lane (AKA Lane Diamond), from whom I've learned so much, and who helped make *Playing with Fire* the best book it could be. I'm also deeply grateful to artist Kris Norris, whose wonderful cover designs have brought the "Uncommon Bonds" series to life.

Additional thanks go out to all my friends and family who served as beta readers to the many early versions of this and future books in the series. Your feedback is very much reflected in these pages and the pages of works that follow.

ABOUT THE AUTHOR

William E. Noland has worked in the fields of human resources and finance. He enjoys music—playing in three different rock bands—international travel, and reading. His writing combines a lifelong love of speculative fiction with a passion for history, sociology, and psychology. He lives in Massachusetts with his wife and two cats.

For more, please visit William E. Noland online at:
Website: www.WENoland.com
Goodreads: William E. Noland
Facebook: @WENoland.Author
LinkedIn: www.linkedin.com/in/william-noland-103804140/

WHAT'S NEXT?

William and his team at Evolved Publishing are fast at work on Books 2-4 of the "Uncommon Bonds series. Stay tuned to the web page referenced below to keep up to date.

www.EvolvedPub.com/UB

HAMMER TO FALL (Book 2)

A grainy photograph and a cry for help begin a new descent into terror for long-separated friends Lotte Schwarz and Eric Schneider.

FROM THE BEGINNING (Book 3)

A devastating flood and a chance encounter trigger a rapid-fire series of events that again pit Lotte Schwarz and Eric Schneider against challenges both mortal and supernatural.

DAY OF JUDGMENT (Book 4)

Be careful what you wish for, as notorious success may lead to unintended scrutiny and even more otherworldly dangers.

MORE FROM EVOLVED PUBLISHING

We offer great books across multiple genres, featuring high-quality editing (which we believe is second-to-none) and fantastic covers.

As a hybrid small press, your support as loyal readers is so important to us, and we have strived, with tireless dedication and sheer determination, to deliver on the promise of our motto:
QUALITY IS PRIORITY #1!

Please check out all of our great books,
which you can find at this link:
www.EvolvedPub.com/Catalog/

Thank you!

CPSIA information can be obtained
at www.ICGtesting.com
Printed in the USA
LVHW112041210622
721764LV00009B/1024

9 781622 537150